THE SANTA KILLER

A DI BARTON MYSTERY

ROSS GREENWOOD

Boldwood

First published in Great Britain in 2022 by Boldwood Books Ltd.

Copyright © Ross Greenwood, 2022

Cover Design by Head Design

Cover Photography: Shutterstock

Every effort has been made to obtain the necessary permissions with reference to copyright material, both illustrative and quoted. We apologise for any omissions in this respect and will be pleased to make the appropriate acknowledgements in any future edition.

A CIP catalogue record for this book is available from the British Library.

Paperback ISBN 978-1-80415-684-1

Large Print ISBN 978-1-80415-680-3

Hardback ISBN 978-1-80415-679-7

Ebook ISBN 978-1-80415-677-3

Kindle ISBN 978-1-80415-678-0

Audio CD ISBN 978-1-80415-685-8

MP3 CD ISBN 978-1-80415-682-7

Digital audio download ISBN 978-1-80415-676-6

Boldwood Books Ltd
23 Bowerdean Street
London SW6 3TN
www.boldwoodbooks.com

In memory of Barry Richards
One in a million
1937 - 2020

In moments of pain, we seek revenge.

— AMI AYALON

1

INGA

Stevenage town centre, four years ago

Inga paid for the macaroons at Coconut Creation Bakery just off the high street, took her change, thanked the lady, and left the shop. She smiled as she gently placed the cakes in her carrier bag on top of the rest of her Christmas gifts. December for her partner, Lucas, just wouldn't be the same without macaroons. He was arriving home in a few days from his air force job abroad, and she couldn't wait. This year, the holiday season would be family only. No one else was needed.

Inga opened her umbrella, put her head down and hastened towards the car park as a squall of rain tried to blast her into the road. A sudden flash of lightning overhead lit up the empty street in front of her. She nipped into a shop front and counted the seconds. The thunder rolled overhead when she reached twelve.

The rain was torrential now, as though the gods were pouring it out of pails, but Inga didn't care about getting soaked. Her daughter, Amelie, was coming back from university tonight and, wet or dry, Inga would be at the door when she arrived. Smiling, Inga put her umbrella down so she wouldn't get electrocuted, then half ran, half scuttled through the sodden streets.

When she was almost at the station, where she'd parked her car, Inga had a dilemma. Even in the middle of the day, she'd usually walk the long way and avoid the scary subways, which had filled with homeless people over the last few years. Yet, if it was possible, the rain was harder now. She checked the top of her bag and noted the packaging for Lucas's macaroons was getting damp. Decision made, she sprinted through the series of underpasses and made it to the car park, where she giggled nervously with relief.

She thought of the new boots in her bag, which her daughter had wanted all year. Inga had told her they cost too much, but she'd secretly spent all year putting a bit aside out of the wages from her part-time job at their local Subway. Amelie was worth every penny.

It was going to be the best Christmas ever after a few lonely ones over the years. In fact, one year she'd had a punch in the face as her main present. Things have a way of working out, she thought. Her smile was wide as she popped the boot, but something caught her attention out of the corner of her eye. It seemed as if a shadow had moved behind her. She didn't even have time to turn before the blow landed.

Thirty seconds later, her mind floated back into her body, and she just about regained consciousness

'Hey, lady,' said a voice that seemed to come from someone many miles away. 'Are you okay?'

As always, Inga's mind was on her daughter. She managed to open one eye, even though it was like lifting a drawbridge, and saw her shopping bags were gone. Two halves of a broken brick were on the ground next to her head, which pounded as if cannons were going off inside it.

Ice-cold water from the deep puddle seeped through her coat and chilled her skin. She gasped. An involuntary keening sound escaped her lips. Blood poured from the wound on the side of her head and filled her eyes, and Inga saw no more.

2

THE SANTA KILLER

Peterborough, present day, three months before Christmas

My fingers are white on the handlebars as I cycle past the river. I force myself to breathe slower, because I'm just on another recce. Soon the time will come. The first message has been sent. The die is cast.

It's cold enough not to seem out of place wearing a winter hat, but I've begun to sweat. The late autumn sun is dipping behind the rooftops, so most of those I pass are also decked in shades. With black jeans and a dark-blue coat on, I really could be anyone. But sadly, I am no one.

I pull up at the bench on the corner of Oundle Road and St Catherine's Lane, where I've often sat to study Maggie's life. She surprised me once with a different routine. It wasn't so cold then, but I was still in disguise.

This time, I lean against the lamp post and pretend to check my phone. It must have been hard to appear inconspicuous before the digital age. I'd look like an idiot now, pretending to read a newspaper or a book, but who really stares at anyone nowadays as they walk down the street? We're too busy focusing on ourselves to consider what others are up to, and that suits me fine.

She won't be going anywhere just yet, because it's exercise class night. She'll leave the house around a quarter to seven and drive to the Swan Hotel Fitness Club. I know she meets Anne-Marie there and they do their class. Maggie doesn't get back until gone nine, because they like to use the pool and sauna. The club is a glass-windowed building on two sides, so you can see the swimming area from the bushes. Must be nice to live so comfortably. My partner always complains about how unfair life is for us when others live so well.

Anne-Marie gets home around the same time as Maggie, because she only lives on Mayor's Walk. I sometimes watch outside her house, too. Anne-Marie has four kids, so I have a touch more sympathy for her, but she still has it easy. I'm afraid she's also on the list.

Maggie is first, though. The situation is intolerable now. I've known for a while it's time to act. We haven't discussed specifically what I should do, but it has to be drastic. Perhaps that's why I'm reluctant. Yet I remember doing it before. Yes, there was guilt afterwards, but there was also satisfaction.

My phone beeps to tell me it's a quarter to seven, so I cross the road to get a better view of her place. She's the fifth house down. They are enormous properties, with lengthy lawns and wide drives. The lucky cow has a double garage for her fancy Audi Q5 to nestle inside. This evening, she hasn't been back that long from work and it's on the drive for when she goes to the gym. She always puts it away last thing at night.

Her mother is there, of course. She has a small red Mercedes sports car. Where does she get her money? They don't deserve to enjoy all the breaks, but they do. I know little about her mother. I tried following her when she came on her bike once in the summer when I'd cycled too, but I couldn't keep up. What the hell is all that about? She's got to be late sixties.

I thought about adding her name to the list, but there are too many imponderables. I think that's the right word. Besides, someone will need to care for the child.

Maggie's huge front door opens. It's the kind that begs for a wreath like they have in those black-and-white American Christmas films. She steps out in her tight T-shirt and even tighter leggings, brunette ponytail swishing, looking the picture of health. Regal even. Maggie has taken it up a notch of late, eating healthy, jogging, and three classes a week, so it's no wonder she looks so good. It's an understated look. Very sexy, but kind of normal.

She's one of those who exercises in full make-up. Maybe nobody knows the real her. Perhaps, like me, she is hidden.

I watch her waving up at the nearest bedroom window. Her strange child is there, motionless, as she often is, and she's the problem. I'm not sure what's wrong with her, but it's something. That observing child is a weak link in my forming plot. No matter. Thoughts of wreaths have given me a brilliant idea.

Maggie gets in her car and reverses off the drive. I turn and push my bike down Oundle Road towards town. She'll be going the other way and only see my back.

I've cycled today. Sometimes, I walk, other times I use public transport, but no more buses. Now my path is set, I don't want to appear on their safety cameras. Coming in a car is no-no, too. I understand enough about CCTV to know that's not a good idea.

Although the detective shows I watch as so-called entertainment are rubbish, I bet the police rarely convict anyone unless they're standing next to the body with a dripping knife. My dad used to shout at the TV for the villains to be smart and keep their mouths shut. I miss that now. Instead, there is silence.

I think of what happened. I consider what I did. The memories circle around in my head, faster and faster, and a storm enters my veins. It gives me the strength to carry on, which is just as well, because I have no choice.

3

MAGGIE

Maggie Glover left her house, breathed a sigh of relief, got in the car and put it into reverse, then backed out onto the road. Pippa was there, motionless, staring out of her bedroom window. Maggie waved, but Pippa didn't return the gesture. She rarely did. Maggie blew out another long breath. If it weren't for her fitness routine, she'd have suffered a breakdown long ago.

Maggie smiled as she indicated right at the top of St Catherine's Lane. Life had been tough ever since Pippa came into it, but they were over the worst of it now, she was sure of that. Her mum, recently single by the time Pippa arrived, had also been a godsend. Maggie had a lot to be thankful for, even though her husband's death had been so unexpected. Poor old James. It was no age.

She accelerated down the slip road and raced towards the Swan Hotel turn off. This car made her smile, too. The crippling sadness that always arose when she thought of her husband had eased at some point this year now six years had passed since he died. Maggie was finally ready for a relationship. She turned the radio on and caught the start of Elton John and Dua Lipa's 'Cold Heart'. Nodding her head, she sang along.

The barrier for the Swan Hotel car park was up, so she zoomed in and went around the rear to the sports club. Maggie spotted Anne-Marie's green Nissan Juke nestling in her favourite spot. Anne-Marie got out of her car when Maggie turned her engine off, then pulled an iron man pose in front of Maggie's bonnet.

'Gladiator, ready!' shouted Maggie as she stepped from her vehicle.

Anne-Marie dropped her pose.

'Permission to proceed straight to the steam room, ma'am.'

'Permission denied,' replied Maggie with a stern look. 'You must proceed immediately to the chamber of death and face the devil.'

Anne-Marie stood nearly six feet tall. She was originally from the Bahamas and her skin looked sun-kissed all year round, but six months ago she'd confided in Maggie at the coffee machine at work that she was pushing fifteen stone.

Maggie had been surprised. Even though they'd worked in the same showroom for years, they had a very businesslike relationship. Anne-Marie had four kids and her husband did nights, so she was flat out busy. Maggie was single and had Pippa, so she was worn down, too, but Maggie's mother always gave her time for exercise, even if she found little opportunity for much else. Anne-Marie had wanted to know how she kept so trim, so Maggie had got her to join the same gym so they could do the classes together.

Anne-Marie was still fourteen stone last time she'd checked, but she barely had an inch of cellulite on her. She was a strong woman. It was typical of life that Anne-Marie envied Maggie's willowy runner's figure, while Maggie would have loved to be so robust and powerful. She regularly joked with Anne-Marie that if she had shoulders and tits like hers, she'd go to work in a bikini top.

Anne-Marie cringed at the mention of the devil.

'No, I can't face him. Lothario is too potent, forceful and dynamic.'

Maggie skipped past Anne-Marie towards the entrance.

'Maybe it won't be him tonight.'

'I hope not. It's tricky to concentrate when he's crouching and grinning in front of me. I bet you hope he is, though.'

Maggie chuckled. She had to admit that he'd swiftly become her favourite instructor. He had such energy.

Lothar hailed from Sweden and had started teaching the odd class at their gym near the end of the summer. He was super friendly and super fit. Anne-Marie reckoned he fancied Maggie, but Maggie wasn't so sure. He was a spandex-clad type with not a hair in sight on his head or body, and surely wouldn't be bothered with her when he could have any number of the footloose and fancy-free youngsters at the front of the class.

The two women were already in their exercise gear, so they just changed their shoes and left their bags in the same locker. When they got to the room where the class was being held, they stood in the middle row. A few older ladies came and stayed at the back and they weren't the only ones who let the odd fart slip out during some of the more difficult stretches.

The instructor hadn't arrived yet. Dead on the hour, the far door opened and Lothar strode in. He always wore Ray-Ban sunglasses perched on his brow, which never seemed to move, and the snuggest pair of leggings possible. Any tighter and the police would need to be called.

'Evening, ladies,' he said, with a big white grin. 'I am going to make you work very hard tonight. You will sweat. You will cry out. There'll be pain and pleasure, but mostly pain.'

Lothar turned around to face the mirrored wall behind him, closed his eyes, crouched slightly, and slowly gyrated his hips to the music that had just started to play. There were good-natured groans from everyone when 'Flower' by Moby blared out of the speakers, with the dreaded line to bring Sally up. It was the most brutal exercise song ever. Their glutes would be quivering jellies the next day.

Maggie looked over at Anne-Marie as they both assumed the same position.

'I reckon he doesn't even need to shower afterwards,' said Maggie.

Anne-Marie winked at her.

'Is that because you're going to lick him clean?'

4

THE SANTA KILLER

Three months later, Monday 14th December 2020

I've checked a variety of stores' websites and they have a range of the things in stock I need, some of which are on offer. That's a result, because money is tight. I planned to buy them a while ago, but I knew I'd feel the urge to use them sooner.

It's a perfect day to go secret shopping with this cold front sitting over the city. There'll be no white Christmas this year, though. Milder weather is due to arrive on Christmas Eve.

I stroll into town late afternoon. Even inside Queensgate Centre, people remain wrapped in hats and scarves. It's a big place, but a poor substitute for somewhere like Bluewater. I spend a minute staring at Santa's grotto. It's contact free this year, apparently.

Young children queue up with flushed and pinched faces. Their parents mentally ticking another thing off their never-ending list.

I wonder what kind of man waits in that little green building covered in tinsel. Is he happy? Has his life turned out how he hoped? Or is he eating mints to disguise his breath? I bet his list is longer than mine.

It's decidedly fresh outside as I walk down the arcade past an abundance of closed shops to Party Outfits, which sits near the end. I push the door open and hear a pathetic tinkle. An old guy looks up from a counter at the bottom of a surprisingly long narrow shop. We share half a wave. I stride to what I want, which is easy to find. They have a large choice of many sizes. They have everything from kids' to XXXXL. There's even one that inflates.

I select XXL, which must be the minimum to be convincing. Three laughing teenagers enter, then two more. While I'm queuing to pay, the little doorbell rings twice more as other people stride in. It's freezing in the shop, though. Maybe the profit margins are slim on this type of merchandise.

'They come up large,' says the shopkeeper without looking at me.

'Perfect.'

He casts a quick eye over my body, but doesn't meet my eyes. He shrugs and nods.

'Twenty-five pounds.'

I freeze behind my scarf for a moment, even though it isn't much money. That's how tight things are. I need a new laptop, but that's wishful thinking. Meat and presents might be slim on the ground this year. There was another argument when we saw the price of a turkey. I don't give a shit what sort of meat it is when it's drowning in salty Bisto.

I shuffle past the throng in the congested shop while avoiding anyone's gaze. It doesn't look like a place that would install cameras, and I haven't seen any. Outside, it feels as if I'm carrying a ticking bomb, but nobody's interested in me.

I wander around to Bridge Street and stand outside the next place I need to visit. This shop stayed open through lockdown, saying it was selling essential items. I guess that applies in my case. A large store like this must have CCTV, so I pull my hat down a little lower and my scarf up when I walk in and peruse the range.

It's not a simple decision. A couple of them feel amazing, but cost over fifty pounds. They might even be too efficient. I select an aluminium one instead that's half price and only ten quid. That should do the job. It's tricky though. I never was any good at physics.

Yet again, the shop assistant barely registers my presence when I hand it over and pay. We really have got customer service off pat in this country. Off pat. That's one of my poor old mother's sayings.

I'd love a pricey but tasty burger from the van opposite the town hall. Instead, I trudge home. Passing WHSmith where the Post Office now is, I allow myself a little smile. They'll have delivered my letter to Peterborough City Radio today, or tomorrow morning at the latest. So, tomorrow night is prime time.

What I've got to do doesn't feel real. In some ways, it seems evil, but at a certain point you have to stand up for yourself and your family. There's a line and we think it's been crossed. Our history drives me to act.

5

DI BARTON

DI Barton looked at his watch and rose from his chair. It had been a tough case dealing with two abducted children, but at least they'd now been returned to their mother. No visible harm had been done, but there were rules, and Dad had broken them. He'd be enjoying processed and reformed turkey on a plastic plate this Christmas.

Only DS Shawn Zander and Barton remained in the office at seven p.m.

'Do you fancy a lift home?' asked Zander.

Barton could stroll to Peterborough's Thorpe Wood police station in less than thirty minutes, so he often did this, to help clear his head or mull cases over. A walk back in the drizzle and dark after a long, stressful day didn't appeal, though.

'Sure.'

They went down to the car park and were soon on their way. Instead of taking the turn to Barton's house, Zander continued straight on. Barton was no fool.

'Why not say you wanted to talk about something?'

'Who said I did?'

'Right. Where are we going, then? Ooh, McDonald's?'

'No, Holly would not be pleased.'

'I'm glad you mentioned her name. She said to remember to ask you and Kelly to come for dinner on Christmas Day.'

Zander and DS Kelly Strange had been close to getting together ever since she'd moved up from London a few years ago, but they'd never quite got over the line. Zander had lost his child to carbon monoxide poisoning not long before Strange had arrived. His relationship had died too, so it hadn't been plain sailing for him. But things had progressed with the resolution of the Fire Killer case and now they were dating.

'Actually, we're going to be at mine. My parents said they'll come over and help with a traditional Christmas to welcome Kelly to the family. Her folks are coming too.'

'The in-laws and the outlaws.'

'Aren't they the same thing?'

'Nope. Outlaws are wanted.'

Zander tutted.

'Oh, very good. How long have you had that up your sleeve?'

'I just made it up.'

'Yeah, right.'

'Okay, it was from a cracker last year.'

'Thought so.'

They arrived at Hampton shopping centre and parked near the entrance.

'I'm getting some flowers,' said Zander. 'Do you want anything?'

'I'm partial to tulips.'

'Ooh, unlucky. Wrong season.'

Zander got out and started walking. Barton caught up.

'Hang on, I'll come with you. Then you can spit it out.'

Zander grinned. They wandered in together. When they reached Tesco Extra and the flower section, Barton twigged.

'Noo! You aren't.'

Zander pretended he hadn't heard the comment. Barton pointed at him.

'Are you going to ask her tonight?'

'No, I'm not. She's cooking for me this evening. I didn't want to arrive empty-handed. Women like flowers. Simples.'

Barton clicked his fingers.

'Christmas Day! You're going to ask her on Christmas Day.'

Zander's eyes darted around before resting on Barton. 'What do you reckon?'

Barton considered his answer.

'I've been married so long that I can't judge if that's cheesy or romantic, daring or desperate, mad or marvellous. Although seeing as you only got together five minutes ago, we can probably throw crazy into the mix.'

'We've known each other for a decent amount of time.'

'It's not the same as dating. I'd hold fire until you've been a couple for six months and the gloss has come off. Wait until the arguments have become vicious, personal grooming diminishes, and sex becomes a distant memory.'

'Talking from your own experience?'

'No, just stuff I've overheard.'

'You always said when you met Holly, you knew straight away.'

Barton smiled. It was over fifteen years ago, but he could still remember that feeling of certainty, that he'd found someone he could share his life with.

'Perhaps I'll buy Holly flowers too.'

Zander laughed.

'Maybe that'll get you some early Holly this Christmas,' he said. 'If you get my drift.'

Looking at the flowers on display, Barton was pleased to find a decent selection of reduced items due to it being late in the day. They both chose a bunch and made their way to the till queues. Barton picked up a Mars bar and put that on the conveyor belt with his seasonal bouquet. Barton had been on a continuous diet since he'd hit his teens, but rarely took it seriously. Zander and he were big men. Well over six feet, but Barton now weighed more than eighteen stone.

Zander shook his head at the chocolate bar. Barton shrugged.

'What? It's not my fault if they put all this tempting stuff at the tills. If the government was serious about helping people maintain a healthy weight, they'd ban these antics and force the stores to have the naughty items in a special over-eighteens section at the rear.'

Zander laughed. 'Good idea. They could call it the aisle of death.'

Barton chuckled as well. 'Exactly. If you asked a shop assistant where the microwave cheeseburgers were kept, she'd shake her head and say, "Ooh, sir, have you lost the will to live?" Then she'd give you a leaflet with a picture of someone having a triple-bypass operation on the front with an 0800 number underneath.'

'Although this is the UK, so she'd then direct you to the aisle of death, telling you that you'll find the cheeseburgers between the cream doughnuts and crystal meth.'

'All of which are buy one, get one free,' replied Barton.

The two men paid for their wares and returned to the car. When they reached Barton's house, Zander cleared his throat before Barton got out.

'Well, John? Shall I go for it?'

'Yeah, why not? Be smart, though. Stack the odds in your favour by getting a load of mulled wine down her neck first.'

He waved Zander off, then realised he'd forgotten to take a key because he hadn't driven his car that morning. He pressed the door-bell. Holly opened the door and stared at the flowers in Barton's hands.

'Oh, John. What have you done now?'

6

DI BARTON

Tuesday 15th December

The next morning, Barton had a meeting first thing to tie up the abduction case with his boss. Barton left DCI Cox's office afterwards with a wry smile. Despite some unpleasant crimes that year, his team's clear-up rate remained impressive. Cox was so impressed she'd just borrowed one of his sergeants off him, specifically DS Strange, and seconded her to the other Major Crimes team, which she said was because they had more cases.

Cox had been promoted above him over two years ago. She must have forgotten about the rumour mill that operated in all police force offices. The other team had one sergeant off sick with gallstones, and the other had taken an immediate holiday, despite them being staff down. Rumour was she'd gone to rehab. She wouldn't be the last. Strange would be going to clear her desk.

There were also people off with Covid, or who'd been in close contact with the infected. Finally, two of the other team's DCs had been injured at the same football match, playing not policing, so it was all hands to the pump.

Barton had agreed to be on call this evening due to the lack of sergeants about. Zander and Strange said they were off to Ikea when he'd asked them and, to his surprise, wouldn't be swayed. Seeing as Barton was working all day, he really hoped he wouldn't receive any calls that night. He was 'acting down' because normally a DS would do it. Usually, Barton would get a DC to 'act up' but he was one of the few DIs who didn't mind doing it from time to time because his team then knew he was putting in extra like they did. When he called on them for more effort and overtime amid serious cases, he was rarely disappointed.

His stomach rumbled. He opened the carrier bag Holly had given him before he left, which contained his lunch. He'd told her not to trouble herself and to focus on getting her other jobs done, but she was wise to that and the contents were healthy and unappealing.

His mobile phone rang, and he gladly placed his tub of ham salad down.

'DI Barton speaking.'

Barton listened to someone sneezing on the other end of the line.

'Sorry, Julian here, I have a DJ to speak to you,' said a quiet young male voice.

'Pardon?'

The line went quiet, then someone much louder came on.

'Tim Tibbles here. I work for PCR, that's Peterborough City Radio, your radio. The radio—'

Barton cut him off.

'DI Barton.'

'Inspector, great to speak to you. Look, I received a creepy letter, very odd, thought I'd ring. Let you know, just in case.'

Barton smiled. It was certainly a voice for radio.

'Before we get to that, where did you get my number?'

'My assistant, Julian, found it. You came in and did a call-out to the public to keep vigilant for a night stalker a few years back.'

Barton recalled the case, but it must have been ten years ago. He supposed he did have the same number. Usually calls would come via HQ and a log would get created. Barton would need to register one if this call turned out to be serious.

'Okay, what kind of letter?'

'Plain white envelope, A4. Addressed to me. By name. I do the morning show. Single white piece of paper, with a short message.'

'And what might that message be?'

'There are three words at the top of the sheet. The Santa Killer.'

'Okay. It sounds like kids messing around to me. Have you had any other similar messages?'

'No, nothing as weird as this.'

'Any crank calls? Any vandalism?'

'No, not for a long time. We get the odd window broken, but that's par for the course on a shopping parade.'

'No staff have felt uncomfortable in any way?'

'No.'

'Do you have someone who resembles Father Christmas? Any shows discussing the big guy?'

'Nope. We used to have a regular guy come in when I worked at Heart FM, but that was decades ago.'

'Okay. I appreciate you taking the time to ring in and tell us about it. Let us know if you receive another one or there's something else worrying.'

'That's it. You aren't going to do anything?'

'No. If we investigated every single message like that, we'd never have time for the serious offences.'

'It's worrying.'

'It's a little worrying. I guess you could argue it comes under the Malicious Communications Act.'

'That's what I thought. Hang on a minute.'

Barton could hear Tibbles speaking to what he assumed was Julian. He began to wish he were eating his lunch.

'Julian says that we got a similar letter three months ago saying that trouble was coming.'

'Have you still got it?'

'Wait there.'

Tibbles came back on after half a minute.

'No.'

'Was it the same writing or style?'

'He can't remember.'

'Look. Nobody's actually been threatened. There's no implicit menace to anyone, imminently or otherwise, except perhaps the good man himself. And he won't be here for over a week yet.'

'Right. Does that mean there will be more?'

'I suppose it's possible. But in the meantime, just be extra careful. Keep an eye out for strange behaviour. Walk to your cars in pairs. Lock the doors. That sort of thing.'

'Okay, great ideas. Detective Inspector Barton, isn't it?'

'Yes.'

'Should I tell my listeners?'

'No, not at this point. We wouldn't want to scare anyone unnecessarily. As I said, you can always call me if any more suspicious post arrives.'

'Okay, I'll keep it to myself, although the three words at the bottom are a concern.'

Barton ungritted his teeth.

'Please, read the whole letter to me.'

'"The Santa Killer. Coming to town."'

7

MAGGIE

With their evening exercise class finished, Maggie and Anne-Marie staggered back to the changing room. It had been a brutal workout under the watchful gaze of Lothar. They sat on a bench next to each other and groaned.

'Think of all the mince pies we've earned,' said Maggie.

'No pies for me until the big day. I'm in the zone. You will not believe how much I weigh now.'

Maggie watched as Anne-Marie peeled off her damp leggings and T-shirt and posed in her underwear.

'Thirteen and a half.'

'Thirteen dead!'

'No way. That's amazing.'

Maggie beamed at her gym buddy. They were becoming closer, and that was a lovely feeling. It had been years since she'd had anything like it. If only they had more free time, she thought. Maybe they could even have a spa weekend together. Maggie smiled ruefully. How the hell was she going to fit any weekends away in? Sometimes life was frustrating.

Maggie pushed those thoughts out of her head. The last few months had been brilliant for her as well.

In fact, if she was honest, it was money she didn't need. James's life insurance had been more than ample, leaving her mortgage-free. Her car had been brand new and the debt on that got cleared as well. They'd also just had a total kitchen refurb, so apart from holidays, which her mother often insisted on covering, Maggie didn't expect any hefty bills in the near future. The pay for a sales-person had been enough for her to live to a decent standard. This Christmas, therefore, was going to be fabulous. Perhaps she'd buy presents for her neighbours and really treat her mum.

'Are you going to the pool and sauna?' asked Anne-Marie.

'Of course,' replied Maggie. 'It's the best bit.'

They got changed into their swimsuits and had a quick shower, then, laughing, they linked arms and walked into the pool area. They chatted as they did breaststroke up and down the twenty-five-metre length.

'You're in a good mood. Is it all that time with the boss man?'

Maggie looked over at her friend.

'Don't start that. I've had a lot more contact with him since I got promoted.'

'Close contact, by the looks of it. He's single, isn't he?'

'I would imagine so.'

'How old do you reckon?'

'I doubt he'll be seeing fifty again.'

'Perhaps that's not a bad thing. He owns the business, has plenty of money, widowed, won't want kids, and he seems nice enough. In fact, he's pretty handsome for an older dude.'

'No, that's true, but it's a bit icky, you know, with him being the owner. He asked me if I wanted to go for a drink after work to cele-brate my figures.'

'Are you sure figures was plural?'

'No, I'm not!'

'You kept that quiet.'

'Yeah, I know. He's kind of overbearing, but I think he's lonely. He isn't my type, anyway. I want someone who wants to keep fit.'

Anne-Marie gave her a huge grin.

'Stop it.' Maggie giggled.

'Did Ken ask you out before the promotion?'

'Yes. Why?'

'Just curious. What did you say to put him off?'

'That I was busy with Pippa. It felt like he'd crossed a line, but at least he was polite.'

'Yes, I suppose it is a little dodgy with him being your boss, but loads of people meet their partners at work. Or maybe at the gym...'

Maggie laughed and swallowed some water. 'That's enough,' she said after standing and spluttering, 'or I'll drown. He looked buff tonight, though. He must get well paid, because I'm sure he has new gear each week.'

They set off swimming again.

'Okay, no more Lothario jokes. How is Pippa? You mentioned she's started talking more.'

Maggie smiled and got another mouthful of chlorinated water.

'Yes, Pippa's coming on leaps and bounds. I thought she was really behind on her schooling, but it's almost as though she's been quietly picking things up while she wasn't speaking. Her vocabulary is limited, but we did some maths the other day and she surprised me. Her drawing is at least where she's expected to be. The only concern we have is reading, but there's nearly two years until secondary school, so it's still possible she can go to the local academy. I just want her to have the same opportunities as other children, you know?'

Anne-Marie wasn't listening. She gestured her head to the

person walking from the male changing room. Maggie glanced over to see Lothar whipping his towel away, then hanging it on a hook next to the showers. He did two swift touches of his toes, then strode around the pool with the grace of a big cat. Maggie got a final gobful of water as she ducked herself under to stop him from catching her laughing at his tiny Speedos.

The women quickly flagged after the tiring class beforehand and clung to the side of the pool. They watched Lothar swim up and down, cutting through the water with powerful strokes.

'Sauna?' asked Anne-Marie.

'Yes, not long, though. Pippa's still waiting for me to get home before she allows herself to drop off, and she had an unsettled sleep last night.'

Maggie felt the waves from someone swimming up behind her.

'Hi, ladies. Can I ask you a question?'

Lothar's English was almost perfect.

'Of course,' said Anne-Marie with a big grin.

'I'm interested in updating the kitchen for my place. I hear you work for a designer and fitter.'

'Yes, we do,' said Maggie. 'There's a showroom at Mancetter Square. Ken's Kitchens and Bathrooms. You can just pop in.'

'Very good, Maggie. Will I see you there?'

'Yes, I don't do Mondays or Saturdays, though.'

'Great. I'll look forward to it. We could have coffee.'

Maggie's face reddened.

'I'll chat to you when you come in.'

'Fine. Good session tonight. You both make wonderful progress.'

Maggie smiled as Lothar swiftly pulled himself out of the water and strutted to fetch his towel. Muscles rippled on his back as his arms swung by his side.

'I'll chat to you when you come in,' mimicked Anne-Marie. 'I don't do Mondays or Saturdays.'

'Are we having that sauna or not?' asked Maggie, trying to look stern.

'I'm not sure we need to. It's rather steamy out here.'

8

THE SANTA KILLER

I feel pretty conspicuous cycling through the streets dressed like this. The huge black windcheater is so big it keeps catching between the spokes. Luckily, it's a dark night. I meet only one other person by the rowing lake. He nearly gets run over because there aren't many lights. He doesn't have a dog, so God only knows what he's doing here.

I cycle through Orton Staunch, where the lock is. It's pitch black and empty. The heavy cloud cover has kept it mild, so I'm sweating like hell. This is the part where I might get seen, so I need to keep my head down and be quick. I race onto Oundle Road, where the traffic is light. Commuter hour is long gone. This is the risky part. She's usually back before nine thirty, but I need a bit of time to get ready.

I've cycled because the plan is to pretend I'm working on a puncture. There are very few cars about when I reach the end of her road. I stumble off the bike, cursing that I wore black wellies, and lean it against the bench. Wellies would be rubbish if I had to run. I'd fear for my chances if anyone fit chased me, like her mother!

It's nine fifteen and a steady drizzle falls. My resolve weakens while I bend over the bike and fiddle, but there's still a core of anger when I spot her Q5. She's cautious in the slippery conditions, and I tense when her headlights light me up for agonising seconds as she turns.

It's decision time. I don't want to do it, but I think I have to. The guilt when it arrives will be hard to bear, but what will my partner say if I fail to go through with it? Where will our lives end up without something changing?

I slide the weapon from my rucksack. Its solid nature gives me reassurance. I stare at Maggie's house. She's parked next to her mother's vehicle and the garage door is rising.

It's the usual routine. She stops on the drive so she can look up to her daughter's bedroom. Pippa stands at the window. The garage door grumbles to a stop. Her daughter doesn't respond when Maggie waves out of the car window. After edging into the garage, she leaves the car. She returns to the driveway and gets no response from another wave.

Maggie raises her left arm and presses the fob to close the garage door. I haul off my raincoat and drop it behind the sign that says St Catherine's Lane. I pass the first few houses on the road as I walk towards her. Their lights are out.

Maggie is only fifty metres away when, for the first time since I've been watching, Pippa places her hands on the glass. She's seen me. Her eyes are on me. Good, let her watch. I pull the hat out of my pocket, put it on, and stretch out my shoulders.

Twenty metres now. It's too late to worry about technique. I have to go for broke. The garage door clunks into place, leaving a heavy silence. Maggie walks towards her front door. She looks at the keys in her left hand. She freezes. I must appear in her peripheral vision, because her head turns in my direction. But I'm already swinging. I'm so close that she doesn't even flinch.

The sound isn't what I expect. It's loud and hollow. The impact jars my arm. She slumps to her knees, but, to my amazement, she twists to grab the door handle. I swing and strike the door instead, then manage to hit her again. She drops to the floor and rolls onto her side. For a moment, I think she's going to see me and scream, but her eyelids droop. Blood trickles past her ear, along her face and pools in the hollow of her neck. Her hand reaches up in a token attempt at defence. I strike it down.

9

DI BARTON

Barton felt his eyelids drooping as he watched the television. He glanced over at Holly as she arranged baubles on the tree in the corner of the lounge. She was a small woman and could pass for a child with her back to him.

As for their children, their eldest son, Lawrence, hadn't returned from university yet despite term finishing. Barton suspected he had a girlfriend. Luke and Layla had been keen on decorating the tree for less than five minutes. Teenager Layla was now texting while sprawled on an armchair. Luke lay on the floor stroking their greyhound. Barton could see the white part of the dog's eyes. Gizmo hadn't yet worked out what species the seven-year-old was.

'Dad, what exactly is a divorce?' asked Luke.

'What makes you ask that?'

'Colin in my class said his parents are having one.'

'I see. How does Colin feel about it?'

'He's sad. He might need to go to a different school.'

'Divorces can be tough on children.'

'Are you and Mummy going to get divorced?'

Barton's gaze moved to Holly.

'That's okay, John. I'll answer that.'

She came and sat beside Luke and placed her arms around him, staring lovingly into his eyes.

'I couldn't divorce your dad because it wouldn't be fair to whoever got him next. It'd be like having your dog adopted by another family because you knew it was getting lazy and windy, and was a bit past its best.'

Holly and Luke both turned to him and grinned.

'Come on, Luke. Put your pyjamas on and brush your teeth,' said Barton, standing.

'Dad! It's early.'

'It's gone nine.'

Barton looked over at Holly. 'Dog or kid?'

Luke replied before she did.

'I want Mum to put me to bed. You never read to me.'

Luke and Holly scowled at him as he and Gizmo left the room.

Barton opened the front door and saw the drizzle. Gizmo had turned into a wonderful family dog over the last few months since they'd adopted him. He wasn't a year old yet, but he'd proven placid, friendly, funny and quick to house-train. The only problem was he was rather selective about where he went for his night-time business. Barton might be outside for half an hour.

His mobile rang eight minutes later, while he was still waiting. It was Control.

'DI Barton speaking.'

'Good evening, sir. I understand you're on call tonight.'

'That's right.'

'There's been a suspected violent incident at number five St Catherine's Lane.'

'Only a suspected violent incident?'

'It's unconfirmed because the details are sketchy. The 999 caller was the mother of the injured party. She found her daughter with her head and face covered in blood at the front door and rang it in.'

Barton's brain fired into action.

'Sounds fairly violent to me.'

'It might have been an accident at this point. No one was seen leaving the scene, and, according to the mother, the victim had only just driven home.'

'Fair enough. What's the current situation?'

'The incident was called in quarter of an hour ago. Luckily, we could divert an ambulance that was two streets away, driving to someone who'd had a fall. The paramedics had seen similar head wounds and noted they looked suspicious. They blue-lighted the victim immediately and rang us en route.'

Questions raced to Barton's mouth, but they weren't urgent. The first priority for the police at the scene was protection of life. If it was an attack or a mugging, the person responsible might still be looking for victims.

'Do we have uniform present?'

'That's a negative. Multiple RTC on Boongate. Various other incidents over the city. You know how it is. One of those nights.'

Barton grimaced. Times were tough all over. People isolating from the virus exacerbated the normal stretching of the thin blue line at this time of the year.

'Anyone vulnerable still at the address?'

'Also a negative. Paramedics spoke to the mother and asked her to follow in her own car with the only child present if she felt able. The house is empty.'

Barton couldn't help asking.

'And the person with the fall from the other call?'

'We sent the last resource we had available, which was a special constable who should have finished an hour ago.'

'Excellent work. St Catherine's Lane is four minutes from me. I'll attend, then continue to the hospital. When I have more, I'll be in touch.'

Barton looked down at Gizmo, who immediately squatted. Barton put his hand in his pocket and gave him a treat.

10

THE SANTA KILLER

As I cycle home, a fire burns inside for the thing I've done. In the dark, I stop and put my big raincoat back over my red outfit. The guttural choking laugh that comes from me is not mine. The leer that distorts my face isn't me. I try to force it into a smile. Even though family comes first, not everyone can step up. Maybe this year will end better now.

I think of the best Christmas I can remember, which would have been when I was around seven. The memories are full of the usual things that remain so familiar. The lights, the tree with too many decorations on, most of which were home- or school-made.

There were parcels underneath addressed to my parents. I remember Mum telling me that adults have to buy presents for each other, but Santa brings the children theirs. There was a Disney film, *Fantasia*, on the TV.

I recall the film because I had no idea what was going on with it, but I never said anything because I didn't want to risk them looking at the clock and realising the time. My parents were drinking something strange-smelling and giggling, so I assumed they understood the movie.

I can even remember being too hot between them. The radiator behind always heated the back of the sofa, and the fire was baking me from the front. It was just the three of us. No one else interrupting. Nothing else mattered.

As my parents laughed some more, I put up with my clothes feeling sweaty. I hoped we'd never move.

Times like that don't last, though. I've learned the hard way, but even back then, I believe that I knew to enjoy the moment. My mum broke the spell by getting up. She chuckled and ruffled my hair.

'Have you been good this year?' she asked.

'Very,' I replied.

I can remember her laughing so much she wobbled. My dad got up and wiped his eyes.

'We love you, son. You're our favourite.'

Well, perhaps I made that last line up, but the rest was true. I'm sure of it. I prayed, as I turned the TV over to find a cartoon I understood, that every year would have this magic.

It wasn't my first memory, though. Most people's earliest recollection is usually something unpleasant. Mine was too.

11

THE SANTA KILLER

Age five

I lean backwards at the entrance to the playground. Every part of me, even my ears, is tensed. I will not go inside.

'Come on,' says my dad. 'You like school.'

'No, I should stay at home.'

'I know, but your mum isn't well.'

'I'll cuddle her.'

He doesn't reply, so I turn and glance up to see if he's weakening. His face is red with embarrassment, though. He apologises to the queue of people behind him who we're stopping getting past. I don't care. I'm still not moving.

My dad picks me up and marches towards our class's entrance. I try to do my plank, but he tucks me under his arm, so I kick and buck. I'm dropped onto my feet at the door to Reception. He crouches down to me.

'You know everyone has to go to school.'

'I'm sick too, Daddy. I am. Really.'

'I've got work to do, and your mum's poorly in bed. I'll be back to collect you at home time.'

He leans forward and kisses me on the forehead. I stand on my tiptoes and scream in his face.

'Won't!'

A large figure appears next to us.

'It's okay. I'll take over from here. You get going.'

It's Mrs Graham, who's usually very nice. She grabs my hand, so I tense, ready to pull back. Instead of pulling me along, she puts her other hand under my armpit and lifts me off the floor as well. My shoes scrape the threshold as she drags me into the classroom and closes the door behind me. I'm so shocked, I let her hustle me inside, remove my favourite red coat, and guide me to my table.

Nasty Tilly is sitting there already. She waits for the teacher to leave, then reaches over and pinches me on the arm. I'm too cross for it to hurt. I want to hurt her in return, though, but I'm not sure how. Instead, I quietly seethe.

We're sent out to the garden later in the morning to play with the sand and water. Tilly stands in front of me, eyes narrowed so much that they're almost shut. I drop my gaze to avoid a fight. Her pink leggings have a big hole in the knee. My eyes rest on her scuffed and battered sandals. She stomps away, and I release a sigh of relief.

A bit later, I focus on my sandcastle. It's a good one. Best ever, in fact. I gently place a shell on the top of it. Then a shoe stamps down and flattens it. When I peer up, a cup of freezing-cold water is thrown into my face. I gasp. Tilly titters. When I clear my vision, I glance around to wait for her to be told off. Nobody comes. No one's interested.

I look down at where my sandcastle was and sniff back the tears. After rooting through the ruins, I find my shell and pocket it. Tilly has returned to the other side of the garden and crouches with her back facing me. I kneel in the sandpit and seethe some more.

After a while, I regain control of my breathing and check who's near me. The teachers are inside talking to each other. Light laughter reaches me through the folding doors. I haul myself to my feet and trudge over to a washing-up bowl, which is half full of water. I pick it up and stomp towards Tilly.

It's heavy. The water begins to move back and forth as I stagger. Waves slosh over the edges of the bowl. My socks are soaked. When I reach Tilly, I pause behind her. Ever so slowly and carefully, I upend the container. Her head sinks beneath her shoulders as if that will somehow escape the drenching. Then she screams. Tilly pushes herself up and turns with a face twisted with rage. I ram the bowl straight into her nose, knocking her backwards. She plonks onto her bum. Then I bash her on the head with a fist.

For the third time that morning, I'm lifted off the ground. There are angry words hollered at me from a stern face as I'm carried past, but I don't listen.

A younger assistant holds my hand outside as we wait for my father to turn up. At least I get to go home. I look up at her, the sun half blinding me, but I can see she's smiling.

'Tilly won't be mean to you again,' she says.

At my confused look, she crouches and whispers in my ear.

'You did the right thing.'

My dad stamps through the gate towards us in his work uniform. I usually hate upsetting him. He's my hero. Although I'm distracted by the kind lady's comments. My dad stops in front of me and glares down. His grimace reflects his anger, whereas my expression would be described as thoughtful.

Even though I'm young, a lesson has been learned.

12

DI BARTON

Two minutes after Gizmo had done his business, he was inside the house, Holly had heard, and Barton was on his way. He pulled off the drive in his blue Land Rover, drove down Orton Longueville village road for a minute, tutted at the lights for thirty seconds, turned right, went over two mini-roundabouts, took a left and he was there. The joys of local policing.

Barton already knew this was a nice place to live with big properties, generously spread out. He parked on the kerb of number five. It didn't look like a crime scene. He got out of his 4x4 and had a quick check around for a neighbourhood watch sign. No joy. There only seemed to be two houses that would have a decent view of number five's front door; both looked deserted. Barton checked to make sure they didn't have doorbell CCTV.

Barton could get one of his team out to help, but if the people involved were safe tonight, he would get more use out of his people if he kept them for tomorrow. He guessed it could be a doorstep mugging, which sadly happened from time to time in the areas with expensive housing. You were at your most vulnerable as you held your shopping in one hand and opened the door with the other. Your mind on the warmth and safety inside, as opposed to the danger behind.

Barton had recognised the voice from Control. It was a woman who'd been doing the job for a long time. When he'd first become a sergeant, he'd wasted time telling capable people how to do their jobs. With experience, he realised that unless they were new starters, they did what was necessary. The paramedics tonight, for example, had saved a lot of manpower by encouraging the mother and grandchild to go to the hospital. They would have known the services were stretched. Their training preserved lives in more ways than the obvious.

Barton also knew that sometimes he forgot all this and asked his detectives to do things they would automatically do. Zander in particular had more investigative experience than he did, and the youngsters were often more clued up with the technology side of things.

Barton focused on the task at hand. If this was a mugging or something personal, it was likely that the attacker would be finished for the night. It was rare, although not unheard of, for anyone to commit more than one attack. Unless, of course, it could be someone desperate for drugs and they might not have taken enough for what they needed.

When he reached the front door, the security light above the garage lit up, quickly revealing to Barton that the unusual pattern on the cream door was a smear of blood. It was raining harder now. By the morning, the block paving wasn't likely to give up many secrets. He scanned the ground and the grass to check for anything out of the ordinary, but came up empty-handed.

He returned to the boot of his vehicle, grabbed five cones and a roll of police tape. After checking the door was locked, he made a small cordon outside it, then got back in his car with a rueful smile.

There was nothing like keeping your eye in, but he seemed to be doing a lot of it lately.

Zander reckoned Barton was the only DI in the country with cones in his boot, but Barton had used them regularly. Once when his car had broken down on a motorway.

He wasn't protecting the scene for evidential purposes, though, because there was nobody to stay with the scene all night. They wouldn't be able to show a court continuity with any item discovered, but it would let people know of the police's interest, which should keep them away from the property and keep the neighbours alert.

He sat behind the wheel, took his mobile from his pocket and updated Control. Then he spun his vehicle around in the road and headed towards the hospital. It could be a long night, especially if the victim died.

13

DI BARTON

Barton drove past eight ambulances parked in a line at the entrance to A & E. He easily located a space in the visitors' car park. It wasn't so simple to find a spot during normal working hours.

He put a mask on and strode towards a nurse who was standing outside the entrance. She was in a heated discussion with a man tenderly holding his arm away from his body. There were other people dotted around. Barton could hear someone sobbing.

The nurse looked up at him. He showed her his warrant card, and she nodded for him to go in. There was a security guard at the sliding door who let him pass. It was surprising what the new normal had become. There was a queue of five women, two of whom had small children with them, at a reception counter with a big screen around it. He walked to the front, pressed his ID against the clear plastic and waited for another nod, which he received. They buzzed him through the next set of doors.

Barton knew where he was going and swiftly found a harassed nurse at another desk. There was a powerful smell of disinfectant. With the coronavirus, this was probably as far as he would be allowed.

'I'm here for Maggie Glover.'

'She's gone for a scan,' said the nurse. 'The skull may have been compromised from multiple blows, but we know little more than that. Maggie's mother, Joan Brown, is in consultation room four with her granddaughter. She's given us her daughter's medical history.'

'Okay. Any other injuries?'

The nurse explained about the damage to the left hand.

'Thanks. You look busy,' he said with a smile.

'We are. The girl has some special needs, so this isn't the right environment for her.' She forced a smile. 'We'd also like the room back.'

Barton gave her a thumbs up and walked in the direction the nurse pointed. The door was closed, so he knocked and opened it. An attractive lady who appeared to be in her sixties jerked her head up with hope in her eyes. She had a large child on her lap, cuddled against her in the same way you would hold a toddler. He showed her his warrant card.

'I'm Detective Inspector Barton.'

That hope dwindled.

'I'm Joan, Maggie's mother. Do you know how she is?' she asked.

'They're scanning her now and the doctors will review her injuries once that's done. They don't expect any serious complications, so it might be better if you waited at home.'

The woman raised her chin.

'I'm not leaving. I need to be here for my daughter. There isn't anyone else.'

Barton gave her a gentle smile, which he hoped showed behind his mask.

'What would Maggie want you to do?'

The lady peered down at the child tucked on her chest, who

seemed asleep. When she looked back at Barton, her face crept into a sad smile.

'I'm in your capable hands, Mr Barton. What should we do?'

'I'll drive you both home. There's nothing more you can do here. If it's a head injury, it's likely she'll be monitored throughout the night. At the very least, they'll keep her in for a few days. Try to get some sleep. You'll be more help that way.'

'My car's outside.'

'We'll sort that out tomorrow.'

'I don't mind getting a taxi here after dropping Pippa at school. In fact, we could walk. The fresh air will do us good.'

'Do you live with Maggie?'

'No, my home's in Marholm.'

'No problem. You aren't far. I'll have someone pick you up when you're ready. We'll probably have some more questions then, anyway,' he said, knowing he would grill her first on the way home. 'Is Pippa's father no longer around?'

'Maggie's widowed. Car accident six years ago.'

'Okay. Sorry to hear that.'

Joan seemed happy to talk, so Barton decided this was as good a place as any.

'Do you have any idea what happened tonight?'

'No, I could make out a strange clonking sound. I was babysitting Pippa like I do three nights a week and was expecting Maggie home, so I assumed it was her. A few minutes later, she hadn't come into the house, so I left the washing up and opened the door to find her slumped in front of it. She had blood all over her face, so I rang 999. I've watched enough TV to know basic first aid, but I don't think she was bleeding profusely. She was just unconscious. The ambulance crew arrived fast and, on their advice, I followed with Pippa.'

'You've done magnificently.'

'I'm a tough old bird.'

That wasn't how Barton would have described the well-groomed woman in front of him.

'So, you saw nothing untoward?'

'No.'

'Can you think of anyone who'd do something like this?'

'Of course not.'

'Okay, that's great. Let's get Pippa back to yours, then, shall we? She's a pretty girl. How old is she?'

'She's ten.'

'I'll see if there's a wheelchair I can borrow.'

Barton opened the door and stepped outside. He could hear shouting, running feet, loud beeps and some kind of alarm going off. He returned to the room.

'Will she be all right if I carry her?'

'Well, I'm not carrying her. I'll lead the charge.'

Barton took a blanket off the bed, wrapped it around the girl's shoulders, and lifted her up. She grumbled but didn't wake. He had a quick word with the nurse he'd spoken to on the way in and left through the chaos at the front entrance. Barton couldn't help a little chuckle as Joan cleared a route for him as if he were royalty.

14

DI BARTON

Barton placed Pippa in the rear of his 4x4 on Luke's safety seat and buckled her in. She was out for the count. He nipped back inside the main entrance to pay for his parking ticket. Barton knew Marholm was only four miles away and the journey wouldn't take long.

'Are you married?' he asked after they'd set off.

'No, divorced. Usual story. He wanted to retire, and I wanted to live.'

'Pippa and Maggie must be very close to you, seeing them so often.'

'Yes. Maggie's husband died at the same time as I left her stepfather. Her real dad vanished a few months after she was born. Her stepfather lives abroad now but they weren't close. So, Maggie and I leaned on each other, but it's easy for me. I have the Women's Institute, Bridge Club, Beetle Drive, and a rambling group. Maggie has a full-time job now and a small girl who needs a lot of extra attention. They say Pippa's autistic.'

'Diagnosis for autism often takes a while to come.'

'Yes, and I don't appreciate the label. Everyone's on the spectrum somewhere, and we move up and down it, depending on what life throws at us. Some simply need more help than others at different stages. That's all. We used to joke Pippa was stuck in her shell, and we had to coax her out, but she's certainly started to emerge over the last year. I hope this doesn't set her back. She hasn't said a word since.'

'When does school start tomorrow?'

'Nine.'

'I'll ring you in the morning around eight thirty. See if Pippa's happy to go to school. We'll have you picked up, even if I have to do it myself. We'd like a statement, where you give us as much detail about Maggie's current and past life as you can. Burglaries and muggings are usually opportunistic. The perpetrator might have been disturbed, or thought the rest of the house wasn't empty, which made him run away. But now I've had time to consider the facts, and having spoken to that nurse, I wouldn't be surprised if it was personal.'

Joan turned and scowled at him.

'Why do you say that?'

'Your daughter's house is fairly secluded in a relatively pleasant area, which fits an opportune crime, but it's down a cul-de-sac. Thieves don't like the notion of one way in and out. Many burglars or muggers attack when they see poor security, or an isolated residence. Maggie's was neither.'

'That still doesn't make it personal.'

'Maggie wasn't hit, she was beaten. Her left hand was hit repeatedly. There were also multiple blows to the head. That can indicate rage, which is often personal. Nothing was taken. They didn't steal her car. She could have died.'

'Maybe the burglar wanted to make sure she couldn't get backup.'

'Thieves and burglars often commit acquisitive offences because they know the sentences for them are comparatively light. Crimes where the loss is only financial aren't generally seen as serious as violent ones and therefore incur lesser sentences, even if the thought of a stranger in your home is incredibly unpleasant. But this was vicious. The guilty party, when we catch them, could receive a life sentence.'

Joan kept quiet as they drove into the village. At The Fitzwilliam Arms, she asked him to turn right for her house. Barton stared at the pub with fondness, but it was more a restaurant than a watering hole now. When they arrived at a dark lane with a line of cars on the verge, Joan pointed at a row of houses.

'That's my home.'

She directed him past them to an isolated but pleasant detached cottage. There was an empty drive, but only two-thirds of his car fitted on it. He left it there anyway, and they got out.

She strode down the side of the property to open the door while he carried the sleeping girl into the house. He followed Joan to a room that Pippa had obviously stayed in many times before. Joan removed around ten stuffed animals from the bed and pulled back the Disney bedspread. Barton laid Pippa on the bed.

'Will you be okay?' he asked as she tucked Pippa in.

Joan's fingers hesitated, then stroked Pippa's head with a slight tremble.

'I'll have to be.'

'It's been a tough night. I'll get going,' he said, giving her his card.

'Thank you.'

'Any problems, call me. I'll speak to you tomorrow morning.'

'Wait a moment. Let me see you out.'

Barton waited near the back door, then stepped outside when Joan reappeared a minute later. She followed him out of the cottage to the car.

'You might think me cold, but this is how my generation cope. We get on and deal with it.'

'That's great. They'll need your strength over the next few days. My mum was much the same.'

Barton had one final go at finding an angle.

'Has anything changed of late in Maggie's life?'

'No, that's why this is confusing. Everything was finally looking positive. Both at work and home, and she was even thinking about dating again. I know I'm biased, but she's a lovely person. She works so hard. Sometimes I despair at how cruel this world can be.'

Barton merely nodded. He didn't need reminding that life wasn't fair. For the first time, Joan lost her poise. Her question came out as a sob.

'Why on earth would anyone hurt Maggie?'

Barton had no idea, but tomorrow he'd begin to find out.

15

DI BARTON

Wednesday 16th December

Barton arrived at the office by eight a.m. and rang the hospital for an update. Maggie had been kept overnight in the intensive care unit as a precaution, but her prognosis was good. It sounded as if her skull had done its job and there was no swelling of the brain, although there appeared to be two hairline fractures on the top of her head. They wouldn't know for certain until the sedatives wore off completely, but she might have escaped with a slight concussion. All the fingers and also the thumb had been broken on her left hand.

Barton caught up with his emails. Only one other case from the previous night had been escalated to Major Crimes, and it was allocated to the other team. Barton was relieved. The incident had been a multiple brawl at a works Christmas Party. It had led to six people getting injured, one seriously. He recalled seeing discarded party hats in A & E the previous night and suspected that was one of the reasons they were so busy. The witness statements would take days. There were five men in the cells. It was an avalanche of work.

He wandered in to see DCI Cox, who was scowling at her computer.

'Sit down, John. I don't suppose you've got any spare DCs hiding in your desk.'

'Only the ones who didn't live up to my high standards.'

She gave him a tight smile. Barton noticed Cox's hair was shorter now and had the odd fleck of grey in it. He'd always thought of her as being young, but she was nearly forty. Time seemed to wear harder on detectives. That applied to all ranks.

'This assault last night at St Catherine's Lane,' she said. 'How serious?'

'Attempted murder might stick because of the severity of the attack, if it's personal, but the victim seems to be out of danger. It's one of those really unpleasant crimes on a woman who certainly doesn't deserve it.'

'Any leads?'

'Nothing.'

'Your manpower.'

'You already have Strange. I've got my new starter, Hoffman, then Zelensky, Malik, and Leicester. And DS Zander, of course.'

'You know what I'm going to ask. The other team is desperate.'

'These are desperate times.'

Cox raised an eyebrow.

'Okay, who do you want?'

'As many as possible. There'll be overtime available for anyone who wants it from now until Christmas day.'

Barton pondered his options. The focus of his team's work for the next two days was writing up their previous case and to prepare for their appraisals in the new year. It was a great week for him to look magnanimous, as nothing was downright urgent. Besides, they'd all like the thought of a great pay cheque in January if extra hours were available.

'I'll keep Leicester. He and I can spend two full days on this assault. Hopefully, a crack will show in that time. You take the rest of my bods and get through the workload from the party. My guys can write up the last investigation on the overtime. Most will work the weekend, then we'll see where we are after that.'

'Very kind of you, John.'

'I'm all heart.'

Barton left her office with a smile. When he reached his desk, there was a Post-it note stuck to his screen telling him that Leicester had called in sick.

16

DI BARTON

The hospital had told him no visitors today unless Maggie's condition deteriorated and then only family, so Barton rang Joan and offered to take a statement at her home in Marholm. She agreed, and he was there in ten minutes. Pippa wasn't going to school, so she would be there, too.

There was a space outside her cottage on the kerb this time, so he parked in the street. Many of the stone houses in that area were built long before driveways were necessary. Even though it wasn't far from the city centre, places like this always seemed isolated to Barton. Years ago, when he and Zander were in uniform, they'd broken into a house in the next village along and found someone who'd died almost exactly a year beforehand. They'd only known because the old man still held that day's paper on his lap.

The police had come because a pane of glass had dropped out of the rotting frame of the front door and the postman had reported it. Barton had met Mortis, the grumpy Scots pathologist who was now nearing retirement, for the first time that day. Mortis had been overjoyed at the prospect of studying the remains. Barton and

Zander had finished their shift and got steaming drunk that night. They'd been close friends ever since.

Barton knocked on the back door and was greeted warmly by Joan, but her tired eyes told of a sleepless night. She left Pippa watching a cartoon in the lounge and made them a cup of tea. He'd decided he was going to treat the case as GBH until he discovered another reason. Seeing as the victim was a woman at home, it was nearly always someone she knew. And that person was usually male, but women could be vicious too.

They went into a small but homely conservatory and sat next to each other on wicker seats. Barton helped himself to a digestive biscuit from the box that had been left on the table and opened his laptop.

'Pippa didn't want to go to school, then.'

'No, she's only ten, but when she knows her mind, there's no changing it. I asked her and she shook her head in a way that we know not to question.'

'Fair enough. I'll type as we talk. Did you both get some sleep?'

'She woke up once, but settled when I got in with her. I've had enough sleep.'

'All right. Please tell me about your daughter over the last ten years. Relationships, social life, and work, her siblings. My questioning might appear blunt, but it's only to get to the fine detail. Have there been any dramas?'

Joan rubbed her eyes. Her earlier bonhomie had clearly been forced. She seemed less a force of nature today, more a tired, elderly woman.

'That's the thing, Inspector. She hasn't had any apart from with her husband and daughter. When Pippa was born, they happily raised her together. As a very much loved only child herself, Maggie led a gilded life, until the car crash.'

'How exactly did he die?'

'He was hit head-on by a truck on a dark road. Killed instantly.'

'And that was six years ago. What about relationships since?'

'Nothing.'

Barton paused.

'For want of a better phrase, she's been celibate for six years?'

'As far as I know. Looking after a child like Pippa, even with my help, is a relentless task, and she managed to carry on working part-time. She made the decision, which she told me about, that she would focus purely on Pippa and her well-being. Then to our delight, Pippa improved so much over the last eighteen months that she could cope with after-school club a few times a week. I pick her up and look after her on the other days. Maggie was able to go back full-time.'

'What does Maggie do for fun?'

'She loves her exercise. It makes her feel strong enough to deal with whatever comes her way. Never one for a gym, me, but she lets off her steam there, and that's enough.'

Barton typed the details into the statement form. It was possible that she hadn't told her mother the truth. Six years was a long time to be single at her age. Maybe she'd been dipping her toe in various dating apps recently but kept quiet about it. He decided not to push that angle for the moment.

'Which gym does she go to?'

'The Swan Hotel. As I said, I stay with Pippa after school until Maggie comes home from her exercise classes. There's a woman she goes with, Anne-Marie, who's a colleague.'

'What's she like?'

'I haven't met her, but Maggie thinks highly enough of her to have given me her number in case of emergency. I texted her last night.'

'Any suitors at the gym?'

'Nope, nothing. I'm sure she doesn't tell me everything, but I hope she'd confide in me on things like that. Her boss, Ken, was a little over-friendly a while back, but it sounded like he was testing the water, and she nipped it in the bud.'

'Where does she work?'

'Ken's Kitchens and Bathrooms.'

'Okay, so Ken was keen.'

'That's right. Ken Wade. He obviously didn't hold a grudge because he promoted her not long after.'

Barton considered her reasoning. Maybe Ken was just trying harder. At least it was somewhere to start.

'No other issues at work?' he asked.

'I think she received a few snippy comments from a couple of the other women when she got promoted, but Maggie wasn't bothered by a bit of jealousy. She's only been full-time for a year, but she's brilliant at her job. People warm to her, so selling comes naturally to her.'

Barton continued his questioning with flagging enthusiasm. Maggie lived a quiet life. Unless she lived a secret one as well, he might struggle to find suspects. He repeated Joan's statement back to her, which she was happy with and stood to leave.

'I can give you a lift now.'

'Thanks, but I'll get a taxi later to the hospital to pick up the car,' she said.

'Are you sure?'

'Yes. Pippa's settled at the moment. Who knows? Maybe they'll let us visit later if I turn up. A few quid on car-parking fees is neither here nor there considering what's happened.'

'No problem. I hope this was just an unfortunate one-off.'

'What happens now?' asked Joan, with some of her drive returning. 'Will they throw away the key when you find whoever did it?'

'You have to admit, from what you've told me, that Hannibal

Lecter doesn't appear to be lurking in her social circle. I'll talk to her immediate work team and boss today.'

'That's it?'

'No, I've requested CSI to have a look at the crime scene, but there wasn't much there, and it was raining last night. I'm going to see a specialist at the hospital to discuss the injuries. Was Maggie left-handed?'

'Yes.'

'That had me thinking on the way over here. She could have used that hand to defend herself, but it seems unlikely to me that all the digits would get broken from a single blow. Crushed maybe, but not broken. Might someone have targeted that hand?'

'What sort of person would do that?'

'I'm not sure. It might be a clue. Would it stop her from doing her job?'

'Not really. She'd type slower, of course. Any brain damage from the beating would have been more of a hindrance.' Joan's jaw clenched. 'How dare he touch my daughter? God, I'd like five minutes with him.'

Barton chuckled.

'I think she'll be okay with you in her corner. You've got my card, but I'll be in touch.'

Barton popped his head around the lounge door to say goodbye to Pippa. She didn't turn away from the TV when he did so. Joan walked him out to the car.

'Do you know what kept me awake last night?' she said.

'No.'

'The sound that I heard outside just before I found Maggie. It was unusual, but it must have been when he was beating her.'

Barton hadn't given the weapon much thought yet.

'What was the sound?'

'There was a light tapping, which might have been her weakly trying to get my attention, but it was the other knock.'

'A knock?'

'Kind of like a woodpecker pecking at a trunk, but slower.'

'It's been a while since I heard one of those outside a cartoon.'

Joan let out a deep breath.

'Maybe it was a woodpecker, although I'm not sure they're out at night. There's a couple regularly in the trees in that area. I just wish she'd have shouted out. When pressed, I'm pretty handy with the contents of a knife block.'

'I can believe that.'

Barton smiled, but his mind was on woodpecker sounds.

17

THE SANTA KILLER

I woke up this morning at five, then went to hide the incriminating evidence in the only place I know is safe. There won't be anyone else about so early in the morning. When I'm there, it's often the only time I can sit and be with my memories and talk. I'm so sick of people pretending nothing happened. It's a shame I can't stay there.

I slip back in the house while it's still dark and climb back into bed. No one seems to bother about anyone else's comings and goings any more. It's only me who watches.

I think of what I did last night. Something took over. It didn't feel like my arm that rained down those blows. It wasn't me that ran away laughing. I'm not like that.

I adjust my earpieces to make them more comfortable and tune into Peterborough City Radio at seven a.m. They must have received my letter by now. Tim Tibbles must have opened it. TT was on the front. I wrote private and confidential and urgent. His morning show is on, but he hasn't mentioned it. Maybe it will be on the news round-up.

It feels as if I haven't slept for years. It's as though I don't deserve any sleep. I am to blame, I suppose, so I must put things right. My list burns a hole in my jeans pocket. I pull it out. There's a pencil on the table. The lead snaps as I cross out the first name.

18

DI BARTON

Barton navigated the busy roads around the hospital when he got back to Peterborough and managed to find a spot not too far from the part of the building where the mortuary was. He took his phone out of his pocket and called the number. It rang for half a minute until a woman with an American accent answered.

'Good morning, is Mortis there?'

There was a cool pause.

'Is this some kind of joke?'

Barton realised he'd used the pathologist's nickname.

Mortis had come about because of Menteith's fascination with the stages of death, which he often cited enthusiastically in his conclusions, that were always detailed to the extreme.

'Sorry, is Dr Menteith in?'

'Hold the line.'

Barton smiled, put a black face mask on, got out of his car, and walked through the entrance. The efficient voice came back on.

'He said to say if it's John Barton, then he's out.'

Barton laughed and cut the call. When he reached the reception area at the mortuary, he was greeted by a slim, tall woman with a blue mask on. He approached the desk. She had elfin short black hair and the biggest, bluest eyes Barton had ever seen. She winked at him. He wasn't sure if it was a flirtatious wink or one that told him he was prey.

'Dr Menteith said he's too old to run. Go straight in.'

Barton walked into the examination room to find Mortis reading a book sitting in a chair next to one of the stainless-steel tables. Sitting there in his immaculate white doctor's coat, with his thinning, light-grey hair, he looked more or less the same as the last time he'd seen him, although there was perhaps a little more weight in his face. Mortis glanced up with a straight face.

'I assume you're here for the cleaning role we just advertised,' he said.

'That's right. You appear to be employing young, beautiful and vibrant employees nowadays, so I thought I'd fit in nicely.'

'Pretty, isn't she? If I was a hundred and forty years younger, I'd be interested.'

'Is she American?'

'Yep, Skylar's from New York. She's a mature student. I wouldn't annoy her. She's streetwise and we have a lot of suitable hiding places here.'

Barton eyed the rows of cabinet fronts, which must have hidden many gruesome sights. He gestured to the book.

'I didn't take you for a big fiction reader.'

Mortis waved the novel at him.

'*Trainspotting*, by the man himself. I went to university around the time this book was set. I lost a few friends to drugs. Good people with promising careers. It wasn't just smackheads, as Mr Welsh liked to refer to them, who perished. I was having a nostalgic moment. We had some fun, but we were reckless with our youth.'

Barton nodded. 'Not as easy for the young nowadays.'

'No, if they're really careless, it ends up on Instagram for eternity. Reading the last chapter of this again has made me think about how we squander so much of our time looking instead of living.'

Barton grabbed a high stool at a workstation and sat on it.

'Go on.'

'When we're young, we waste time focusing on the future. To Christmas, our next birthday, leaving school, university, first jobs, first relationship, coming foreign holiday, but don't pass much thought to what we're up to generally. Then it tilts. We start to waste our time looking forward to when that great job will come along, or getting out of the rat race, or to when we're going to be thin, or happy.'

'Ah, I see. Because those things aren't guaranteed.'

'Well, I suppose none of it is, but at least the first list is the natural scheme of things. The second list is fleeting possibilities. At your age, John, you start to look around. Parents are dead or fading, friends your own age have also passed. You begin to understand that it's stupid to spend your life staring at the horizon because the right now is all you're guaranteed to have.'

Barton nodded. Mortis was on the money.

'You're spot on. I never took the time to appreciate nature or my health when I was younger. Nowadays, I often notice trees, or gaze around at parties or gatherings and appreciate being there in a way that I didn't before.'

'And then there's my stage, which is the staring back. It's easy to reminisce with sadness or anger, but once you reach your sixties, the past often becomes more rose-tinted. It's very reassuring to know that you've lived and laughed.'

Mortis slowly closed his book and rested it on the lethal-looking tray of tools next to him.

'Now, what do you want? We've got charades starting at midday.'

'I had a few questions about violent head trauma.'

'Okay, when will they be wheeling our subject in?'

'This one's still alive.'

Mortis's eyes widened. He rose from his seat, put his hand to his heart, and pretended to stagger.

'John, finally. I'm impressed. Obviously, it's taken a while, but that really is policing for the twenty-first century. Robert Peel would be proud. Fancy, trying to solve the crimes while they're still alive.'

'You know, every moment in this room is a joy.'

'That's how I feel. Go on, then, spit it out.'

'I have a victim with every digit broken on her left hand and two linear fractures to the skull. Victim is concussed but seems to have got off relatively lightly. No weapon was recovered.'

Mortis hummed to himself as he thought for a moment.

'Broken fingers and hands are common when fending off an attacker, but it's rare for them all to be damaged unless it's a crushing injury.'

'Nope, I think they'd have said crushed if that was the case.'

'So maybe that hand was targeted and repeatedly hit. Interesting. And the two linear fractures were to the top of the head?'

'Yes.'

'That would mean the victim was probably attacked from behind by someone at least as tall if not taller, or the swipes would be from the side, unless, of course, they hit them after they'd fallen.'

'How hard is it to crack a skull?' asked Barton.

'Unfortunately asking that is like inquiring how easy it is to crack an egg. The bone is strongest when it's intact, so the first crack is important. Age of Jane Doe?'

'I didn't say it was a woman.'

'Aren't most of them?'

'Thirty-eight.'

'Her skull should be strong, which means you need to focus on the weapon.'

'Right.'

'Linear fractures are common from falls. If you fall off a climbing frame and hit a blunt object, such as the ground, a fracture often occurs. There are four types of skull fractures.'

Barton took a deep breath in preparation for Mortis's latest biology lesson.

'A linear one cracks the bone but doesn't move it. Recuperation is swift, surgery is usually unnecessary. That should apply in your case. Then there are depressed fractures, where the skull sinks in from the trauma, which can damage the brain. Obviously, that's serious, but it can also be more dangerous because of swelling. Risky surgery might be needed to correct the deformity.'

'That would be caused by a harder impact.'

'Yes, a higher fall, or being hit by a more solid object, perhaps swung at a faster velocity. There are also diastatic fractures along the fuse lines, which we generally see in infants and young children. Basilar fractures occur at the base near the spine and are deadly because they can affect the blood supply to the brain.'

'So, our victim was probably hit by something light and blunt from above.'

'Excellent, John. Glad you're keeping up. Yes, an ice pick would depress the skull into the brain. A chair leg probably wouldn't. Do you remember your physics lessons?'

'I'm not sure I can recall what I watched on TV last night.'

'What is force?'

'Luke Skywalker's special power.'

Mortis shook his head in mock disgust.

'Force equals mass times acceleration. Something relatively light wouldn't normally depress the skull due to its lower mass.'

'Unless it was swung by someone who was incredibly strong.'

'Correct, or there was an undiagnosed weakness in the skull.'

'Ah.'

'Also, if you hit me with a tyre iron, or a thick piece of lead pipe, I could die, but if a child or elderly attacker did it, then I might get away with a bruise. Women are generally lighter and smaller, so their impact might be less, but those are stereotypes. If your attacker was Brigitte Nielsen, then all bets are off.'

'Yes, but it gives us a starting point.'

'Correct. If your person was intent on murder, they'd have used that ice pick, or, if they were able to sneak up on their victim, surely a knife would be easier, cheaper and more accessible.'

'There's one more thing. The woman inside the house heard a strange knocking sound. Higher than a solid blow would cause.'

Mortis snorted.

'I was joking about playing charades, or are we playing Cluedo here? If you tell me in a minute there was gunshot and CCTV, you'll be seeing your giblets early this year.'

'Sorry.' Barton laughed.

'A higher note would obviously indicate that a lighter object was used. A noticeably higher sound hints that it was hollow. A bat, for example.'

Barton smiled. 'A bat?'

'Just a guess, but how many things do you swing? An aluminium baseball bat fits your attack. It's light to carry, easy to buy, and would make a higher sound than a wooden bat.'

'Don't aluminium bats hit harder than wooden ones?'

'Unless Babe Ruth is your man, I wouldn't obsess about that. Pathologists rarely see victims from baseball bats. They are terrible as a weapon, but they've been made popular by American movies. You need space, time and technique for maximum impact. Not ideal in a speedy assault, and unless you got a good blow in first, you might not even incapacitate the victim. A hammer makes a much more effective instrument, although then the risk of murder is higher.'

'I'm thinking that a younger person might make the mistake of choosing a weapon like that, having seen it in a film.'

'Good idea, although I seem to remember one being used in *Carlito's Way*, which was about thirty years ago. Considering the rest of this conversation, assume the age of your assailant to be fifty or under, and I reckon you're on to a winner.'

'Great,' said Barton. 'I should have this sorted by teatime.'

'I'm glad to have cleared that up for you. Now, you could have phoned for that. Why are you really here?'

Barton slid a Christmas card out of his suit pocket.

'You and your wife have a wonderful Christmas, Mortis.'

'Stop trying to soften me up. We're not sending any this year.'

Barton chuckled and waved goodbye. Mortis's wife had already sent him one.

19

DI BARTON

Barton grabbed a cappuccino from Costa near the hospital entrance after settling the parking bill and trudged back to his car. He checked his phone for missed calls or messages, but there weren't any. Considering he didn't have any staff, that wasn't surprising. He was tempted to nip into his office, but all that was there for him was a container of green soup and a slice of rye bread.

Barton drove out of the car park and managed to make his way to Ken Wade's kitchen showroom without stopping at the McDonald's on the way. The showroom was based in Werrington on Mancetter Square. Barton considered it an industrial estate, but the sign outside now declared him to be arriving at a retail and business park. It didn't appear that different from when he'd brought his rusting cars along to be patched up over twenty-five years ago. He parked in one of the spaces at the front of the estate, rang Control and confirmed his location, then got out of his vehicle.

The third unit had a dazzling clean white sign, with just the word 'Ken's' in big red letters. The front was mostly glass, and, despite the inclement weather, he could see clearly into a spacious showroom full of what looked from a distance to be quality products. Barton had barely stepped through the door when a slim man, who seemed to appear out of nowhere, greeted him and put a mask on. His name badge declared him to be Ken. He reminded Barton a bit of Fred Astaire and moved as agilely. Up close, Barton noticed he had unusually coloured eyes, which were a yellow and green colour.

'Morning, sir. Welcome to Ken's Kitchens and Bathrooms. How can I help you today?'

'Would it be possible to use one of your bathrooms?'

'Pardon?'

'I've been out of the office for a while and need to go.'

Barton showed his warrant card.

'Oh, sorry. Of course. You must be here about Maggie. Come this way.'

Barton followed him down the showroom.

'Heidi,' said Ken. 'Keep an eye on the shop. I'm just going to take this officer out the back.'

A middle-aged woman, whose upbeat name clearly didn't suit, slouched past Barton with the weight of the world on her shoulders. He never would have believed someone could look so utterly miserable wearing an elf's hat, especially with 'All I Want for Christmas Is You' playing over the tannoy.

'Morning,' she said, as though it were her last.

Ken guided him through a door at the back and pointed at another door with a unisex sign on it. It contained a small toilet, and Barton took advantage of the facilities. He walked out and found Ken laughing in a spacious office next door with six desks. All had women sitting at them. There was a bigger desk at the head of them, which made Barton think of a schoolroom.

A slim woman with stylish grey hair and bright red lipstick strolled up to Ken with a Post-it note. She had a multitude of gold rings on her fingers.

'Message for you, Ken.'

He gave her a wide smile.

'Thanks, Judith. Make us a coffee, please.'

'Sure thing.'

Ken beckoned Barton to follow him and walked into another room next to the main office. This windowless room was smaller, spartan, and had only one entrance.

'I've heard of minimalist interior design, but this is something else,' said Barton.

'This smaller office is for meetings when we need privacy.'

Ken left to grab another chair and returned with Judith, who carried two coffees in plastic cups. After she'd left, Ken shut the door and removed his mask. Barton did the same, gave him a tight smile and took a seat. He put his laptop bag on the table and opened it up.

'Tell me about Maggie.'

Ken sat down with a humph.

'Maggie is just wonderful. I call her my best girl. She's been a real trooper too, what with the disabled child and her husband. We only had her part-time for a few years, but she's full-time now. Or was. How is she?'

Barton raised an eyebrow at the plentiful information and dated terminology.

'I think she's going to be okay. It'll have been an unpleasant experience for her.'

'I bet. Her mother rang us. It was a terrible shock. Well, we'll look after her when she's back.'

'Do you know which handed she is?'

'Pardon?'

'Right or left?'

'Oh, erm, I'm not sure. Everything's computerised nowadays, so you mostly see people typing with both hands.'

'One of her hands has been damaged, so she might struggle to type as fast. Will she be okay to do her job?'

'Of course. She's front of house with Anne-Marie and Heidi, so they do the greeting and selling. The admin team out there does all the processing and chasing. Some of them can type.'

'Do they ever sell?'

'They don't need to with Maggie here. That's why she's so important to us. She's irreplaceable. I never want her to leave.'

The way he said that made Barton look up from his notebook where he'd been writing.

'Was she thinking about leaving?'

'I hope not.'

'Why say it, then?'

Ken's cheery manner slipped for a moment, and Barton detected a hint of sneakiness or even anger.

'The bathroom and kitchen business in this city is surprisingly insular, so we all have a feel for what the other companies are up to. We've been doing well for years. I won an award, as did Maggie and I'm pretty sure gets approached from time to time.'

'Do you know by whom?'

'No, she said she hadn't, but I reckon she had.'

'Why wouldn't she tell you?'

Again, the sly expression slipped across his face like a small lone cloud on a breezy summer day.

'Because she's a lovely person. She hates any animosity. Her mantra is life is too short for bad feeling.'

Barton let out a deep breath.

'Okay, you gave her a promotion recently.'

'Yes, and it was well deserved.'

'Has she been here the longest of those who work in the showroom?'

'No, Heidi's been with us for twenty years. Anne-Marie started about a decade later, but she's been part-time for long spells. Maggie's the most recent to join by far. Heidi was actually my first employee.'

'Did either Heidi or Anne-Marie get the arse, if you'll excuse the expression, from being passed over for promotion?'

'No, I don't think so. Perhaps some healthy rivalry, but Maggie is perfect for the position. She's a complete role model.'

'One whom you asked out on a date.'

'Pardon?'

Barton leaned back in his seat and watched Ken squirm.

'Who told you that?'

'Does it matter? Surely the important thing is whether it's true.'

'I don't see what that's got to do with anything.'

'Well, people are more liable to get the arse if you've been promoting people on looks, not talent.'

Ken leaned forward. Definitely anger in his eyes this time.

'I promoted her on ability. Anyone who says different is a fool.'

'But you did ask her out before you promoted her.'

Ken sat back down and took a deep, calming breath.

'I asked her if she wanted to go for a drink. She's had a tough time of things. I thought it'd be nice to be wined and dined.'

'Just wined and dined?'

'It's not illegal.'

'No, but there should be boundaries when it comes to manager and employee.'

'No boundaries were crossed, Inspector Barton. Anything else you'd like to know?'

Barton couldn't quite decide what type of guy Ken was.

'Are you married?' he asked.

Ken laughed out loud.

'Widowed. A long time ago.' His smile dropped. 'I hope you're not trying to fit me up for this.'

'Where were you last night?'

'At home.'

'Can anyone corroborate that?'

'No, actually, yes! My neighbour came around about seven thirty. He'll confirm I was there.'

'How long did he stay for?'

'Not long, five minutes, maybe. This is ridiculous. Why would I attack my most valuable employee?'

From what he'd just heard, Barton could think of one obvious reason, but, rejection aside, it didn't seem as if Ken knew the time of the assault.

There was definitely something slippery about him, though.

20

DI BARTON

Barton made Ken sit with him while he finished typing out the statement, just in case any last queries sneaked to the surface. In his experience, guilty people didn't like silence. Ken managed to remain quiet.

'Final few questions, Ken. Do the women generally get on well, both admin and sales? Or are there points of regular conflict?'

'No, we're successful. They rely on each other to hit the targets, and smash them, we do.'

'Ah, so they receive bonuses.'

'Everyone wins if we do well. The sales staff can earn much higher rewards, but their basic salaries are lower.'

'Does that annoy the admin staff?'

'No, I don't think so.'

'Do Anne-Marie, Heidi and Maggie all approximately earn the same?'

Barton peered up when a reply didn't come.

'No,' said Ken slowly. 'It's performance related. Maggie is the best, then Anne-Marie.'

Barton's mind cast back to the surly Heidi. That wasn't the greatest surprise.

'Are the three of them a good team?'

'Anne-Marie and Maggie are. Heidi struggled to pick up the new IT system, and her husband has been in and out of work. Family commitments have also got in the way somewhat, so she's not as focused.'

'Sorry, I can't get my head around the differences. How much would Maggie earn compared to the others?'

'Thirty thousand for her, Anne-Marie twenty-five, Heidi twenty.'

Barton wrote the figures down and put that it was a sizeable difference.

'Could I talk to Heidi in here?'

Ken looked at his watch.

'No, she's asked to finish shortly. Midday is common for her to go home during the week unless we're flat out. Her husband, Cameron, needs a lift to go to a job interview in Huntingdon today. I'm very flexible with her hours at the moment.'

Barton quickly connected the dots.

'Why doesn't he drive himself?'

Ken shrugged and studied his nails. Barton noticed they weren't that clean.

'Is Anne-Marie covering?'

'No, I'll cope today. It's me and Anne-Marie in tomorrow with the part-timer, then all three of us and Heidi over the weekend when we're busiest.'

'You have a part-time sales assistant.'

'Yes, she normally works weekends, but we get busy before Christmas.'

'People buy kitchens as presents?'

'Yes, some do. Beats perfume.'

Barton didn't reply. Holly was getting perfume.

'Okay, do Anne-Marie and Heidi live in Peterborough?' asked Barton.

Ken reeled their addresses off as though he went around their houses regularly. At least it saved Barton filling out the data-protection paperwork.

'Do you mind telling me how old you are?' asked Barton.

Ken's eyes narrowed and looked to the side, as though he were being asked to reveal his innermost desires, which Barton suspected might be disturbing.

'Fifty-three.'

Barton smiled. He shook Ken's hand and left the building. He'd made a decision about Ken by that point and decided that he might not be guilty of assault, but he was definitely a shifty weasel.

21

DI BARTON

Outside, Barton was about to get back in his car when he noticed the end unit was a café. His stomach rumbled. He sauntered over to read the menu in the window, but the glass was too steamed up. A chuckling woman left the premises, giving him a waft of fried food. He was drawn in, almost on tiptoes, as if the Pied Piper were playing.

There were only two other patrons; a trucker type who was as wide as he was tall, and a rake-thin youngster in Network Rail overalls. They were both leaning over large plates brimming with greasy-looking food.

A plump woman came over to him with a smile. She had an accent that sounded Greek.

'You come for breakfast?'

Barton didn't want to seem rude.

'Okay. What have you got?'

The lady pointed to the menu on the wall. There was a light breakfast, a vegan breakfast, a large breakfast and something called The Colossus. Barton looked over at the trucker, ploughing manfully through his food.

'One Colossus coming up,' said the waitress, grinning. 'Starting this week, if you eat it all, then you get your next one for free, but there's a snag.'

She widened her eyes at him, then left. Eight minutes later, Barton's eyes bulged at the plate that hit his table with a clonk. He got stuck in. The trucker belched next to him and pushed his half-eaten breakfast away. He went to the counter and paid. Barton smiled as he heard him and the waitress laughing.

The railway worker, surprisingly, persevered. Barton couldn't help chuckling as the man wiped the last bit of bean juice up with his final chunk of crusty bread. The waitress stood next to him.

'Wow, well done, Lonnie. Impressive. Are you sure you haven't put any in your pockets?'

'Nope. Hollow legs, me. You said if I finished, I got a free breakfast, but there was a catch.'

'Yes. You do get your next one for free, but you have to eat it now.'

22

DI BARTON

Barton managed to stop after two-thirds, otherwise he'd have had to slither up a tree like a snake for the afternoon. Anne-Marie was next on his list. She and Heidi lived on the same street, Mayor's Walk, but it was a long one, which had very different houses at each end. Anne-Marie's was at the Thorpe Hall end. He pulled up onto a spacious drive when he arrived, between a rusty truck and a smaller car, which was only a few years old.

A gangly black lad who looked to be in his late teens answered the door with his arms crossed. He stood eye to eye with Barton.

'Yo!'

There was a shout from the back of the house before Barton could reply. The teenager's attitude vanished.

'Good afternoon. How may I help?'

'I'm here to see Anne-Marie.'

'Who shall I say is calling?'

'Detective Inspector Barton.'

The kid's face fell.

'Wait there, sir.'

The door was pulled but didn't sneck, which allowed Barton to hear the kid whispering loudly.

'There's a cop out there asking for you.'

'What the hell have you done now?' he heard a woman shout at the top of her voice.

'Nothing, Mum. Honestly.'

'Just pulling your leg, baby. He'll be visiting because of Maggie. Here's the cinema money for being fairly polite and helping with the cleaning. Off you trot.'

The door opened to show the very tall baby giving his mother a sloppy kiss on the cheek. He pretended to doff his cap at Barton, then ran past him, laughing.

'Come in, please,' said Anne-Marie.

Barton followed her in. She was a big-framed woman with curly hair and a large smile.

'We'll talk in the dining room, but you'll need to walk past Bagpuss.'

She opened the lounge door. Barton strolled by a thin man about his own age with short, greying dreadlocks, who was quietly snoring in an armchair. The fire was roaring, which made Barton glance longingly at the other empty armchair.

He followed Anne-Marie into a lovely dining room, which looked out onto a small tidy garden. There was a rusting swing in the corner. Barton had one similar in his own backyard.

'Take a seat,' she said, noticing his gaze. 'I can't bring myself to throw it away just yet, even though my youngest is eight and only wants to stare at computer screens.'

'Snap,' said Barton. 'What age are yours?'

'The others are twelve, fourteen and Marlon, who you met, is eighteen.'

'Mine are seven, thirteen and eighteen.'

'Nice! Marlon was shorter than me a year ago. Look at him now. Time flies.'

'Yes, it sure does.'

'Would you like a coffee?'

'No, I won't take up too much of your afternoon. You've heard what's happened.'

'Yes. Maggie's mum, Joan, is really on the ball. She texted me last night and I told Ken, even though she probably messaged him as well. I can't believe it. You read about these things, but it's something else when it happens to someone you know. I was so angry for her I barely slept an hour.'

'I'll need to record what we talk about, if that's okay.'

'Of course, whatever you like.'

'You and Maggie are friends, is that right?'

'Yeah, work and gym. We've got closer lately, so we grab the occasional meal now and coffee, but we're both bogged down with family life. I'm sure we'd do more together if we had time.'

'Any idea who might have done it?'

'None at all. She's a fab person. Everyone likes her.'

'Even Heidi?'

Anne-Marie laughed. 'Maybe not Heidi. She doesn't like anything or anyone, but life's tough for her.'

'And you don't mind Maggie getting paid more than you?'

'No way, I learn from her. You daft men are putty in her hands!'

'Cheers.'

'Sorry.'

They both chuckled.

'She regularly gets job offers from other companies. I wish I was in such high demand.'

'Popularity has its curses, which links into what I'd like to ask you. I'm looking for some kind of motivation as to why someone would hurt Maggie. Nobody has a bad word to say about her yet.'

Anne-Marie smiled but didn't reply straight away. When she spoke, Barton got the impression she was genuinely affected by what had happened to Maggie.

'Did you meet the boss?'

'Yes.'

'Oily fucker, ain't he?'

Barton laughed out loud.

'A little.'

'Luckily, he's out and about most of the time. Look, I just rang the hospital. I said she was my sister. They told me there doesn't seem to be any swelling, so they should have her on a step-down wing soon, and she might even be allowed home on Sunday or Monday morning if everything improves as expected.'

'Thanks. Saved me a job.'

'Have you put a guard on her?'

'No.'

'If it was personal, maybe they'll go back to finish her off.'

Barton had considered that, but the chances of anyone wandering onto an intensive care unit nowadays was very remote, even more so with all the precautions.

'I'm not getting an organised crime vibe here, but it's worth a call to the hospital. To be brutal, if someone really wanted her dead, they'd have done it last night. I think the assault was either to take something from her or the house, unrequited love, or it was some kind of warning.'

'Warning about what?'

'She's a pleasant, pretty person, and good things tend to happen to people like Maggie, like promotions, but that sometimes causes bad things to arrive at the same time. Someone looking in might be jealous. Or maybe their man has been obsessing about her. Perhaps it's a weird neighbour who's secretly fantasising they're going to be lovers.'

'People are attracted to Maggie. She's always getting attention at the gym.'

'Anything creepy?'

'No, I don't think so. Nothing that's particularly bothered her. She hasn't felt as though she had time for any of that, but she always lets them down nicely. I think she fancies the fitness instructor, Lothar, but it's more one of those admiring from afar things.'

'Does he like her?'

'I'm not sure. I'm pretty sure he likes himself.'

They both grinned.

'Okay, as I said, if it wasn't an opportunistic crime, it's hard to imagine someone balanced hurting her.'

'I suppose that fits in with what you mentioned that nasty things can still happen to nice people.'

'Correct. We need to find this person because they'll probably do it again sooner or later. Although you never know what's going on in people's lives. Maggie could be a serial Tinder dater with a dark and devious personal life, or be secretly providing Peterborough's underworld with drugs and guns.'

Anne-Marie guffawed.

Barton was packing his laptop away when a young girl appeared at the conservatory door.

'I want something nice for dinner,' she said with a stern pout.

Anne-Marie beamed at her and got out of her seat.

'This is my second youngest, Hungry Hannah, who often comes home for lunch because she ate her pack-up early.'

Barton rose with a grin.

'I'll get out of your way. Here's my card. Ring me about anything you think could be important. I was hoping to speak to Maggie because she might have an idea who it was, but that might have to wait until next week. That should focus our investigation, but hopefully it's just a random, petty crime that got out of hand.'

'I'll walk you out.'

They tiptoed past her husband, who'd sunk lower in the seat. He grumbled a little, then smiled in his sleep.

'You know,' said Anne-Marie, 'You know, I don't understand you men. My man, Drew, is a hard worker. He does nights at Booker's cash and carry. Has done for years, and he never complains. I told him his luck was in this afternoon with Marlon at the cinema and when Josie went back to school. Josie loves her mum's cooking and often comes home for lunch. Anyway, we had two or three beers, then I made us all a pleasant pasta dish. And there he is snoring away. If he doesn't wake up soon, he'll have missed his chance!'

Barton winced.

'What?' she asked.

'At his age, three beers? Then a big meal. You'll be lucky if he wakes up again this year.'

Barton closed the door to another bout of Anne-Marie's infectious laughter. Sometimes dealing with the public was a joy.

23

THE SANTA KILLER

Aged 11

My dad pokes his head into my bedroom.

'That lad's here again,' he says.

He points a finger at me when I slip past him.

'Behave!' he shouts as I clatter down the stairs.

I yank the door open and bump fists with Jamie. My dad's not happy about our friendship, but I think Jamie's great. He's so funny and always looking for exciting things to do. Although I'm not at all keen on his latest plan.

'Okay, I'm going to do it now.'

'Why bother?'

'I told you. He keeps chatting my girl up.'

The blonde in question doesn't appeal to me in the slightest. She has teeth like a crocodile.

'Why don't you talk to her about it?'

'Because, smart-arse, I don't need to. He's getting whacked with this.'

Jamie opens the carrier bag and pulls out an empty wine bottle.

'How will that stop him from talking to her?'

'It's a warning. I whack him over the back of the head with it. He passes out and we run away.'

I give him a sceptical look.

'Don't you want him to know you did it?'

'He'll know. We've argued about my woman already, but this way, he won't be certain, so he can't grass us up.'

We leave and I walk alongside him, pleased that I'm the much faster runner. The kid he's planning to hit is enormous for his age. He has a moustache. I have two pubes. The real reason Jamie's doing a sneak attack is because his ass would be kicked in a straight fight. I've not met any kind of girl that might have me poking the hornet's nest that Jamie's about to.

We get to the street where Jamie lives. His nemesis, Marvin, lives about twelve doors away, so Jamie sees him delivering the local free paper every Friday after he's had his tea. There are some dodgy flats on his route, where he has to press the buzzer to get in. That's where Jamie's surprise will occur. My task is lookout and to provide a false alibi if Marvin tells on us. Our word against his, apparently.

We stand around chatting while we wait for him to come into view at the bottom of the avenue. We'll spot it's him in the distance by his fluorescent bag. We sit on the kerb in the street while Jamie smokes a cigarette, looking cool. He glares at an old dog walker, who no doubt is surprised that someone his age is smoking. I have a quick puff, but don't inhale. I'm wired, and I notice Jamie is, too.

'There he is. You know what to do.'

I cross over to the other side of the road and sit on a garden wall. My legs jiggle. It seems to take Marvin ages to do all the houses on the road, but he strolls by without looking at me. I give a thumbs up to Jamie. I lick my lips as Marvin saunters up the path to the flats. Jamie sneaks out from behind the tree with the bottle already raised.

I watch as Marvin puts one hand on the handle of the entrance door and presses the buzzer with the other. Jamie wallops the bottle into his skull. The world tilts on its axis when Marvin doesn't fall over. All he does is move his fingers slowly to the rear of his head. The surprised, pained expression when he turns around is soon replaced by one of fury.

Jamie takes a step back. Marvin then points his finger at Jamie who whacks the bottle against the wall. I can't help smiling as the bottle smashes into smithereens and drops from his hand. He spins and runs towards me. His eyes look as if they're about to pop out of his head.

I'm already in the set position. I pin my ears back and race down the road faster than I've ever run playing football. It's like I'm flying. I overtake two kids on their BMXs and don't stop until I reach home.

I barge through the door, leap inside, slam it shut, and pull the bolt across. My heart is pounding and I have to put my hands on my hips to breathe. My dad has the racing on the television. He looks over and raises an eyebrow.

'Who's chasing you?'

I'm gasping so hard, I can't lie, even if I could think of something to say. My dad stands up and walks over to me. He takes my hand and guides me to the sofa.

'Sit down.'

I plonk onto the seat and lean back, avoiding eye contact, desperately trying to slow my gasps.

'Did you win?' I splutter, gesturing to the TV.

'Nice try. Spit it out. What happened?'

I still can't figure out a lie, so I tell him the truth. I hoped I'd feel better after, but the look of disappointment on his face will last long in my memory.

'Never do anything like that again, you hear?'

'But—'

'No buts. You aren't that kind of boy. We aren't that kind of family.'

I nod, make my excuses, and leave to go to my room.

When I get to school after the weekend, I see Jamie in the playground for the first time since the incident. It looks as though his face has been used as a punchbag. He rolls his eyes and grins, not being the type to hold grudges.

'I take it he caught up with you, then?' I ask.

'Yeah, he got me at my front door as I was putting the key in. Gave me a right old hiding. My bloody dad was watching through the window.'

'No way. Didn't he come out of the house?'

'Nah, he'd been drinking. Didn't half gimme a lecture after I'd managed to drag myself out of the rosebush. More or less told me to learn from the experience while he bandaged my hand.'

'Did you mention the bottle?'

'Yep.'

'What did he say about that?'

'Said I should have used a baseball bat.'

24

DI BARTON

Barton took his time driving back to the police station. This was becoming an intriguing case. There was something odd about how everything was stacking up. The victim seemed to be a nice lady who shouldn't have had any enemies. Yet the location of the incident made it unlikely to be random, and the nature of the attack seemed too individual and frenzied for it not to be personal in some way. Barton had a sense that it might not be an isolated incident. He would check to make sure there hadn't been anything similar recently because he reckoned someone out there was either very angry or they'd lost their marbles.

Barton had just pulled a seat up at a desk when his phone rang. It was DC Leicester.

'Afternoon.'

'Hi, guv. I thought I'd explain about my illness. I feel terrible for letting you down.'

'Don't worry. If you're sick, you're sick. What's up?'

'Explosive diarrhoea.'

Barton shook his head. Was there any other kind?

'We can talk about that when you get back, if it's really necessary.'

Barton wondered for a moment if Leicester had something serious on his mind, but it appeared not.

'I'm bored,' said Leicester. 'There's nothing wrong with me apart from the fact I can't be more than a few metres from a toilet. I was wondering if there was something I could do for you from home.'

Obviously, there was, but Barton resisted.

'Enjoy a relaxing day at home if you can. Do you need me to pick up anything? Imodium, maybe. Or a cork?'

'No, Malik's been around with fruit and medicine. It's just I exercise in most of my free time, so I'm at a loose end.'

Barton couldn't resist.

'You certainly seem to have one,' he said.

'Good one, guv,' said Leicester without meaning it.

'Okay. Do some research on baseball bats for me. It's a bit of a long shot that I usually wouldn't bother with at this point, but something like that might have been used. An aluminium one in particular. If you've got the runs, don't come back until at least Friday.'

'Do you mean look at who sells them? That sort of thing.'

'Yeah, I can't imagine too many places would locally, but ordering online must be easy.'

'Okay. What's the case?'

Barton explained about the assault and not having much to go on. He pictured Leicester thinking, because he had a way of running his hands through his hair when he was absorbing information. Barton still remembered Leicester's first day, all ginger hair and fresh skin, but even he was over thirty now. Zander reckoned he looked like a young Boris Becker.

'Have you thought about recent customers of Ken's Kitchens?' asked Leicester.

'Do you mean oddballs stalking the pretty woman who was assisting them?'

'Them as well, but having a new bathroom or kitchen fitted is a costly and expensive process. Perhaps she sold someone a kitchen, and the fitters were useless, and it fell to pieces. This Ken sounds like he might wind people up. Maybe they complained about the workmanship, and they were brushed off because they'd already paid.'

'Would that make someone angry enough to go round the salesperson's house with a bat? How would they know where she lived?'

'Who knows? Nothing like having work done or DIY to make folk act crazily. They could have followed her car after she'd finished her shift one night. I'll have a look on Google reviews, Facebook and Trustpilot to see if they've had any angry punters or whether their feedback is generally good or bad. I'll email you if I find anything.'

It was more unneeded proof that investigations ran better with teamwork. Barton cut the call and rang Ken's Kitchens and Bathrooms. Judith answered the phone but said that Ken had popped out. She'd ask him to ring Barton back. Barton decided to get everything he'd done so far on the computer.

By five, Barton was up to date and planning his next day's schedule. Ken hadn't returned his call, which was annoying and naturally made Barton suspicious. He'd be getting a visit tomorrow if he wasn't back in touch.

The other obvious line of inquiry was Maggie's neighbours. If he'd had the manpower, he'd have done that today, but it couldn't be helped. Barton huffed. He would do it himself early tomorrow morning. There were only twenty houses in the street and only a few with a view of Maggie's house. It'd been a busy day, and he was looking forward to getting home to dinner. Holly did a proper meal on Wednesday nights now to coincide with Luke's football training after school.

Barton's phone rang with an unrecognised number, but it registered in his mind.

'Barton speaking.'

'Hello, Inspector Barton, it's Joan. Maggie's mother.'

'Hi.'

'Um, well, I wasn't sure whether I'd be wasting your time, but Pippa wanted to do some drawing this afternoon. She seemed content, so I left her to it.'

'Okay.'

'I really think you need to see what she's done, because it doesn't look good.'

'What? The picture?'

'She's drawn what looks like somebody attacking a woman in front of her house.'

25

DI BARTON

Barton blinked a couple of times as his brain engaged.

'Are you saying she's drawn the picture of her mother's assault?'

'It seems like it.'

'What did you tell her about Maggie being in hospital?'

'I said that her mum had banged her head and was having some tests, but she was fine and would be home soon.'

'It's highly unlikely she'd have imagined this, then. Could she have seen it?'

'Yes, I'm afraid so. She sometimes watches from the window as her mum leaves and arrives.'

'It would have been nice if you'd told me that yesterday.'

'I had a lot on my mind, Inspector. I'd also been in her room about five minutes beforehand and she'd been in bed asleep.'

'Maybe she was pretending.'

'It wouldn't be the first occasion, and it's a decent explanation.'

'Can you send me an image of it?'

'By post?'

Barton smiled.

'Do you use WhatsApp?'

'No. I text and ring. The rest is wasting your time.'

Barton glanced at his watch. It was rush hour, so the ten minutes to Marholm might be considerably more.

'How has Pippa seemed after the incident? Is she upset?'

'Pippa doesn't show much emotion. I reckon she gets it from me. She was getting more demonstrative, but it was a slow process and now she's hardly spoken since it all happened. You saw how subdued she was, but I thought it was her picking up on the stress of the situation as opposed to having seen the assault.'

'Okay. What's happening in the picture?'

'It looks like an old man attacking someone with a sword.'

Barton considered his options. He needed to look at that picture and he wanted to talk to Pippa about what she'd seen. Interviewing a minor was fraught enough as it was without there being concerns around conditions such as Asperger's or autism.

'I'll drive there now and pick the drawing up. I'd like to have a professional ask Pippa some questions around what she saw. How do you feel about that?'

'At the police station?'

'No, we have a different building for those sorts of interviews. It's all very low-key with specially trained officers.'

'No way! I dread to think how Pippa would respond to something like that. I'll ask her before you get here. I think you'll find that even though my granddaughter struggles with new places and people, she's much stronger within her own home. And I want this nutter found.'

Joan cut the call. Barton put his phone down with increased respect. DCI Cox was walking through the busy office as he pulled his coat off the back of his chair. It seemed as if the entire department was ploughing through the paperwork and interviews for the mass punch-up.

'Ma'am, how are we doing for manpower?'

She raised an eyebrow.

'Is your assault case proving troublesome?'

'Maybe. I can't help thinking whatever this is, it isn't over yet.'

'Good news on that front. One of the goons we picked up from the party had videoed the brawl on his camera, so we've been able to shorten the interviews now we can see who was directly involved. You'll have your team back on Monday.'

'Excellent. The victim's daughter, Pippa, appears to be on the autistic spectrum, but it seems she might have seen what happened. Grandma's looking after her but won't let any strangers talk to her.'

Cox winced.

'Yes, she's sort of non-verbal, but it looks as though she's drawn a picture of the attack.'

'I don't suppose Pippa's eighteen and at art school.'

'Ten and at junior school.'

'Fabulous. I'm sure I don't need to tell you to tread carefully, then. This has alarm bells ringing.'

Barton hustled out of the office, booked out a car, and was immediately in heavy traffic. When he was younger, he sometimes pounded the steering wheel with frustration. It often occurred at the culmination of cases when minutes mattered. Nowadays, he used the peace as an opportunity to run things through his mind.

It was gridlock at the Thomas Cook roundabout, so he tried calling Ken's Kitchens and Bathrooms again. The call went to voicemail. Barton supposed he could have left, seeing as it was almost six p.m.

Once he got through the junction, the traffic eased a little and twenty minutes later, he was parking under a tree down the road from Joan's picturesque home. The bushes and trees were well trimmed and there was an array of ornaments in the garden adding character. Joan opened the door and took him into the lounge.

Pippa was eating some white bread sandwiches, crusts removed, cut into perfect squares, while sitting on the floor watching *SpongeBob*.

Joan passed him the picture of Maggie's house. It wasn't bad. The house had four windows, and the front door was situated in the correct position. Even the garage was proportionate. Barton looked at what appeared to be a grey sword in the attacker's hand.

The people didn't appear as the right ratios, though. Maggie seemed child-sized compared to her much larger assailant, who was in an enormous yellow coat with massive black boots. He had a grey beard on a large misshapen head with a yellow hat. The mouth was full of sharp teeth. The stuff of nightmares.

Barton and Joan sat on the sofa.

'Do you want to ask Pippa some questions about what she's drawn?'

'No, my training's not up to date for interviewing juveniles. That's why I said I'd like to have someone talk to her at a place we have for just this sort of thing.'

'I don't mind if you talk to her.'

'I'm afraid it doesn't work like that.'

'What a load of rubbish.'

Joan called Pippa over and showed her the drawing.

'Tell us about the picture, please, sweetie?' asked Joan.

Large doleful eyes looked from her granny to Barton. She shook her head.

'Why did you draw this, Pippa?' tried Joan.

Pippa's gaze returned to Barton. She seemed to be sizing him up. She took her picture back, analysed it, cocked her head, then stared at Barton, but didn't comment.

Joan reached forward and pointed a finger at the man in the yellow coat.

'Who's this?' she asked.

Pippa whispered something, but it was too quiet to make out.

'Sorry, Pippa,' said Joan. 'I couldn't hear that. Say it again, please?'

This time, she spoke with force.

'Bad Santa!'

26

DI BARTON

Barton and Joan looked at each other for a moment. Both of them realised they were on wafer-thin ice. How did you question a ten-year-old who still believed? Or did until she saw what happened to her mother.

'Why do you think it was a bad Santa?' he asked.

Those eyes stayed on his face, but she didn't say anything. Barton leaned back in his seat. Was there any point in probing further? Pippa was unlikely to be able to tell him much more. Not unless Santa's sleigh had a number plate.

'Would you like a tea or coffee?' asked Joan.

Barton wanted to get home, but it'd give him time to see if any more questions sprang to mind, or perhaps Pippa might open up with him being there for longer.

Barton was pleased he stayed when Joan brought out a box of Marks & Spencer Extremely Chocolatey biscuits. Now it was Christmas, he thought. Joan offered them to him and he took two. Pippa came over and stared at the ones he'd chosen. Her eyes widened. She chose two of the same and returned to *SpongeBob*.

Barton picked up her drawing again. He spoke quietly to Joan.

'Why has Santa got a yellow coat on?'

Out of the corner of his eye, he watched Pippa get up off the carpet and grab something off the fireplace. It was a red felt-tip pen. She drew a line down the side of her picture with it, then threw it on the floor. The pen had no ink.

27

DI BARTON

Thursday 17th December

His alarm went off the next morning at six. It was his turn to walk Gizmo, but he lay there for a few minutes. Barton hadn't got back to his house until nearly eight p.m. the previous night. Holly had left him a big plate of home-made curry on the kitchen table, although someone had pressed a small Santa figure into the centre. Luke, he reckoned, but Luke denied it. Holly broke under questioning. He felt her arm on his back as she pushed him out of bed.

Downstairs, he grabbed the thrower and ball and slipped on the dog's lead. Outside it was pitch black except for the street lights, but mild. Barton thought of Maggie and her family having their Christmas ruined.

He walked the dog to the field and shone his torch into the ball so it glowed. With pent-up anger, he launched it like a missile. The greyhound watched it disappear into the distance, then sat down. Barton traipsed after the ball, then trudged back to his house.

While he went for a quick shower, Holly set a place for him at the table and was stirring a pan of porridge on the hob. She ladled some into his bowl.

'Here we go, Daddy Bear.'

'Cheers.'

'Why was Mother Nature frustrated after making Yogi Bear?' asked Holly.

Barton chuntered under his breath. Holly beamed at him.

'Because on her second attempt she made a Boo Boo.'

Barton growled and spooned in his breakfast. Holly sat next to him.

'Hey, big guy. Why so gawumpy?'

He told her about Pippa's drawing.

'Wow, that is a nasty thing to do on many levels,' she said. 'I hate to think of children not having happy Christmases.'

When he'd finished, he took his bowl to Holly, who'd started filling the dishwasher.

'Did I mention that Zander and Strange aren't coming for Christmas Day?'

'Yes, you said. It's a shame. I love it when there's a non-family member here. It kind of adds something to the occasion.'

'Yes, it's a pity.'

Barton sat back in his seat to drink his cup of tea. He frowned as he reflected on his mother, who would be missing for the second year.

'Shall I go to the homeless shelter, see what they've got?' he asked.

Holly came and kissed him on the forehead.

'Ah, don't be silly. Just because Santa's gone rogue.'

Barton shook his head. Never a truer word said in jest.

At half-seven, he began the ten-minute walk to the scene of Bad Santa's assault. It was only then that he remembered the call from the radio presenter. The Santa Killer. Coming to town. Barton shivered despite the mild weather. He reached the first house in the street and saw a sold sign. He looked through the lounge window and all the furniture had gone.

The second house appeared deserted. He knocked on the door, to no avail. The third property didn't answer either. He was just knocking again when a door opened at the next house along.

'They're at their caravan at the seaside,' said an ancient-looking woman, who was smoking out of the front door.

Barton wandered over. He was surprised when he realised she was smoking a small cigar. She had frizzy grey hair and thick foundation on, which hadn't been rubbed in properly, but her eyes were bright and shrewd. He wasn't sure whether she had a housecoat on or if it was a shabby dress.

'Are the campsites still open?'

'Owners only.'

'Okay, thanks. Don't suppose you know where the people from number two are?' he asked.

'Pair of lesbians. Both catch the train to London first thing and get back late.'

'And number one?'

'Divorce. Nasty one. Been empty for months.'

'Is there neighbourhood watch around here?'

'Are you taking the mick, sonny?'

Barton chuckled.

'No, I'm a police officer.'

'Ah, you're here about poor Maggie. I popped over when I noticed the ambulance that night.'

'Yes. Did you see anything else?'

'No, I can barely see you from this distance, and you seem quite large.'

Barton forced his smile to remain on his face. Another long day loomed.

'My husband reckons he did, though,' said the old lady as she dropped the butt into a pot next to the door.

'Is it okay to speak to him?'

The woman tipped her head back and laughed.

'You won't get any sense from him. He's as mad as a mongoose. I've just taken thick bacon sandwiches up for him. He'll be asking for his breakfast in five minutes.'

'Could I have a word, anyway?'

'Okay, but you must have nothing better to do. I'm Abbie Wainwright.'

Barton followed her in. There was a Stannah stairlift on the stairs, which Barton stopped next to.

'Don't even think about it,' said Abbie with a crinkle of her face.

She climbed the stairs surprisingly fast. Barton suspected she wasn't as old as she looked. That was the price of smoking. Sure enough, the man upstairs in the front bedroom who gave him a brief glance only appeared to be in his mid-sixties. He had blue and white striped pyjamas on and was sitting at the window in a large rise and fall armchair. After a shrug, he turned back to stare out of the window.

'He likes to watch the trees. He's always liked that. Haven't you, Henry?' Abbie shouted the last bit, to no response. Barton stood next to him and peered out with him. He could see the front of Maggie's house.

'Abbie tells me you noticed something a few nights ago,' said Barton.

Henry's head slowly swivelled towards him. 'When's breakfast?'

Barton looked back at Abbie, who put her finger to her forehead and spun it around.

'I told you. He's not all there.'

'What did he say he saw then?'

Aggie laughed, which turned into a deep-throated strangling cough. Barton watched, horrified, wondering if he should try to catch her lungs when they came out. When she'd recovered, she looked at him through watery eyes.

'He said Father Christmas ran across our lawn.'

28

DI BARTON

Barton got out his notepad and perched on the edge of the bed.

'Tell me more.'

'That's kind of it. I thought he was messing around. We occasionally get flashes of the old Henry, before the strokes, but not so much recently. He's lost huge patches of his memory now, and more goes every day.'

She stood next to Henry's chair and placed her hand on his arm. He shrugged it off.

'Why didn't you contact the station and tell us?' asked Barton.

Aggie chuckled.

'It's him that's mad, not me. I can just imagine you lot sniggering down the phone when I let that out. Besides, you get a lot of tomfoolery this time of year.'

'Fair point. You didn't hear anything on the radio about it?'

'No, I only ever used to listen to music in my car, and we haven't had one of them for five years. We like our peace, don't we, Henry?'

Henry looked up at his wife with a blank face.

Barton thanked the couple for their time and walked into work. As he strolled through Ferry Meadows past the joggers and cyclists, he pulled out his phone and found Peterborough City Radio. He clicked on listen and put it on speaker.

'Wow, what a song, an all-time best, certainly one of mine, what do you say, who doesn't love, "Jingle Bell Rock"? You're listening to Tim Tibbles on PCR. Let's pick up the traffic news for those of you who are driving to work at Christmas.'

Barton smiled at Tibbles' DJ style. He might not be getting a visit from Santa this year, but he could expect one from Barton.

When he reached the office, Barton went straight to see Cox and told her about the communication the DJ had received. Then brought her fully up to speed.

'What's your plan?' she asked.

'I'll ring this shifty sod at the kitchen place this morning. If he doesn't pick up, I'll go and see him first thing. Tibbles' morning show finishes at twelve, so he'll have my face pressed up against the glass by eleven. The station is based at the shopping parade on Oakleigh Drive, Orton Longueville, so that's easy. Then I'm going to visit Heidi. She's the other one who works at Ken's, who might have had some rancour with Maggie getting promoted ahead of her.'

Cox drummed her fingers on the table while looking sideways out of her window at the office blocks beyond the car park. She turned her head back to Barton.

'It's not very festive, is it?'

'What isn't?'

'A baseball-bat-wielding Father Christmas.'

'Right, no, most unfestive. If the letter's connected, it could be quite worrying.'

'Yes, my thoughts exactly. No one's been killed yet, so does that mean that whoever's responsible isn't finished?' asked Cox.

'It's more likely someone unhinged trying to instil fear. I bet they expected the presenter to reveal they'd received that letter. Possibly even broadcast it over the air.'

'Wouldn't most sane people suspect that any normal radio station would get the police involved first before blurting it out on air? Maybe this criminal isn't very bright.'

'Luckily, not many of them are, but we don't have much to go on. The pandemic made our jobs harder by giving everyone a reason to wear a mask. This isn't that different, because any witnesses still won't see a face. I could do with some of my team back.'

'I think you have everything covered at this point. Your gang can come in Sunday, assuming nothing happens in the meantime. At the moment, all you've narrowed it down to is someone large and jolly. Even though it sounds like it might be a jealous female colleague responsible. Besides, many hands make light work, and we'll have the other case put to bed by the end of tomorrow.'

'What about too many cooks spoil the broth?'

'How about the boss is always right?'

Barton knew when he was beaten. In fact, he was pretty sure they'd had this same conversation before, and he'd lost. No wonder they'd made her DCI.

'I wonder how many Santa suits are sold each year,' he said. 'I assume you'd buy them from party shops. We only have a couple in the centre and, surely, they can't sell loads.'

'I fear you'd be surprised. People love dressing up. Why don't we give The Santa Killer what he wants?'

'Which is?'

'Ask Mr Tibbles at the radio station if he can mention it on air..'

'Might that cause panic?'

'I don't think so. It's only an ambiguous letter, but it could flush him or her out, or satisfy their lust for attention. Make sure Mr Tibbles tones it down. Mention how communications like the one he received are illegal and any further messages will be investigated thoroughly. Ask the public if they've seen the man himself running around looking suspicious. A tooled-up Santa tends to stick in the memory.'

'Okay.'

'And, John. Don't grow a white beard or buy a red coat, or you might end up spending Christmas on remand.'

Cox was humming 'Jingle Bells' as Barton rolled his eyes and left the room.

29

DI BARTON

Barton grumbled to himself. It wasn't even nine o'clock, and he'd already had enough of strong, feisty women outmanoeuvring him and generally taking the mickey. He checked his emails and saw one from Leicester asking him to ring him.

'Morning, boss,' said Leicester.

'Hi, how are you feeling?'

'Improving. Bad night, though. My stomach was so dodgy that I daren't fall asleep, if you get my meaning.'

'Does that mean you haven't had any sleep?'

'No, I fell asleep.'

Nasty. Barton didn't wish to hear any more.

'I'm on the mend now, though.'

'Great. How did your research go?'

'As we expected. You can buy baseball bats online virtually anywhere, but only a few shops sell them in town. Argos and Sports Direct being the main ones. Unless we get further intel, it's probably not worth pursuing because they're busy stores. The bat could have been bought months ago with cash, but it's good we already have the facts for when things pan out further down the line.'

'Okay, that's great. Well done. Do you fancy looking for Santa outfits?'

'Eh?'

Barton explained.

'Sure. I can do it all from here and I'll talk to you soon about what I find out.'

Barton told him about overtime on Sunday and finished the call, then rang Ken's Kitchens and Bathrooms. Apparently, Ken was out of the office today. Barton went to book another pool vehicle out. He used his own if he had no choice, but it was always better to use a 'company' car because you never knew what might happen.

He pulled out of the car park in a grey Insignia saloon and accelerated away. When he reached Ken's Kitchens and Bathrooms, he could see through the window, the elusive Ken speaking to a bald guy. Oily indeed. Anne-Marie was also at work at the back of the store, talking to a young Asian woman in a hijab.

Barton felt his temperature rising, so sat in his car for a moment. He watched Ken chat jovially with the customer, then shake his hand. When the man stepped outside the store, Barton strolled in.

He wasn't surprised when Ken glanced over and took a step backwards. Barton walked straight past him.

'Office, please.'

Ken followed him to the smaller office out the back of the shop with a face like thunder. Barton got the feeling that Ken believed very much that this was his domain, and he didn't enjoy being made to appear weak.

'That was rude,' said Ken.

'Not as rude as avoiding my calls.'

'I'm a busy man.'

'Too busy to help find the criminal responsible for assaulting one of your employees?'

'That's your job, not mine.'

Barton stared at Ken, as he considered how best to play this. Ken was irritating, but he might clam up if Barton let his annoyance show.

'Fair enough. I shouldn't barge in here. Let's go to the police station where we're out of view.'

Ken folded instantly.

'No, sorry. I should have taken your call, but I didn't know what to say.'

Barton smiled.

'Perhaps that's because you did it.'

'What? Why would I?'

'Being spurned in love drives people to distraction. I've arrested people on weaker motivational grounds.'

'Maggie was my best salesperson. Because she's out of action, I've had to promote Anne-Marie to supervisor in case I'm ever out, which obviously has a cost implication, although Anne-Marie has just done a mega deal.'

Barton shook his head at Ken's focus on the bottom line.

'Why Anne-Marie, not Heidi?'

'Anne-Marie's the better seller.'

'Forgive me for playing devil's advocate here, but the best seller, or the best of many roles for that matter, doesn't necessarily make the best manager.'

'Trust me. I've made the right call.'

Barton stared hard at him. This guy got under his skin, but it was difficult to imagine him battering someone.

'Ken, do you have angry customers?'

'As opposed to happy ones?'

'Let me rephrase that. Do you have people who aren't thrilled with your product or service?'

'A few. Not many. We're priced fairly. We only use decent manufacturers and I've worked with the fitters for years, so jobs tend to run pretty smoothly. You get a few arseholes who love complaining, or the occasional bit breaks. It is mostly wood or MDF, after all.'

'What do you do then?'

'Sort it out. Bad reviews can really affect referral sales, so it's best to take the odd hundred-pound hit for something like that on the chin.'

'Right, fair enough. I'll need your direct mobile phone number from now on.'

Ken gave him his business card without a fuss. Barton followed him into the busy admin office on the way out. He stopped at the door, turned back, and cleared his throat. The woman who Barton remembered as Judith, who was red-carpet-ready despite being in an industrial estate in Werrington, slowly rose from her seat as if she had a gun trained on her and switched the radio off. Barton cleared his throat when the presenter was cut off mid-sentence. The other women looked up at him.

'I'm Inspector Barton. If I call here in the future, it's serious. I expect my questions to be answered truthfully.'

Barton looked around at their faces as they all nodded. Judith's face bloomed bright red.

Barton smiled at them, then wandered through into the showroom. Anne-Marie waved at him, clearly flushed with success. He waved back. She was the obvious person who gained from this situation. He noticed the young woman in the scarf was now at one of the computers. She must be Ken's part-timer. She was very pretty. Barton left the shop with the dawning realisation that every single employee of Ken's was female and apart from Heidi, attractive as well.

30

DI BARTON

Barton was experiencing again just how much running about there could be at the start of an inquiry. Mistakes were easily made. Enthusiasm could rapidly win over progress and send the investigation off in the wrong direction.

He put the radio on and listened to a few carols while he drove around the parkways to where they broadcast PCR. It was an up-and-coming station. Heart FM was a national radio now, so PCR was one of only two that were solely for Peterborough. In fact, it was tough to pick the signal up outside the city limits. Barton tried to imagine Tim Tibbles for a bit of fun.

He plumped for thirty years old, dodgy Hawaiian shirt stretched over a hairy belly, and a cowboy hat. Barton parked up and walked to the entrance. He passed Fishtastic, the chip shop, and resolved not to even glance in its direction on the way back to his car. The door to PCR was locked so he pressed the bell and looked around.

Longueville was one of the more pleasant areas of Peterborough. There were a lot of decent-sized bungalows and a variety of pretty houses. Three different dog walkers strolled past while he waited for a response. They were all older people with small pets. Christmas tree lights twinkled in many of the windows of the properties surrounding the shops, and there were a few with decorations in their gardens. They were classy and understated, not like someone had brought Blackpool illuminations to the area.

Barton turned around on hearing the door opening behind him. A slightly dishevelled man around his mid-forties appeared.

'Police, for Mr Tibbles,' said Barton.

'You must be here about the letter, I'm Julian,' he said with exaggerated mystery. At least Barton thought it was exaggerated. Barton followed him into a messy room with tables and chairs higgledy-piggledy as if a giant had thrown them inside from a distance. The guy, who had extremely long hair scraped back into a ponytail, which did little for his small-featured face, handed Barton the letter with a big grin. It had been laminated.

'I told Tibbles to return it to its envelope and leave it alone until further notice.'

He leaned forward and whispered, 'Between you and me, he's scatty. We had something similar a while back, but I think it just got thrown away. The listeners love him though.'

Barton wasn't sure what laminating would do to their hopes of removing fingerprints, but it couldn't have improved them.

Barton suppressed his annoyance. It was unlikely anyone nowadays would send a threat to kill in their own handwriting and not wear gloves. Saying that, the writing looked spidery and distinctive, which was something. If they found a suspect, this would add weight to the prosecution. It was also worrying. No attempt to disguise the writing meant either the person didn't care, or they were only planning to do it once, which would then make the case more difficult to solve.

'Where's the envelope?'

'Not sure. Tim thinks it might have been thrown out.'

Barton shook his head. 'Where is he?'

'In the studio, doing his morning show. He'll put three songs in a row on soon, so we can grab him then. Is this to do with the woman who got assaulted?'

'How did you know about that?'

'My friend lives at the bottom of her street. He walks past the houses at the top to get to work. He messaged me an hour ago that an old lady who's always outside smoking told him a bloke in a Father Christmas suit did it. It's all over our WhatsApp group.'

Barton wondered if he'd misheard for a moment.

'Say that again.'

'It's all over it,' he said with even more enthusiasm.

'What exactly is over your WhatsApp group?'

'Clips of Santa with a machine gun. Check this out.'

Julian got his phone out. He fiddled with it, then gave it to Barton, who then watched a short video of a female Father Christmas type in a fur-lined bikini shooting a large machine gun. The sound was on. Santa spoke to the cameras afterwards in what sounded like Spanish. Was this the modern equivalent of the jungle drums? Gossipy biddy, thought Barton.

'Sweet, eh?' said the grinning man.

'No, it isn't. Was the note anything to do with you?'

'Of course not.' Julian seemed a little disappointed by the suggestion.

Tibbles came out of the recording studio with a huge smile on his face. He was around seventy-years old, had obvious false teeth, and wore a cheap grey suit with the sleeves rolled up.

'DI Barton. Nice work. Come in, take a seat.'

Barton found himself opposite Tibbles, sitting on a low stool while Tibbles returned to his big chair. He reminded Barton a bit of Ken, who also felt he was the king of all he surveyed.

'So, John—'

Barton put his hand up.

'Why didn't you keep the envelope like I told you to?'

Tibbles was taken aback.

'You didn't mention it was important.'

'But I did say keep it.'

'I suppose.'

'Was it addressed to you personally, or the station?'

'It just had TT written on the front. I sometimes call myself that. Oh, and the name of the show was on it.'

'Okay, well, I'm sure you've heard from your colleague out there that someone dressed as Father Christmas was seen leaving the scene of a badly assaulted woman.'

'Yes, crazy times.'

'Not crazy. Worrying. Aren't you at least concerned that you're going to be next?'

Tibbles' face quickly matched his suit.

'Eh?'

'Who's to say that the person, who was lucky to escape with non-life-threatening injuries, didn't receive a letter like you did a few days beforehand?'

Tibbles swallowed.

'Did she, then?'

'We're looking into it. Now, I'm happy to share some details with you on the show, but it's important that we don't panic the public. All I need to get across is if anyone knows anything, or has seen anything, they need to contact us immediately.'

Tibbles hadn't thought of doing anything live on air, but it instantly appealed to his idea of being the centre of attention

'Right on. If you pull that microphone over to you, then you can talk from there. Try not to lick it or touch it with your nose because it causes feedback.'

Barton gritted his teeth as 'Stop the Cavalry' finished.

'Listeners, do I have some news for you. We have Detective Jake Barton from downtown Thorpe Wood police station, in the flesh, in the studio. He's here to tell you an important thing for the holiday season, and that is that you'd better watch out.'

It swiftly went even further downhill after that.

31

THE SANTA KILLER

I wake up shouting out his name. After gasping and clawing at the duvet, I manage to control my breathing. A layer of greasy, cold sweat is like a thick film on my forehead, but I'm not the only one who screams in their sleep here.

After I've settled, and the tension and horror have seeped from my bones, I develop a sense of acceptance. I don't deserve to forget, so maybe my subconscious is teaching me a lesson.

I knew that it was a good idea to get Tim Tibbles involved. He's such a great guy. I imagined he'd be cool like Jon Bon Jovi, so seeing him through the window performing last week was a bit of a surprise. Nevertheless, he'll play his part. I will need to play mine, although if I don't manage some sleep tonight, I'll be too weak.

My message is out there now. That should make it easier for me to escape justice. People must understand. I, we, are to be listened to. Why can't we be on top for once? Otherwise, what's the point? I'm so sick of the lucky getting richer. Why do only they get what they want? We deserve a break.

The next on my list is about to experience what happens when the luck runs out. This will be a Christmas they won't forget.

32

DI BARTON

Barton sat in his seat with his mouth opening and closing after Tibbles had finished the interview and cut for the next songs. Barton crossed his arms.

'Did we not mention beforehand about not causing panic?'

'Yeah, relax. Don't worry about all that Santa's-coming-to-get-you crap. It's radio, man. People love it. Just a bit of fun, great for the ratings, fab for me.'

Barton felt a surge of rage that he hadn't experienced in many years. He stood, picked up the microphone he'd been talking into as his words had been twisted, and snapped it in half. Tibbles became the goldfish.

'I'm beginning to think that you sent this letter in yourself, or maybe it's one of your colleagues who's responsible. More a rating winner than a Santa Killer.'

'My fans are my friends. I'd never jeopardise our relationship.'

'Well, never do anything like that again. And if you cared about what's fab for you, then I'd keep an eye out for men in red suits waiting for when your shift finishes.'

Barton left the station feeling marginally better, but he still hoped PCR didn't have a big audience. In particular, any listeners who were DCI or above. Next stop was Heidi Hulse's house. He recalled the bedraggled woman who Ken had asked to look after the shop when Barton first met him.

His phone beeped. Joan, bless her, had sent him a lengthy, detailed text saying that Maggie had rallied. There was a superficial skull fracture, but the rest was soft tissue damage. The very slight swelling they'd seen on a scan had vanished. Maggie would be on a normal ward by tomorrow and hopefully home by Monday morning at the latest, although there were to be no visitors. That was good news. Unless they got a break, she was the most likely person to be able to direct Barton's investigation. There were some emails he needed to respond to, which would give Heidi time to get home.

The parking was always bad at the top of Mayor's Walk. It was nearly all residents only. He located a space outside Ferrari's café, a popular spot in the area, but he could only stay there for an hour a traffic warden in the distance was scanning the road. He found Heidi's house. It was a Victorian terrace. Most of the houses in this vicinity were. Heidi's appeared to be the most dilapidated, despite some strong competition.

He pushed the thin metal gate open, but it only opened thirty centimetres before it wedged against an uneven paving slab. Barton squeezed through and cursed as the gate left a trail of green slime on the thigh of his blue suit trousers. The garden was small with metre-high weeds. Despite that, they'd managed to fit an old microwave, fridge and dishwasher in it.

Heavy traffic edged through the narrow road behind him, filling the air with thick fumes. It was a far cry from Anne-Marie's place, just half a mile away. Barton poked the doorbell, expecting it to not work, and looked around. To be fair, many other residents had tried with their gardens and there were numerous new front doors and clean double glazing.

The city's house prices were accelerating, even though they were still a long way below most places between Peterborough and London. It meant there was a shortage of affordable homes to rent or buy for those on lower incomes. Many people felt lucky to have a roof over their heads. Barton pressed the doorbell again. There was a crack and his finger went into the wiring. He knocked instead.

He heard voices approaching the other side of the door, which then became shouting. A teenage girl opened the door in a Bretton Hills uniform, which was a local school. It was hard to gauge her age as she had plenty of make-up on. Barton noticed the glazed expression. She seemed young for smoking marijuana at this time of day, but that would be his guess. Dead eyes stared at him without consideration. She stopped on the doorstep and spun around theatrically to shout inside.

'I told you not to fucking touch it, Glenn.'

A taller lad, also in school uniform, scowled at Barton before replying to the girl, who had turned her back to him and was stomping along the path. She kicked the gate open.

'What difference does it make, Ashlynn?' the boy shouted. 'You can't wear DVDs out by watching them too many times.'

He quickly followed the girl, who had to be his sister, down the street in the direction of their school. Barton listened to them arguing. The f word was used frequently. He turned back to the front door, which was still open.

He stepped inside, where it was cooler than outside. Stale smoke lingered in the air. He edged into a lounge, which could only be described as a dumping ground. There were cups and plates on top of newspapers and carrier bags full of clothes piled up under the bay window. The TV looked relatively new, but the screen was damaged in the bottom right-hand corner. The fabric sofa had shiny arms. Barton stepped to the next door, which was ajar. He shouted out.

'Hi, is anyone home?'

Seconds drew out with no reply. Barton pushed the door open and strolled into what was a nice open space, but that was the only nice thing about it. The kitchen and dining room had been made into one room. Someone had attempted to keep it tidy, even if they were fighting a losing battle, but the smoky aroma was fresher here and thicker. The atmosphere oppressive. After a few seconds, the damp had a hand around his throat.

At a table in the middle of the room sat a stooped figure constructing a thin roll-up. She looked up at Barton with the same facial expression as the young woman who'd just walked past him.

Her eyes were vacant, too, but not through drugs. Something else.

'What do you want?' she whispered.

He thought of the warmth and cosiness of Anne-Marie's house. It'd felt like a home the moment he'd stepped through the door. This place was the polar opposite. Polar was the right word, too.

'I've come to talk to you, Heidi.'

'Oh, what about?'

'Do you remember me?'

She put the cigarette in her mouth, then lit a match. The flame danced from a hidden draught. Heidi cupped the flame as the match was burning down, taking her time lighting the rollie, perhaps relishing the heat. After a quick inhale, she blew a thin stream of smoke towards the window as though it were open.

'No.'

'I met you at Ken's Kitchens.'

She squinted as smoke billowed around her face, then looked him up and down.

'Sorry, I do recall you now. You're the policeman.'

'That's right. I have some questions.'

She gestured to the table. 'Pull up a seat.'

Barton felt a twinge of pity for the relatively young woman. Her clothes were ill-fitting but seemed okay quality, clean at least, but her hair and face looked as though they'd received no loving care in years. Thread veins covered both cheeks. The wrists that jutted out of the thick jumper were worryingly thin.

'I'll shut the door,' said Barton.

He walked back to the front door. His gran used to have a property with a layout like this. She called the front room the parlour, and nobody ever sat in it. Barton placed his hand on the radiator in there. Stone cold, same as the one in the dining room when he returned there.

'Pretty chilly in here,' he said.

'Boiler's broken. We can't afford to fix it.'

'When did that break?'

'I'm not sure. It's been a while. I left the oven door open last Christmas to spread some warmth through the house. We've got fan heaters upstairs, but they aren't cheap to run, and no hot water.'

Barton looked up at a photograph on the wall. He recognised the boy he'd seen earlier, and possibly the girl, but it had been a few years since the photo was taken. There was another taller lad who must be the older child, with the girl, the youngest. Then there was Heidi and a shortish, heavyset guy. In fact, Heidi herself was much curvier in the picture to the point of being quite overweight. They all beamed at the camera.

'The family?' asked Barton.

Heidi nodded. 'Three years ago. Happier times.'

'Good one of the kids.'

'Yes, that's Ronnie, and you just met Glenn and Ashlynn. We don't usually have anyone home for lunch, but I had nothing to put in their packed lunches this morning. I had to go to a food bank, so they could have a bowl of beans.'

She took another deep drag of her fag. Barton frowned as she then stubbed it into the ashtray with her thumb. Maybe her hands were too cold to burn.

'You know about Maggie?' said Barton.

'Is that why you're here?'

'Yes. I'm trying to get some background. She doesn't seem the type to be assaulted in a quiet lane.'

'No, must have been quite a shock for her.'

Barton wasn't sure if he detected the hint of a smile when she made that comment.

'Don't you like her?'

'She's okay. Too corporate for my liking. Licking the boss's ass, and all that, but she isn't a bad person.'

Barton noted the tension in Heidi's jaw when she was thinking about Maggie.

'She got the promotion,' he said.

Heidi seemed to concentrate on the conversation for the first time.

'Yes, that should have been mine.'

'I thought she was the best salesperson.'

Finally, Heidi showed some energy.

'So what? Twenty years I've been there, with Ken the pervert.'

Barton raised both eyebrows.

'Yes, I didn't always look like this. Times change.' Her top lip curled. 'I remember when it was heating or eating if you ran out of money. Now I can only afford to smoke.'

'Do you think you should've been promoted?'

'Damn right. For years, that shop was just me and him in the shitty, cheap unit around the back of the parade from where we are now. No heating there either. No bonus, minimum wage. He always told me when he reached the heavens, I'd be going with him. That was his mantra. I gave him everything.'

Heidi looked away as she said that. Barton decided now wasn't the time to dig too far into what everything meant.

'So, you were a bit annoyed when Maggie was given the extra responsibility.'

'Yes, well, pissed off is closer, although my family has had plenty of shitty luck. It's been tough for us. I probably wasn't at my best when the promotion came up to give it my best shot, but I'm getting there. If only my husband could find a job, or at least stick at one. Maybe something good will come of this Maggie thing. We could really do with some extra money.'

Barton decided not to tell Heidi that Anne-Marie already had the gig.

'What about Anne-Marie?' he asked.

'She wanted the position, too, but she wasn't that bothered when it was given to Maggie.'

'Why's that?'

'Who knows? Her husband has a solid job, they have a lovely house. She's got enough money.'

'Do you get on well with her?'

'I suppose.'

Barton pondered whether to mention that Ken had hinted that Heidi hadn't been on her A-game for a considerable amount of time. He decided he owed Ken nothing.

'Your boss said Maggie was by far the best person for the role.'

Heidi bared her teeth in a cold smile.

'Did he, now?'

'He alluded to the fact you'd had some recent challenges.'

'He should mind his fucking business. I'd have less challenges if he paid me a decent wage and gave me more hours instead of giving them to Zahra.'

Barton heard the front door open. Then it was slammed. A short man, who Barton guessed had different vices from his wife due to his width, scraped against the wall as he came through the lounge door. He had an ugly snarl on his face, but it dropped when he saw Barton. He glanced at Heidi with genuine concern, then back at Barton.

'I'm the husband, Cameron. Who the bloody hell are you?'

'Detective Inspector Barton.'

Cameron pulled out a chair next to Heidi on the other side of the table from Barton. He didn't hold Barton's eye contact.

'What does he want?' he asked Heidi.

'I'm not sure. Ken's been shit-stirring since Maggie got attacked.'

Cameron's eyes narrowed, but he put his fist over his mouth, which Barton suspected was to stop him blurting anything out.

'Ken is not a nice person,' he finally said. 'He pays on looks and he takes advantage of his staff.'

Barton noticed Heidi cringe, even though she tried to hide it.

'I've been hearing things,' said Cameron, with a sneaky smile.

'Don't,' said Heidi.

'Shut up, woman. Screw Ken,' snarled Cameron.

'Like what?' Barton leaned in to listen.

'I've just been for an interview as a supervisor at a large joinery. The boss didn't tell me straight out, but I got the impression Ken wasn't one of his best payers. I also heard something similar from a fitter that I know that he'd turned up for a job and half the kitchen was missing.'

Barton filed that titbit away. Cameron looked again at Heidi. He put his hand on her arm and seemed to squeeze a little too hard.

'How are the kids? Doing a better job with them?' he whispered, although Barton could decipher each word. He suspected Cameron didn't care he was talking too loudly.

'I'm trying. It would help if you were here more often.'

'I'm looking for work,' he replied, his voice rising. 'It's all I fucking do. All day and every day, so don't give me any crap.'

'Did you get the job?' asked Barton to distract Cameron and defuse his surging anger.

'I find out tomorrow.' Cameron's face dropped. 'There were a lot of people there for interviews, but I did a similar role eight years ago. We could do with a break. Perhaps Ken will come good and promote Heidi now, like he should have done to start with.'

33

DI BARTON

Barton's head was spinning when he left the house. It was a relief to step outside into the relatively fresh air of the busy road. He'd heard some kind of motive from the Hulses for an attack, but it wasn't particularly strong. These people weren't having it easy, which Barton knew from experience could lead to anger and guilt. Barton had taken a sneaky picture of the family photograph on the wall when they were bickering with each other about Ken.

Barton suspected if Zander had been with him, he'd have tried to help Cameron and Heidi Hulse, but Barton had less sympathy. Tobacco wasn't easy to give up, but you'd have thought that providing your kids with a decent packed lunch would come before having a fag. Cameron didn't seem to be going too short on calories either.

Barton also understood you never knew what hardships people had suffered, so it was wise not to be too judgemental. After all, his own six-pack remained well hidden. Thoughts of food made his stomach gurgle, but he still only nipped into Ferrari's for a coffee. It was warm inside and there was a chatty atmosphere amongst those sitting beneath the Christmas decorations.

When Barton stepped out of the café, he found a traffic warden next to his car. Barton had a minute left, much to the guy's displeasure. By the time Barton returned to the police station, it had gone two and he decided to set up an incident room. There was little he could do at the end of the day on his own, apart from update the computer system.

He grabbed a whiteboard and put Maggie's name in the middle. The best direction for the inquiry that Barton could see was her work. If she left hospital on Monday, he'd talk to his team first thing, then speak to her. There could be hundreds of different avenues for the investigation to go in. He hoped there wouldn't be anything more serious over the coming days.

Leicester had sent him an email saying that a lot of places sold Santa outfits. A few even rented them, making that particular detail another needle in the haystack without further intel.

Barton called his contact at the council. Barton hoped to catch the manager, Bob, who he'd known for over a decade. He had a warped sense of humour, but had proven a valuable asset in the past. Bob answered his call.

'Hi,' said Barton. 'I've had something unusual come up. Maybe you can help.'

'Sure, John. Thanks for the card, by the way. Brilliant.'

Barton had posted him a Christmas card with a joke about peeping toms on it. What's the difference between a peeping tom and a pickpocket? One snatches watches... The card disgusted Holly when she saw it, but Barton knew it would tickle Bob, and he was a good man to have on side.

'Starting from now,' said Barton, 'can you keep an eye out for me for people who are in fancy dress and looking suspicious, or actually committing crimes?'

'We do that anyway.'

'Yes, but let me know if you see anything I might be interested in.'

'Anything or anyone?'

'Both, just ping me an email.'

Barton heard a chuckle from the other end.

'Do you remember the Easter Gunny a few years back?'

Barton grinned as he recalled the headline from the local paper the following day after a man had attempted to hold up a bookmaker's dressed in an Easter Bunny outfit.

'I do.'

'People, eh? It was so obviously a toy gun that all the customers in the betting shop threw pens at him.'

Barton quietly snorted. There'd been some good jokes that Easter, although it hadn't been funny for the guy who'd been trying to rob Ladbrokes. They'd arrested him for having an imitation firearm with intent to commit an indictable offence and he'd later received two years.

'Yes, focus in particular on those dressed Christmassy.'

'Ah, right. I understand now. Is this related to the Bad Santa that was on Tim Tibbles' show this morning?'

Barton smiled. It seemed more people listened to local radio than he'd thought.

'Something like that.'

Barton spent the next couple of hours inputting his witness statements. He was just contemplating an early finish when his email box pinged with a message from his boss, DCI Cox, asking him to come to her office. Apparently, the detective chief superintendent's wife had been listening to the radio that morning.

34

DI BARTON

Barton went straight to Cox's office, knowing he'd only stew in his seat otherwise. She grinned at him from behind her desk.

'Afternoon, John. How's the case going?'

'Something stinks. Maybe most of it.'

'And the woman, Maggie?'

'That's the only positive news. She'll hopefully make a complete recovery.'

Cox nodded.

'I suspect more by luck than judgement,' replied Cox. 'Considering her improvement, I'm wondering how important this is.'

Barton understood straight away what she was thinking. The CPS might downgrade this to an ABH for a guilty plea instead of GBH. That didn't even guarantee a custodial stay if the attacker had no similar previous, and the accused could afford a quality solicitor. With resources stretched, this investigation could end up on a back burner.

'Do you have any strong leads?' she asked.

'I'm afraid it's another one of those cases where facts and background are pouring in, but it's all circumstantial at this point. I should be able to chat with Maggie on Monday. She might say then that an ex has been bothering her, or a person addicted to drugs has been sleeping nearby. It could be anything.'

'And your explanation for the radio interview?'

Barton couldn't gauge if Cox was annoyed or not. He explained what had happened.

'Nothing gets in the way of a good story,' Cox drily commented afterwards.

'No, and my idea of not causing a panic and his were different. At least he didn't mention the word killer, which was on the note he received.'

'Well, I'm reasonably happy with your performance, even if others at HQ might not be. The custody sergeant had someone joking about the show to him an hour ago. With this sort of case, publicity might not be a bad thing.'

'What if it encourages high japes and fancy dress over the weekend in the pubs and throughout the town centre?'

'That's par for the course at this time of year. It wouldn't be the same if we didn't have at least one soiled Father Christmas in the cells covered in vomit while dropping the f-bomb.'

Barton chuckled, but he feared the worst.

'Go home, John, and enjoy some downtime. I'm afraid I need you in HQ tomorrow morning for some strategy meetings, but don't worry about coming back to the office afterwards unless there's been a disaster. You seem uncharacteristically stressed of late, although I'd appreciate you keeping your phone on. Speak to Maggie Glover when the hospital releases her and see what she has to say. Your team has done well this year and you have to take a lot of the credit for that.'

'Thanks, ma'am. My team are going to come in Sunday, so I will too. It's likely Maggie will be out on Monday. Anyway, you know the tradition.'

Cox smiled. The department often came in the Sunday before Christmas to try to clear the decks for a fresh start after the holiday. They never managed it.

'If I'm paying overtime, I want backlogs being consumed, not just coffee and cake.'

Barton chuckled and stood to leave.

'There's also this letter for you. Read it tonight,' she said, sliding an envelope slowly across the desk.

He picked the envelope up and put it in his suit pocket.

'Pay rise?'

'Don't be silly.'

'I'll chat to you later.'

'I'll be in Sunday as well, but wait a minute. Everything you've said has made me think of something national that's come up. Do you recall that body found outside the victim's house in Stoke about six months ago?'

'Yes. Young woman killed with an axe or similar.'

'Spot on. It was an awful crime with seemingly no motive. If you're not safe in daylight, something's gone badly wrong.'

'I don't remember hearing anything about them solving that case.'

'That's because they didn't. Little progress was made.'

Barton nodded, waiting for the reason why Cox was mentioning it now.

'Another body was discovered in Leicester a few weeks ago. They suspect a heavy sharp blade of some kind on the top of the head.'

'Same method of dispatch.'

'Yes, and it's a similar story. Quiet woman, few friends, lived alone. In fact, I think she worked from home three days a week.'

'I don't see the connection to Maggie,' said Barton after a moment's thought.

'A lady came forward this morning to say that someone in a mask attacked her in Liverpool about fifteen months ago.'

'She obviously survived.'

'Yes, but she said she was hit on the back of the head when she returned from the shops. Hard, but not enough to do more than concuss her. It was outside her house.'

'Ah, that's closer to what we have here. What kind of mask was it, and why did she wait so long to tell us?'

'She was pretty drunk and embarrassed. It might have been a cartoon mask, possibly Spiderman. The guy was disturbed by a taxi arriving for next door. She decided she just wanted to forget it, even though she had some considerable bruising.'

'Right. You want me to speak to someone up there?'

'Not at the moment. They're trying to talk to her now, but she's cautious about getting involved. She's a foreign national and only reported the incident because she was struggling to move on and was worried a monster was running around. It was the computer system, HOLMES, that linked the cases.'

'I suppose our weapon doesn't match the earlier incidents, but we should keep an eye on it.'

'Yes. The other thing is if you draw a line from Liverpool to Stoke and then on to Leicester, it's almost straight.'

Barton turned to the map on the wall, found Liverpool and did just that.

'Keep going,' said Cox.

Barton didn't need to. It wasn't a completely straight line, but he could see that the next place might well be Peterborough.

35

DETECTIVE WALLINGTON

Stevenage Hospital, the day after the assault, four years ago

Detective Sergeant Wallington stood next to the hospital bed. An incredibly beautiful young woman, who had confidently introduced herself as Amelie, held the patient's hand.

'So, Inga,' he said to the older woman, 'I came right here to tell you that we have some good news for you. We've arrested the culprit and it looks like we managed to get all your items back before he had time to move them on.'

Inga had the biggest set of panda black eyes that he'd seen in a long while. She tried to smile.

'What did you find?'

'We recovered a bag with some battered cakes, a brand-new pair of red leather boots from Next, and a telescope, and your handbag, which still had your bank cards and driving licence inside. What we believe is your phone was under the man's makeshift pillow.'

'What do you mean?' asked Amelie.

Wallington smiled at the young woman who positively shone compared to the ill people surrounding them in the six-bed ward.

'When the man who found you on the floor rang the police, we turned up en masse. There are a lot of homeless people down there, some are known to us, and a couple have convictions for street robbery. We picked up a guy later that night when he was fast asleep. He had what we think were all your possessions, but he was too doped up to interview. We spoke to him this morning.'

'And he admitted to doing it?' said Inga. 'He could have killed me.'

'He said he couldn't remember, but he's a pragmatic man. After ten minutes' thought and considering the stolen items were on his person, he confessed. He was remanded into custody at lunchtime today. He'll get a long sentence for this crime, considering his previous convictions.'

'And it was definitely him?'

'Of course. Why? Do you think someone else could have been involved?'

Inga thought for a moment, then shook her head.

'No, it doesn't matter.'

Inga seemed to sink back into her pillow, but then she raised her right hand and waggled her ring finger.

'They stole my ring as well. It was a simple gold one. Did you find that?'

Wallington's face fell. He'd seen the full list of what had been retrieved, and there was no mention of a ring. Inga's head dropped.

'I'm sorry,' he replied. 'No. Jewellery is the easiest and quickest thing for them to move on. Was it valuable?'

There was a brief pause before Inga turned her gaze to him. Then she looked out of the ward window for another moment. When she replied, her voice was soft and sad.

'Yes, it was.'

36

DI BARTON

Sunday 20th December

Barton didn't leave HQ until mid-afternoon on Friday, then went straight home. He enjoyed the remainder of the day by doing very little, but he'd been distracted after opening the envelope his boss had given him. He kept what he read to himself. Even so, the contents popped into his head at regular intervals.

The family had a long walk with Gizmo through Ferry Meadows on Saturday morning, and he'd booked a festive early evening meal at the Gordon Arms, which made Holly happy, and the kids were on their best behaviour, as he found they often were in the run-up to Christmas.

The most fabulous thing of all was there were no further phone calls from work. Luke had unearthed an old board game, The Game of Life, and insisted everyone join in. To his surprise, Lawrence, who'd returned from university at last, and Layla agreed, and even as Barton was laughing and playing, he knew it would be a day he'd never forget.

It was only late Saturday evening that his mind turned to work. It was rare for him to keep his mind away from Peterborough's caseload. Usually, the lure of the office proved too strong, and he snuck in for at least a few hours. He wondered whether he was losing some of his drive and commitment.

The weather had taken a turn for the worse, so he took his car to work on Sunday morning. Not long after he got in, he received a text from Joan to say that Maggie would be home by midday. Joan also said she'd be looking after her today at Maggie's place, so he could drop by if he wished. Barton was really beginning to like Joan.

Barton had all his team back, and they filtered into the office in good spirits. He gave his people an hour to prepare for the ten o'clock meeting. They gathered in the incident room, where Barton brought them up to speed on Maggie Glover's assault.

'Any thoughts?' asked Barton.

'It doesn't feel like something for Major Crimes,' said Zelensky.

'No, I agree. As time has gone on, the severity seems to have diminished. The good news is there's been nothing else for us so far over the weekend, so we have the opportunity to see if we can get a result. The next murder or similar will knock this right down the pecking order unless something else happens with this case, so let's try to solve the puzzle before either of those things occurs.'

'What's the plan, then, boss?' asked Zander.

'All of you spend the next hour reading the notes. Annoyingly, but not totally unexpected, we had four arrests of people dressed up as Santa on Saturday night.'

'I assume they're unlikely to be our guy?' said Malik.

'Yes, we'll check, but two were steaming drunk and got into a fight with some other youngsters. They reckoned they only got their outfits in the last few days. The other two were students who just came back from uni last week. They were fairly tipsy and fighting with each other. The *Peterborough Telegraph* already has hold of this because of my radio interview, and there's an article about it online. We could get more copycats. All of which gives the culprit cover and makes it less of a surprise to spot someone dressed as Santa.'

'The attack might have been a one-off,' said Zelensky.

'Correct. I'd like you and Malik to spend this morning analysing the social media accounts of everyone who's mentioned on the case file. Check the PNC for any previous for those people too. Also, it's possible we might want to look at their emails, bank records and maybe even Amazon accounts for purchase histories in the recent past, so make sure that's in the back of your mind.'

They both nodded.

'Zander, have a quick word with DCI Cox about the murders across the country. See what you think. We'll liaise this afternoon.

'Leicester and I will visit Maggie shortly. I've had contact with her mother, and she's told me Maggie's being released this morning.'

'Is she returning to the place where the assault happened?' asked Malik.

'Yes, but I'll discuss that with them both. Her mum is on the ball, so hopefully she'll agree to having them stay at her house in Marholm while she convalesces. When we've seen Maggie, I'm going to drop Leicester in town so he can visit some of the retailers. Then I'll nip by and see the guy at the council's CCTV centre.. He said there was a boisterous crowd out at the weekend. It'd be good to check where the cameras are around the city again and maybe have a general chat about fancy dress and other disguises.'

After the meeting, the team dispersed. An hour later, Zander came out of Cox's office with a strange expression on his face. Barton called him over.

'Everything okay?'

'Yes, she explained about the other murders, and I agree, it doesn't link too closely even if Maggie has a similar background to the other women.'

'Anything else?'

'We had a chat about something non-case related. She said she'd catch up with you later in the week.'

Zander pulled a mysterious expression at Barton, leaving him wondering what was up, but the case in hand soon pushed any concerns to the back of his mind.

Leicester booked out a car, and at midday he and Barton were turning into St Catherine's Lane. It was the type of street that rarely had cars lined on the kerb, but there was a battered blue Fiat Punto parked at the top of the road and next to Maggie's house was a very nice black BMW 4-series coupe.

Joan's red vehicle was on the drive besides a green Nissan Juke, which looked familiar to Barton. Leicester drove past the BMW, did a three-point turn, then stopped behind it. They got out and admired the impressive vehicle.

'Sweet,' said Barton. 'You're into cars. How much does one like this cost?'

Leicester stared at the wheels and the trim, then pressed a hand against the tinted glass and peeked inside.

'Looks fully loaded. At least fifty grand.'

'Very nice.' Barton looked at all the vehicles. 'This seems like a lot of visitors, though, for someone who just got out of hospital.'

Leicester smiled.

'Perhaps we should wait in our car. Check who comes out. It'll also give us an idea of the traffic up and down the road.'

They returned to the car. Barton knew little about Leicester apart from the fact he and Malik went to the gym a lot. Barton didn't probe too much if his guys were quiet about how they spent their time off, but this was a decent opportunity if Leicester wanted to talk.

'I see you like to keep your home life and work life quite separate.'

Leicester grinned.

'Do I need a lawyer present?'

Barton put on a serious face.

'Off the record, of course. I just need to know who you've killed.'

Leicester laughed.

'If I'm honest, I don't have that much of a home life. My mum died pretty young, so my dad raised me. He's a quiet man. He moved to the coast, to a retirement community, and keeps to himself. We exchange cards and presents. I visit him a couple of times a year.'

'Christmas?'

'We used to spend it together but stopped. We both found it depressing, you know, watching crap TV, not much to say. He's not a drinker, but he used to get hammered, I think, so he didn't have to endure the tension.'

Barton laughed.

'Happy memories,' said Leicester, but he didn't seem too bothered.

'What do you do instead?' asked Barton.

'I lived with a girl for five years until fairly recently, but we split up a little over a year ago. You see, I love this job. Sometimes it's exciting, other times it's challenging. It's always real and raw and that means I don't want the rest of my life to be electrifying. She wanted to head out most evenings, whereas I preferred to read books on true crime or go to the gym. I enjoy pushing my body. I did karate for ages. Anyway, we had a gigantic row at The

Boathouse when we went out for an early Christmas dinner, and now I spend it alone. Last year I watched all eight episodes of *The Mandalorian* on my own and reheated a Chinese that I'd bought the night before. The tofu was a bit soggy, but apart from that, I enjoyed it.'

Barton frowned at the thought of soggy tofu, but he'd found Holly's next victim.

'I didn't know you did kung fu,' he said. 'You still do it?'

'Karate. No, I broke my writing hand striking a dummy in the dojo a few years ago. There was no reason for that to happen. A little finger just snapped, so I stopped because the injury interfered with work.'

'Does that make you Bruce Lee hard, then?'

Leicester chuckled. 'It's largely defensive. When most people attack, they're less balanced with a higher centre of gravity, so they're also more vulnerable to a counter punch. Not many could beat me hand to hand. Although, fighting someone of your or Zander's size would be tough, purely because of the weight.'

'And our finely tuned physiques.'

'That goes without saying.'

Leicester pointed towards the house. When Barton looked over, the door was opening.

37

DI BARTON

The man who stepped from the house was grinning widely. He had a shaven head and was wearing high-end exercise gear. Even from a distance, Barton could tell he was light on his feet and fit. Anne-Marie came out after him. She was also smiling. Barton remembered then the Nissan Juke had been parked on her drive.

She said something to the bald man, who tipped his head back and laughed, then walked off up the road towards the battered Punto. Barton frowned as he watched him get into the car and slowly accelerate away. It was the same guy he'd seen talking to Ken at his showroom. Barton was about to ask Leicester to take a record of the car's registration when he heard the click of Leicester's phone camera next to him.

Anne-Marie went back into the house but didn't shut the door. Barton thought for a moment it was because she was giving them a subtle message that she'd seen them, but she soon returned. This time she was shooing Ken, her boss, outside, but he seemed less willing to leave than the other guy. Anne-Marie stood on the doorstep with her arms crossed, even delivering a slight finger-waggle to Ken as she spoke.

Ken finally walked towards the BMW. He had a slight scowl, which dropped further when he saw Barton parked behind his vehicle. He quickly changed his expression to one of neutrality. Barton got out of the car.

'Quick word, please, Ken.'

'I'm in a rush, so could you make it fast?'

Barton smirked at the obvious lie.

'Lovely motor.'

'Thank you.'

'Things must be going really, really well, to afford such a luxury.'

Ken's eyes flashed with anger, but he kept his mouth shut.

'Although I hear things aren't going so well.'

'Who told you that?'

'Are you saying that's not true?'

'The business is extremely solid. We've had a few supply-chain issues, but nothing more than that.'

Ken swallowed hard when he finished talking.

'Why are you here?' asked Barton.

'To visit Maggie. I wanted to make sure she was okay.'

'On the day she gets out of hospital? You must be desperate to see when your star seller is coming back to work.'

Ken spoke through clenched teeth.

'I came in a personal capacity with some flowers. Now, if you don't mind.'

Barton stepped back from the BMW so Ken could open the door and get in. The car purred as it pulled away.

Anne-Marie was coming out of Maggie's home and pulling her coat on by the time Barton and Leicester reached it. Barton introduced her to his officer. She was in high spirits.

'It's great to have her home,' said Anne-Marie. 'It's made me realise what a good friend she is.'

'What were those two doing here? Anything dodgy?'

'No. Lothar's from the gym. They all heard about the Santa attack. He did a whip-round and bought some chocolates and a card. It's a little OTT. In fact, it was a little creepy seeing him away from the gym. They aren't that close, but he reckoned he was only intending to post it through the letter box.'

'Would the box have fitted through the letter box?'

Anne-Marie paused, then smiled.

'Not without tap-dancing on the chocolates first.'

'I saw him in Ken's showroom.'

'Yes, I think he popped in but I was busy. Lothar said he was thinking of getting a new kitchen, although they didn't acknowledge each other just now.'

'And Ken?'

'Ken, on the other hand, somehow knew that she was at home, so I've lobbed him out.'

'So, nothing dodgy about this Lothar guy?'

'No, apart from wearing scary budgie smugglers, he seems okay.'

'Do you know his surname?'

'It's a bit odd, begins with Q.'

'What is it?'

'Sounds a bit like barnstorm, but with a q.'

'Quarnstrom?'

'Yeah, I think so. Oddly enough, there was another bloke who seemed interested. He was a Q as well. Quigley.'

'What was his first name?'

'Cliff, and no, he hasn't dropped any presents off. I felt sorry for him. He came over from Dublin for business, so he doesn't really know anyone. We call him Quiffley because he has a ponytail and a quiff.'

Barton pulled a face,

'Yes,' said Anne-Marie. 'No wonder she's not keen.'

Barton made a mental note of the names for the file.

'Is Maggie still okay for a chat?' he asked.

'Yes, she was watching a movie when the worshippers turned up. Come in.'

Barton and Leicester followed her in. Anne-Marie introduced them all to each other. Barton thought Maggie looked extremely well, considering, especially without make-up. There was the hint of a black eye and her left hand was in a thick plaster cast, but she gave them a big smile, which lit up her face.

'I'm going to head off,' said Anne-Marie. 'I don't usually work Sundays, so Drew and I watch a cheesy movie on the sofa in the afternoon. It's our special time, which we keep reserved. Then I go out and get fish and chips for everyone when they return from their friends or come down from their rooms. The girls at the showroom pull my leg about it, but we love it. Sunday evenings generally suck, so this is how we combat the gloom.'

Barton decided to have a quick word with her outside.

'Look after the lady,' he said to Leicester as he left the room.

Barton caught up with her at the door.

'Anne-Marie. Have you any idea how profitable Ken's business is?'

'I have a gossip with a girl in Accounts every now and again. They set the payments up, but he needs to make any final adjustments. She says it's going great guns, but Ken takes a big wage. You saw the car.'

Barton recalled the flash vehicle.

'Thanks.'

Barton waved her off and returned inside to find Leicester sitting next to Maggie on the sofa, with the pair of them smiling at each other like love's young dream. Barton sat down in an armchair opposite. They both blushed when they looked back at him.

'Okay, Maggie,' said Barton. 'Are you up to talking to us?'

'Yes, I had worse hangovers when I was younger.'

'That's the spirit.'

Her gaze sharpened, which reminded him of Joan's expression.

'I want him caught,' she said.

'Okay. My colleague will record the details, I'll ask the questions. Can you explain in your own words the events of that night?'

Maggie couldn't tell them anything new, except she'd seen a red reflection in the glass panel of the door just before the lights went out. There had been no dodgy suitors or threatening communications of any kind. Barton rubbed his hands as he thought.

'Can't you think of anyone who might even be a touch upset with you?'

'No. I try to be nice to everyone. I've always been that way, but I'm more like it since my husband died. You never can tell how people are struggling.'

'Forgive me for asking, but I assume there was nothing suspicious about your husband's death.'

Maggie's face fell.

'I don't believe so. His brakes were worn although still safe, but the crash damaged both vehicles extensively, making concrete conclusions tricky. It was an unlit slippery surface and one or both drivers ended up on the other side of the road. I was told it was mercifully quick. The truck had been reported stolen from Manchester the previous night, but the driver ran off, never to be seen again.'

Barton gave her a few seconds to compose herself.

'Are you happy staying here after what happened?' asked Barton.

'I want to stay here. Pippa doesn't mind it at my mum's, but she's always brighter here. Listen.'

Barton could hear both granny and granddaughter laughing in the adjoining room. It sounded as if they were playing snap.

'My mum thinks it will be safer at hers and won't take no for an answer, so I'm heading there for a few nights. I'll up my security here in the meantime. A guy around the corner is a locksmith.'

Barton shook his head at the lack of suspects. He was hoping for something more. He had one last question.

'Obviously, if this wasn't random, we'd look at your personal life. That means the gym and work, or maybe someone you see at the school gates. Any recent changes?'

Maggie nodded.

'I get asked out a bit, but I've always said no. I didn't think it would be fair to see anyone with my other commitments. I was just considering whether it was time to date again. Obviously, I don't want to be on my own forever. I've had a job offer from B&Q kitchen department too, for a lot more money. Anne-Marie was encouraging me to accept it, but it's more hours, so we'll see.'

Barton tutted.

'Fair enough. Have a think and let me know if anything pops into your head, however small it might be. I'll just say hi to your mum,' said Barton.

He left the lounge and closed the door, finding Pippa and Joan playing cards at a dining-room table. Joan didn't see him at first. The way she stared at her granddaughter was a treat to observe. Pippa won a hand and squealed in delight. A beaming Joan turned to him.

'Hi, Inspector,' said Joan. 'Any news?'

'No, not really. So err on the safe side and ring 999 if you're suspicious in any way.'

'Do you have anything solid, or is it policeman's intuition?' she asked.

'Perhaps the latter.'

Joan winked at him and touched her nose.

Pippa leaned into Joan. 'He's very tall.'

'I think he's a giant,' whispered Joan.

Barton chuckled, left them to their game, and found Leicester and Maggie deep in conversation. He looked them over with a quizzical eye.

'Have you two met before?' he asked.

'We've seen each other before at parkrun,' they replied as though synchronised.

Barton trudged from the room. That was just what he needed.

38

DI BARTON

Barton and Leicester got into the car and began the journey into the town centre. Barton's phone rang. It was Zander.

'The early Christmas peace and goodwill to all has finished, John. There's been a nasty domestic involving a blade. I'm in the car, heading there now.'

'Is the incident over?'

'It's hard to say. A couple are inside, but we don't know exactly what's happened. There's an injured minor outside. Uniform has the scene under control. I'm pulling up there now.'

'What's the address?'

'It's The Swamp.'

'No way. After all this time? I'll meet you there.'

Barton finished the call and turned to Leicester.

'Drop me at 222 Benland, then continue as planned. Nip into the CCTV control centre, then check those retailers. You'll be working on this "domestic", as Zander so politely called it, for the rest of the week, unless something else happens.'

'What's The Swamp?'

'It's what we nicknamed the address of a rowdy couple over in

Bretton when Zander and I were in uniform. Just a nightmare pair who've been together since they were at school, but they used to like to get drunk, then split up every ten days or so. To be fair, I haven't heard about them for ages. Back then, we were at the point of asking for a restraining order to keep them apart when the woman got pregnant. She stopped drinking, and he toned it down. It went quiet, but we must have been there twenty times one year.'

Benland wasn't the best area of town by a long stretch. Leicester dropped Barton off and left. Barton made his way to the cordon and showed his ID, even though the officer was already letting him through. There were a lot of emergency vehicles, including two ambulances, and plenty of gawkers.

Zander was talking to a time-served uniformed sergeant Barton knew called Clarke.

'Greetings, Clarkey. Why have I got déjà vu?'

'Afternoon, John. Nice to see you. Neighbours reported it after an almighty row,' said Clarke. 'You'll obviously know the place.'

'Yeah, I thought they'd gone quiet.'

'They had. We picked him up a few times drunk in town over the last few years, nothing too heavy, but we've had quite a few calls to here recently. The daughter's at senior school now. From what I can gather, she's very much on her mum's side.'

Barton nodded. He'd seen this type of thing before. A simmering status quo, while unpleasant to the outside eye and any peace-loving neighbours, kind of worked for some couples, even when young children were involved. Teenagers, though, brought new pressures, and they could prove very toxic in an already volatile environment. Barton guessed their daughter would be about fifteen now.

'What's the current situation?'

'No idea,' replied Clarke. 'Next door but one rang it in. Said she heard a blood-curdling scream. We turn up just as the mother throws her daughter into the front garden and locks the door. The girl's refusing to say anything at all.'

'Injuries?'

'The daughter's in the ambulance, covered in blood.'

Barton stared at the stationary vehicles.

'Why isn't she on the way to the hospital?'

'Only a little of it appears to be hers.'

Barton looked back at the house and swore.

'Negotiator?' he asked.

'Half-hour,' replied Zander with a shake of the head.

Barton peered into the ambulance. There was indeed a lot of blood on the girl. Time was against them. People bled out fast. He'd have one attempt at resolving the situation by having the parents come out, or they'd get a team to move straight in. Barton was about to talk to Zander about the plan when the front door opened. A woman in an off-white dressing gown, which was stained red, strode into the street.

'What the fuck are you waiting for?' she bellowed. 'He's dying.'

39

THE SANTA KILLER

I glare at my partner and shake my head. The news is poor.

'Well, that didn't work,' I say. 'Maggie's out of the picture and Anne-Marie gets the gig.'

There isn't a response, only a knowing smile, but the implication is clear. I stand and walk to the door, then return and grab the TV remote.

'I don't want to do any more,' I shout. 'I might have escaped detection with this one. There's no guarantee that another attack would work, anyway.'

'It has to. Who else is there?'

'The Asian girl, Zahra.'

'Very funny. Just do it.'

I turn the TV off, throw the remote on the floor, then sit on the sofa and place my head in my hands. Rocking helps. As does repeatedly running my fingers through my hair. Doing them together is even better. I'm left alone. It's dusk by the time I gather my senses.

I walk through to the kitchen, my stomach growling, but I know there's little point in opening the fridge door. The question is whether I put water on my cereal or eat it dry.

I suppose I don't have much choice in the matter. Not really. How can I say no? This situation has to end.

I place the bowl under the tap and turn it on. The tap judders and spits before a weak stream of freezing water trickles out. I stare out of the window. It looks bleak outside, although BBC weather said the temperature won't drop below zero.

I trudge upstairs, drag off my two jumpers and my T-shirt. Shivering, I root through the bag of clothes in the corner to find some more layers that fit. A vest will do. I try not to think whose skin it was last on. My T-shirt goes back on, followed by the jumpers, then another for good measure. I pull my mac on, then stamp down the stairs. I wonder, briefly, where the others are. It's stupid. If you had anywhere else you could be, you'd be there, not here. Maybe I'll go to the library at the weekend. They always crank up the radiators.

First, I need to fetch my kit. I step outside and start to walk. I try to move my legs quickly, but I'm so tired. The assault on Maggie gave me a small boost, but another doesn't seem to make sense. It's as though I can't reason with anything now, making me putty in others' hands.

I find myself humming one of Elvis's ancient songs that I heard a few months back. No wonder it stuck in my mind, but I was singing the lyrics wrong. They were actually 'And Marie' and he was singing about his latest flame. My jingle is a little different.

Anne-Marie's the name, and she's the next to blame.

40

ANNE-MARIE

Anne-Marie snuggled closer to her spouse on the sofa as the closing credits for *Casablanca* scrolled down the screen. Then she stared with revulsion at the pile of foil wrappers in the half-finished Roses tub. A tub they'd only opened just before the film started. Drew pulled himself out of their embrace, rose from the seat, and stretched.

'Do you want me to get the fish and chips tonight?'

'How can you think of food after this afternoon's disgusting debauchery?'

He shrugged and ambled off towards the hall.

Anne-Marie smiled. Her husband's hollow legs were part of the reason she'd struggled with her weight. Still, Christmas was the season for loosening your belt in most regards. She rolled off the sofa and quickly shovelled up the thrown wrappers that had missed the tin, then went to hide all the evidence in the kitchen. Her children were fit and trim. She didn't want them learning any bad habits. With another guilty twinge about being healthier, she shouted out to her husband.

'It's okay. I'll walk down when you get back.'

She heard the front door go as Drew left to collect their eight-year-old, Ronan, from his friend's house, so she prepared the table for their dinner. There was nothing like fish and chips from the chippy itself. She laughed to herself, feeling slightly crazed as her mouth watered. Although Drew heated their own baked beans and mushy peas on the hob while she was fetching them to save a bit of money.

Soon, all the gang had returned from their mate's homes or had come downstairs from their rooms and the house was back up to its normal levels of noise and activity. Ronan had made a Christmas decoration and wanted it put on the top of the tree. Her eldest daughter, Melanie, was giving him some good-natured leg-pulling about the type of family who'd have a dalek up there.

Anne-Marie pulled on her coat and a pair of strong shoes. She usually tried to walk to pick up the takeaway, because she'd burn a few calories and could have a few extra chips.

It was chilly outside, and she was tempted to grab her car keys, but the parking was bad up at the parade, so it was always hit and miss if she could get a space there. She pulled her coat around her and removed a thick hat from one of the pockets and set off. Twenty minutes later, she reached her destination. It wasn't that busy on a Sunday night, so she was soon on her way home.

The food would be lukewarm by the time she got back, but the kids wolfed it down whatever. She often stuck hers and Drew's in the microwave after the children had been sorted.

Anne-Marie had a strange feeling come over her as she walked the last few yards and was about to turn up her drive. A sensation that made her think she was being watched. She stopped dead, then quickly turned around to find a man at her shoulder.

Mr Singh, from next door, jerked backwards with his mouth open.

'Sorry, Ajeet. I thought I was being followed,' said Anne-Marie.

'I was behind you, but only with my dog.'

She reached down and petted the collie, who tried to stick his nose in her warm carrier bag. Ajeet had to drag the pining hound away. Anne-Marie walked up to her door. All this business with Maggie was making her paranoid, but Drew said someone had knocked back his truck's passenger-side wing mirror a few times in the last couple of months while it was on the drive. The children had denied it. She grinned to herself. She supposed they would.

The door opened before she could press the handle. The three youngest kids stood there with suspicious eyes, as if she might have bought fruit instead.

'Come on, Mum. We're starving to death while you're chatting with the neighbours,' said Ronan.

She took one last look behind her and walked inside.

'I'm going to faint if you don't hurry up,' said Marlon, who was already seated, cutlery in hand.

Anne-Marie gave him a big smile, but something felt wrong.

41

THE SANTA KILLER

I know her movements on Sundays almost as well as my own. It must be nice to have such a happy routine. I can virtually see the love from inside leaking out of her door as she steps into the house. If only I could bottle some and take it home. I sneak closer and peer through the edge of the dining-room window. There they all are. The four kids sit at the kitchen table, laughing and joking, while getting stuck into thick, long chips and tall glasses of juice.

Drool pours out from the corner of my mouth. Watching this is what they must mean by pleasure and pain. I'm sure I can smell vinegar out here in the stale, cold, winter air. Imagine the guilty crunch of the salt. Their father comes to the table and sits at the head. Anne-Marie carries his plate out. Woah! Look at the size of that. That really is heaped up high. My hand involuntarily makes the same movement as his as he squirts tomato ketchup in a big splat on the side of the dish. My eyes follow his fork as it rises filled with battered fish. I clamp my teeth together to stop myself from chewing when he does.

Anne-Marie brings in her plate. She's shown some restraint, but I'm still mesmerised by the steam pouring off it. I hunted through the greasy paper and ate the scraps out of their bin once. The chips and batter had even retained a little heat. Afterwards, I licked my cold, oily fingers in the dark.

My stomach rolls. I would do it again right now.

My gaze follows the smiling faces around the room. The laughter filters into the street. I'd steal some of that, too, and release it in our home, but there'd be no point. It wouldn't want to stay.

I guess the heat from the radiators and food is causing the window to mist up, or perhaps it's my breath, which is the only part of me that's warm, because the picture fades from sight. It was a scene from Christmas past. Why, why, why can't this image be ours again?

Instead, *this* is the only way I can help. To watch, to wait. To know her routine.

42

ANNE-MARIE

An hour later, the kids were full and sleepy, as was she, and Drew had taken a shower and was leaving for work. She walked with him to the door.

'Shame we can't have a cosy early night,' she said.

'We've both got Christmas off this year. You'll be sick of the sight of me by Boxing Day.'

She stood in the doorway, watching as he reversed off the drive.

'Were you born in a barn, Mum?' asked Ronan, who was going upstairs behind her.

Cheeky little sod. Although she'd been saying that to him for years regarding leaving doors open. She went back into the house to bring the rubbish out. She hated the wrappers lying in the bin because it stank out the room. After returning to the kitchen, she changed the plastic bag in the pedal bin and went outside, closing the door with a smile.

Her breath puffed out ahead of her. She waited for some passing cars to disappear into the distance, then stepped onto the drive. Don't be daft, she thought. There's nobody out to get you.

She headed to the side of the property and grabbed the handle of the wheelie bin. It was collection day on Monday, so putting it on the road was all part of the routine. She pulled it towards her and saw a bulky red object rise from the gloom behind as Father Christmas stepped forward. Something long and glinting came into her vision and flew directly at her head.

43

THE SANTA KILLER

She wasn't expecting me, that's for sure, but I'm so cold and stiff that my blow lacks venom. I merely clonk her on the head. Panic surges in my chest. She staggers to the side, eyes wide as I step around the bin. I have more room now and, this time, I really get speed into the swing. She puts out a hand but, in the dark, she misses the bat. There's a strange crack when my weapon hits the top of her arm. She lets out a gasp, then a cry, and drops to her knees.

She looks up through watering eyes, face filled with pain.

'Please,' she gasps in desperation.

The vision of her laughing family is at the forefront of my mind. Is this right?

She opens her mouth to scream, so I jab the end of the weapon into her mouth, not having time to pivot and swing. It has the desired effect. But now, when her head is bowed, I stop. Should I make sure? She's not the only one who's desperate, but is it too late to change my plan?

I clench my jaw, then raise the bat as high as I can. I gasp with effort as I hammer it down.

44

ANNE-MARIE

The crack her arm made snapped her out of the stunned state into which she'd slipped. Even as the agonising pain caused her to drop to her knees, her mind was on her family. She placed her hand on the floor so she could look up.

'Please,' she gasped.

She thought of her innocent children, cosy inside the house. A blur of possible images of their graduations, weddings, and her grandchildren flashed through her vision like a passing Intercity train. A burst of horror at the thought of not being there with them, or for them, had her mouth opening for a piercing scream. The thud of something hard, jarring and unforgiving into her lips and teeth, knocked her head back and silenced her tongue.

Blood poured into her mouth. Anne-Marie looked down and, as she spat it out, she realised her front door was unlocked. The next blow was misjudged and hit her on the back as well as the head, sending a bolt of pain along her spine. She felt the warm embrace of oblivion.

45

DI BARTON

It had been a demanding afternoon. Barton left Zander at the scene of the stabbing and returned to manage the various tasks from the station. It was one of those crimes that he hated. There would be a lot of work, but a clean conclusion was unlikely.

The husband from The Swamp was in a bad way. He'd been stabbed in the back and had been barely conscious when they'd entered the house. Although Barton suspected that was more due to alcohol than the attack. He had been bleeding profusely by the time the paramedics had got to him.

Barton had sent a uniformed PC with the ambulance. The victim had had surgery and would live, and the daughter's cut to her leg was superficial. She, too, had gone to the hospital with Malik and Zelensky. They were bringing her to the station when she was released, but A & E was busy, and she wasn't a priority.

The mother had shouted at the top of her voice to her daughter that her father had fallen. 'Don't say nothing,' Mum had screamed as Zander had put her in the rear of a police car, and the daughter hadn't. Families like this understood to stay quiet. It made the police's job almost impossible if the only witnesses were also the perpetrators. The team could spend weeks processing the case with no chance of getting a conviction.

Barton's mobile rang. It was Control. He listened with growing horror.

'I'll have someone on the way immediately.'

Barton glanced around at the still busy office even though it was gone six p.m. Leicester was the obvious candidate. His work in town hadn't proven beneficial. Barton had been hoping to put The Santa Killer to one side. What he'd just heard meant that was unlikely. Leicester must have felt eyes on him, because he looked up. Barton beckoned him over. Leicester pulled a chair over and sat down.

'With perfect timing, there's been a further incident in the Santa case.'

Leicester's face fell. 'Not Maggie?'

'No, well, I don't believe so.'

Barton got his phone out and searched for Joan's number.

'What, then?' asked Leicester.

'A woman's been attacked outside a house at the bottom of Mayor's Walk. It's likely to be Anne-Marie.'

'Is she all right?'

'I don't know. It's being dealt with as we speak. We were triggered when the address was put in the system.'

'Okay, who's going?'

'Me and you.'

'Have they caught who did it?'

'There was no mention of an arrest, so I'd guess that's a negative.'

Barton watched Leicester look into the distance as his detective's brain clicked into gear.

'It's got to be the Ken's Kitchens angle. Three women who work in sales. Two down, one to go.' He looked at Barton's face. 'Unless the remaining one did it.'

'Yep. Book a car out. I'll be with you in a minute and we'll discuss it on the way.'

'PPE?'

'No, uniform are already there. Actually, take it. This might point our investigation straight to the culprit.'

Barton hit dial, but Joan's number went straight to voicemail. He left a message that he hoped would be enough to encourage her to be cautious as opposed to petrified.

Barton stood up and had a quick word with Zander. He was pulling his coat on when Strange appeared in the office and wandered over to him.

'I return tomorrow, John, you lucky boy. Cox just said you've got your hands full all of a sudden.'

'How about you return now?'

He gave her a thirty-second rundown.

'Erm, sure. I was only planning to go home for a nice bath, then slip into my jim-jams and get cosy in front of the fire. Maybe a glass of wine and a few slices of pizza.'

'You've had a lucky escape, then.'

Barton and Strange met Leicester in the car park, and they left for Mayor's Walk. Barton rang Control for further updates as Leicester drove. The victim was still alive, which was at least something, but they had no more information. Mayor's Walk had been cordoned off, so Leicester parked on the pavement at the entrance to Thorpe Hall.

The scene seemed relatively calm to Barton as they strode over, which reassured him slightly. He found Anne-Marie sitting up in the back of an ambulance with Marlon standing beside her. Barton couldn't help grinning.

'I feared the worst,' he said.

The paramedic was a grey-haired lady with big bags under her eyes. She was holding a bandage over Anne-Marie's nose, but Anne-Marie's eyes were looking at him.

'How is she?' he asked the paramedic.

'I suspected a fracture to her left forearm, but now I'm not as certain. She's a strong one. There's a loose tooth, which they should be able to cement back in. Very large egg on her head, too, but I'm pretty sure the skull is intact. I'll treat her here. A & E is jammed, so there's no rush. If she seems okay, I'll get her arm X-rayed at the urgent treatment centre instead, but we'll keep an eye out for concussion.'

'Good work.'

A uniformed PC came up to Barton with purpose.

'Sergeant Adil has asked if this might end up as one of yours.'

Barton ushered the young female PC out of earshot of the ambulance.

'What exactly do you know?'

'It's another assault, sir,' she replied. 'We were first on the scene. A young man, Marlon, noticed his mum pawing at the front door. He quickly rang 999. We got here at the same time as the paramedics. The victim was conscious, and she said she'd been assaulted by Santa and asked for you by name. Control had already informed you. Um, we put out a BOLO for Father Christmas, but as yet nothing.'

Barton raised an eyebrow, which knocked the tiny smirk off the PC's face. A BOLO was a be-on-the-lookout-for message. Then he smiled to let her know not to worry. It obviously did sound surreal.

Barton didn't bother looking up and down the street. He'd walked these streets in uniform and cycled through them as a kid. There were four roads and two paths off the junction thirty metres away. It had been nearly half an hour since the incident, so the perpetrator could be on the other side of Peterborough by now depending on his mode of transport, or hiding in any number of front gardens or even the grounds of the large hospice nearby, Thorpe Hall.

Barton needed a forensics team, but the local vans were probably still working on the earlier knife incident. This attack was almost identical to the one involving Maggie. Barton didn't think this scene would help much, either.

Barton knew precisely where he was heading, though. Leicester was right. This had to be a work issue. He found Sergeant Adil and pulled him to one side.

'Process the scene as normal, please,' he said. 'I'll confirm later that we'll be taking it on, but I have a firm idea about who's likely to benefit from this attack, so I'm going straight there.'

'Where's that?'

'The other end of this road. I have two of my guys with me, so we'll make the arrest, but I'll need two of yours with me in case we need to force entry or things become volatile. We'll also require a search team and forensics in that house as a priority, not this one, which we aren't going to get this evening. I need someone posted at the door overnight, too.'

Adil chuckled.

'You're aware how thinly we're stretched.'

Barton tried to appeal to Adil's better nature, but he had little chance. Years ago, many units worked nights, and uniform would regularly protect crime scenes, but the cuts had done away with a lot of that. Barton might be able to bribe one of his team, but then he'd lose them tomorrow.

'I'll find a volunteer, sir,' said Adil. 'But it's your budget, time and a half.'

Barton grimaced, but gave him the go-ahead. He walked back over to Anne-Marie in the ambulance, who was now holding the bandage over her nose.

'Anne-Marie. Just nod to answer. Is there anything you can tell us that will help?'

Anne-Marie didn't nod. She took the bandage off to reveal an angry, flushed face. A drop of blood dripped from her nose. The paramedic, who had been sorting through one of her cabinets, tutted. Anne-Marie silenced her with such a withering glance that she turned away.

'I reckon he planned to kill me.'

'Was it definitely a he?'

'I think so, but he had sunglasses and a white beard. It was just the way the bat was swung and how he carried himself. I'd guess not many women would play baseball. Not in England, anyway.'

She tried a smile, but winced.

'Was it definitely a baseball bat?' he asked.

'Yes, but it looked silver, not wooden.'

'Do you have any other clues which might help us to identify him?'

'Sorry, I don't. It was so quick and frenzied. Bastard made me throw up my fish and chips.'

Barton put his hand on her shoulder.

'You must have had your Weetabix this morning.'

A tear rolled down each cheek at the same moment as another trickle of blood ran from her nose. She furiously wiped her face with her sleeve. The woman who he'd met a few days ago seemed much changed. She was dirty and dishevelled. Missing buttons and the mud on her cheeks and forehead made her look like a victim. Barton noticed Anne-Marie recognise the pity in his expression as he turned to leave.

The young female PC from earlier and a tall lad who looked even younger strode over to say they'd leave with Barton. The lad said he could also protect the scene through the night. Barton smiled as the female lifted an enforcer out of a van as though it were a loaf of bread. She'd do. He explained to them that they were insurance and he wasn't expecting trouble. Barton headed to his car.

'Wait, Inspector.'

Anne-Marie pushed herself off the seat of the ambulance and limped down the steps.

'I was dizzy after he attacked me, but I reckon he wasn't that strong. After he walloped me on the head for the last time, a future without me flashed by. God. I don't know where I got the strength from, but I think it was the thought of my children in the house. Something roared inside, and I leapt up as he was about to hit me again. I kind of fell over on top of him. He was weak and flabby and dropped to the floor easily.'

'Was he tall or short?'

'Shorter than me. I have no recollection of what happened next, but apparently I was trying to get back in the house.'

She cringed with pain from moving her arms in the motion of the memory of scratching at the door. Barton smiled at human nature. Anne-Marie's and Maggie's only thoughts had been to protect their children. Marlon, who was watching his mother with concern, came to support her as she wilted.

'It's okay, Anne-Marie. You're a very brave woman,' said Barton. 'You, too, Marlon. Great work.'

'No, it's not okay,' bellowed Anne-Marie. 'This is our home. It's my sanctuary from the madness. You nail this fucker to the wall for me.'

46

DI BARTON

Barton, Leicester and Strange got back in their car. With Mayor's Walk cordoned off, they would need to drive the long way around to Heidi Hulse's house and come in from the Edwalton Avenue end. Barton spent the eight minutes it took them to arrive to contemplate how the Hulses might react. When they were parked outside Ferrari's, Barton waited for the marked police car to arrive behind them and for the PCs to get out. Barton turned to Strange and Leicester.

'Listen in. Speak up if your view differs. I believe that Heidi's husband, Cameron, in desperation at their financial predicament, has taken it on himself to knock out of action the other members of Ken's sales team, presumably in the hope that his wife would get more shifts or a promotion. Cameron fits the physical description. He's not particularly tall, is flabby and looks weak, but he has a temper. He may have been pushed to the end of his tether by their living conditions.'

Barton looked at the other two, who nodded.

'I don't suspect that Heidi is involved as well, but she might be. There's no risk of her absconding seeing as they can barely afford the bus to town, but we'll need to search the property for the weapon and the outfit. I'll get a PolSA team to do a full sweep tomorrow. I want any computer devices we find in the house tonight, so glove up. We'll obviously take Cameron's phone, but let's grab Heidi's mobile, too, assuming she's got one.'

'Is there any risk of him attacking us?' asked Strange. 'I'm not quite up to speed with this.'

Barton thought back to when he'd met Cameron before.

'No, but we brought stab vests and spray. I'll go in first, then Leicester. While they are appalling crimes, they're also a chaotic and slightly ridiculous series of events. Where else would we look when both of Heidi's work colleagues have been assaulted? I wouldn't be surprised if he's expecting us.'

'I agree,' said Leicester. 'It does seem daft, so maybe there's something we're missing. Let's hope he hasn't saved his shotgun cartridges for tonight.'

Barton scowled.

'I checked the shotgun register for the city. No hits.'

'Excellent. So, what's the upside for anyone in all of this? I'd be very shocked if whoever was responsible was thinking clearly, so let's be cautious. I'm going to pound on the door, then arrest Cameron in front of his wife. Let's gauge her response. He doesn't work or have any money, so he's likely to be at home. Hopefully, the kids will be out or in their rooms.'

'Are you sure it was him, not her?' asked Strange. 'She might feel more rage towards Maggie and Anne-Marie due to working with them. You said the boss passed her over for promotion after decades of loyal service.'

'Possible, but unlikely. Heidi seemed defeated and exhausted. It didn't look like an act when I last spoke to her. I got the impression she'd prefer to take it out on Ken than the other women.'

'Okay, how thorough a hunt do we do? And where will we keep

the family while we do it?'

Barton had a quick think. The PolSA team, which stood for Police Search Advisor, would have the place stripped in the morning.

'Just a brief look for computers, obvious clothing and the bat. We're short on manpower and I'm aware that the children have had a tough time of it. We'll keep whoever's present in the front room with one of the PCs. Leicester, see if anyone who's about is talkative. Strange, I'll stay with Cameron and work on him. You go through the house with the other PC and hopefully find what we think is an aluminium bat, then we'll take Cameron back to the station.'

'We need to consider what to do with the wife and kids after that,' said Leicester. 'You mentioned their home is virtually uninhabitable. We can't keep them in the front room all night.'

Barton had already considered that.

'I'll contact the crisis team. There was a case recently where they stuck a family in the Travelodge for a few nights at our cost. I doubt anyone will put up a fight when they hear there's heating, warm showers and flatscreen TVs.'

Barton took two twenty-pound notes out of his pocket.

'I don't think they will have had enough food either, so they can walk over to Tesco and get a couple of days' worth. I'll hopefully sort this on expenses. Perhaps they'll sing like canaries with gratitude at finally being warm. We'll talk to Cameron when we get back and keep him in the cells overnight. I'll be in touch with Heidi tomorrow morning to see how she's feeling, then I'll ask someone to take the youngsters to school if necessary.'

They got out of the car. Barton and Leicester pulled on a stab vest and took a baton each. Barton strode towards the front door and knocked. A biting wind cut through his clothing. It was the daughter who appeared in the doorway. She had an unusual half-smile on her face.

47

DI BARTON

Ashlynn folded her arms and stood in the doorway.

'Well, if it isn't the police again. When life's going from bad to rotten, you can always rely on the cops to come around and make it worse.'

She tried to brush past Barton. He put his arm out and stopped her. She struggled, so he virtually lifted her back into the house with one hand. Confused, Barton looked down. His hands felt damp and cold. Ashlynn was wearing a newish blue and white tracksuit. She scowled and spat her response to him.

'There's no tumble dryer and the radiators don't work. Call yourself a fucking detective.'

'Language, young lady. Where are your brothers?'

Her scowl strengthened.

'Not content with just targeting my parents?'

'Ashlynn.'

'Okay, okay. Not surprisingly, they've been sleeping at friends' houses. Only someone with a death wish would sleep in this crypt.'

'Why are you still here?'

'I need to keep an eye on those two in there.' She jerked her finger backwards. 'They do have a death wish.'

'Take me through to them, please,' said Barton.

Ashlynn turned and flounced back to the dining room. Barton followed and found Cameron and Heidi slumped at the table. It looked as though Heidi was reading something on her lap, but her straggly hair hung down and concealed whatever it was she had there. Smoke drifted in the cold air like a winter's mist. Cameron glanced at Barton, then at Leicester when he came into the room. He didn't look at Strange when she walked in.

'Evening, plod,' said Cameron. 'Fancy a drink? If it drops a couple of degrees, I could probably rustle up a snowball.'

'Cameron, this isn't a social call. I'm arresting you on suspicion of grievous bodily harm with intent. You do not have to say anything...'

Barton finished the caution after a few pauses due to the hacking cough that came from Heidi, but she didn't glance up throughout the process.

'Do I have to come with you?' asked Cameron.

'That's usually how it works,' said Barton. 'Although I am happy to take a confession here.'

'My wife's not well. I'm worried about her.'

'Yeah, she sounds terrible,' said Ashlynn, who was hovering in the kitchen.

'Cameron, we're looking to put your wife and Ashlynn in a room somewhere like the Travelodge for a couple of nights while we look into things. They'll receive some money for basics, and it'll definitely be warm and comfortable. Meanwhile, we'll search this place from top to bottom. If there's anything here, give it up now. I can talk to the council about temporary accommodation after that. People shouldn't have to live in places like this.'

Barton had worked his way around so he could peer at Heidi's lap. He was concerned she might have a weapon. She looked up as he closed in on her.

'This isn't a council house. It's ours,' she said.

The only things on Heidi's lap were scrawny hands with prominent blue veins.

'DC Leicester will stay with you in the front room while we wait for support, then we'll get you sorted out, Heidi. I understand your sons are with friends at the moment. Will they be able to continue to stay there, or will you need accommodation for them?'

A look of confusion passed over Heidi's face.

'It won't be a problem. I'll text them and sort it,' said Ashlynn, while staring hard at her mother.

'Cameron,' said Barton. 'I'm going to cuff your hands in front of you. Please remain in your seat for the moment. I need to confiscate your mobile phone and computers. Where are they?'

'What's he done?' asked Heidi.

'We suspect him of assaulting two women.'

Heidi stared at Cameron, who dropped his gaze to the floor. Barton could sense there was something very off here. Surely Heidi must have linked the recent assaults with the police being here to arrest Cameron. Then he remembered Heidi wouldn't have heard of the attack on Anne-Marie.

Barton analysed Cameron's face for guilt or innocence, but neither were present. They'd found Cameron's criminal record, but it only contained a DUI two years ago, which explained why Heidi had to drive him around. Barton turned his gaze to her. Did she know something about what was going on? Ashlynn was staring at her father, but with an expression of pity rather than disgust.

Barton waited for someone to respond, but nobody did.

'Anne-Marie was assaulted an hour ago,' he stated.

Cameron looked at Heidi, but she'd returned to looking at her lap.

'Where were you an hour ago, Cameron?' asked Barton.

Cameron scrunched his eyes tight, but kept quiet.

'Does anyone want to say anything before we take Cameron away?' asked Barton.

Heidi's head rose, but only for her to shake it. Ashlynn took her phone out and started texting. There was no point in any more questions because anything they said would be inadmissible until they'd been offered legal counsel. Barton took a last look at Cameron, who raised his arms to be cuffed. He smiled.

'I'll come, but I won't confess.'

48

DI BARTON

Cameron Hulse caused no trouble on the journey to the police station, nor when the custody sergeant booked him in. In fact, he seemed overly accepting of his fate. Barton took Strange to interview room two for a chat beforehand. They'd found nothing incriminating in their quick search of the house.

'Okay, Kelly. If you do the honours, we'll see what he has to say. Cameron's either a very cool customer or he's got no remorse.'

'Or he didn't do it,' she replied with a smile.

'Yes, that looks possible. But he knows something. It's late, so let's give it no more than an hour. We'll have another crack again in the morning. Maybe a night in the cells will loosen his tongue.'

'It'll defrost his tongue after being in that house.' She smiled.

'Yes, it's hard to believe that people in this day and age live without a functioning boiler.'

'Yeah, luckily we don't see it as much nowadays. It's sad people like the Hulses get overlooked. They tried to do the right thing getting on the property ladder, but who keeps three grand hanging around in case the boiler blows?'

'A large proportion of the population doesn't have a buffer anywhere near that.'

'Me included,' replied Strange. 'I suppose I could always borrow it, or bang it on a credit card.'

'But if your credit rating is shot, and you can't find work, what do you do?'

'You sit and suffer, and it's liable to make you desperate.'

'But would it make you stupid?'

Barton pondered the facts for a moment. Cameron seemed sane and had no similar previous, which was concerning. Most of those who committed these types of crimes at this level of violence had been troubled for a long time. These were offences that men escalated to, not started out at, unless there was a catastrophic collapse in someone's well-being.

'Leicester said there was a locked loft door that Heidi said she didn't have the key for,' he said.

'Seems unlikely.'

'Let's see if Cameron's bothered about us going up there.'

Barton left the room, walked through to the custody desk, and asked for Cameron to be brought to interview room two. He signed the custody record. When he'd returned to Strange, he opened his mouth to have a quick word before Cameron arrived, then closed it. She scowled at him.

'Were you going to give me some instructions?' she asked.

'Nope.'

'Shall I ask him plenty of personal questions first? See if we can get a baseline for his honesty.'

'Whatever you think's best.'

They grinned at each other. Cameron appeared five minutes later with the duty solicitor. He'd taken his coat off and seemed much slimmer in just a checked shirt and loose jeans. Perhaps some of his padding had been down to wearing multiple layers to combat the effects of living without central heating. Strange went through the preliminaries and Cameron confirmed he understood.

'How are things, generally, Cameron?' asked Strange.

'Do you mean my health, my family, or work?'

'All of them.'

'Well, they're all falling apart in one way or another, or perhaps they're broken beyond repair.'

'Explain, please.'

'You saw my wife. She's on the brink of a complete breakdown, but we can't afford for her to have any time off.'

'Doesn't she get sick pay?'

'Not for the first three days, which might not seem like much, but our finances are on the edge of a precipice.' Cameron clicked his fingers. 'We're ready to fall.'

'Could you ask for a payment holiday for your mortgage?'

'We've already had two of those, and that's the maximum our provider does. We were behind anyway, and we've taken out as much equity as we could. It's lucky house prices keep going up, or we'd already be dead and buried.'

'How does that make you feel?'

'A man should be able to provide a warm home for his family. It kills me that I can't.'

'Are you at the end of your tether?' asked Strange.

Cameron gave her a ghost of a smile.

'Close to it, but not as near to meltdown as my partner is in all of this bullshit.'

'Are you married or common-law?'

'Married. We tied the knot last year. The kids wanted us to do it to move on from our troubles, but we had no money. We managed it all for £120 which included a meal at KFC.'

Cameron beamed as he thought about that day.

'It was still kind of special. My partner always dreamed of a big white wedding, but she never complained. Not once.'

'Do you often call her partner instead of wife?'

Cameron's smile slipped.

'It was from the beginning when the children were young. We used to shout, "Howdy, partner," to each other as we crossed ways. I did nights, and she did days. We were partners in crime, partners in everything. The kids say it too. They loved cowboy films. For me and Heidi, it was us against the world, until the world stopped caring. That's when it all went tits up.'

'What happened?'

'I had a small security firm, me and two employees. I used to look after building sites, factories, and warehouses to stop stuff from getting nicked. My knee started playing up around three years ago from an old car accident and I struggled to get about. One of the sites got robbed, and I lost the contract. Then a few others didn't renew, and my business tanked. Basically, we had some bad luck. Personally, and professionally. I drank too much for a while. That was a few years ago. I stopped drinking altogether because, jeez, that really didn't help. It's not been easy since.'

Strange paused after that. Barton suspected she was wondering if Cameron's business went under because of his knee or due to boozing.

'Have you worked recently?' asked Strange.

'Yes, well, kind of. I've had quite a few jobs. There was Amazon and I tried a couple of other warehouses, but my knee couldn't cope. I've done a bit of temping, some Christmas work, but I'm pushing fifty now. No one wants to give a knackered old man with a dicky leg a permanent job with benefits when they can pay a twenty-year-old next to nothing and they'd do it faster.'

'How are the youngsters coping with everything?' Ashlynn said they stay at friends' because of the cold. That must be hard,' asked Strange.

Barton watched the same expression pass over Cameron's face as had passed over his wife's earlier. It was one of sadness and weary acceptance.

'It's been very tough. They sneak showers at school, whereas my wife and I just stink. It's like we're treading water with someone's boot on our heads, stopping us ever getting out.'

'Do you have family or friends who help?' asked Strange.

'No family for either of us nearby, or who gives a damn. Friends tend to slip away when your hand is always out.'

'A promotion at work would have helped for Heidi,' said Barton.

'Yeah, it would.'

'Does she like her job?' asked Strange.

'Did you know she slept with him?'

Strange hesitated again.

'No, I didn't know that,' she replied.

'Greasy shite got her drunk at the Christmas party not long after she started. Although, calling it a Christmas party was a joke, seeing it was just the two of them.'

'That must have been tricky to move past with her still being employed there. You must have been livid.'

'She was so sorry that I had to forgive her. We tried to find her another job but I guess he felt guilty, because shortly after he offered her better hours that really worked with getting the kids to school and back. Jobs like that are gold dust for any working family. We couldn't turn it down, even though it pissed me off to think of him staring at her at work. Then the years ticked by, and here we are.'

'Is your marriage strong?' asked Strange.

'I'm a lucky man. I can't bring myself to go to the food banks. It's too embarrassing, but she does.' Cameron's eyes filled, but he blinked the tears back and, after a few seconds, continued, 'Heidi has a friend who gives us bags of second-hand clothes from the charity shop she volunteers at. We wear this new-to-us stuff, because it's been cleaned when they get it. Then we don't pay to wash our own at the launderette. We just re-donate it.'

Barton thought he'd heard of most things before, but even that was news to him.

'What do you have to say about the charges we believe you're guilty of?' asked Strange.

'Nothing.'

'What do you mean, nothing?'

'I reckon you have nothing, so I'll be saying nothing. You lot solve most of your crimes through confessions, so you won't get one from me. Prove I was there. Prove I did it. Show me the weapon that was used. I heard the news. Where's the Santa suit I was wearing?'

'There's a strong motive for doing it,' interrupted Strange. 'With Heidi's colleagues unable to work, Ken would look to his longest-serving employee to fill the breach.'

'What's in the loft, Cameron?' asked Barton.

Cameron flinched, then gathered himself.

'Nothing,' he said. Then he leaned back and closed his eyes.

49

DI BARTON

It was well past eight when Barton plodded out of the station with Strange. He left his car in the car park and took Strange's offer of a lift home so they could talk. He'd had little chance to chat with her of late, so he asked her in for a coffee or a Christmas tipple. When they entered the house, Gizmo heroically drained his reserves of energy to drag himself off the sofa, which he wasn't supposed to be on, to allow Strange to stroke him. Then he sauntered back to his spot.

Holly came out of the kitchen with a flushed face.

'Kelly. Lovely to see you. Excuse the smell, I've been feeding sherry to the Christmas cake.'

Barton smiled. 'Looks like the cake had some company while it was getting drunk.'

'Actually, Holly, can I have a quick word?' asked Strange.

'If you're struggling with what to buy me for Christmas, I've plenty of ideas,' interrupted Barton.

'I got your tie in last year's January sale, John,' said Strange.

'I expect she wants to know what the kids want,' tutted Holly.

'Typical bloke, thinking it's all about him. Maybe Kelly will find me something on my list, namely a new husband.'

'The number one wish for women this Christmas,' said Strange, with a smile as the women warmed to the theme.

'Out with the old, and in with the new,' sang Holly.

'It's a great idea. You could take him down to Webuyanyhusband.com, see what you get for him,' said Strange.

'It's funny you should say that,' said Holly. 'That would present a moral dilemma. Do I declare he's in perfect working condition, or should I come clean about the considerable problems under his bonnet?'

'Don't mention the exhaust.'

Barton folded his arms.

'Hey, I am listening! Besides, I'm still a desirable model. They don't make 'em like me any more.'

Barton laughed as the jeering women closed the kitchen door on him. He found Luke and Layla watching *Scrooged* in the lounge. The fire was on and the lights were twinkling on the Christmas tree. There were already plenty of presents under the branches from various friends and work colleagues. Barton saw where Luke had been putting them into piles, and no doubt shaking them as he did so.

Barton couldn't help picturing the Hulses' house. There'd been no tree. He hadn't even seen any cards. He considered how he'd feel if he was unable to provide for his own children. Would he resort to crime?

'Dad,' said Layla. 'Luke keeps farting.'

'I don't. It's her.'

Barton watched them enjoying their argument with not a serious care in the world. The Hulses were wondering about their next warm meal.

'I'm going to leave a sign out the front telling Father Christmas not to risk coming inside because you smell so bad,' shouted Layla.

With that, she stomped out of the room. Luke chased after her and bellowed up the stairs.

'Maybe you should ask Santa for a new personality because you keep getting dumped.'

Barton chuckled at the low blow. He sat down next to Gizmo on the sofa and rapidly solved the mystery of who was responsible for the heady aroma. Gizmo looked lovingly up at Barton.

'Blame it on the sprouts,' whispered Barton.

He glanced at his watch. They could hold Cameron for twenty-four hours, but it wasn't like in the movies where they held people for the maximum detention time seemingly at a whim. As soon as they had enough evidence to charge, they must do so. They could only keep a detained person under lock and key if they were securing evidence to charge them. Custody sergeants like Donald would simply release them without charge if they felt the rules were being bent, because it was their necks on the block. And at the moment, they certainly didn't have enough to ask for a superintendent to give them an extension without more convincing proof.

Barton had to hope that CSI found something in the house that his team had missed that put the family in the frame. The problem with that was they were as overworked as his team was. They might not even get to it until late or in the morning. They weren't dealing with a murder. Leicester was going back first thing to have a look in the loft when it was daylight. The possible contents of it had been the only reason that Donald hadn't bailed Cameron already.

Barton let the details of the case filter through his mind. He thought of the letters that had been sent to the radio presenter. He didn't like that one iota. It implied a level of malevolence, or possibly a God-complex, which added an extra danger to proceedings.

He switched the TV over to *Sky News*, catching the back end of the sport. Strange popped her head in five minutes later.

'I'm gonna get going,' said Strange.

'No time for a beer?'

'I need to do some shopping for your children. Holly's given me plenty of options. I presume you'll be joining us Christmas Eve after work for a couple, so we'll have a good catch up then. You can tell me all of Zander's dirty secrets.'

'My lips are sealed,' he replied. 'Until my third pint.'

Strange waved and closed the door. He couldn't be bothered to get up. His eyes were drooping when the main news came on again. Another woman had come forward to the police to say she had been assaulted in Anglesey in similar circumstances to the attack in Liverpool. Police in Leicester had also found similarities between their case and the ones in Liverpool and Stoke. He increased the volume.

'Police are investigating in all of the areas and expect to have further information for the media over the next few days. Meanwhile, they would urge those partying on the run-up to Christmas and the new year to be aware of your friends and surroundings. Drink sensibly, and, most importantly, ensure everyone in your group gets home safe and sound.'

Barton felt a chill across his shoulders. He looked to see who'd opened the lounge door, but it was still shut.

50

DI BARTON

Monday 21st December

For a change, Barton wasn't one of the first in the office the next day due to struggling to get up after a poor night's sleep. He turned his computer on to see what the criminal elements of Peterborough had been up to the evening before but thankfully it had been a quiet night. There had been a few drink-driving incidents and a couple of domestic disputes, but nothing to interest Barton.

As he checked his emails, one appeared from Tim Tibbles. He clicked on it. The title was Letter. It said they'd received another one that morning. Barton emailed him back and told them not to touch it. He grabbed a pen and paper and made a list of what he needed to do.

The first job was to interview Cameron, but that wouldn't take long if he declined to say anything. Then he was going to ring Leicestershire Police and find out what they knew about the spate of assaults and killings that might be heading their way. His brain had finally woken up and was in top gear. He was less worried about the link between the murders in Stoke and Leicester now that Anne-Marie had also been attacked. The Peterborough bat incidents seemed to have a work angle. He just had to discover what it was. Otherwise, the other likely connection for the two victims was their gym which Maggie's admirers attended.

He emailed the team there'd be a meeting at midday to discuss the latest on both this case and the domestic stabbing over at Benland. Barton was interested to hear if anything came up from any social media profiles for those involved in Maggie's case. Men and women posted some strange stuff, not knowing that it would be on the web for eternity. People also liked to drink alcohol at home. Many a crime got solved by trawling through people's feeds and posts.

He opened an email from Sirena next, the Crime Scene Manager. She'd overseen the crime scene investigations at Maggie's and Anne-Marie's houses. There was a fair amount of detail, but Barton could tell there wasn't anything that would help him right now. She was spending the day at the Hulses'. Leicester was the final member of his team to arrive after being at the Hulses' house and Barton beckoned him over.

'Anything in the loft?' he asked.

'No, nothing except for a whole load of family stuff. Boxes and boxes of photo albums, framed pictures of the children when they were young. Old school reports. That sort of thing.'

'Great. How did it go last night with the crisis team?'

'Heidi and Ashlynn have been given a room at the Travelodge. Two nights, that's it. I went with them and it was pretty sad. The mother just got into bed. I put the heating on full blast and left her there. Ashlynn was excited, especially when she saw they had a bath. She took the money for the food and ran off to the supermarket. I dread to think what she spent it on.'

'It's a shame we can't do more for them. What are your thoughts on them being involved in some way?'

'I guess I'm like most detectives and usually have an inkling, but the only feeling I have at the moment is that people aren't telling the truth, or are at least keeping their cards close to their chests.'

Barton nodded.

'I assume the fact I didn't hear from you means there were no confessions and nothing else incriminating turned up at the Hulses' house.'

'No, Heidi's phone was broken and there were two ancient laptops. I was tempted to leave the one for Ashlynn's homework, because she'll be without it for a while. Ashlynn said her parents never used them.'

'And you believe her?'

'Yes, their broadband was cut off a year ago.'

Barton thought about how the Hulses would have managed with home schooling throughout the pandemic. Leicester cleared his throat.

'If you want,' said Leicester, 'I'll visit the hotel today. I was going to leave Ashlynn's phone with her so we have a means of contact, but I've checked her messages because it's her I trust the least. She was really measured when she answered my questions, although she gave me the brothers' mobile numbers in case we want to talk to them.'

'That was the right call. Annoyingly, her father wouldn't give us access to his phone. It's not an iPhone, so we can extract the data easily if we have just cause, but right now we might not have enough. I'm glad you're here bright and early because Peterborough City Radio has received another letter. Your first job is to get down there and bring it back. Tell Tibbles not to mention it on air unless I've given him permission.'

Leicester shook his head in disbelief.

'No way, another letter turned up?'

'Yes, although this one is a little more aggressive.'

'What does it say?'

'"Santa Killer has come to town. Now more women will frown."'

51

DI BARTON

Barton phoned Leicester police and eventually got through to the detective sergeant who was dealing with the murder there. Leicester's was a much bigger force than Peterborough's, so it wasn't unusual to have a DS in charge of a case this important.

'Hi, this is DI John Barton, from Peterborough. Is that DS Smith?'

'Big John, no way! It's Albie. We played inter-force rugby against each other about fifteen years ago.'

'You're kidding. The guy with the wild hair?'

'Yeah, that was me. Now I'm a guy with no hair.'

'I remember! I owe you some bruises.'

'Don't give me that. I think I still have your footprint on my chest.'

The two men reminisced for a few minutes.

'I recall you saying in the bar afterwards you were going to remain single and stay a beat plod forever,' said Barton. 'You wanted the easy life, remember?'

'They were wise words that I ignored. Two kids and a wife now. Ruined everything. Horrible woman keeps pushing me. She wants me to make the best of myself before I check out and leave her as a merry widow.'

Barton chuckled, but it was time for business.

'Good for you. Now, what have you got? I assume even you lot joined the dots together.'

'Yes, it's clearly a pattern. We've taken detailed statements from both the surviving women in Liverpool and Anglesey. The four attacks are similar, just a different weapon was used in the first two. We're pretty certain it's the same guy.'

'Any kind of description yet?'

'No, you know how it is at this point. The collection, inputting of data, interviews, chasing around, but I don't like it at all.'

'What's worrying you most?'

'The perpetrator is smart. He doesn't want to get caught. I've got my best analyst on it.'

Barton smiled. They would probably only have one analyst.

'There must be a few other assaults like that in the country.'

'Yeah, we've scoured the national database for similar MOs, but there aren't many. There are a few that match, but the perpetrators are inside after guilty pleas. There's a definite pattern southward for our guy. He attacked the earliest victim over a year ago. Then he moved on. Second assault three months later.'

'I take it the third attack was three months later, and the fourth, three months after that.'

'Correct.'

'I don't suppose it's to the day, or on some sort of lunar cycle.'

'No, it's not that specific, so we can't predict that the next woman is going to get it Friday or anything like that, but he's methodical, which shows planning and cool.'

'That's assuming no other victims come forward, and that we've found all the bodies.'

'Yes, that's a chilling thought, but possible. We think hammer or similar for the first two incidents. Perhaps he was intending to do worse with the second attack but someone disturbed him, so he moved on to a weapon that could more easily do the job with a single blow. Although it's possible he was interrupted during both attacks. He might have always been a killer.'

'Right, he may well have got the taste for it after the initial incident, then gone on from there.'

'That's what we think. Which means whoever he targets next is in deep shit.'

'Maybe the fact it's hit the papers will keep him lying low,' said Barton, even though he knew it was unlikely.

'You know what these nutters are like, John. He's angry, and he'll want the world to know why at some point. They all do. I bet he's jerking off now it's on the news. It's possible he'll make a mistake with the next one, but he's been very disciplined so far, which is worrying.'

Barton didn't have to say it. A disciplined murderer, moving at a relatively quick pace across county borders, who was butchering people he'd never met, made him the textbook serial killer.

'We need to stop this guy, John, or some poor fucker's going to die before Christmas. I reckon that's a certainty.'

'What do you have?'

'Both women who survived didn't see the face of who attacked them. One said she had the impression from her peripheral vision that he was tall, but she's pretty short, so take that how you like.'

'And neither of them had anything obvious from their past or current lives that linked them?' asked Barton, shaking his head.

'I'm uncertain for the first lady, but the second one went into detail. The perp didn't get into a relationship with her beforehand. She said her life had nothing different from her normal routines. Hopefully he's selecting them for a reason, because if they really are random, it'll make it that much harder.'

'So, you've found no links at all?'

'Nope, the victims don't seem to be related in any way. I don't think they've finished talking to the Anglesey woman yet.'

'I only heard about that case on the news last night. Sounds like a bit of a mess.'

'Yes, we've got a specialist up from the Met, though, and she's picked something out from the other files. The women appear to be struggling generally or have quiet social lives.'

'Struggling how?'

'They were isolated individuals who had few close contacts. Whether that was through choice, I'm not sure. They don't, or didn't, have great support. Any children had left home, and they lived alone. The Anglesey victim was a pensioner, but the others were working long hours and had poor or non-existent social lives. They were all without partners. He's selected them because they were lonely.'

'Clever,' said Barton with a wince.

'Yes. I'm not entirely convinced this Anglesey case is connected, though. The victim is much older, and the attack seems less brutal, but we haven't got a lot of specifics yet.'

'Okay. And nothing from CCTV?'

'There's so much of it to look through and very little close to the scenes because they were done in residential areas. We're looking, but it's so manpower-intensive, we need something to narrow it down.'

'Can you keep me posted?'

'Sure. What's your interest in this, apart from the possibility of the murderer heading to Peterborough?'

Barton picked up on the word *possibility*.

'Does that mean you now think it probably won't lead here?'

'Yes, the Anglesey addition makes it more likely the line is curving. My guess is somewhere like Bedford will be next to have an unwelcome visitor rather than your city. After all, where will he want to end up?'

'Where the lights are shining on him,' replied Barton.

'Yes, London has to be his destination. Imagine the damage he could do in a place like that full of folk wearing masks. If he's looking for solo people living isolated lives, then the capital is the spot to be. He could kill or maim dozens before we caught him.'

'He'll slip up. They always do, or their luck runs out. He's smart, but he'll have a weakness.'

'I hope so. I assume you've not had anything similar.'

'No. We also have what I reckon is a loony attacking women, but it doesn't match what you have. I think it's a more local case dealing with local issues, but he could be so clever he's running two lines of attack.'

Barton thought of the letter that the radio station had received. The change in tone was concerning. He exhaled deeply.

'What's your next focus?' asked Barton.

'More analysis. The profiler is trying to persuade the two women who were attacked first to meet. She wants them to have a chat about their lives. See if anything matches. Maybe they both like books, or music or live bands, or exercise, or a local pub, or one of their closest friends had a new boyfriend which gave him access to their inner circle, or the postman was new, or a new neighbour, or please, God, something.'

Barton laughed.

'I'll email you as soon as I find out anything.'

'Appreciated, Albie.'

'Take care, John, because if Peterborough's next in line, I wouldn't be surprised if the killer is already there amongst you.'

52

DI BARTON

Barton thought of Cameron in the cells below as he put the phone down. He couldn't believe he was the guy Leicester police were looking for. He didn't think he'd be able to afford the travelling for a start, although he might be lying about their finances. House prices had risen a decent amount, so it was possible he took a fair-sized sum out of the equity. It was unlikely, though, judging by the conditions his family was living in. Barton collared Strange.

'Kelly, let's see if Cameron has turned into a canary overnight.'

'Sorry, boss, but I've got a meeting with your boss.'

'It feels like you're avoiding me,' he shouted at her retreating back.

She turned around and sang a song line to him.

'Too much Barton can kill you, just as sure as none at all.'

Barton tutted. Seemed as though everyone was losing their marbles.

'Zelensky, are you sane enough to question the husband with me?'

'No, boss,' she replied with a straight face.

'Ah, well. Just take notes, then. I doubt anyone will notice.'

She grinned as they headed towards a vacant office so they could prepare.

Cameron arrived at the interview room looking like a different man from the day before. After the preliminaries, he stretched as though he'd enjoyed a break at a health spa.

'How are you feeling, Cameron? Troubled night?' asked Barton.

'Yep. Troubled by not being with my family at a tough time, but it was warm and toasty in those cells. I've not slept so well in months.'

'People have been injured. You are aware of that,' said Barton.

'What I'm aware of is that you're going to have to release me soon.'

'Where were you on the night of the fifteenth?'

'I'm not a fool.'

'How do you feel about your wife's work colleagues getting hurt?'

'Do you know what, Mr Barton? I don't feel much at all any more. It's cold at the bottom where we are. Our feelings don't matter. If you feel, you suffer. Perhaps they pissed the wrong person off. Maggie stole that promotion off my wife, that's true. Did they offer a hand or show any interest in our sinking ship while they were riding the crests of their waves? No, they did not.'

'You don't care, then,' stated Barton.

'Interview's over, Mr Barton. I've had every bit of bad luck there is.'

Cameron couldn't keep the end of that statement coming out as a snarl. He closed his eyes and seemed to focus on his breathing.

Barton paused and raked his brain for something to get this guy going.

'It must be tough with a broken boiler. Can't the council help?'

Cameron opened his eyes. His jaw tensed as he met Barton's gaze.

'As I told you, there's support for council houses, but we own our home.'

'There's also assistance if you have young children.'

'Correct. They put us in touch with a charity who gave us the electricity-eating heaters we have upstairs. A plumber came around from I don't know where to try to get the boiler going, but it was no good. The circuit board and both switches had shorted, and the radiators are gunked up. What we need is a new combi, but because the old boiler is tank fed, all the pipework has to be changed, so it's the best part of three grand.'

'Can't you borrow it?'

'Even the Krays would turn their nose up at our credit rating. We were introduced to another organisation who might have been able to help, but they went under with the lack of funding events due to the lockdowns. We were lucky last winter, if you remember. It was wet, but we only had a few weeks of proper freezing weather. Besides, there are worse things than being cold.'

As Barton digested that cryptic comment, Zelensky cleared her throat.

'Cameron,' she said. 'You were saying that you'd had every bit of bad luck there is. Does that also apply to your wife?'

'What's that supposed to mean?'

'Maybe you are innocent. Let's look at the facts. Anne-Marie beaten. Maggie beaten. Perhaps this monster wants to ruin Ken. He can't run his business without sales staff. If I was the attacker, I know who'd be next on my list.'

Cameron leaped out of his seat. His solicitor, Barton and Zelensky all leaned back.

'You let me the fuck out of here, right now!' roared Cameron.

And just like that, Barton knew for certain what he'd already suspected. He picked up the room's phone and rang the custody sergeant.

'Custody.'

'Barton here. Please arrange the immediate release of Cameron Hulse.'

53

DI BARTON

Barton and Zelensky stayed in the interview room until Cameron calmed down. They got back to the office at the same time as Leicester returned from the radio station. Barton had a quick peek at a photocopy of the letter that Leicester was holding. The rest of the team were present, so it was a good moment for their meeting. When they were gathered and seated, Barton gave the floor to Leicester.

'For those who don't know yet, the radio station received an unstamped letter.' Leicester waved the evidence bag. 'It says, "Santa Killer has come to town. Now more women will frown."'

Leicester passed the bag around so everyone could have a look.

'First thoughts?' asked Barton.

There was a pause. Barton could see Leicester had a view, but he'd had more time for his brain to engage. Zander shouted.

'He's escalating. He wants the city to fear him.'

Barton shrugged. 'Anything else?'

'It's a bit unusual using a rhyme. I reckon whoever it is has a high opinion of themselves,' said Zander.

'Some people love poetry,' said Barton. 'Although, I'd have put money on the Hulses not being that sort.'

Leicester, Malik, Zelensky and Hoffman all spoke at the same time.

'He's getting careless. It's risky going back to the radio station to post another letter,' said Zander, as they all paused.

Barton curled his lip. 'Anyone else?'

The new detective, Hoffman, spoke out.

'Wasn't the other letter posted via Royal Mail?'

'Excellent. Taxi for Zander. What else?'

'Where's the envelope?' asked Zelensky.

Barton looked at Leicester.

'No envelope, guv. It was folded and posted into the little letter box on the wall at the address. Apparently, the postman doesn't use that. He usually knocks on the door and hands them to whoever's there. This wasn't delivered the same way.'

'It's also different writing,' said Hoffman. 'Remember, the writing in the other letter was spidery, and had a lighter feel. This is blocky, or even angry.'

'Excellent,' said Barton.

'Didn't the other message also say The Santa Killer was coming to town?'

'Correct, Mr Hoffman, well done.'

Zander put his hand up.

'Sir, I don't like the new guy.'

'I'm sorry, Constable Zander, but Sergeant Hoffman is staying.'

The team laughed, Zander loudest. Barton realised Zander had been in a great mood recently.

'I'm sure you'll agree this suggests that someone else is responsible for this letter,' said Barton. 'But before we have Mr Hoffman knighted, let's also remember that whoever was responsible could have disguised it deliberately to confuse us, or had a partner do it for him. Let's assume it is someone unconnected. Any guesses as to who wrote it and why?'

'Another person with mental health issues,' said Zelensky.

'I suspect that's a given,' said Strange.

They all chuckled again.

'I'd be willing to bet this letter isn't linked to the first guy, so it might be a sicko having fun at our expense. Back in the day, we used to call them shit-stirrers,' said Barton.

He looked around the room before he spoke next.

'Earlier today, I had a chat with Leicestershire Police.'

Barton gave the team the relevant details of the phone conversation. He paused for a minute to let them process the information. Malik was fastest off the blocks.

'You think it could be connected to our attacks?'

'No, I don't, but this letter could be anything.'

'I've read about the guy who killed the women across the country. He's no fool,' said Zelensky. 'If he's coming here on his way to London, leaving a few dead bodies on the way, and he sees the news is full of a nutter running around dressed as Father Christmas and attacking females, he's going to be thrilled. It's the perfect cover.'

'Great. That's a nice angle. Let's put that to one side for the moment and refocus on the crimes we know are happening here, as opposed to just ones that might. What about social media for the Hulse family or anyone else involved?'

'It's sparse for all of them,' said Malik. 'I can't find anything at all for the lads. Ashlynn is on there, but she only has around forty friends and doesn't seem to post much. That's not unusual. We all know that the kids don't think Facebook is that cool. People our age and older love it because it helps us keep in touch with anyone, anywhere. It's a link to our past. Schoolkids don't generally have a past. All their mates are at school with them, and there are cooler ways to keep in touch.'

'What about the parents?' asked Strange.

'Cameron has an account. He used to use his frequently. His security settings are decent, so I can't see many comments, but I can see a lot of photos. There appears to be very little for the last three years. In fact, it seems he abruptly stopped posting.'

'That's when he said his business folded and he got done for drink driving, so perhaps it isn't surprising. Some people use Fakebook to boast about their lives. Perhaps he had nothing much to say. Then things only got worse,' replied Strange.

'And the mother?' asked Barton.

'Zip. No social media imprint anywhere that I can locate. Same for the boys. They could have pseudonyms on sites like Pinterest, TikTok or Insta, but I haven't been able to find them. Anne-Marie has a page, but the security is so tight all I'm able to view is the profile picture. Nothing for Maggie across the board either, except a LinkedIn account.'

'Right. Well, we've let Cameron go. He can look after Ashlynn. We should speak to Heidi next, or do we start on the gym angle? I think—'

Barton was interrupted by his mobile ringing. He didn't recognise the number.

'Barton speaking.'

'It's Ken. You gave me your card.'

'Hi, Ken. What's up?'

'There's something I should have told you but didn't.'

'Okay, fire away.'

'No, I don't want to say it over the phone.'

'Okay, I'm at the station now.'

'I've taken the morning off with the stress of it all. Can you visit my house?'

Barton grumbled, but knew whatever Ken had to say might be important.

'I'll send an officer around shortly. What's your address?'

'117 Portman Close, but I'd like you to come, personally.'

Barton chuntered some more.

'This better be worthwhile.'

'It will be. I suppose it's a confession of sorts.'

54

DI BARTON

Barton wound up the meeting, then Leicester and he left the building and took a pool car to visit Ken. Leicester drove as Barton picked up another message from his phone. It was Abbie Wainwright from the house that overlooked Maggie's. She'd rung to say her husband had seen some suspicious behaviour in the street. Barton shrugged. He might as well swing by her place on the way back from Ken's.

Barton assumed Ken was going to confess to the affair with Heidi, but he could say something else. It was interesting that the stress was getting to Ken. It was also possible that he could reveal a detail that would change the focus of the investigation. Barton's phone rang again. He recognised Ken's number this time.

'He's here. He's bloody here.'

The voice was a strange mixture between a whisper and a snarl.

'Who's there?'

'The Santa Killer. He's outside my fucking house. Please, send someone quick.'

'Okay, Ken,' Barton spoke slowly and loudly. 'Control will

despatch a response vehicle immediately. A colleague and I are also on our way. We'll be three minutes. How do you know it's him?'

'He was banging on my front door. I could make out the red coat. He was hammering at the glass like a crazy person. I saw the white of the hood as it went past my kitchen window. What do I do?'

'Dead-bolt all the doors.'

'I've bloody well done that.'

'Go into the bathroom and lock yourself in. We'll be there in just a couple of minutes. Lean against the door if necessary.'

Barton heard a muffled thud. Then he caught the distant but unmistakable sound of breaking glass.

55

DI BARTON

Barton shouted into the phone.

'Ken, talk to me.'

The line was dead. Barton rang Control.

'DI Barton. Be advised, call received from 117 Portman Close, the home of Ken Wade. An attacker is on the premises. Breaking glass heard. Please advise other units, CID team of two en route, ETA two minutes.'

Leicester tutted as he had to give way behind parked cars on Ledbury Road. He accelerated hard when the route cleared, then indicated right into Portman Close. It was a street with nearly all bungalows in and as they sped down the quiet street, Barton was surprised that Ken lived in such a place. He spotted Ken's posh car on a drive at the bottom.

Barton was in a slight quandary. Leicester and he had no PPE. A response vehicle would be there in minutes containing uniformed officers with stab vests, batons and PAVA spray. Taser units would also be on their way. A minute might make a big difference to Ken, though.

Leicester and Barton got out of the car. Barton smiled as

Leicester fearlessly jogged up the path. The bungalow appeared unloved. There was peeling paint on the windows, which weren't even double-glazed. Leicester tried the handle of the front door, but it was locked. They both looked at each other as a wild shriek came from inside the property. It was a woman's scream, but it was hard to discern if the emotion powering it was fear or rage.

Leicester pushed the low gate open that led to the rear of the property. The back door to the house was locked, so they edged into the garden. They saw what was responsible for the broken glass sound. Someone had thrown a brown terracotta plant pot through the large conservatory window. Another shout came from inside, followed by a solid thumping noise. Barton suspected the sound was hammering on a door. He hoped Ken was safe behind it.

Leicester hopped agilely through the hole in the window and moved inside the building. Barton was more careful due to his size. He noted a few drops of blood had dripped on the floor, so the assailant was probably injured. The wail of approaching sirens indicated the cavalry would soon be there.

'No!' came a voice from beyond what Barton guessed was the door to the kitchen, then another slapping sound. Leicester opened the door and assumed a crouching, defensive martial arts pose, but with no sign of the attacker he relaxed and stood up. He walked to another internal door in the kitchen, which was open, and looked into a hall. He took up another cautious pose. Barton peered over his head and saw the attacker. It was a pasty-looking Heidi, who turned to look at them. Barton edged around Leicester.

'It's okay, Heidi. I'm here now.'

Her puffy face, under a thick, fluffy white hat, had sunken, bloodshot eyes. A string of snot or drool hung from her chin. She made a strange bleating sound, then hit the door with an open hand, but the strike lacked power. A bloody imprint remained on the cream door where her hand made contact. Barton moved closer.

'That's enough, now, Heidi. Come on. Let's get you away from that door.'

He put an arm around her shoulder and guided her through another door into the lounge, then sat her on the sofa. She peered at him for a few seconds, then the light in her eyes dimmed. Her head drooped as she covered her face with her hands. Heidi's shoulders rose in tandem with her breathing, which was rapid and shallow.

After responding to a shout of 'Police', Leicester brought in two young uniformed women.

'Is there an ambulance?' asked Barton.

'Yes, sir. It's just pulled up.'

'Get them in here. This is Heidi Hulse, and I'm worried about her.'

'What happened?' asked the older PC.

'It looks like she's come to have it out with her boss. She's been struggling emotionally, and it seems she's finally snapped.'

Barton heard a lock being drawn back, then the door Heidi had been banging on opened. Ken popped his head around it.

'Has that bonkers woman gone yet?' asked Ken.

Heidi looked up and across at him. Barton was ready to place his hand on her shoulder to stop her from getting off the sofa, but her head dropped again and she began to sob.

'Get Ken out of here for the moment,' said Barton to Leicester. 'Put him in our car and ask him why he thought The Santa Killer was here.'

Barton glanced down at Heidi, who had a dark orange coat on. He supposed through the glass it could have looked red and her hat was white. Ken must be close to the edge if he was imagining the worst like that.

The paramedics came in and attempted to check Heidi over, but she'd gone into some kind of trance. Her breathing was still fast.

'I'm going to take her to A & E,' said one of the paramedics. 'Is she under arrest?'

'No. I'll send a PC with you to the hospital, but I suspect they'll keep her in.'

Barton had a final attempt to get Heidi to speak.

'Why did you come here, Heidi?'

Heidi didn't respond. Barton wasn't too worried. Ken would know.

56

DI BARTON

Barton returned to his car, where Ken was sitting in the rear. Leicester shook his head when Barton mouthed if he'd said anything. Barton got in the front passenger seat and turned around to Ken.

'We came for your confession, Ken. What is it? This has all gone on long enough.'

Ken looked up through rheumy eyes. He had the same defeated expression that Heidi and her husband had worn. He took a deep breath. Leicester got his notebook out.

'I'm lonely,' said Ken. 'I have been for decades. About twenty years ago, I was widowed. A real nasty cancer, but I cared for her until the end. I'd just started the kitchen business and was struggling to juggle everything. I used to fit the kitchens as well as sell them back then. Funny, isn't it? I spent most of my time working to provide a better life for my family and ended up without one.'

'Cancer can be very cruel,' said Barton.

'Yes, it can. Then my mum became ill. I moved back in here with her because she was almost housebound with COPD. It wasn't too bad. We kind of had each other. She was mean by the time Alzheimer's had won the war, but that's a cross you bear.'

Barton nodded. 'It can be a tough time.'

'The business was picking up, though. I advertised for a sales assistant, Heidi started, and we developed feelings for each other. In the end, we had a quick affair, but I broke it off. She had young children and felt guilty. Her husband has a bit of a temper, but I could imagine how it would feel if it had been done to me. I didn't want to break someone else's family up.'

Barton was a touch surprised by what he was hearing. He'd not expected much depth from Ken.

'Wasn't it awkward her carrying on working with you after that?' asked Barton.

'No, we still got on well. I've looked after her too. She had a mini breakdown about ten years ago and was off work for about six months, but I paid her as normal. Then they had more bad times, and her husband lost his licence. When my mum died quite a while ago, Heidi helped me through that with her kindness. Heidi feels like family. We argue and fight, but we don't give up on each other.'

'So why didn't you promote her?'

Ken took another deep breath.

'You were right. My business is struggling. All the way through the pandemic, I paid everyone's wages. I have a brilliant team at the moment and can't afford to lose any of them. The furlough from the government helped but now we've got supply-chain issues and the fitters are so in demand that I've even had them quit mid-job to take a higher-paid one for another company.'

'Do you think your business could go under?' asked Barton.

'I hope not. It might be tight, but that was why I promoted Maggie, not Heidi. You've met Maggie. She's brilliant. The customers love her.'

Barton felt as though they had got to the crux of the discussion.

'But those feelings went beyond those of an appreciative boss?'

'Yes, I misread the signs, which was daft of me. Why would anyone like her choose to be with me? I've been a fool, but, as I said, I've been so lonely. I tried internet dating, but I'm hardly handsome. The only people who seemed to be interested were searching for a meal ticket.'

'Instead, you've been looking for love at your business premises,' said Barton. 'That's tacky, at best. Women shouldn't have to come to work thinking their boss is going to hit on them. I noticed that all your staff are female.'

Ken finally showed some emotion.

'I resent that implication. I only asked a couple of them out and I was never pushy.'

Barton looked out of the car window as the paramedics stretchered Heidi into the back of the ambulance. She was strapped in and her eyes were shut above a steamed-up oxygen mask. He watched a PC climb in with her. Heidi's vengeance, if that was what it was, was over.

'Why did Heidi come here to confront you?' asked Barton.

'All along, I said there'd be a promotion for her. She needed the money, but I was desperate for Maggie to make the sales. It was a business decision. You've seen how Heidi is. Would you buy a kitchen off her?'

Barton shook his head.

'I prefer not to press charges. That family has been through enough. You can tell she isn't in her right mind.'

'Ken, a crime has been committed here. Your opinion on whether she's charged or not is irrelevant. It's not a gigantic leap to say she attacked you after she assaulted two of your sales staff outside their homes.'

Ken frowned.

'Heidi wouldn't have done that. She came here for answers.

That's what she shouted through the door. I don't think she'd have hurt me. She didn't bring a weapon, did she?'

'What exactly happened?'

'I've been nervous after all that's occurred. What if I was next? I've seen strange people hanging around outside the shop. Sometimes I get silent phone calls.' Ken paused for dramatic effect; eyes wide. 'Someone threatening was in my garden a year ago. When I challenged him, he said he was lost and ran off.'

'What did he look like?'

'A young black lad.'

'Really?' said Barton, with his mind whirring. 'You didn't know him, then?'

'Nope. I struggled to see him clearly because he had a scarf wrapped around his mouth and nose, but my heart was pounding.'

Barton's obvious thought was Marlon.

'Was he tall or short, thin or overweight?'

'Slightly taller than me.'

Barton filed the titbit away for a moment.

'Okay, so let's talk about today. What happened?'

'I heard the doorbell go, but I'd been having a shave. When I got out of the bathroom, whoever was there began to hit the window of the front door. I spotted a red coat, which made me panic. Then I saw the top of a hat. I ran back into the bathroom after speaking to you. Whoever it was pounded the toilet door, then screamed at me. It was only then that I thought it sounded like a woman. When I next opened it, you were here.'

'What did she shout through the door at you?'

'Not much. It was all mumbled. She called me a bastard a few times. I suppose Heidi could have been the one who's running around attacking people. She almost hit a customer a few months back who was rude to her. The office girls at work made a joke about it because she stood to gain if the other salespeople were incapacitated.'

Barton couldn't imagine Heidi swinging a baseball bat in rage combined with complicated and devious planning, but she had come here. A thought came to Barton's mind.

'Was she happy at work lately?'

'Not particularly, and she wasn't much good. She moaned a lot. Anne-Marie told me that she overheard her complaining to a customer that she'd been there twenty years and had never been promoted.'

'Could that have got back to Heidi?'

'Which part?'

'That Anne-Marie told you she was being unprofessional. She might have seen Anne-Marie as undermining her.'

Ken shrugged.

'Maybe. Who knows? It's a close team, so some gossiping is to be expected. I had one of Anne-Marie's kids in the shop recently when he came to pick his mum up. He gave me grief about her pay, so perhaps she's been bad-mouthing me at home.'

Barton didn't want to jump to conclusions, nor have Ken do the same, but he had to check.

'Had her son been in before?'

'Don't think so.'

'It's not too bad if a kid sticks up for his mother.'

'It is when they're practically men and right in your face.'

The information connected in Barton's head, and he blew out his cheeks. Finally, he reckoned he had the case solved.

57

DI BARTON

Barton got out of the vehicle, went around to Ken's side and opened the door.

'I need you to come to the station tomorrow and sign a statement,' he said.

'Of course. What happens here now?'

'Ring a glazier so you can have your conservatory made safe and secure. I'll let you know what we decide to do with Heidi. Just one last question. Have you had any other threats at all?'

'What kind of threats?'

'Maybe a feeling of being followed or a falling out with a customer.'

'No, although some idiot broke the aerial off the back of my BMW a month ago, and someone smeared shit on my car door handle the day before Halloween.'

'Did you report it to the police?'

'You're joking. About eight years ago, someone smashed the showroom window. I reported that, but the person who came and took the details only got back in touch to say that he wouldn't be taking it any further without more evidence. My brother got acid poured on his Volvo a few years ago and none of you were interested in that, never mind a snapped antenna.'

'Okay. I'm sorry to hear about that. We'll be in touch. Keep hold of my number. You did the right thing calling me. If anything else strange happens, ring me again.'

Ken wandered around to the rear of his house, and Barton got back into the car. Leicester had a small smile on his face.

'I even feel a little sorry for him. Where to now, boss?'

'Travelodge.'

Leicester was surprised, then he twigged what Barton was thinking.

'You reckon one of the Hulses' kids did it?' he said.

'Correct.'

'I don't trust Ashlynn, but I can't see her as a baseball-wielding psycho much more than I can her mum.'

'It might be Ashlynn, but she didn't appear guilty and kids aren't usually that cool. I do think she knows more than she was letting on though.'

'One of the brothers, then, and she was aware, or at least suspected they were up to mischief.'

'Yes. We would have got to them eventually now we don't suspect Cameron or Heidi.' Barton rubbed his chin. 'I wouldn't normally have considered children for something like this. It isn't the type of crime they commit.'

'No, it's a lot of planning. So why do you think it's one of them?'

'That whole family is under incredible pressure and living in unacceptable conditions. The kids are probably hungry. It's hard work filling up teenage boys even with a healthy bank balance. Most children don't have any idea what's going on in their parents' lives, which is why divorce is often such a shock. That's the way it should be. You protect them from money worries. You try not to quarrel too forcefully in front of them. It's what parents do.'

'I thought it was healthier now to argue in front of the kids so they don't get an unreasonable view of what marriage is like.'

Barton chuckled.

'I would say the jury is out on that. What I think is that Cameron is an angry man, while Heidi is at the end of her tether. Ken gave me the clue back then when he said Anne-Marie might have been bad-mouthing him at home.'

Leicester glanced over at Barton and nodded.

'SoHeidi and Cameron would likely have been doing the same at their house, but with more of an axe to grind,' he said.

'Exactly,' replied Barton. 'I bet they're arguing like mad, or, at the very least, he's been shouting at her. I should think the subject of promotion and her job has regularly come up, and the young-sters will have heard all about it.'

'They've listened and decided if they knock out the competition, their mum would get promoted instead.'

'Spot on. The two assaults are related. A similar weapon was used. Mortis implied that a male youngster was more liable to use a baseball bat.'

'They might have got away with the first one.'

'Yes. Getting dressed up as Santa was reasonably clever, but repeating it was not.'

'That makes sense. A youngster might not have the experience and understanding to know that when a pattern is formed, it makes our jobs much easier.'

'Right.'

'So which child is it? Or both?'

'I haven't even met Ronnie, so it's hard to say. He's eighteen and been staying elsewhere. The younger one seemed a little odd, but I only saw him in passing. Maybe Ashlynn is a tomboy.'

'What about the campaign against Ken? Having a lad in his

garden is concerning. Hasn't Anne-Marie got a son in his late teens?'

'Yes, Marlon, but Ken said the lad was shorter than him.'

'Kids grow.'

'True, his mother said he'd shot up lately. I might have a word with him.'

'Only might?'

'Yes, let's focus on Heidi's boys first.' Barton gave Leicester a stern, jokey look. 'You know I'm the best judge of character on the planet.'

'Of course, boss.' Leicester smiled.

'I'd be willing to risk my plums, and yours, on it not being Marlon.'

Leicester's smile disappeared.

'You're that sure?'

'Yes. You haven't met them both yet. You'll understand if you do.'

'Fair enough, boss.'

'It doesn't feel right, and I don't want to accuse him if I'm not certain. Maybe I'll mention what's been occurring in a roundabout way. Let him know those kinds of crimes might only be summary offences, but prosecution and a criminal record would follow if we found the culprit. I can't see him being involved with Maggie's assault, and he certainly didn't bash his own mother up.'

'Agreed. Who do you plan to speak to first?'

'They should all be at school, but I wouldn't be surprised if Ashlynn's still at the Travelodge with Cameron. I'm hoping those two will fold now and tell us what they know, which will be very helpful for when we confront the brothers.'

'Okay.'

'On second thoughts, Ashlynn gave you contact numbers for the two boys. I'm going to give them a ring before we catch up with her.

Would you answer your mobile to an unknown number if you'd been up to no good?'

Leicester reached in his pocket as he was driving down the parkway towards the Travelodge in the town centre and passed Barton his notebook.

Barton rang the younger brother's number. Glenn's phone was turned off. The call went straight to a message in Glenn's voice asking the caller to leave their details. Barton cut the call and rang the older brother. His phone was off, too, but the recorded message was different.

'This number is no longer in service.'

58

Barton frowned. Had Ashlynn deliberately given them a wrong number? He looked over at Leicester, who was deep in thought.

'What are you thinking?' asked Barton.

'Isn't it a bit of a leap to believe that one of the boys would buy a bat and leather his mum's work colleagues with it?'

Barton pondered the question for a few moments.

'People sometimes commit crimes for the weakest of reasons, but you're right. This is a serious offence with aggravating factors. There was a significant amount of planning and the assaults were relentless. Even with no previous I'd expect an adult to serve five years. Finding a juvenile is responsible would be shocking, but I have seen similar. Some of the child criminals in the past have been bad to the point of evil.'

'It just seems idiotic, though. Do they want to get caught?'

This was an angle Barton hadn't considered yet.

'That's a thought. Maybe there's something else at play here. I suppose if Heidi and Cameron have depression and or anger problems, then it wouldn't be surprising if one or all of the children did, too.'

They pulled into the car park of the Travelodge and walked inside. Leicester knew the room's number, so they got in the lift and went up. Leicester knocked on the door of 320.

Ashlynn opened it with a smile after a few seconds. She looked much healthier than before, with a glow on her cheeks, but her grin soon fell away.

'Pleased to see us? Or were you expecting someone else?' asked Barton.

'I was hoping it was my mum or dad.'

'We released your father first thing. Isn't he back yet?'

'Yes, he came here, but Mum, who was acting dodgier than usual this morning, had already gone for a walk, so he left to look for her.'

'Any idea where he was heading?'

'No.'

'How about your mum?'

'She mumbled something about getting some fresh air, but she's been ages.'

'We've found Heidi. She went to see her boss, Ken.'

Ashlynn frowned.

'What for? She told him last night she wasn't going into work for a few days.'

'We're not completely certain, but it appears she broke into his house and threatened him.'

Ashlynn slumped onto the edge of the bed. 'Oh, Mum,' she said in a hushed voice.

Barton whispered an order to Leicester.

'Get Malik, Zelensky, and Hoffman down here with Zander. Two cars. Tell Strange I'll be bringing the children to the station. Social services will need contacting. We'll need a family liaison officer and an appropriate room. Let's find the father, fetch the kids, and keep them all in one place until this is sorted.'

Barton turned to Ashlynn.

'Okay. The time for games is over. What do you know?'

Ashlynn shook her head and wiped tears from each of her cheeks with the sleeves of the dressing gown she was wearing. She started to sob but clenched her fists and steeled herself. She took two deep breaths, then peered up at him.

'You don't understand what it's like.'

'Tell me.'

'I'm trying to hold us together, but I can't. We're all running from each other.'

Barton squatted down in front of her so they were at eye level.

'I understand what you're attempting to do, but you're only a child. It's not your job to keep the family intact.'

Tears dripped off her chin in a rapid cascade.

'But no one else will do it. They've given up. I had to try.'

'Tell me what you know,' urged Barton.

'Why has nobody helped us?'

'We're helping now.'

Ashlynn's face twisted as she fought her emotions.

'You won't understand.'

'I've been doing this job for over twenty years. There aren't many things I haven't seen.'

Ashlynn glanced up. She wiped another stray tear away.

'I don't really know anything. I just suspect.'

'Suspect who? Your brothers?'

Again, Ashlynn narrowed her eyes as though judging what to tell him.

'Is my mum in trouble?'

'A little, but I presume she isn't well. It appears she's committed a serious crime at Ken's house.'

'That's your fault. If you hadn't arrested my dad, she wouldn't have gone anywhere. You're so stupid for arresting him. He's spineless. That's part of the problem.'

'Explain the problem.'

'No.'

'Tell me about your brothers.'

Ashlynn raised her chin.

'Okay, it'll be him. It's always him. He caused all the strife in our family, and he always will. He destroyed us. I can't forgive him.'

Barton didn't like where this was going.

'What do you mean?'

Ashlynn tried to wipe the torrent from her eyes, but it was a pointless task. She set her jaw, then stared hard at Barton.

'Ronnie plays football at school every Monday afternoon. Arrest him. He's responsible.'

'Just Ronnie, or is Glenn involved as well?'

'Just Ronnie.'

'Why didn't you tell someone if you knew what he'd done?'

She snarled her reply.

'He didn't admit to it. I saw the news, and I remembered he'd been out. My parents had been complaining about Ken and his lies. My dad is full of shit. He was always saying that he was going to smack Ken, but he never did. He'd throw the fact my mother shagged him years ago in her face all the time. And he'd say it in front of us. His latest thing was to blame Mum for not earning much commission. She stupidly told him that Maggie had been promoted. We all heard.'

Ashlynn stopped, knowing her mouth had got away from her. She gasped and held her head in her hands. Barton rested his hand on her shoulder.

'What happened then?'

Ashlynn whispered through her fingers.

'My dad wished someone would go and knock that sissy cow out.'

Barton just about made out what she said.

'Your father was all talk, but Ronnie was listening, and he took it on himself to do it instead.'

Ashlynn removed her hands and let out a wail.

'I'm going to be sick,' she said.

She raced past Barton and slammed the door shut. Barton's street sense was a little too late to stop her. The door lock slid into place.

'Shit,' he said.

'What?' asked Leicester, who'd been watching after finishing his call.

'She's gone in there with her phone.'

59

DI BARTON

Leicester looked back at the door.

'Shall I kick it down?'

Barton shook his head.

'I don't think her texting either brother is life or death. Besides, it wouldn't look too good if she really is being sick or is on the toilet.'

'I suppose so. If Ronnie's playing football, he won't have his phone with him, anyway.'

There was a knock on the room door, which Leicester opened. It was the team. They entered, and Barton gave them a quick rundown of that day's events.

'Right, Zander, take Hoffman and meet me outside Bretton Hills school. You'll go to Reception and ask them to pull Glenn out of his lesson. Follow whomever they send in case he runs. If he's not there, join us on the field, assuming that Ashlynn was telling the truth that Ronnie had football in the afternoon. I doubt I'd have known what lessons my siblings would have had on any particular day. She could be covering for either brother.'

The door of the bathroom opened, and Ashlynn stepped out.

'I do know actually because he's always moaning about not having a dry football strip to wear.'

Barton watched as Ashlynn strode into the room. Her eyes were bloodshot, but she had pulled herself together again. He detected a hint of defiance.

'Zelensky and Malik. Give it half an hour here to see if Cameron shows up. Call Control and get uniform and CCTV in town to search for him. Take Ashlynn and Cameron, if he's found, back to the station and we'll talk to them there.'

Barton turned to Ashlynn.

'Phone, please, Ashlynn. Who did you text?'

'Glenn.'

'What did you say?'

'They know. They're coming for you.'

'Why were you warning him?'

That little smile again appeared on her face.

'I wasn't. I was letting him know to be ready for you.'

She offered her phone to him.

'Unlock it, please.'

The phone was too old for finger recognition and she typed in a code, then passed it over with the messaging app open.

Barton checked the last text, and the message was as Ashlynn had said. He rang Glenn's number, which went to voicemail. He handed the mobile to Hoffman but glared at Ashlynn.

'Ashlynn. If you're interfering in this investigation, we'll charge you with perverting the course of justice. It's an extremely serious offence.'

Ashlynn's expression slid to one of disdain.

'You can't hurt me. Nobody can.'

60

DI BARTON

Barton and Leicester left the hotel with Zander and Hoffman, then followed them around the parkways to Bretton Hills school. Both cars parked up, and they got out. Zander and Hoffman headed for Reception, while Barton and Leicester wandered to the games field, which was down a path through a small wood.

Over the years, Barton had been to the school many times. Mostly for talks to teenagers on community policing and to encourage the children to think before offending. Sometimes he'd also come to arrest kids.

When they reached the playing fields, there was a team of older boys with a middle-aged Asian man. There were about twenty of them doing shuttle runs, switching each time when the whistle blew. Barton got his phone out and found the picture of the family photograph he'd taken a few days back, but which now felt like months ago.

He used his fingers to enlarge the photo. Ronnie was a tall, pasty lad, but he was rake thin with a long neck. There'd be no mistaking him on the field. Barton showed the picture to Leicester.

'I hope you've warmed up,' said Barton.

'What for?'

'Well, there's no chance of me catching him if he does a runner.'

They both looked over the children. The sprinting had stopped, and the lads were separated into two teams. Barton couldn't see anyone that resembled Ronnie. He walked onto the pitch towards the teacher. The boys had seen them by then. One of them shoved his mate in the back.

'Here he is, officer,' he hollered. 'He's sorry about what happened outside the girls' school, but his belt broke.'

All of them laughed, except the victim of the jape, but they were nervous titters. Barton recognised the lad who'd shouted it out. He was from a family known to the police. Barton had put his dad in prison for handling high-value stolen goods a few years back.

'Are you still being a well-behaved boy, Jonathan?' shouted Barton. He smiled as the lads around Jonathan gave him some good-natured abuse.

Barton and Leicester reached the man supervising them, who had a cautious expression. Barton introduced himself.

'I'm Mo Javid. Give me a moment,' said the teacher.

They watched as he got the teams set up playing one-touch football. When he returned, he stood in front of them with his hands on his hips.

'Which boy is it?'

'Ronnie Hulse.'

The teacher frowned.

'What about him?'

'We need to talk to him right now.'

The man seemed to pale in front of them.

'Is this some kind of joke? You are police, aren't you?'

'Yes. What's the problem?'

'Ronnie died two years ago.'

61

DI BARTON

Barton briefly looked to the heavens. He almost chuckled as he considered the implications of them not being told this simple fact. He recalled Cameron and Heidi's behaviour, then Ashlynn's. It all made sense.

'I take it you didn't know.'

'No, what happened?' asked Barton.

'Complications from an accident in a condemned building. It was very sad. He was in hospital for around a year.'

Barton looked at the young lads, laughing and running. He vaguely recalled an incident where a child was seriously injured after a fall some years ago.

'Can you talk for a moment about it?' he asked.

'Of course. Perhaps if you explained why you're here, I'll be able to help, but I'm guessing it's to do with his brother.'

'You're right.'

Barton turned to Leicester.

'Give Zander a hand, please. Ring him to tell him you're on your way. We might well have a furious young man on our hands.'

Leicester reached into his coat pocket and pulled out his phone.

He sprinted towards the main building with it attached to his ear. Barton stood next to Javid, who was wearing a worn tracksuit and a beanie. Barton smiled as they watched the chaos on the field. His games teacher at school had sported the same attire as Javid.

'Tell me about Ronnie and Glenn, then?' asked Barton.

'I hate to speak ill of the students, but Glenn was a handful. Always fighting, always arguing, always running. Nothing too bad. Just a ball of mischievous energy. He was a talented football player, though. Quick and a bloody good throw-in, which is rare at this level. In fact, he was decent at most sports. Over time, he seemed to run out of enthusiasm for any of it. His head was turned by the older kids.'

'Oh dear.'

'Yes, he stopped coming to the after-school clubs and often skipped lessons as well. Ronnie, though, was outstanding. Good enough to make a career out of football. His God-given talent was heading. Scored goals for fun. He had a temper too and could be mischievous, but sport kept Ronnie on the straight and narrow. Without that focus, he might have got into more serious mischief like his brother.'

Barton grimaced. 'What is it with kids and dangerous buildings?'

'Who knows? Boys being boys, I guess. Glenn rang 999, but he couldn't face his parents. The ambulance arrived and took them to hospital. There was damage to Ronnie's brain.'

'Were the brothers close?'

'Kind of. Ronnie used to look out for Glenn. I think he considered it his job to protect him, so he got into some fights because Glenn wound people up. Ronnie was more a joker than a fighter, but he was tall and could throw a punch. Glenn has been very odd ever since Ronnie died. It's such a shame. They were both intelligent kids.'

'Odd, how?'

'Keeps to himself. Talks to himself. Dropped his friends. Occasionally he hangs around with his sister. He doesn't engage in classes. It's like he's in a daydream, but what can you say?'

'He comes to school every day?'

'Yes, well, he's here in person. What exactly has he done?'

'Sorry, I can't discuss anything at this stage.'

Javid looked off to the right at a shed in the corner of the field.

'May I ask you a question, Inspector?'

'Sure.'

'Do you think he was being abused at home?'

'No. Now I know the facts, I think the whole family are struggling with life. Ronnie's accident will be the event that set it all off.'

'Good,' replied Javid. He paused and sniffed. 'I better show you something.'

Before he moved, he shouted over to his class.

'Ten minutes, then get yourself into the changing rooms.' Javid grinned as he walked towards the shed. 'They'll still be playing when I return. A lot of them would play in the dark.'

Barton paused to look back at the students before moving into stride with Javid.

'I guessed it might be Glenn, but there were other suspects,' said Javid.

'Suspects for what?'

'Sleeping in the equipment shed.'

They'd reached the shed by then. The door was around the side and out of view. Javid pointed at a latch with a bolt and a small padlock. Barton nodded for him to continue.

'I lock it every night, and it's always back in place when I next return, but a couple of times it's been a little loose. I thought it was getting old, but I found the heater inside was in a different position from where I left it.'

Javid put the key in the padlock and opened the door. It was a large space with a mower taking up the bottom fifth of the room. Every wall had floor-to-ceiling shelves which were crammed full of equipment. Barton could make out cricket bats and pads, rugby and footballs, a variety of rackets and even a shelf laden with metal balls for shot-putting. There was also a battered office chair against a deep wooden table. On it were piles of exercise books and a few lever arch folders. At the back sat a dirty-looking white kettle on a fridge with two steel containers, which Barton guessed held teabags and coffee.

Barton felt nostalgic memories trying to distract him from the job in hand. The damp cold air and mildewy smell jogged his memory to his rugby-playing days. An image of him and other laughing boys racing into the sports shed to grab the balls for practice sprang to his mind. He thought of what Mortis had said about that time being all about the future. Barton walked further into the room, which made the floorboards creak. He stared down at the oil-filled radiator next to the chair.

'That's the one,' said Javid. 'I'm overcautious because it's a wood building, so I always triple-check it's switched off, and I turn it off at the plug as well as on the side of the radiator.'

'How long ago was this?'

Javid transferred his weight from foot to foot as he waged an internal dilemma.

'I probably should have reported this earlier. My suspicions were raised when it first got cold. I found a chocolate wrapper in here. My vice is crisps, so I knew it was one of the kids. I thought they'd crept in here instead of doing games, or maybe while the others were running around the field. Then I noticed the lock, then the radiator. I've been at this school a long time and it's happened before.'

'Glenn was sneaking in here overnight?'

'It's a possibility. The reason I haven't reported it yet is because we have quite a few students from troubled homes. Glenn wasn't my top pick, because usually the ones who've sneaked in here in the past have visible signs on their bodies of what the situation is like at home.'

Barton didn't need him to explain further.

'Others,' said Javid, 'are so thin that it breaks your heart. Anyway, I left a trap. Some bread, cheese slices, instant soup, chocolate biscuits and bottled water. Apart from the water, all of it had been got at. Clever, really. He only took a bit of each in the hope I wouldn't realise.'

'Why didn't you report it straight away?'

This time it was Javid who shrugged.

'Hell,' said Javid. 'I come here a lot myself. It's quiet for writing reports and us men sometimes need a little space away from our families from time to time.'

Barton and Javid shared a smile that spoke of the experiences of marriage and raising children.

'We do,' said Barton. 'They enjoy the break from us, too.'

'Yeah. Anyway, I suspect the kids are usually early teens, which isn't far off being able to leave home. If it's a one off or just a few times, then I'm not sure reporting it is the right thing. This is a safe place. It's warmish. People freeze to death in weather like this. We lost a child five years ago from sleeping rough. That chair is okay for napping in. Safe and warm might not be the words to describe where they live. If the father is angry and abusive, then a visit from the authorities won't make him any happier.'

Barton glanced around as he considered what he'd heard. Large comprehensives like this one held a huge range of children from all walks of life. Some families were violent. Others were troubled in specific ways, such as grieving. Many kids skipped school, but plenty didn't want to go home. In some ways, teachers weren't much different from prison officers. A similar skill set was often needed. Barton knew all too well that sometimes turning a blind eye was the correct decision.

'It's funny, though,' said Javid. 'Usually I'm worried about them nicking stuff. This time, I got extra.'

'I don't follow,' said Barton.

Javid walked over to one of the shelves.

'Whoever it was left this here,' he said, picking up a long silver baseball bat.

62

THE SANTA KILLER

My phone takes its time turning itself on after I leave the toilet. There's only ten minutes of my lesson left, so they won't expect me back. I wander out of the building and walk towards the only place where I seem to have any peace of late. Ronnie is never here, so my thoughts are my own.

My mobile beeps with a message from Ashlynn. I smile. She's still trying to save our family. That's as daft as playing football with an egg. The end result will be the same. Her text is brief.

They know. They're coming for you.

Run and hide, or stay and fight? Both are laughable, but I have nowhere to go. I'm just a kid. The shed isn't even an option any more. Not after I ate all that food. It was obviously left to see if someone was staying in there, but I was so hungry that I couldn't stop myself.

The wind blows my hair around and its icy fingers reach through my thin coat. Ronnie is quiet. I can't sense him anywhere nearby. Now I want his insistent urgings, now that I need his advice, he is elsewhere. I put my hand in my pocket and feel the weight of the penknife I used to unscrew the shed lock.

I can only assume they'll be here soon.

63

DI BARTON

Barton's phone rang. It was Zander.

'John. Glenn was in today. He walked out of his lesson less than twenty minutes ago, saying he needed the toilet.'

'Have you looked in the toilets?'

'That's why I'm ringing. Do you want us to?'

Barton groaned at the irony of it happening again.

'I know where he might be,' interrupted Javid.

Javid explained and said he'd show Barton. Javid sent the kids to the showers. Barton texted Zander with the details of where to meet them. Barton found himself walking across a playground towards a small garden at the far side of the school. Javid said they'd built it as a peaceful remembrance spot for the children and teachers they'd lost over the years. It was a place for quiet contemplation. He often saw Glenn on one of the benches.

As they neared the area, a head popped up from behind a wooden screen. It was Glenn. He burst out from the garden to stand wide-eyed at the edge of the playground. He stared at Barton, then Javid, then turned to his right and sprinted away.

'Damn, he's quick,' said Barton.

Before he could encourage his knees into action, Zander and the others came out of the door that Glenn was heading towards. Glenn skidded as he desperately tried to stop, eventually losing his balance and bouncing on his backside. He scrabbled around, managing to get to his feet, and pumped his legs back in the direction he'd come from. He was so quick, Barton didn't even have a hope of intercepting.

Glenn raced past him and Javid at such a rate of knots it was like being at the dog track. Leicester, though, was not far behind with a high-arm action that reminded Barton of the second *Terminator* film. Barton saluted at Hoffman, who raced by next, showing good speed. Zander thundered by in last place like one of the rhinos from *Jumanji*. He gave Barton a filthy look as he passed him.

Javid and Barton turned and watched as Glenn reached the grass slope down to the field. He slithered a bit on the grass, then rapidly powered away towards the gated exit. Leicester, however, was gaining. It was a surreal scene with a schoolboy being chased by a man in a suit, both with jackets open, against the leaden sky and the bare branches of the surrounding hedges.

'Letting the youngsters steal the glory this time?' asked Javid.

'I think that's only fair,' replied Barton. 'It's no good for team morale to have me flashing past everyone with ease and taking all the plaudits.'

Glenn slowed slightly when he neared the gate, as if he was going to hurdle over. As he approached it, his stride widened for the attempt, but, with metres to go, Leicester rugby-tackled him to the ground.

64

DI BARTON

Barton asked Javid to come with him so Glenn could see a friendly person he trusted. When they reached Glenn, he was face down and cuffed from behind. Hoffman and Leicester had control of his shoulders, so he couldn't move, but his chest wasn't restricted. Gone were the days when backs were knelt on for any duration because it stopped the ribcage rising.

Leicester was finishing the caution and had already recovered his breath. Barton knelt next to Glenn.

'Glenn. Are you okay?'

Even though he wasn't breathing especially hard, Glenn's skin was pallid. There was a look of utter exhaustion and little else. Tears dropped from both eyes like a trickling tap, which unnerved Barton with a lack of any other emotion.

'Let's take him back to the station now before a school bell goes. Any further deterioration in his condition and it could be a trip to A & E.'

Barton decided Leicester and he would escort Glenn. He left Zander and Hoffman to secure the evidence in the shed and inform the headmaster. Glenn was quiet as they walked towards the vehicle, but when they were about to put him inside, he twice whispered to himself. He spent the journey with his eyes closed.

Glenn was booked into the custody suite under constant observation, while Barton considered what to do with him. He asked the custody sergeant, Donald, to request a mental health worker.

When Leicester and he returned to their office, Strange, Zelensky and Malik were there. They all grinned at him.

'Afternoon, guv,' said Strange. 'We have Cameron and his daughter downstairs in an interview room.'

'Custody told me. Glenn's there as well.'

'I heard Leicester saved the day while you hung around at the back holding your hamstring.'

Barton scowled. He would have his revenge on Zander.

'How did you find Cameron?'

'Uniform found him in the town centre walking towards the hotel.'

'What did he say?'

'Nothing. He said he wanted to chat with his family first before he talked to us. What do you reckon? We can find an appropriate adult to sit in with Glenn instead if we think that Cameron is just going to tell him to clam up.'

'I've requested healthcare to confirm Glenn's fit to be interviewed.'

'Is he that bad?'

'I'm not sure. At the end of the day, we believe he committed the assaults, so we need to follow the process. You and I will talk to Cameron and Ashlynn first. Then we'll fetch Glenn up for them to have a word with him. Did you hear Glenn's brother died a couple of years ago?'

'Yes, Zander told me,' said Strange. She shrugged. It was rare they got the full picture at the beginning. Investigations weren't chronological tick boxes.

Half an hour later, Barton and Strange sat across from Cameron and Ashlynn. Barton resolved to get straight to the point after cautioning them both.

'Cameron. Your son assaulted Maggie and Anne-Marie outside their homes dressed as Santa with a baseball bat. He left his bat where he's been sleeping in the school equipment shed.'

Cameron put his hand to his mouth but didn't comment.

'Sergeant Zander has informed us he found a Father Christmas outfit and some wellies stuffed in two carrier bags. They were hidden behind a pile of goal nets. Glenn's DNA will be all over them.'

'I've told you. We don't talk to police.'

'The time for that kind of bullshit is over. If you don't play ball right now, any sympathy I have for your case will vanish.'

'What's that supposed to mean?'

'If nobody talks, then I charge Glenn with these two offences. They are serious, so bail is unlikely. Glenn will stand in front of a youth court where they'll remand him to a young offender institution while he awaits trial. While there, he'll be surrounded by hardened criminals, some of whom will be murderers. That is his fate, unless you or he tell me a reason why that shouldn't happen.'

Ashlynn moved to put her hand on her dad's arm but stopped herself.

'Dad, please. Glenn needs help, not prison.'

Cameron looked as if he was in pain for a moment.

'Let me speak to my son.'

65

DI BARTON

Two hours later, Barton had a meeting with the mental health worker. Tom Rolands was a slim but boisterous northerner who always wore cheap suits and pronounced his name Roarlands. Barton often worked with him and had found him fair to both sides.

'Tom, how's things?' asked Barton.

'Busier than ever, which is really saying something. There's nothing like lockdowns to unsettle people's minds.'

'Yes, we've had the lull, but now it's the storm. Okay, Glenn, is he fit for questioning?'

'Yes, I'd say so. He didn't want to reveal anything he did. All he stated was his brother ordered him to do it.'

'I assume you said that seems unlikely, considering the fact he's dead.'

Rolands smiled.

'Yes. He knew that, but he reckoned he often saw him in the corner of the room where he'd talk to him. Other times, Ronnie spoke to him through the TV. That's how it started.'

'And he seemed lucid telling you this?'

'Yes. I asked if he saw any other dead people and he replied no. He confirmed he understands it isn't normal, but that explains his behaviour.'

'Was he point-blank refusing to reveal anything about what he'd done?'

'Yes, his dad told him never to talk to the police because they know nothing unless you confess.'

Rolands had agreed to be the appropriate adult for Glenn at the interview, because his father might be involved somehow, but Cameron would be present as well. It was unconventional, but Barton suspected it was the best way of getting to the truth.

He returned to his office, grabbed Strange, and the two of them walked down to the interview room where Cameron, his son, the duty solicitor and Rolands waited. Strange went through the preliminaries, explained the interview was being recorded, then leaned casually back in her seat. She and Barton had prepared their tactics.

'It's confession time, Glenn,' she said.

'We won't be saying anything,' interrupted Cameron. 'If you want evidence, you'll have to look elsewhere.'

'I think we've enough evidence. We have the weapon used and a motive. There'll be enough DNA on the bat and Santa suit to lock Glenn away for a long stretch. If he doesn't speak to us and reveal the truth, then we have to assume he is simply a violent danger to society and that prison is the best place for him.'

Cameron's eyes blazed at Strange.

'He's already explained to the psychiatrist person that Ronnie asked him to do it.'

'His dead brother?'

'Exactly.'

'Sadly, Glenn isn't the first suspect to sit in that seat and say someone else told him to do it.'

'Why would he lie?'

'It's even less plausible when the person he's referring to is no longer with us.'

Barton watched Cameron grinding his teeth.

'That solves it, then, doesn't it?' shouted Cameron. 'He's lost his mind. Glenn doesn't understand what he's saying or doing. He's ill.'

'If that's right, let Glenn talk to us about what he did and why. Then we can make a decision. We aren't the enemy here. We only need the facts.'

'Don't give me any shite. You want an easy job. No doubt you'll pin some other stuff on him as well.'

'Cameron. You're obviously an intelligent man, so I'm sure you don't really believe that,' replied Strange. 'Let me explain to you how this works from now on if Glenn continues to remain silent.'

Barton could see Cameron's rate of breathing had increased, but he managed to nod.

'If Glenn doesn't talk, then there's no point in us keeping him here at the police station. He'll be off to the magistrates' court first thing in the morning. All the magistrates will hear is that Glenn has committed some awful offences where the evidence is damning. The Crown prosecutor is going to request bail be denied, because they have no idea of the risk levels involved because Glenn has kept quiet. Who's to say that if they released him, he wouldn't go back and attack those women again or choose another target?'

'He's too young for prison.'

'Correct. I'll repeat what we said earlier. He'll be remanded until his trial in a young offender institute. If he doesn't confess, then the case against him will need to be prepared. That's a lot of cogs turning, and it's a lot of costs rising. All of which are unnecessary, seeing as Glenn committed these offences. In today's environment, I expect he'd be looking at around a year before any trial.'

The solicitor leaned over to Cameron and whispered in his ear. Cameron exhaled as though he were blowing out a candle.

Strange continued.

'Silence is not a defence. It's an admission of the worst guilt possible, because if there were any extenuating circumstances or reasonable explanations, then surely, you'd give them. Neither does silence get you a third off any sentence like a guilty plea does. I'm sure you've seen prison programmes on TV. Young offender institutes hold some of the most troubled children in the country. Many describe them as the hardest jails to serve time in. If Glenn talks to us, it might be more appropriate to take a different course than throwing away the key.'

Cameron puffed himself up, then slowly deflated, but his voice still had an edge to it.

'My boy's not a killer. He doesn't deserve the rest of his life in jail. It's that psycho on the news who's killing people. He should be in prison. Spend your time catching him and give my son the psychiatric help he needs.'

'Maybe you'd be able to put it in better words than Glenn,' said Barton.

'Why don't you tell us why he did it, if you know him so well?' added Strange.

Cameron's right eye twitched. He looked at Glenn next to him, who was still staring at the desk with his head down. Cameron turned his ire on Strange.

'Look, you stupid mare. Can't you see? Why are you so incapable of understanding what's in front of your fucking nose?'

Barton was tempted to step in, with Cameron so close to the edge, but this was the point when they were most likely to get the truth. Besides, Barton was more than happy to give Cameron a piece of his mind if he got too far out of line, although he suspected Strange would beat him to it.

'No, I can't see it,' said Strange. 'Why don't you stop shouting and tell me?'

Cameron rose from his seat. His solicitor put a hand out and held his arm. Cameron stared down at his son. Glenn started to shake his head rapidly. Cameron's eyes widened, but his voice was little more than a whisper.

'Our lives ended three years ago.'

66

DI BARTON

Cameron lowered himself back down and was quiet for a few seconds while he composed himself. When he spoke, it was in a monotone.

'I don't think I can properly explain to you what it was like to receive a call to say my son was in intensive care and that I needed to get to the hospital as quick as possible. My heart leapt straight into my mouth, and, even now, it's still there.'

A small smile rose on his face as he remembered his boy.

'Ronnie was a wonderful kid. I basked in his brilliance, his potential, then it was all gone. He was in hospital for nearly a year. Doing better, doing worse. I bet I never took a deep breath during that time. You'd trade your soul to the devil to swap places with your child. I pleaded with God. I begged. I offered a deal that, if he survived, I would be a nicer person. God broke that deal and, as Ronnie began to fade, so did my wife.'

Barton pushed over the box of tissues that they kept in the room, but Cameron shoved them back.

'I have no more tears, Mr Barton. I ran dry a long time ago. I've watched my partner like a hawk ever since. Heidi said that if Ronnie went, she was leaving too. It would be the right thing to do. Even in my grief, I could see that she was only seconds from the edge. She only managed to not go over because we have Glenn and Ashlynn.'

Barton looked across at Glenn, whose head was still bowed. Tears were forming a wide puddle on the table under his chin.

'I was outside on a deckchair staring at a full apple tree when they rang to tell me that he'd passed. I remember the view down the garden when they said those words as though it's a photograph in perfect technicolour. It's stuck forever in my mind. I see it every morning when I open my eyes after exhaustion has closed them for a few hours. I have nightmares where the fruit and leaves drop off in front of me and the branches twist, blacken and fall. I wake up drenched in sweat, with such profound guilt. How dare I sit on the grass in the sunshine when my son was dying? What kind of father am I?'

'It must have been devastating for you all,' said Barton.

'Heidi folded in on herself. She became a robot with no feeling. Any remaining warmth that was there leached away over that year, leaving her a cold, empty shell. Life dumps on you, then it shits on you some more. How could she be upbeat and sell anything when her child is in pain? It was no wonder Ken didn't promote her. I suppose we should be grateful that he hasn't sacked her, although, as you can imagine, I have few kind thoughts towards Ken.'

Barton considered what Ashlynn had told him about her father's cruel comments to Heidi. There were always different versions of the truth.

'I was wondering,' said Barton. 'Why don't you do a call-centre job or charity work?'

Cameron gave him a sad smile.

'You don't understand. I'm sure you've heard of the seven stages of grief. Shock, denial, bargaining, guilt, anger, depression, and hope. Well, I haven't got to hope, but the rest have been regular house guests. What's just peachy about friends like these is that they appear over and over again. Sometimes they stay for days. Other times, they pop in and out hundreds of times a day. And I always go to bed with one of them. When I wake up, more have crept in during the night. It's an orgy of misery, from which there's no escape.'

Cameron blew out a breath when he'd finished. It was clearly a rant he'd delivered before, but Barton was surprised by how eloquent he was and wondered what else he'd got wrong about Cameron.

'Does that mean you don't know how you're going to feel on any given day?'

'Exactly. My knee hasn't helped in some jobs, but I struggle to concentrate. I make mistakes.'

Barton couldn't help thinking of Zander, who'd lost his little boy around the same time as Ronnie's accident. He had often been distracted after it first happened.

He nodded his understanding. 'You're suffering from depression. You need help.'

'I'm just so angry,' said Cameron. 'With myself, with others, with God. What sort of fucking world is this, where innocent children are punished and killed? I hear people moaning in the street about nothing. When I pass pubs, I look inside at everyone laughing and relaxed without a care, and I know, without a shadow of doubt, that I'll never be like that again. How can I feel any joy when I couldn't protect my child? My life is grey. Only the memories before that day have colour.'

Barton hadn't been expecting to hear Cameron open up in this way. Glenn had seemingly stopped crying, but his head was so bent over it was almost touching the desk. The solicitor wiped tears from his eyes.

'There are organisations now to help you through this challenging stage,' said Barton. 'CRUSE does some great work with those who've lost loved ones.'

'They offered me counselling, and I rejected it all. What I wanted was more time with my boy and nobody could give me that. There is no God, because no God would do such a thing, so there is no heaven. There's no chance I'll ever see him again. He is gone, and that's a heavy anchor to drag around each day.'

Barton gave Cameron a brief spell to compose himself. Barton hated what he now had to do. The problem with cases involving the suspect's mental health was that there was a fine line between having a personality disorder, which many criminals did, and having a mental health issue that mitigated the suspect's guilt. The law deemed a personality disorder as untreatable and not a mental illness. People couldn't be detained under the Mental Health Act with a personality disorder. Proving or disproving either state beyond reasonable doubt was hard. It usually ended with the provision of a prison bunk instead of a hospital bed.

'Ashlynn and Glenn will be struggling as well,' said Barton.

'To my shame, I've ignored them. Grief swamps you. Sometimes it's all you can do to keep your own head above the waves, even if you're aware others are drowning. I've finally found some peace recently. That's why finding a good job is so crucial. My family's shipwrecked. I need a good salary to save them. You see a flabby, washed-up bloke in ill-fitting clothes, but I got a first at university. I'm a fraction of the man I was.'

'Time with your children is just as important as money.'

Cameron seemed to shake his head, but Barton wasn't sure. Glenn's head finally rose. He slowly turned his gaze across to his father. His voice was the same as his father's. Quiet, but there was an extra edge of what Barton suspected was pent-up anger, so the words sounded as though they were being forced out.

'You are mean to everyone because you can't stand to see anyone else happier than you, but you've always been like that. You hate me because he was your favourite.' Glenn's head swivelled towards Barton. 'And I killed him.'

67

THE SANTA KILLER

Three years ago

I hold the fence back for Ronnie.

'Come on, it'll be fun.'

'It looks scary, not fun.'

I peer up at the big house with the crumbling bricks as the light dwindles in the background. Then the clouds glide away from the dipping sun and a beautiful sunset casts the large building in an orange glow. I beckon Ronnie forward.

'I reckon we'll be able to spot our place from the top. Other kids have been in there. Look, the board over that window at the side has been pulled off.'

Ronnie finally edges through the gap in the fence. He's thinner than me, but he has to dip his head further because of his extra height. It's strange to have a brother who's so much taller than you. Maybe that's why I'm always trying to pull him down to my level.

He gives me a nervous smile as he passes.

'Only for a few minutes, okay? I've got loads of homework to do.'

I nod. Ronnie's nicer than me, too, and more studious. He and Mum are so alike, it's unreal. They can sit in silence for hours and hours doing crosswords or reading. With neither of them ever getting bored. I feel excluded when they exchange the odd grin as if they are sharing secrets.

Although if I'm honest with myself, an environment like that has my skin crawling after a few minutes. Dad's the same as me. We need background noise and drama, which we provide to each other by arguing. I don't know why I make him so angry. I'm not that naughty. The police haven't charged me with anything yet, even though they prosecuted the older boys for that fire. I'm just easily influenced if a mate wants to do something for a laugh, especially if it's dangerous.

I hasten after Ronnie, who's weaving through the building debris in front of the house like he does with a ball on the football field. They say he could turn pro. Dad gives him an easy ride because of that. I've seen his little cardboard folder where he keeps the local paper's articles about Ronnie's goal-scoring.

I jog to catch him up, then race by. Why am I always so competitive towards him? He's never been anything but decent to me, but I do things to annoy him all the time. I cut the shoelaces of his boots before he went to a seven-a-side tournament last weekend, so when he pulled on the ends to tighten them, they would have come straight out in his hands.

I was in the lounge when he came home with the trophy. He never mentioned the laces, which made me feel terrible. Did he just not want any conflict, or did he genuinely not think his own brother would do anything so spiteful?

I jump up and sit on the windowsill, then lean into the building. Inside, most of the internal walls have been knocked through. It doesn't appear like good pickings for nicking anything. I drop down with a thump on the exposed wooden planks. My footsteps echo as I walk along them. They groan under my weight.

'Careful, Ronnie. There are needles on the floor here,' I say.

'Then why the hell are we going inside?' he says, following me in. 'Christ, it stinks of piss in here.'

He isn't wrong. Piss and something else. A thick, cloying smell, which I suspect will linger in our minds long after we go back outside.

I stride down a hall towards a closed door. It's a peculiar house. More like a factory or warehouse really. One of my mates said someone bought it to fix up but ran out of money. A room on my left is still carpeted, but the door has gone. There are crumpled foreign lager cans piled in the centre.

When I reach the end of the hallway, I slowly open the door. It creaks, but swings back easily. It leads into a stairwell. There's a lot of broken stairs and some are missing. I put my hand on the banister and keep to the left as I step up them. They don't seem too bad, but I move lightly and slowly. I hear creaking all around me.

Ronnie trips over a tin of something downstairs, sending it skittering. I chuckle and continue climbing to the next floor.

This level is very different. It's almost open plan except for two tall chimney-type things, which I assume are to support the ceiling above. People have definitely been staying up here, judging by the scattered sleeping bags and odd pillow. There's even a dirty mattress in the darkest corner with a rucksack leaning against the wall. The windows are unboarded and more intact, but it's still dark with the filth all over them. My mind begins to work overtime.

'Good venue for a party,' I shout, even though it's not. This place is oppressive. 'Let's go to the roof.'

I cross the room towards a set of iron stairs in the far corner, keeping my eye on a bundle of material nearby. It looks as if there could be a body under it. Up here, there seems to be much less sound. I get within twenty metres of the pile of rags and breathe a sigh of relief. There's nobody there. It's a mass of clothing, some of which appears to be women's underwear. I swallow, drily.

A cloud of powder drops off the stairwell as I climb up it, finding myself on the edge of an attic. A cool draught and weak sunlight make their way through holes in the high roof. A flutter up there makes the hairs on my neck stand up, but it's only a pigeon moving around the joists. I take one step forward. What I thought was heaps of dust on everything is actually old bird shit.

All the flooring is exposed. I carefully step along the central beams to the first brick column, then move across another beam to a dormer window. I lift the handle and, after a little resistance, push it open wide. Sweet, rainy air blows into the room. I take a deep breath.

When I get my bearings, I'm disappointed that I can't make out our house after all, but the view over the houses and gardens is impressive. It makes me feel strange as I look below on other people's lives as they rush home from work, or pull washing off lines as the drizzle comes down.

'Can you see our house?' shouts Ronnie from behind me.

I turn around as he reaches the central beam.

'Careful, Ronnie! That bird shit's slippery.'

Ronnie grins, takes another step and his right foot slides straight off and vanishes through a sheet of thin wood. He teeters to his left side, ending up lying on the remains of the panel. He stretches his long arm back and hooks his hand over the beam.

'Don't move,' I whisper.

There's a dry, ripping crack. His eyes bore into mine. Then he disappears.

68

THE SANTA KILLER

The detectives, Barton and Strange, look sad. I've never told anyone that story before. I said afterwards that it was Ronnie's idea to trespass, and that he went first. To be fair to my parents, they never challenged it. I suppose there wasn't much point. Ronnie was dying, and that was that. Even though I'm ashamed of revealing what I did, I can feel a weakening of the band that's been across my chest ever since that day. The big policeman in front of me is right. I must confess to all my sins.

'There was another crash as he dropped through the floor below. I ran down the beam and looked through the hole he made in the ceiling. I don't think he fell that hard, but he'd hit his head on one of the paint tins. There was a growing pool of blood. It was my fault. He would never have been in there. I can't move past that fact. I never will. He talks to me in my dreams, and I see him on the edge of my vision every now and again.'

'And does he tell you to do things?' asks Barton.

'Yes, I think so.'

'You only think so?' asks Strange.

'Yes. Look, I know how it sounds, but it's as if I get a message from him. The first time was when I was watching TV. Dad had been ranting about the bitches at work getting paid more than Mum. When I turned the TV off, it was as if I knew that Maggie was the enemy. I started hiding outside her house. At Anne-Marie's place as well, but I'd just watch.'

'I didn't say to hurt anyone,' says Dad.

I ignore him. Even now he's lying.

'It was as though my dad could see how Mum was struggling, but still moaned at her. She used to earn decent money with bonuses, but she isn't the same person any more. None of us are.'

'Did you ask anyone for help?'

I shake my head.

'What for? Nothing can bring Ronnie back.'

The older detective takes a deep breath as his brain churns through the choices ahead of him. For some reason, it feels like he's more on my side than my father.

'Are you giving us a full confession and a complete statement of the facts?' he asks.

The solicitor, who has been listening quietly, speaks up.

'Can I speak plainly?'

Barton nods.

'This is clearly a mental health matter, but I accept those types of issues cause as many problems as they solve. I've explained to Glenn and Cameron that these are serious offences and it's best for us to co-operate fully now. Maybe while he awaits sentencing, my client can receive some help. I dread to think what prison would do to him.'

'A confession starts the ball rolling. I'll talk to the CPS and see what they want to charge him with, but there's no getting away from what he did.'

'He's ill,' says Dad. 'And he's sorry.'

Barton's face is almost apologetic.

'I'm afraid sorry isn't going to be enough.'

69

DI BARTON

Barton and Strange spent over an hour taking a statement from Glenn. He lifted his head from the table and admitted to everything, giving them dates and times, even some of his thoughts and reasons. The only thing he didn't admit to was being involved with the other letters the radio station received, and he also said he wasn't aware Maggie was left-handed. He just hit what was in front of him. Barton decided it was time to cut to the chase.

'How did it make you feel, Glenn?'

'Which part?'

'When you were planning the attacks, or when you were actually hitting those women with the bat.'

Barton's eyes narrowed as he watched Glenn search for feelings that should have been there, but weren't.

'It felt like I was helping.'

Barton turned his gaze on Cameron. It was hard to believe he could sit there next to his son and not display any emotion after listening to his son say that. Yet Barton knew the death of a child was the worst thing imaginable to anyone. The only daughter of a sergeant from Huntingdon had been diagnosed with cancer, but she'd luckily beaten it. Her child was treated at a famous children's hospital. The mother said that one of the things she could never forget from her many overnight stays was hearing howls of pain and screams of rage. Not from the children, but from their parents.

Cameron leaned towards him.

'You think I'm a monster, don't you?'

'No. It's hard for me to understand what you've been through.'

'I know what you're thinking, but I just can't give him comfort. We're just too angry with him. I can't let it go. Every time I see his face, I'm back on that deckchair being told that Ronnie's dead. We knew whose idea it was to go into that building.'

'Unfortunately, we help a lot of families affected by premature deaths. Time often softens the edges of people's grief,' said Strange.

'That's what they say, but when? I'm still waiting.'

'Your luck will change, too. When should you hear from that job?' asked Barton.

'I already did. It was the perfect position for me. Thirty thousand pounds per year. Enough money so that Heidi wouldn't have to work as many hours, even have some time at home. We could get her better, focus on the children, get them better. They told me my commitment and enthusiasm shone through at the interview.'

'Isn't that great news?' asked Barton, genuinely pleased.

'I had all the suitable experience. There were hundreds of applicants. I should be happy to have made the shortlist of two.'

Cameron closed his eyes. He shook his head from side to side in the same manner that Glenn was doing next to him.

'I'm sorry,' said Barton.

Cameron spoke while keeping his eyes shut.

'Second best, again. That position would have saved our family. Now I have no job, a wife heading for the nuthouse, and a homicidal maniac as my sole surviving son. It's no wonder I'm furious.'

'Your daughter seems healthy and someone to be proud of,' said

Barton. 'She's fighting for your family, too. Don't give up on it, or her.'

Cameron opened his eyes and seemed to steel himself.

'She's a good kid. She watches Heidi like a hawk, like I used to.' He sighed. 'Right, what happens now?'

'Glenn still goes to the magistrates first thing in the morning. Probation will be there. They'll do a report that day to see if he's fit for trial, or whether he should be remanded or released on bail.'

'Does that mean he might still get remanded in custody?'

'Yes.'

'Bloody hell. This is bullshit. What was the point in confessing?'

'In my experience, because we're now aware of what we're dealing with, if he's remanded, Glenn will get sent to the institute's healthcare wing, where he'll be fully assessed. It's the first step on his journey to getting the right care for his mental health.'

'It's a joke.'

Barton felt for Cameron, but he'd had enough of him now. He wasn't the only one who was suffering. Innocent people had been hurt.

'It's time for you to accept the situation, Cameron. Yes, you've had the worst of things, but you heard your son just now. There was no remorse. He's hearing the voice of a dead person. He's a danger to the public and to himself.'

'I talk to Ronnie as well. Am I crazy too?'

'Does Ronnie talk back?' asked Strange.

Cameron shook his head.

'Cameron,' said Barton. 'You and Ashlynn are free to go. Be at the magistrates' court at ten tomorrow morning. I expect your Glenn to be remanded because what if Ronnie is still around? What happens when someone else interferes in Glenn's life? Maybe Ronnie is just the realisation of Glenn's anger, and the next time

Glenn perceives that somebody has done him a disservice, Ronnie might tell him to kill.'

Cameron blew out his cheeks. The fight was gone for him, but he tried.

'He's sick. He needs looking after.'

'I agree,' replied Barton. 'But you also need to acknowledge one important fact. Even if he was hearing voices that were telling him to hurt those women, he still could have said no.'

70

DI BARTON

Four hours later, when after a team effort most of the paperwork was completed, Zander and Barton left the station.

'Do you want a lift or are you walking?' asked Zander.

'Lift, please. It's a ploy of mine to save money on petrol. I walk in, one of you lot drive me home.'

They walked down to the car park. Barton's phone had died, so he plugged it into the charger Zander kept in his car and turned it on. It beeped numerous times as Zander manoeuvred out of the tight space. He put his messages on loudspeaker. There were two hang-ups, then one from Holly.

'Ring me, asap.'

'That's not good,' said Barton.

Zander widened his eyes as Barton picked up the phone and rang Holly's number. She connected and spoke to him for about thirty seconds. Zander grimaced.

'That sounds bad.'

'It's an absolute disaster. Only you and me can save the day.'

Zander briefly glanced at him as the exit barrier raised.

'That sounds terrible. What is it?'

'Layla wasn't happy about our intensively farmed turkey purchase last year. She made us promise to buy an organic one from a local farm. Holly agreed, even though I suspect human meat would be cheaper. Anyway, they rang earlier today and basically someone broke in last night and released the flock, so they can't fulfil our order.'

'That's heartbreaking news just a few days before Christmas. You'll have to have some kind of nut roast instead. Nice for your blood pressure, disappointing for your taste buds.'

'Holly wants us to pop to Lidl, see if they have any big frozen ones left.'

'Woah! What's this "us" business? I'd rather perform my own dental surgery than go near a supermarket in the run-up to Christmas.'

'Zander. You are a strong, capable, resilient, young man. There's nothing to be scared of.'

'There's loads to be scared of. Some of the shoppers in there will be mean.'

'We rush in, locate the turkeys, grab one, then leave. Like a bank robbery. In and out.'

Grumbling, Zander indicated left at the Gordon Arms pub and drove a few minutes down Oundle Road to the supermarket. The car park was jammed. Zander had to leave his sports car in the space that was furthest from the entrance. They trudged towards the shop with the same enthusiasm as soldiers going over the top. All the baskets and trolleys were gone. Through the glass, they could see a swarm of people inside. Barton chuckled.

'Kind of reminds me of when Millwall played Peterborough in the FA cup all those years ago.'

'Didn't someone die that day?'

'No, I don't think so,' said Barton, looking at the pinched faces in front of him queuing to get in. 'Many were injured, though.'

They stepped into the store and shuffled along with the crowd to the freezer section. Zander and Barton looked around at the tense expressions surrounding them. Violence was in the air.

'When I visit a supermarket with you,' said Zander, 'which, by the way, happens much too often, I always have the impression that people think we're a couple.'

Barton stopped shuffling forward. He raised an eyebrow.

'What are you saying? That you're ashamed of me?'

'I'm not saying that. I just get the feeling people are staring at us, so don't do anything weird.'

Barton smiled as they finally reached the freezers. The lid of the ones that were supposed to hold the turkeys had steamed up. Barton held his breath, then yanked up the lid. He stared into the abyss.

'Oh dear.' Zander chuckled. 'The hunter goes home empty-handed. Grumblings of dissent will filter through the pack.'

Barton collared a passing worker.

'I don't suppose there are any turkeys out the back?'

'Nope.'

'Poop.'

The lad smiled, then moved away into the throng. He stopped after a couple of paces, then returned to them.

'Actually, sort of depends on how fussy you are. Someone bought one a little while ago, got home, and realised it didn't have giblets, so they brought it back. I wasn't sure whether to put it out again.'

'I'll take the risk. Give the bird to me. We'd be defrosting it by now, anyway.'

The young lad nodded, went through a plastic sheet into what Barton assumed was the warehouse, then reappeared with the biggest frozen turkey Barton had ever seen. There was a thirty per cent off voucher on it.

'Here you go. Seeing as it's already got some mileage on it, I put a discount code on the label.'

Barton took the turkey off him with a massive grin. He held it aloft, like when Rafiki presented Simba to the other animals in *The Lion King*, and weaved his way through the throng towards the tills. Zander caught up with him.

'I'm not sure I've ever seen you so happy.'

'At my wedding?'

'No, not even close.'

'Just goes to show, there is a God. And I'm his favourite.'

The queue was long, so they waited in line. Barton handed Zander the turkey.

'Hold this for a moment.'

After a minute, Zander frowned.

'Why am I carrying this?'

'It was making my hands cold.'

Zander shoved it back to him. They eventually got to the front and Barton plonked the turkey onto the conveyor belt. He patted it.

'We'll have to form a family scrum to nudge this bad boy over the finish line and into the oven.'

Zander shook his head and grabbed a packet of gum from the shelf behind him.

'Won't it defrost too soon?'

'No, something this size takes three days in the fridge.'

'Fair enough. You know, I'll miss being at yours on Christmas Day. Kelly said the same.'

'We'll miss you, too, but that's what happens when you have your own families. It's a good thing.'

They stood in companionable silence for a moment, but, as when all detectives got together, their minds lapsed back into work mode.

'So that's it,' said Zander. 'The case of The Santa Killer has been solved.'

'Pretty much. It's another one of those cases that feels very unsatisfying, but at least there'll be a conviction, which we won't be getting from whatever the hell occurred in The Swamp. It'll take a while to unravel what the rest of the Hulses knew, but there are never any winners in situations like these, us included.'

'Well, I'm glad it's case solved. I could do with a nice quiet Christmas.'

Barton was paying for the bargain turkey when his phone rang.

'It's Abbie Wainwright. I called you earlier.'

Barton recalled the feisty elderly lady who lived next to door to Maggie. He also cringed. He'd forgotten she'd left a message with all the drama at Ken's house and after.

'Hi. I'm sorry I haven't come back to you. I've been tied up on another case. What can I do for you?'

'It's my husband. He reckons he saw Father Christmas on the lawn again.'

Barton said he'd be there within the hour and cut the call. He told Zander what Abbie Wainwright had said while they walked back to the car.

'Is this the guy with dementia?'

'Yep.'

'Not the strongest of sources, then?'

'No. I've had better.'

'Don't we have The Santa Killer in custody?'

'Yep.'

'Oh dear.'

'Yes. All things considered, it's not a great call to receive.'

'Maybe he imagined it.'

Barton smiled as he put his purchase in the back of the car. They got in and drove away.

'That was the shortest quiet Christmas on record. I've got to walk the dog tonight. I'll wander round with him and have a chat with Abbie. Might well be nothing, but I have a really uncomfortable feeling about this.'

'Oh, no. Not the Barton belly.'

'Yep, it's grumbling into life like one of those nasty old tractors you get at the seaside.'

'I'll bet there's a similar smell, too. I'd better drop you off at home, pronto.'

Barton laughed loudly. Zander smiled.

'That's good to hear, John. You've been a bit down of late. Are you sure everything's okay?'

'Has it been that obvious?'

'I'm afraid so. You've been a little tetchier.'

'Tetchy? Moi? Well, this is a horrible case. I'm surprised you aren't more affected.'

'You know what? In some ways, it kind of helps.'

'Really? How so?'

'I struggled so much when my son died. It's an awful thing to get over. Part of it was the anger over why it happened to our child, you know? And why it happened to us. But these investigations prove there's heartache everywhere. We have sad crimes to solve as well as dramatic or exciting ones. This job saved me. It gave me a reason to go on. All I want to do now is help people. Help folk like the Hulses.'

Zander turned into Barton's street and bumped up onto the kerb outside his house.

'Cox handed me a letter recently,' said Barton.

'Yeah?'

'There's a position come up at HQ in the Divisional Development Unit.'

'What the hell is that?'

'It's a project role looking into future training and development for CID. It's about getting the best out of the next crop of detectives. They want someone experienced and successful involved.'

'I assume they couldn't find anyone like that and asked you instead.'

'I was their first choice.'

'Very modest.'

'Cox's words, not mine.'

'She must be desperate.'

'Not desperate enough to ask you.'

Zander chuckled.

'I might have known,' he said. 'You remember when I went in to see her?'

Barton nodded for him to continue.

'Cox mentioned there were a few changes coming up. She asked if I was ready to step up to cover a DI position if the position arose. I assumed she was talking about the other Major Crimes team.'

'That was sneaky of her, although I suppose it's quite clever if I take it. They've given me the first refusal for the role. I also got the impression Cox thought I needed a break. After all, I let a disc jockey get the better of me. I must be losing it. Maybe some time away from the front line will refresh my enthusiasm.'

'Yeah, right. Whoever came back from an HQ desk job?'

'Fancy coming in for a beer?'

'Tempting, but Kelly's expecting me soon. We might need to wrestle over who gets your job.'

Barton undid his seat belt.

'Wait,' said Zander. 'You haven't told me what the Barton belly is telling you.'

'It's these other killings across the country. The Hatchet Man case.'

'When did they start calling it that, and who's to say it wasn't a female?'

'The moniker was in the *Telegraph* today. And when was the last time you heard of a female serial killer running around killing other women with an axe?'

Zander paused for a moment.

'Joanna Dennehy.'

'Killed three men.'

'Oh, yeah. Okay, never.'

'Right. My belly is good at anticipating things, such as nice lunches, but it's also detected something whiffy about this Hatchet Man case. The resolution of The Santa Killer isn't sitting right either.'

'None of us like the fact that a murderer might be heading here.'

'It's not just that. Bits of the cases are similar, so maybe that's what's making my brain link them. The victims of The Hatchet Man have been vulnerable women who led relatively lonely existences. You could apply that to Maggie, so perhaps it's that which is sparking my intrigue.'

'Cameron was bloody angry today. Who knows where he's been disappearing to?'

'Exactly. Now we hear that Mr Wainwright saw Santa again. Maybe it was Cameron. Perhaps he went straight around to Maggie's after we released him to finish what his son started, but couldn't get in. Then we find him in town. Obviously, he doesn't mention it.'

'I would say it's more likely the old guy mistook the postman. It's a similar outfit.'

'He's got a poor memory, not a drinking problem. I wouldn't be surprised if Cameron has been up to no good, or perhaps was more involved.'

'That's not ridiculous, but I can't see it. Cameron's still at that angry stage. It's all consuming, but it's more like a frozen rage. Very little breaks through. It's hard to get motivated to do anything apart from stew. I'll visit him in a few days to see how he's coping. Hopefully his wife will have stabilised by then. Maybe I can help him look to the future.'

'That's nice of you.'

'Actually, it helps to talk about my son now. I don't want to forget I had one. Besides, I might find Cameron sharpening his extensive range of expensive cutting tools in the backyard. It is possible he's smart enough to reap his revenge against women well away from his own front door, but you didn't detect animosity from him towards females in general.'

'No, just towards Heidi's work colleagues, who happened to be women.'

'I can still check ANPR for the last three months. It might be as simple as seeing where their car's been. If it says their vehicle went to Leicester at the time of that killing, it's a home run.'

Barton nodded.

'You're a genius, Zander. Anyone ever told you that?'

'A few. Not enough.'

'Did you know Cameron doesn't drive at the moment?'

Zander frowned, while Barton grinned at catching him out.

'He's banned from driving,' replied Zander. 'It doesn't mean he hasn't been driving.'

Barton grinned at him again.

'Cocky sod. Okay, while Cox was pitching me about this project job, I was asking her if we could look at The Hatchet Man case. She's given us from now until Christmas to work on it. Let's delve into the nitty-gritty.'

'You've had some involvement already. What have they turned up so far?'

'It seemed very little, but that was a few days back. Maybe they've made more progress since then.'

'It's a scary thought that someone so unhinged is freely wandering around. No wonder the news is all over it. This really is serial-killer territory.'

'Yes, the sergeant in Leicester reckons he's amongst us now. I'd put money on the attacker doing something before Christmas. It will appeal to his ego to be all over the news on the big day.'

Zander considered that fact.

'That third letter to the radio guy is concerning. Did you believe Glenn when he said he didn't send it?'

Barton clicked his fingers. 'Yes, I did, although I didn't probe too hard because it wasn't so important. We're not going to charge him for malicious communications when he's looking at much more serious offences. That could be the link. The Hatchet Man might have been planning on coming to this city, anyway. He's intelligent. Let's assume he sent it, because this latest letter muddies the water and casts doubts all over the place. He'll probably know that we get copycats and jokers with this type of crime. If he turned up in Peterborough, in or out of a Santa suit, killed a woman, then disappeared, he'd be tough to catch.'

'It's a shame we released the news that we have someone in custody for the assaults.'

'I reckon Cox was under pressure to achieve a result before Christmas.'

'Okay, well, he'll know we won't be blaming The Santa Killer for any new attacks if we already have him banged up. It's a lot to think about.'

'Yes, if this is my last case, I want it to end well. This guy might prove to be our deadliest adversary. He's been killing one person in each place, so another worry is that if we don't catch him here, he'll disappear to another city for his next victim. On that cheerful note, I'll see you tomorrow.'

'Hang on. Are you thinking of moving to HQ, then?'

Barton nodded.

'Would it be permanent?'

'It could be. Cox said I could do it for a year if that was all I wanted, although there are more projects in the pipeline. She said there'd always be a role at Major Crimes for me, but that's flannel. If there isn't an open position, I might have to switch forces for a similar role. It's the right move, though. It's time for me to take a step away. We've had tough stuff to deal with over the last few years.'

'Peterborough's grown so fast with all this immigration. It's no wonder we've been flat out.'

'True, and a lot of the pressure for results rests on the DI's back, as you may well find out if you become one. Maybe I am carrying some baggage. I know we're detectives, and it's our task to go through folks' lives with a fine-tooth comb. But just lately, I've felt like a vulture, picking at the bones of other people's misery.'

Zander nodded.

'You'll be missed if you do go. When's the job start?'

'New year.'

'Passing on your skills is important,' said Zander.

They were both quiet, then Barton got out of the car and took the turkey off the back seat. He held it under his arm while he watched Zander disappear out of sight, then glanced down his street at the twinkling lights. It was so peaceful here. He peered inside his lounge window and saw Luke jumping up and down on the sofa as he laughed. Barton could almost hear the springs ripping through the material. Was it the right moment to step away from the job? Few escaped with their reputations intact.

He wasn't finished yet, though. Barton had read the post-mortem reports of the gruesome hatchet attacks whose perpetrator might be heading to Peterborough. They were grim reading. He frowned as he opened his front door. Hopefully, The Hatchet Man would stay away, but Barton had a strong feeling that this year it wouldn't only be Santa who was coming to town.

72

THE HATCHET MAN

It seems the authorities have worked out my little route to London and let it slip to the press. They've guessed that Bedford or Peterborough is my next destination. *The Sun* newspaper even said that I was clever. It's nice to be appreciated.

'Just here please, mate.'

The taxi driver stops a hundred metres up from the railway station. I pay him in cash and get out. You've got to love this mask-wearing lark. Everyone's forced to cover up and nobody dare look at anyone any more. The driver glanced at me once during the entire journey. Judging by the state of his car and the sounds of his engine, I doubt he'd want any involvement with the authorities anyway.

I pick up the large Manila envelope on the seat next to me and leave the taxi. Turning away from the station, I walk towards the new estate where I know a lot of the commuters live. Pausing at a bus stop, I pretend to analyse the timetable. The train from London coasts into view behind a row of trees. It's the one I've been waiting for.

The commuters trickle out of the station. Many go to the car parks, others head into town. They're a raucous bunch tonight.

Christmas get-togethers are perfect for lowering people's inhibitions, and their caution. A man and woman stagger past me, arms entwined, clearly worse for wear. They seem so happy. He'll only find out the truth when it's too late. I feel like screaming out and warning him. She will leave you, mate.

One of the stragglers is a woman. She's more promising. I watch her approach for a moment. No, she's too with it. Too focused and fit-looking. A more suitable prospect is behind her. This one looks tired and anguished, downtrodden even. She walks past without noticing me. I'm about to stroll after her when I catch where her bags are from. Smyths Toys. They're full. I'm still tempted to follow. The children could be at a nanny's, I suppose, but at this time of night, it's likely that her husband is at home. She has a lucky escape.

The one thing the police got wrong was the three-month timeline. They suspected I planned it to spread the cases out, but that's not so. After scouting the town or city to locate a convenient area, it's then necessary to hunt for a suitable victim. It all takes time.

I've perfected the procedure now. Ideally living alone, the lucky woman will come home on an early evening train or bus. Not too late, because I want the anonymity of a crowd. I need to follow them at least once at a distance to confirm they're the one. There have been four in Bedford so far, but none that I've seen again. It's an expensive business, but so worth it. I'm in no rush. If I have to wait until after Christmas, so be it. They won't catch me.

Another female strides past with her nose in the air. Snooty bitch. If I didn't care about getting caught, I'd chop her down in the fucking street. She briefly glances at me, but she can't see my bared teeth behind the mask. That taunting expression on her face so reminds me of Maggie.

The news said they have someone in custody for the crimes against her. I bet she thinks her ordeal is over.

73

THE HATCHET MAN

I'm about to sit down on a bench and wait for the next train, when a woman I've followed before stumbles out of the station. She was merry last time, but she's steaming tonight. She'd have to be to wear that flashing reindeer jumper. Luckily for her, she doesn't live far. It's such a perfect location that I almost did it on the first night. I haven't evaded the authorities by being impulsive, though.

She walks past, also laden with bags, but these are from mid-range clothes shops. Presents for friends at best, more likely treats for herself. I dreamt of what was going to happen to her for a good few nights after our first 'meeting', but then she was nowhere to be seen.

Then an unexpected thing happened. The news that Maggie Glover had been assaulted was in the local paper with a line that said everyone spoke highly of her and couldn't believe what had happened. I wonder where they got that from, or did they just make it up? No one's that nice. I know that for a fact. Anyway, it inspired me. Maggie grabbed my focus, just as this lady did.

The drunkard staggers by, oblivious of my interest. Like many commuters, she wears trainers under her crumpled suit. I'm swamped by what I think is cheap perfume, but I'm no expert. She has a prominent nose that looks red, even with a fair amount of make-up, which I suspect hasn't been touched up since this morning.

When she's fifty metres away, I follow. Her house is a three-minute walk. There's time to collar her. She weaves a little, and I catch up too soon. I pull back. There's only one other person around; a dog walker who's disappearing into the gloom ahead. Even the street lights seem to have lost any enthusiasm for life around here. I bet most of the residents can't believe they've ended up living in all this toytown blandness.

I hear her phone ring when she's almost at her house. Ignore it, I urge her, but she stops and answers it. Shit. I'll have to walk past. Just before I pass by, a bag slips from her grip. She drops the phone as she attempts to catch it. I manage to grab her mobile before it slides into the gutter. It's an Apple handset, but it's well loved with a cracked and scratched screen.

'That was close,' I say as I hand it back.

'Thank you. Butter fingers, or should I say beer fingers.'

She slides it into her coat pocket probably having forgotten it rung, then picks up her bag. Her eyes are glazed. Christmas really has come early. For both of us.

'Are you okay?' I ask.

'Yes, I only live there.'

She points to where I know she lives. Her expression changes slightly. It's probably because I'm outside wearing a blue medical mask.

'No worries,' I reply.

I turn and cross the street. After counting to twenty, I crouch to pretend to tie a shoelace. Looking over my shoulder, I can see she has just headed through her gate, which she leaves swinging. The area remains empty of pedestrians. I let a car pass, then jog over the road. The temperature in my chest builds as I catch the gate and walk up behind her as she tries to put her key in the door. She giggles.

My hand is already in the Manila envelope.

I only allow myself a single blow nowadays. With all the practice, I consider myself a professional. It's like a challenge. One attempt should be enough. My arm is swift and true. The hatchet wedges in her head with a thud, while her hair prevents any splatter. She drops to the floor without a sound. I let out a sharp gasp. It's similar to an orgasm, but over every inch of my skin.

After a deep breath, I put my foot on her shoulder to lever the hatchet out. I drag the body behind two wheelie bins. Perfect. I sweat under my hat as I stroll in the opposite direction from the way I came. There's another taxi place a twenty-minute walk away, which I haven't used before. Then it's back home to Peterborough.

74

DI BARTON

Barton opened his front door, went inside, and found Holly cleaning the kitchen work surfaces. The house was quiet. She looked at the turkey in his arms and grinned.

'Wow, you are going to get very lucky later,' she said.

'Talking to me or the bird?' asked Barton.

'Both.'

'Hmm. I might be the first man in history to turn down a threesome.'

She moved to the microwave and turned it on. Then she pulled out a chair for him. After opening the fridge, she handed him a can of Birra Moretti. He moved it to the side.

'Are you going out again?' she asked with a frown.

He nodded. She pushed a few escaping strands of hair away from her face. She was wearing faded blue jeans, which she had probably had on most of the week. White T-shirt with the odd stain here and there. The slippers he'd bought her last Christmas. Loose now, after so much use. He almost stood to hug her, but he sensed something was playing on her mind.

'Everything all right?' he asked.

'I was just thinking about what you missed tonight. Luke got a prize for his drawing of Father Christmas,' she said without emotion. 'He was so excited to show everyone at dinner time.'

'Sorry.'

'Layla wanted to ask you why young boys were so horrible.'

Barton nodded and rubbed his forehead. Holly gave him a sad smile.

'I'm here all the while, and she never wants to speak to me.'

'I'll talk to them.'

'I know I asked you to buy a turkey tonight, but you would have missed it, anyway. You miss a lot.'

The microwave pinged, and she tutted. A few seconds later, she slid a plate of steaming food in front of him. Shepherd's pie. His favourite. He picked up a fork.

'Cox spoke to me about development.'

'Great. More training? What next? Parachuting, or abseiling?'

Her right cheek was raised, pulling her face into an angry wink, while she furiously dried a cup. He looked into her eyes.

'Nine-to-five, project role at HQ.'

It took a few seconds for the words to register. She tried to hide her smile. The moment was fleeting. She knew to push those feelings away because they'd been there before. What he'd noticed most amongst that brief flash of hope and joy was relief. She turned, opened the cupboard, and put the cup inside with a clatter.

'What did you tell them?' she asked without turning around.

'I told them I'd think about it tonight.'

Holly placed her hands on the work surface, bowed her head, and let out a deep breath.

'I said I'd discuss it with you,' he said. 'See if you were happy for me to take it.'

She spun around. Hope was back. He bobbed his head.

'Yeesaahh!' she yelled. 'Daddy's coming home!'

Holly walked towards him and did a couple of fist pumps, then a spin.

'About time, too,' she said quietly.

'Do I get a hug?' he asked, standing.

'Nope. You can have more than a hug when you return from wherever it is you're going tonight.'

'Ooh, a promise.'

'Yes, it is, so you'd better not eat that plateful, or you'll be too sleepy later,' she said, pointing at his dinner. 'You do remember the cheesecake calamity.'

Barton felt a touch of heat come to his face. A few years ago, he'd been complaining that they hadn't had any 'special' time of late, so one night, when they'd known the older kids were at friends', they'd planned an evening in together.

Barton had been involved with a complicated kidnapping involving a foreign national and had been exhausted. They'd enjoyed a nice meal with candles and wine while Luke had watched TV. Holly had put Luke to bed and changed into something suitable. When Barton hadn't come upstairs, she'd gone to look for him and discovered him fast asleep at the table, snoring quietly, with his forehead resting on his half-eaten cheesecake.

'That was different.'

'We'll see. When would you start this new role?'

'New year.'

He sat back down and picked his knife and fork up. She pointed a finger at him.

'Brilliant. Right, you big galumph. Be extra careful from now on. Don't be a hero and get hurt on your last week in the job.'

75

DI BARTON

Barton set off thirty minutes later, having cleared his plate of Holly's shepherd's pie, and he'd also found a smallish bar of Toblerone in the fridge after a successful little forage. Gizmo trotted along at the side of him. Barton slowed to allow him to sniff a variety of wet patches against various walls and posts, while he admired the outside Christmas decorations along the village road. Gizmo peered up at him and seemed to smile. He was teaching Barton to live in the moment.

Barton tried to recall the days when his children were born, but the memories were hazy. Was that because it was so long ago, or because he hadn't been completely present? Whenever there was a big case, some of his headspace remained absorbed in it. If he had to solve a serious crime like a murder, he found it hard to relax. It felt almost selfish to have downtime at the weekends or evenings if cracking the case a few days or even hours earlier meant a life could be saved.

When the kids were young, Holly had often said she felt guilty that she wasn't doing enough. That she should be giving more of herself. He sighed. Back then, he'd given her lots of good advice about celebrating the small wins, that nobody was perfect, and how it was important not to do too much yourself. All great advice, which he should have been taking himself.

Barton had always struggled with the idea of letting go of his hands-on role. Not getting the recent promotion had been a relief at the time, but now he was ready for a different challenge. He could feel the tension leaving his shoulders as he strolled along Oundle Road towards St Catherine's Lane. When he arrived at Mrs Wainwright's house, she was standing in her usual spot at the front door, fag in hand.

She looked up as he walked down the drive. Her eyes shifted to his dog.

'It's a greyhound,' said Barton.

'You don't say. Maybe I should get one.'

Barton was about to laugh when he noticed her thick white make-up had wet lines running down it. Bloodshot eyes stared into the distance.

'Your husband?'

'Yes, he was tired an hour ago and got back on the bed. I went to fetch him a hot drink, but when I returned, he'd slipped away.'

'Sorry to hear that.'

'Well, don't be. The outlook was bleak for both of us if he lingered on.'

Barton wasn't sure how to reply to that. He barely knew the woman, yet he felt compelled to ask.

'Do you need a hand with any of the formalities?'

'No, I did it for both my parents and his. It's just a few phone calls. I want one last night with him first, anyway.'

'Fair enough. I'm happy to help or advise. My mum passed recently. You've got my number.'

'No wonder crime's going up if you're running around helping old biddies.' She cracked a smile. 'What are you doing back here?'

'You rang me, remember? Said your husband had seen Santa dashing across the lawn again.'

'Oh, yes. Sorry. Doesn't look as though he'll be able to tell you much now.'

Barton couldn't help smiling.

'I guess not. I don't suppose he was the haunting type, although I've found the courts aren't all that keen on evidence gathered by Ouija board.'

Wainwright grinned.

'I know I'm rude, son. Ignore me. You coppers have hard jobs in this day and age. Are you on a night shift or something?'

'No, I don't live far, so I thought I'd pop over.'

'Really? You're not getting paid to be here?'

Barton shook his head.

'What the hell's wrong with you? Why aren't you at home with your family? Treasure every moment, Mr Barton. You'll be standing here like I am before you know it.'

'Will do,' he replied. 'Have you got somewhere to go for Christmas?'

'Yes, we always visit my cousin. He's a moaning grumpy guts, so we get on well.'

Barton kept a straight face. Thank God for that. Even Holly might not be charitable enough to have Mrs Wainwright over for dinner.

'When was it he noticed this second Father Christmas?'

'He told me just before I rang you, but it could have been any time. His memory stopped working how it was supposed to, so something he said he saw that morning may have been from years ago and vice versa.'

'Did he give any kind of description? Tall, fat, or perhaps how fast he ran,' asked Barton, thinking that a youngster would probably be thinner and quicker.

'No, nothing like that, sorry.'

Barton didn't want to grill Mrs Wainwright in light of what had happened. It was hard enough to think of her going inside to sit on her own with a dead body, but he'd sat with his mother, and it'd helped a lot with saying goodbye.

'I'm sorry for your loss. You can still ring me if you see anything else, or even if you just want a chat. Thanks for your help.'

'No problem.'

'Come on, Gizmo.'

He was halfway up the drive when she shouted out.

'Wait, there was one thing he said about their appearance.'

'Pardon?'

'What my husband actually said was that he saw another Santa near Maggie's house.'

'Another?'

'Yes, I don't think it was the same one.'

76

DI BARTON

Tuesday 22nd December

Barton got to the office early the next morning, even though he'd had another restless night. He wanted to help catch The Hatchet Man and go out in style. Even just assisting a different force in solving the case would be enough. Then he could leave feeling the slate was clean.

Barton's mind kept concluding that someone was still up to no good in Peterborough. Who was running across the Wainwrights' lawn when Glenn was in custody? Glenn had confessed to sending the second letter to Tim Tibbles, so who posted the third one?

If the old man had seen correctly, then who was running across his lawn from Maggie's place? It was time to go back and study her life again. He'd spoken to her work colleagues; next stop was the gym.

Zander and Leicester arrived, so he grabbed them and ran through his thinking.

'Zander, you've already had some contact with the forces in Anglesey and the others. See what else they've found out. There might be connections between the women, which could help us. Leicester, start looking into those guys who were interested in dating Maggie.'

'Ken and that Swedish guy?'

'Not Ken. The Swede and the Irish bloke with the ponytail.'

'Lothar and Cliff. Okay, I'll get their car registrations and search ANPR, have a good look at both of them.'

'Actually, we'll check Ken too. See where all three have been driving. If Cliff and Lothar have been out of the county recently, it'll show up. Anne-Marie said Lothar had moved up from London, but is that true? Check on the electoral registers.'

'Do we have enough to bring them in?' said Zander.

Barton thought about it. He felt the clock was ticking. It was three days until Christmas.

'Let's check their records first. We'll haul them in if there are any anomalies. Who knows? One of them might have something glaring.'

'Isn't Anglesey off the coast of Wales, so there'd probably be a ferry to Ireland?' asked Leicester.

Barton's stomach did a turn.

'Yes. I'll speak to our police friends in Sweden and Ireland. See if they've had any similar unsolved crimes or if either of our potential suspects are known to them. You've got until one o'clock, then we'll have a meeting to pool our knowledge. There'll be a connection, we—'

Barton stopped as Strange walked in. She had a concerned look on her face.

'What is it?' he asked.

'It's just come through. The Hatchet Man has struck again.'

77

THE HATCHET MAN

Aged 12

My mother stands before me. She holds the two halves of the broken vase. Her nose is scrunched up under her tired eyes. I almost chuckle even though I'm in a lot of trouble.

'How many times have I told you about playing football in the house?'

'Two or three. Maybe more.'

'What's wrong with you? It's like you're possessed. That vase was my mum's.'

'I don't think she'll mind.'

'I mind. That's all I have to remember her by.'

She lets out a deep breath, but I can tell she's furious.

'Please, try to be good.'

'Does good get me the bike I want at Christmas?'

'No, I explained to you it's too much money.'

'Where's Dad?'

'Why?'

'Just wondering.'

'Searching for work.'

'Looking for drink is closer to the truth. That's why that bike is too expensive?'

'How dare you talk about your father like that? He provides for us.'

'I hate him, and I wish he was dead.'

The sound is like a crack. It surprises her, and she's not the one who's been slapped around the face. For a moment, I'm tempted to reciprocate. Then I slink away. I run up the stairs and storm into my bedroom, slamming the door behind me. I feel childish, but what else can I do. Why do I talk back to her? She's my world.

I need to be nice. My father rejected me years ago. Mrs Torrington had me moved from her class. I won't give my mum reason to leave me. She must understand. We need each other. She's all I have left.

78

DI BARTON

After dropping her bombshell, Strange took a seat.

'What did Cox say?' asked Barton.

'Not much. I'd only popped in to see her to sign for those two sick days I had off. It's the same MO. This time it was in Bedford. It has to be the same guy. A woman delivering leaflets this morning found the victim behind some bins. She had a deep chopping-type wound to the head.'

'Recent?'

'Depends on what you mean by recent. They reckon from the night before.'

Barton knew they'd have a decent idea of the time of death by the state of the body and any blood that had been spilled.

'That makes it unlikely that The Hatchet Man is coming here for Christmas after all,' he said.

'Yes, that's what Cox thought,' said Strange.

Barton looked out of the window as he reflected on the news.

'Maybe we've had a lucky escape, but I still don't like what's going on here. The third letter that was sent and whoever was running around near Maggie's are both frustrating and concerning incidents. I want whoever's responsible caught.'

'What do we do about Lothar and Cliff?' asked Strange.

'The plan remains the same. Let's see if Leicester comes up with anything. If he does, find out where they are today and visit them. See them at work if necessary. I can't imagine this has anything to do with Glenn. Let's keep an open mind, though, in case he roped in a friend, but from what the games teacher said, that's not likely. If the sender of the letter and person seen in the Santa suit are time wasters, I still want to talk to them.'

'If we visit Cliff and Lothar at their places of work, they're liable to get annoyed,' said Hoffman.

'Yes, my young apprentice,' said Zander. 'If they're innocent, that is, but at least we've covered ourselves in case something else is occurring.'

'I knew that. All I'm saying is that if either are violent, a visit could set them off.'

'Smashing point, Hoffman, so everyone be careful,' said Barton. 'If they turn up clean, we've only got a couple of days until Christmas, so we might not have any more suspects. Any spare time, get your year-end appraisals ready.'

'Should I pop round and see Maggie and Anne-Marie? They might have something to add,' said Strange.

'Good idea. I'll check Europol as well. Make sure one of Europe's most wanted isn't running step classes in our local hotels.'

Barton was secretly relieved after a quick search that neither Cliff nor Lothar were on any list. That would have been just his luck.

He requested a check from the Irish Garda and Swedish police on both men. Then he read his emails. The DNA report and the analysis of both letters had been completed. It was what he'd expected. No retrievable DNA from either, and the handwriting was clearly different. The type of paper used was common, but the quality of the paper was hugely contrasting. One was cheap and had a low gsm. The other was much more expensive. The lower grade one was Glenn's.

An hour later, Zander reported back to Barton.

'Okay. Staffordshire Police has taken the lead. They've found some loose similarities between the cases, but little else. The women involved were all between thirty and forty, except for the first incident. That was a very elderly woman. The second victim worked from home, but they suspect she was assaulted as she came back from a regular shopping trip. The final two were office workers who got attacked in the early evening on their doorsteps when they returned from their jobs.'

'Interesting. Perhaps he realised that if you're going to attack someone, doing it just as they put their key in the door is a good time.'

'Yes. The older woman was a retired teacher by the name of Torrington. The others were an accountant, a solicitor, and an administrator of some kind, which makes them all professionals, but there are no obvious links through their work. Of the four, three lived alone and the other had a lodger who often worked away. One might have had a recent boyfriend who could have been Polish, that they've been unable to trace.. Another was seeing a mixed-race guy called Alan who has a reasonable alibi.'

'The oldest victim, Joslyn Torrington, had escaped serious injury because of the thick woolly hat she'd been wearing. The rest had been bare-headed. It was possible that the perpetrator had learned from that first experience, because the police suspect that a hammer was used in the first two incidents.'

'Then he progressed to a hatchet, rather than an axe?' asked Barton.

'They think so. The smaller head of the weapon matches the

wounds, but I don't believe there's a standard. I suppose the press felt The Relatively Small Axe Killer didn't have quite the same ring as The Hatchet Man.'

'A hatchet, assuming it isn't some kind of home-made weapon, is deadlier because it's much easier to wield,' said Barton.

'Yes, they told me the second woman seemed to have either a thicker skull or the technique had been poor, but she survived without brain damage from the hammer as well. The attacker probably got a thrill again, but realised he wanted to go further. Hurting them wasn't enough.'

'So, he ups his weapon and possibly even works on his technique?'

'Yes, they think the Stoke victim may have crawled for a bit before dying, but the Leicester victim was killed instantly. The poor soul in Bedford looks like she received an instant end too. The guy in charge informed me that the might of the Met are now clunking up the gears in anticipation of the arrival of The Hatchet Man in London.'

'And they can't find any suspects on CCTV at the scenes or nearby?'

'No, and that has them really concerned. CCTV is being scrutinised all over the country, but they have nothing. Number plates are being cross-checked, but no luck. There's obviously CCTV on buses and trains, which they're looking at, but it's a gigantic task. Who's to say he didn't get a train first thing in the morning and sit in McDonald's planning his attack? Specialist officers are being called in to better interpret the road-camera data, but that will take time. There's also a special programme running after the news on BBC1 later today.'

Barton shook his head.

'A fast-moving fugitive is going to be tough to track.'

'Yeah, this latest murder ticks all the boxes for the worst type of serial killer. The public's imagination will light up. We'll be under the spotlight. It won't take much to create a panic.'

There wasn't a lot Barton could do about The Hatchet Man if he wasn't coming to town, but he could spend the last few days hunting around with what he had. He was just debating his next move when Leicester came over to update him about Cliff and Lothar.

'Obviously, neither of the two surnames are very common. There's only one Cliff Quigley in Peterborough, and he checks out. He's on the electoral register with a woman who has the same surname. I'd guess it's his wife, but might be sister or mother, seeing as he's been asking other women out.'

Barton thought of Cliff's joke name of Quiffley and suspected he lived with his mother. Zander had overheard.

'A serial killer and a cheat,' he shouted. 'No heaven for that guy.'

'Sadly, he looks clean,' said Leicester. 'Quigley's car is registered to that address, has a valid MOT and current insurance. Lothar, on the other hand, isn't on the electoral register. I rang the gym to ask when he was next in. What sounded like a young lad told me he was doing a class and said he'd be in tonight. He happily gave me Lothar's address when I mentioned I needed to speak to him. The vehicle Leicester took the photo of at Maggie's address is in Lothar's name, but the MOT expired start of Jan, and it's registered to an address in London, not the address that I was given.'

Barton gave the facts a thought for a moment. Lothar wouldn't be the first guy to turn stalker after a rebuffed request for a date. That could be a reason for him hanging around Maggie's house. Maybe he got dressed up as Santa in the hope he'd be seen. With Maggie already scared after what Glenn did to her, she might start to feel she needed a big, strong man about the place. Step forward, Lothar the gym bunny. That might also explain the letter to the radio station, although that was harder to believe. From what Anne-Marie said, Lothar was no criminal genius.

'Right. Leicester, Malik, Hoffman, Zelensky and Zander, find this guy and ask him to come in for questioning. Strange and I will visit Maggie and Anne-Marie. Cameron is only up the road from Anne-Marie, so I'll swing by there afterwards and get an update from Cameron about Heidi. It'll be interesting to see how he and Ashlynn are doing now Glenn's not in the house and everything's out in the open. I'll also let him know about his visitation rights and the things he's allowed to send in for Glenn, with him being a remand prisoner, not a convicted one.'

Barton's brain normally started to plan the next few weeks ahead and look at his resources. It was only as he and Strange got in a pool car that he realised he wasn't doing it.

'Everything all right?'

He nodded. Strange looked focused, whereas Barton felt the first edge of something unexpected. It was tension leaving his shoulders. He steeled himself. Now he'd confirmed to Cox he was leaving, the last thing he wanted was a mistake during his last few days.

Strange drove slowly out of the station, then kept quiet as she cruised down the street. She blinked rapidly with her mind clearly going into overdrive.

Was there anything they were missing? He closed his eyes and quickly came to an important conclusion. It didn't matter that the last attack was in Bedford. After all, it was only forty miles away. The most important aspect of all of this was that there was a killer at large.

Barton realised with a grimace that if this were chess, the police would be losing.

79

THE HATCHET MAN

It's great that the papers are full of The Hatchet Man. That's me! One strike and revenge is mine. Or is it justice? I should send them a photo of me in shadows. They'd love that.

Why have I put up with people leaving me all my life? I've always skulked away like a beaten dog instead of fighting back. I will admit that I'm really enjoying the new me. They called me a cunning killer in one article. It's clear they've made no progress in finding me. Am I too good for them? I think so. My parents never thought I'd amount to anything. It's almost a pity they aren't around to see this. I'm sure they'd be proud.

It's funny how things work out. Funny how seeds planted years ago can lie dormant, then sprout when the skies finally open. The rains have fallen and now I'm alive. All this power is quite a buzz.

After Anglesey, it all fell into place. The plan was to finish in Stevenage and chop up my ex-wife, Inga. Finish the job, perhaps on Christmas Day. She bloody deserves it too. But I can't. My daughter knows nothing about me, but I still love her. I can't leave her without a mother. I'm tempted to introduce myself, but it might be a touch too risky, considering what I've been up to.

I bet they'll think I'm heading to London, but that's not the plan. It's tempting, though. London's so big and anonymous, I could do ten a night.

I still think I'll finish by Christmas, but first it's the bonus round. The thought of the big day makes me look towards the Santa outfit hanging out of view in my wardrobe.

My stomach gurgles as I consider tonight. Anne-Marie must have received her piece of paper by now. I sent it first class two days ago. It'll certainly be her least Christmassy one. The clock is ticking, but I've scoped out the house. The hatchet has been sharpened. I've even had more practice on the tree perfecting my technique. That hatchet and I have travelled quite a journey since my first glorious effort on the girl in Stoke. I felt bad afterwards that she was able to crawl away for a bit, but even Tiger Woods had to study his swing. I'm learning as I become more disciplined. I think the police know that, and it will make them fear me more. If they're too stupid to notice, I'll send another letter.

I'm Mr One-Shot. There's no messy injuries like poor old Glenn managed. He made the same mistake I did when I started. It's about planning and efficiency. I've enjoyed it so much that maybe I should do a few afterwards in London. I know some of the areas quite well. That'll drag all their resources away from Peterborough at least. Then I can retire from my little hobby. I'll still have my memories, but I'd better focus on earning and saving some money next year or everything really will fall apart.

I tap my hands against my knees. If I'm honest with myself, I don't give a shit about work any more. I just want a special someone. Why does nobody choose me? Rejection could be my middle name. The best I seem to be able to manage is to be on the periphery of other people's lives. It's not enough. Not any more.

Maggie practically laughed in my face when I mentioned a

drink together. Well, she didn't laugh in my face, but I suspect she had a nice joke with Anne-Marie about it afterwards.

There's a twinge of sympathy for the others who are going to get hurt, but the urge to strike out now and level the score is too strong. Perhaps if I'd struck back at my mother, then I wouldn't have ended up where I am now. Maybe if I'd been more normal, Maggie would have wanted me. We'd have been great together. I'm sure of it. Lovers and friends.

It's such a shame.

80

DI BARTON

Barton and Strange visited Maggie's house first. He expected her to be at home. The schools were closing today for Christmas but he reckoned Pippa would be here while her mother was recuperating. When they arrived and knocked on the door, Barton spotted it was new. The door opened only a few inches as the chain did its job. Little Pippa scowled at them through the crack. Then she slammed it shut. Maggie appeared half a minute later.

She gave them a warm smile and looked relaxed in leggings and a thick, Fair Isle jumper. As they followed her to the kitchen, Barton noticed her hair didn't look quite right at the back. They must have cut some away when they cleaned the wound to prevent infection.

'Sorry about that. I wasn't aware the little rascal could open it. It's frustrating that I was attacked out there, because I paid for a new door with last month's bonus and upped the rest of the security as well. I received more than I expected, so we also had new window locks throughout. The windows were all triple-glazed at the rear apart from the kitchen, so that was replaced. The guy fitting it reckoned that a burglar would struggle to get in with a crowbar. I've decided to get an alarm fitted as well and that's happening tomorrow, and he's putting a seven-lever lock on the back door.'

Barton smiled, although burglars were probably the least of her worries.

'That's brilliant. We'll keep the tag on your line, so if you ring us, we'll know to be here asap. He'll still be trying to enter when we pull up.'

Maggie's face dropped.

'Won't Glenn be locked away until the trial?'

'Yes, of course. I meant the burglar.'

'Oh, right. Good. I feel safer knowing that, although I feel sorry for Glenn, too. Is that weird? What is that? Survivor's guilt?'

'It's called having a heart. Not everyone has one. I don't suppose you've had any visitors?'

'What kind of visitors? I've had a few robins in the garden.'

Barton chuckled.

'I was more interested in people. You had Ken and Lothar just after you got hurt. Have either been around again or posted anything? Anyone else been to see you?'

'No, nobody. Only my mum. That's pretty poor, isn't it? Anne-Marie rang. I need more friends. I kind of hoped the officer you came with before might be back.'

Barton glanced away as she blushed.

'Maybe when this is all over.'

He had a thought.

'I got the impression dating wasn't a priority for you. Anne-Marie said you weren't too bothered with either Lothar or Cliff.'

'I wasn't sure if I was ready to date until I spoke to your colleague. The other two weren't really my type, anyway. I'm not a big fan of ponytails and Lothar seems flakey to me.'

'Flakey?'

'I'm being polite. He looks the type to kiss himself in the mirror.'

Barton laughed. He hadn't told Maggie yet that another fleeing Santa was seen by the confused, dying man, but if she was back after being at her mum's, he had to tell her.

'One of your neighbours saw someone else in a red outfit running past their house recently. It wasn't the most reliable of leads, but you should know.'

Maggie's fists clenched, and she stood up.

'Who said that?'

'Mr Wainwright.'

Maggie sat down slowly.

'Okay. Mr Wainwright knocked on my door last year and asked when we were going on holiday together. Not sure who he thought I was. What you've said is still concerning, though.'

'And I'm afraid I also have some sad news. Mr Wainwright has died.'

Maggie's chin dropped.

'What? Someone's killed him?'

'No, I think his heart gave out. It was a peaceful death.'

'I see. That's still very sad. He was a gentle, quiet man, well, before he became ill. I'll pop over later.'

'That's kind of you. Do you mind if I ask whether Cliff or Lothar are the sort to come around uninvited?'

'I wouldn't have thought so.'

'I'm wondering if you'd be better off at your mum's.'

Maggie put her hands on her hips.

'I will not be scared out of my own house. Don't worry. I'll be very careful. We won't leave the house at night and we have everything we need. My feisty mother arrives on Christmas Eve for a few days.'

Barton looked at Strange to see if she had anything to add.

'Maggie,' said Strange. 'Have a lovely Christmas. Be on the lookout over the next few weeks. We always get confidence tricksters trying to get into people's houses. Thieves often target properties at Christmas when the residents have nicely wrapped and stacked the goods in one place. Don't open your door if you're not certain who it is. Talk through the letter box. I wouldn't let anyone in unless you know them very well and trust them.'

Maggie's grin faded.

'Okay,' she replied. 'Only my mum and I have a key, and we have a chain on the front door now, but I'll check through the letter box. The chain's too high for Pippa to remove and we only let people in the front.' The smile reappeared. 'The kitchen's too messy,' she whispered.

Barton and Strange declined an offer of tea. He gave Pippa a thumbs up as they left, which she ignored.

'How's she doing?' he asked Maggie at the door.

'Back to normal now we're home,' said Maggie, chuckling.

'And how are you doing?'

Maggie followed his gaze to the cast on her left arm.

'I probably haven't dealt with it all yet. Pippa's routine was my concern. To be honest, it helps to know it was Glenn. I had a call from a liaison officer who explained about the mental health issues that were present with Glenn's offending. It sounds like what he did wasn't personal because he just wanted to help his family.'

'That's a good way to look at it,' said Strange.

'Merry Christmas,' said Barton.

Maggie gave them a wave and closed the door. When Barton reached his car, he turned to Strange before getting inside.

'You laid it on thick back there,' he said.

'Yes. I haven't been too involved with this case, and in theory the danger to Maggie is much reduced. But something feels wrong.'

Barton nodded. He couldn't have said it better himself.

81

DI BARTON

Strange drove smoothly around the parkways. The traffic was light. Barton suspected most people had knocked off for Christmas or were working from home. He caught Strange deep in thought as they turned into the street where the Hulses lived. Good coppers had hunches. That was why they were the best. Hunches didn't help prosecutions, but they kept you in the game. They kept you focused. Any break might be a small one. You needed to be ready and looking.

Barton knocked on the door, and Cameron opened it. He seemed in decent spirits as he let them in even though the house was still cold and retained a particularly non-festive feel. They followed Cameron into the dining room. There was no offer of a drink.

'How's Heidi?' asked Barton.

'Much better, actually, but they're still assessing her at the hospital. They gave her some sleeping tablets and more or less knocked her out for twenty-four hours. She's groggy but with it. I assume taking her out of here has helped. I reckon she had a feeling that Glenn was up to mischief or he'd lost the plot. She says not, but I suspect she's just protecting her boy, you know?'

Barton did know.

'Did you attend magistrates' court to see Glenn remanded?'

'Yes, he didn't look well. The magistrates were good, though. They made it clear there were mental health issues in play. They seemed pleased that I'd turned up and even explained for my benefit that Glenn would be assessed at the young offenders' place and his treatment would go from there. They said it was the best place for him.'

Barton nodded. The magistrates rarely saw either parent in the worst cases put before them. It was always an encouraging sign if one attended. It was even rarer for a father to be present. As for Glenn being in the best place? That was doubtful.

'Will he be prosecuted if they find he's insane?' asked Cameron.

'You'll find it more helpful to say he was struggling with his mental health rather than use terms like that. I wouldn't describe Glenn like that anyway, so it's highly unlikely he'd be found unfit to stand trial, or incapable of admitting to his guilt, if that's what he wants to do. Sentencing will go ahead. The wheels of justice have to turn. He still committed those crimes, even if he's found to have had diminished responsibility.'

'Right,' replied Cameron, not looking particularly bothered.

Barton noticed a few differences in the house as they left. It wasn't tidy, but it was tidier. It smelled fresher, too.

'I need to ask if you've been around Maggie's place since we arrested Glenn.'

'Why would I go there?'

'Maybe to apologise.'

'You know me better than that. I'm sorry she got hurt, but that's where my sympathy ends.'

'Are you okay for Christmas?' asked Strange. 'Will Heidi be out of hospital?'

'Yes, we'll be fine. Actually, there was a bit extra in Heidi's pay cheque. Not much, admittedly, but enough for a few basics. We'll visit Heidi if she isn't released. I might have some good news too, although I daren't get my hopes up.'

'Oh, yes?' asked Barton, turning as he stepped outside.

'You remember that job I applied for?'

'The position where you came second.'

'That's it. They rang and told me the successful candidate had a few issues with a notice period in his current role. He's on three months, not one. They're considering some kind of preliminary post for me. Maybe look to keep us both on. Anyway, they wanted to know if I was still available.'

'That's fabulous news,' said Barton. 'Hopefully something to celebrate with Ashlynn.'

'Fingers crossed,' said Cameron.

'Is Ashlynn about?'

'No, I've not seen much of her. I think she's finding it hard. Her and Glenn weren't really close. They argued like mad, but they were very protective of each other. She's gone unusually quiet.'

82

DI BARTON

Barton and Strange drove to Anne-Marie's house. Strange tutted as they parked outside.

'I didn't warm to him much,' she said.

'Cameron?'

'Yep. He seemed off.'

'Yes, but some of that is down to what's happened. You remember how Zander was when you first met him?'

Strange paused to think.

'A bit prickly? I suppose he wasn't quite connected, or not at least to me.'

'It's the opposite now,' said a beaming Barton.

Strange didn't take the bait.

'It's true that losing a child is something that's never too far from the surface, especially if it's fairly recent. Some people cope by being down, distant or edgy, others overcompensate. Eventually nice things begin to happen and they can move on a bit, but it might be a long time. Zander seems in a good place now.'

'Yep. Maybe he had a win on the horses.'

Strange slapped Barton's arm.

'I heard about the training job,' she said.

Barton scoffed. 'One, it's not training, and two, who told you that?'

'John. It's a police station, not a monastery. We all know. I think it'd be good for you.'

'So you can get your feet under my desk?'

'Zander's shoes will fit nicely.'

Barton gave her a quick glance to see her expression.

'Aren't you interested?'

Strange let out a deep breath.

'I was angry when I came here after a shitty time with the Met, but the drive I brought has dissipated somewhat. I wanted to prove myself and feel respected, and now I do. I love the job and the team, but I want to do something else for a while. Next year's a big one for Zander and me. I'd like to step away from the pain and torment that we investigate. At least for a while. I can always come back to it, as I assume you might do.'

'Wow. Lots of changes,' replied Barton.

'Yes. Perhaps a few tears, too. I think about what happened to Pigs in the Fire Killer case all the time. We put our lives on the line when we join the police. It's healthy to step away every now and again. The team won't be breaking up. It'll change, that's all. We'll look back on this Christmas fondly and maybe a little sadly.'

Barton could agree with that. He often thought of Nicola Pignatiello.

'I always remember Ginger and the others at this time of year.'

'Stop it, John. I'm emotional enough without you heaping it on. Joe Public doesn't expect us to turn up weeping, but we have lost some good people over the last few years.'

They got out of the car at the same moment as Marlon was opening the front door. His mum had a large bandage on her head and her arm in a sling. She looked particularly unhappy as she kissed him goodbye. Marlon left at speed.

'Everything okay?' asked Barton.

'No, it bloody well isn't. I appreciate you coming, though. Great work, seeing as I haven't even called you yet.'

Strange and Barton followed her into the house. Barton smelled home cooking, caramel perhaps. There were cake tins on the side, greased and ready to go. When they reached the kitchen, she handed him a small folded business-card-sized piece of paper. There was a big red number one on the front. Inside were five words.

You're next, but one. SK.

83

DI BARTON

Barton recognised the handwriting immediately as being the same as that of the second letter to the radio station.

'That's not good,' said Strange.

'That's not good for him,' shouted Anne-Marie. 'If he gets in my house, I'll chop him up myself. Practice for the bloody turkey. In fact, he'll be going in my fucking oven. I've got my brother-in-law arriving tomorrow. He wouldn't even notice if I served something different. He'd crunch him up, bones and all.'

'No one saw anything?' asked Strange.

'Of course not. Or I would have said,' roared Anne-Marie.

She bowed her head for a moment, then looked up.

'God, I'm sorry. It came by post. It's just my children are buzzing around the place, all excited, and I don't know what to think. Is this for real?'

'We'll examine it, but it's clearly concerning.'

'Do you need it for prints? I'm sorry, me, my husband, and the oldest touched it.'

'Yes, we'll take it, but I assume whoever sent it is too smart to leave proof.'

'Do you have a suspect, then?'

'No, a radio presenter got a similar communication.'

'And what happened to them?'

'Nothing, so we don't need to panic, but we should be vigilant.'

'Okay. Shit. I thought with Glenn in prison, all this was over.'

'So did we. Whoever wrote this obviously knows where you live. Have you considered staying elsewhere over the holidays?'

'What? No, I haven't. My sister and her husband are coming tomorrow afternoon. We've got the only house that's large enough. I'm not ruining Christmas because a crank sent me a letter.'

'Okay. We'll put some precautions in place. Give me a minute to think.'

'Fine. Would you like a coffee? I've just brewed some. You can have my husband's and mine. We need something stronger.'

Five minutes later, Barton and Strange had spoken in the garden and were now sitting on armchairs with a really strong coffee each and a plate full of mince pies. Barton had never been mad on mince pies, so he only had two, so as not to look rude. He swallowed appreciatively and stifled a burp. Not bad.

Anne-Marie and her husband huddled on the sofa with a whisky each. Barton would have loved an Irish coffee on a chilly day like this. He was struck again by the contrast between here and Cameron's place, even Maggie's. This house was how a family home should be at this time of year. There were cards everywhere. They hung on string around the coving and were lined up higgledy-piggledy on the mantelpiece. The kids had covered the Christmas tree in loads of old crap that would mean the world to the parents in front of him. Whoever sent that note needed their holiday plans ruined instead of these people's.

'Right, Anne-Marie. We have nothing concrete to tell you, but the positive, if you can call it that, is as far as we know there's been no first. Your address is logged on our system, as is Maggie's. I'll ask for patrol cars to drive past at various times over the next few days. If we get more intel, we can adjust.'

'Do you think she's in danger, too?'

'I don't know. She hasn't received a note saying she's first, so I suppose that's something. Don't go out alone. It certainly looks like you're a target, but nothing's definite.'

Anne-Marie put her hand to her mouth. Her husband knocked his drink back and placed his arm around her.

'Is this anything to do with this guy they're talking about on TV, The Hatchet Man?' he asked.

'I've received no solid facts to believe it is, but it's an extra worry that someone like that is running about attacking vulnerable women. Bedford isn't far away. I wouldn't have said you fit the bill for that guy's victims, but you've received a horrible message.'

Barton had an unpleasant thought that whoever was first might already be dead. If this was posted a few days ago, then the woman in Bedford could have been the first. Either that, or maybe the body hadn't been found yet.

Yet this killer was crafty. He'd be aware first-class post would probably take longer at Christmas, so Barton suspected he would have put that she was next, not next but one. That was if it was the killer. The killer might well be sharpening his wares in a London hotel somewhere, and these letters could just be an oddball getting off on causing panic. It had surprised Barton at the start of his career how thrilling it was for people when they did this type of thing. They became drunk on how it made them feel powerful.

It was important not to jump to conclusions, because sometimes those responsible were quiet types who believed they'd been unjustly overlooked by society. People like that were harder to catch. It was usually easier if it was a misogynist who was convinced of their own brilliance, which often led to them leaving clues.

Barton looked at Anne-Marie. He could tell she felt backed up to the wall, but she did not appear vulnerable in any way, shape or form. Barton had seen less savage faces in medieval war film scenes.

'It goes without saying to be careful answering the door,' he said. 'We'll have an armed response vehicle on standby. You hear anything, call 999. The ARV will be on its way if it's not at another emergency.'

Anne-Marie stood and paced, eyes wild.

'There's no chance he's getting inside here. No fucking chance at all.'

84

DI BARTON

Barton and Strange returned to their vehicle. Strange was about to start a conversation when Barton cleared his throat.

'Just give me a minute. The old Barton brain has dragged something out of its bowels.'

Strange's lip curled.

'Please try to keep whatever it is out of the car.'

'Sorry, I mean depths. I've just had an idea. Let me roll it around in silence while we drive back.'

They reached the office at the same time as Zander and Leicester. Zander was about to say something when Barton raised his hand.

'Let's wait for the others and let everyone hear everything together in the incident room. I have something to say as well.'

Leicester, Malik, Zelensky, Strange, Zander and Hoffman traipsed into the room. Barton had a moment as he looked at his people. It was the team he was leaving behind. He quickly updated them about events at Anne-Marie's house.

'I've also had an inkling that the person responsible for the hatchet attacks might live in our city. Some of it is a gut feeling, but

I'm betting a few of you have it, too.' There were many nods around the room. 'Let's discuss the case. I reckon they committed the first crime in Anglesey and it released a load of pent-up anger and vengeance. Any thoughts?'

He glanced around, but no one commented.

'It's classic serial-killer behaviour. He assaults the first woman but messes it up somewhat. Maybe he didn't plan to kill. But it felt good. So great, in fact, that he had to do it again. He's bright and wants to get away with it, so he takes his time. That might be more the reason why there's a gap between crimes than any three-month sequence. He's thinking, planning. I've never even been to Anglesey. It's a weird place to start off, so what does that mean?'

'There has to be a personal connection.'

'Spot on, to Anglesey and to Peterborough. All the letters went to a local radio station. I bet nobody outside Peterborough has heard of Peterborough City Radio. Let's flip it. How could he be connected to Anglesey? Shout them out.'

Barton took a whiteboard pen and wrote each one down.

'Family. School. Partner's old place. Holiday memory. Killer is a genius.'

Barton spun around at the last comment.

'Explain that, Zelensky. I don't think this guy is a complete Einstein because there's very little that connects Anglesey and Peterborough.'

'That's what I meant, boss. Maybe he chose Anglesey knowing we'd look for a connection. It'd be absolute genius if he'd never been there before.'

'God, that would be worrying. No, I'd say Anglesey was personal. He's planned the rest, including leading us to London, but the other victims were unknown women. In effect, he's probably been laughing at the police as we follow him down the country. We couldn't see the pattern until he did Leicester. Now he's hit Bedford, so we think he's off to London, which will be easier for him because his next victim might be one of an unofficial ten million.'

'But you reckon he could kill here?' asked Zander.

'Maybe. Assume he was here all along. Let's try to solve it as if it were our case. This man hates women, for whatever reason. It'll no doubt lead back to his youth, perhaps his mother.'

'Or his school life,' said Hoffman.

Barton clicked his fingers.

'Brilliant.'

'This Joslyn Torrington was a teacher and so could she have taught him? When did she retire? Who did she fall out with during her career? Who threatened her?'

'That list will be massive if she's been an inner-city school-teacher all her working life. Those jobs are hardcore,' said Strange.

'Correct. It might be long, but what do we do with the names on that list when we get it?'

'See which ones link to Peterborough,' said Leicester.

'Yes, but there's one other thing. This woman's retired. What does that tell us?'

'That the list will be really long,' said Zelensky.

There was a brief chuckle, but the focus was instantly back.

'That the perpetrator is unlikely to be young,' said Zander.

Barton nodded and wrote it on the board.

'Anything else?' he asked.

'He might fit the demographic for Anglesey,' said Zander. 'A detective up there said there were only around one per cent who aren't white.'

Nobody else replied until Malik put his hand up. Barton smiled at his formality.

'Maybe we should ask her if she remembers any psychos. These crimes are pretty off the scale.'

Barton bobbed his head. 'I'm betting this was repressed rage.

Something happened within the last few years that released it. The person who attacked the teacher may well have only been a little scary when she knew him, but was still unbalanced. If someone poses a question about unusual children as opposed to violent ones to her, she might well remember him. The rest of the victims were selected for a reason, but there might not be a personal link to the murderer or the other victims.'

'Which means that any other future targets will be random as well, which is worrying,' said Zander.

Barton knew it was very worrying. A man who took his time to kill people he didn't know was a hard man to catch, even in this day and age.

'Wait. I don't get the connection to Anne-Marie and Maggie,' said Zelensky. 'I missed the start of this case. I can understand that the killer lives here and commits his attacks elsewhere to evade suspicion, so why then do it in his home town?'

Barton was about to explain when Leicester clicked his fingers. Barton gave him a thumbs up.

'Glenn attacking Anne-Marie and Maggie in the killer's city strikes a chord with him. Maggie, in particular, matches his target victim. He'll have seen an opportunity. The first letter that Glenn sent added to our confusion. I bet it annoyed him when we caught Glenn, or Glenn could have taken the blame. Our investigations would have been all over the place.'

'Right,' said Barton. 'What do most serial killers eventually do?'

'Make mistakes.'

'Precisely. They do something too close to home, or they assume they're smarter than us, or they just get unlucky. The trick is to catch them before they kill someone else as opposed to finding them when they're long retired, but this might not be as hard as we think. Do we have an Einstein here, apart from me, of course?'

Leicester stood up, his enthusiasm getting the better of him.

'The connection between Anglesey and Peterborough will lead us to the killer. If that murderer goes after Anne-Marie and or Maggie, then it's what connects those two women. I know a bit about Maggie's life. She doesn't do much socially. Gym, running and work. Anne-Marie doesn't run. The only things they do together are work and the gym. Our person of interest is likely to frequent one of those places.'

'Very good. I know we keep saying man, but it could be a woman. It might be a person who knows them socially, someone who works with them, or someone who works out with them. It could be another gym member, or a person employed there.'

Zander cleared his throat.

'Now's a good time to announce what we discovered on our trips to see Cliff and Lothar. Cliff was at home. He'd been back to Ireland for a few days, so he definitely wasn't running around Bedford with an axe. We saw the paperwork. He even had a receipt from the airport.'

'There's still that connection with Anglesey and Ireland being so close. We keep talking about a lone killer,' said Barton. 'He doesn't have to be.'

'Yes,' said Leicester. 'We thought we'd probe around that.'

'I asked him if he knew Lothar,' said Zander. 'The change in expression on his face was immediate and it was distaste.'

'He admitted to knowing him, but found him creepy,' said Leicester. 'I asked him whether that was because Lothar also has feelings for Maggie. He denied that, but he looked sad. He'd wanted to ask Maggie out for a while, but every time he spoke to her, he choked or was too vague.

'The vibe was that he was a decent bloke, despite a dodgy pony-tail. When I said we had concerns someone was stalking Maggie, he appeared genuinely concerned for her.'

'Okay, what about the Swedish meatball?'

'Lothar, on the other hand, wasn't at home. The guy who rents the room to him was, though. His name is Xin Bai.'

'Wait, I just remembered something,' said Leicester. 'When I was talking to Maggie not long after Lothar and Ken had been around to see how she was, she mentioned that Lothar had told her he was interested in a new kitchen.'

'Yes,' said Barton. 'I also saw him at Ken's showroom.'

'Unlikely,' said Zander. 'Seeing as he owes two months' rent. The owner sneaked a look in his room when he was out of the house recently. It seems Lothar's taken anything of value out of his room. Bai says he thinks Lothar planned to do a runner a while ago and has deliberately left a few bits and bobs, so it looks like he's still there. He also had quite a few visitors to the house who didn't appear to be friends. He wasn't sure, but he suspected Lothar was selling stuff.'

'Drugs?'

'He thought so, but then an old watch of Bai's went missing. It's valuable and a family heirloom. CID paid them a visit but there was no proof. Lothar denied any knowledge of it. Bai also said Lothar had a habit of being out very late at night as well.'

There was a hubbub of noise as people all commented at the same time. Zander continued, and they quietened.

'When he first moved in, the landlord said Lothar told him he worked at Apex House just over the road, so we popped over to see if Lothar was in today. There are only two companies based in there. Neither of them employs, or have ever employed, anyone matching the description or going by the name of Lothar.'

85

THE HATCHET MAN

Tonight is the night I play my cards. I could hardly concentrate today. I can feel myself getting out of hand. Who knew this would be so addictive? I have the best of both worlds. I get pleasure from my actions and I also teach women a lesson. It's not all females I hate, just the ones who use you. Those who let you down and don't give you a chance. I guess that is quite a lot of them.

I've planned tonight like a military exercise. The few bumbling police on duty won't have a clue what's going on. They aren't committed like I am. I bet ninety per cent of them will have left for the day by six. They probably go home and pretend to be Magnum, P.I. in the mirror.

So, it's the last two attacks. Bang, bang. Although I might treat myself to one more in London, so all eyes turn there. Hitting London would be fabulous. I can feel my pulse quickening in my chest. God, there'll be thousands to choose from. Although it might be a little trickier. With all my lovely news coverage, surely nobody in the capital will ever put their key in their front door again without looking around first.

I walk into the back garden and urinate on the spot where I

buried my mother's personal stuff. I can't help frowning. Hindsight is a wonderful thing, but I should have considered burying her ashes here, or, better still, the body.

A dark thought trickles into my mind. What if I get caught? They'll throw away the key if I'm successful this evening. I push any fear away. The familiar warming sensation returns as I think of the final few moments when I'm raising my arm.

86

DI BARTON

Barton grinned as he watched his team arguing so vigorously. This was what being a detective was all about. The buzz in the room was an addiction just like any other. Barton would need to find something to replace it. He rapped his knuckles on the whiteboard to get their attention. Everyone quietened.

'Did Bai have any idea where he might have gone?' he asked Zander.

'No, Lothar had been acting sneaky for the last week, but he occasionally saw him in his gym gear, so he's probably still doing classes or at least working out.'

'Ring them now, please.'

Zander picked his mobile out of his pocket and pressed two buttons. He'd clearly called the Swan Hotel gym already. After a long minute, he put the phone away.

'It's ringing out. Same as before.'

'Okay, get down there. Take Malik, Leicester and Zelensky. You better take PPE as well, just in case. Be careful. Strange, report all this up the chain and to Comms. Hoffman, you help her. Let's have uniform on the lookout. I'm going to look at the case notes and check if there's anything there. I'll call North Wales Police and see if I can find someone to go and have a word with the teacher. This might blow my theories around linking Peterborough and Anglesey out of the water, but I want to check both angles.'

The team dispersed, leaving Barton to log on to his computer and locate The Hatchet Man investigation. As he expected, there were files and files, then a load more sub files. There were interview notes and photographs. It would take him days, which he didn't have, to read it all. He found a contact for a sergeant who'd done some interviews and gave the station in Wales a ring.

After a few minutes of being passed around, he was put through to her department. A man answered, then told him the officer he wanted was out of the office. Barton asked to leave a message and explained why he was calling.

'I can give the teacher a call for you,' the man replied in a soft Welsh accent. 'We all know the case.'

'That's brilliant. Let me explain my thinking.'

After he'd finished, Barton could almost hear the smile as the man replied.

'That's a nice angle. We did ask her if she had some enemies from her school days, but she's been retired fifteen years and didn't want to get anyone into trouble, which was pleasant of her but frustrating. I spoke to her myself the last time, when we were looking for links to the other cases. We had a chat about her background, but it turned out that she lived a quiet life with just a few routines. I think she wanted to put it all behind her.'

Barton suspected those very routines might have made her vulnerable.

'Ring me with anything you find, please.'

'I'll call you when I've spoken to her. This case has been infuriating from the start. Her assault, while unpleasant, seemed different from the others, so we didn't push too hard. It appears every few days of late, something else turns up, making it into a spreading nightmare, but it's complicated with so many forces involved. The Met is taking over the whole thing now.'

'Yes, but it'll take them a while to get organised, which could be the difference between life and death for one poor woman.'

'The teacher will be in this evening, don't you worry. She doesn't go out at night any more.'

Barton shook his head as he cut the call. Even those who recovered their physical health after an assault often carried deep emotional scars. He flicked through some of the interview notes, but his mind kept picturing Lothar. Had he been in Anglesey? It was an unusual place for a Swedish national to end up, and he was too young to have been taught by Torrington anyway. Barton pondered a name like Lothar Quarnstrom.

He drummed his fingers on the table. They might hear from the Irish police about Cliff Quigley fairly fast, but he had no idea how swift the Swedish would be with regard to Lothar.

He had a sneaky idea how he could move that along. Leicester had checked the PNC for Quigley or Quarnstrom and come up empty-handed, but there was also Cambridgeshire's records. When police forces investigated alleged crimes, they retained investigation records on their own database. Fingerprints had to be destroyed, but the rest sat on the system unless deletion was requested by the persons involved. Obviously this fact wasn't advertised.

Barton accessed the system. If Lothar Quarnstrom had given a statement when CID arrived a few months back after the watch had vanished, then his statement would have been scanned. Barton swiftly found it and read the document. The watch had allegedly been worth over a thousand pounds. Quarnstrom had declared that he knew nothing about its existence. Short of finding the watch in his possession, they had nothing.

What Barton was after was the identity document. There was an email address, date of birth, and a place of birth on each form. It was filled in for Lothar. He was born somewhere called Storuman. Barton brought up a page with a map for Sweden. It told him Storuman was a locality in the seat of Storuman Municipality in Västerbotten County. Barton couldn't help a bitter smile when he spotted it was in the province of Lapland.

There were around two thousand residents. He googled the police station, then called the number on their website. Barton had found in his experience that people who committed violent crimes tended to leave a trail behind them.

While the number rang, he remembered speaking to the Swedish Police a few years before. There was no language barrier for Barton, but the Swede had struggled with Barton's Peterborough accent, which was pretty unique. Peterborough being near the centre of the UK meant it had a mix of dialects, but it was influenced quite heavily by the fens. Londoners had also moved up in their thousands as overspill in the sixties when the capital became overcrowded.

He spoke slowly when the call was answered.

'Good afternoon. My name is Detective Inspector John Barton from Peterborough in England. I'm after background on a man who was born in your town a little over thirty years ago.'

'Good afternoon. We only have one detective on duty today and she's out doing rounds.' She gave Barton an email address. 'Send her the full name and date of birth of your interest. I work Reception, so I'll see that she looks out for it. Obviously, we're restricted with what we can tell you if it's not through official channels. What is it you wanted to know?'

'I guess if he's wanted for anything over there. I don't need specifics. Lothar Quarnstrom is a person of interest regarding some serious crimes.'

Barton froze as he wondered if the woman would take the bait. He heard a chuckle.

'This is a small place. The older generation, which includes me, all know of him here, but he's been gone for many years.'

'Was he violent?'

Again, there was a pause.

'Sometimes. Dishonest and unscrupulous would better describe him. He was like a cuckoo, if you get what I mean.'

'I'm not sure I do.'

'He befriended and charmed people, then moved in with them before bleeding them dry, emotionally and financially.'

'Not a nice guy, then.'

'If you need more, we'll need to see an application from your intelligence department. If you've already completed it, forward your confirmation and I should be able to find it on our system with the relevant authorisation. I'll fast-track it if it hasn't been done.'

Barton thanked her. He was putting the phone down when Zander rang his mobile.

'Barton.'

'John. Lothar wasn't at the gym, so we told them to ring us if he came in. As I pulled out of the car park exit, Lothar drove straight past and inside. I turned around when I could and drove back to the car park. His car's here outside the gym. What do you want us to do?'

'Arresting him is the traditional option.'

'Yes, very funny. What about the risk if he's homicidal and armed? It's a public place.'

Barton grinned. Zander was covering his arse, which was fair enough.

Lothar was likely to work out for a while, giving Barton time.

Confronting him on an exercise bike, or barefoot in his Speedos in the pool, were good options. Better than waiting for him to come out to his car.

'Apprehend him if he leaves, but otherwise wait outside. I'll be there in ten minutes.'

87

DI BARTON

Barton rang Control and updated them. The armed response vehicle was at another job in King's Lynn. Another unit could attend but it would be an out of county one. ETA ninety minutes. He declined and sat quietly. The team could handle Lothar.

Five minutes later, stab vest on under his suit jacket, he drove out of the compound and headed to the hotel gym. Doubts pecked at his concentration. Was he doing this because it might be his last chance to get his hands dirty?

Barton considered himself an excellent judge of character. If Lothar was a confidence trickster and a fraud, that wouldn't surprise him. The big question was whether Lothar was so angry inside that he was prepared to drive to different parts of the country and kill people.

Barton didn't think so, not without someone else being involved. That lessened the risk, and, even if he was their man, it was unlikely he'd take any weapons with him to work out. Barton parked up next to Zander's vehicle. He wound down his window, and they wound down theirs on Barton's side.

'I've been inside this gym before,' said Barton. 'It's got one exit at the front here and you can also go through to the main part of the hotel. Malik and Zelensky cover that. Zander, you and I will enter and nick him. He's a fit guy, but we aren't too past it yet. Leicester, there's also a fire exit out of the pool building. That's an option if he gives us the slip, but it's a glass door. Stand behind it and he'll think there are more of us out there.'

'There's only one person in the gym,' said Leicester. 'The windows are heavily tinted, but it could be him.'

'Good. We need to act now because he's a definite flight risk. Can anyone see any possible problems apart from the hatchet of Damocles?'

'He might have taken a weapon to the changing room, but not into the gym itself,' said Malik.

'He won't be the first to have a small knife in his pocket,' said Zelensky.

Barton nodded and acknowledged those possibilities. He and the others got out of their cars and removed their equipment from their car boots as inconspicuously as they could.

The team strode towards the building. Barton could see a bald-headed person was on a fast-moving cross-trainer while looking away from them at a raised TV. Leicester peeled off to the fire escape. The rest walked through the front door. Malik and Zelensky took up position to block the main door and the gym entrance to the hotel. Barton strode up to the counter with Zander.

A middle-aged man in a tracksuit with Mark on his name badge, looked up from a fitness magazine. He peeked at Zander, then at Barton.

'Scan your passes, please. The steam room is being cleaned at the moment, but you have full use of the sauna and the jacuzzi.'

Barton brought his index finger to his lips and showed his warrant card. He took the piece of paper out of his pocket that he'd scribbled on when he was still in his office and slid it across the desk. On it was written:

Where is Lothar?

'Gym,' replied Mark loudly.

Zander waved his baton at Mark as they left. Barton recalled the gym as a modest one situated about fifty metres along the corridor. There were some free weights and about twenty-five machines scattered around. Barton had been a member here once. He was extremely familiar with the sauna, steam room and the pool. Not so much with the gym. They reached the entrance, and Zander and Barton stood in the doorway. Lothar was now on a stair-climber, with sweat pouring down his face.

He glanced over and took less than a second to work out the threat. The weights were behind him. He jumped off his machine and picked up a medium dumb-bell in each hand before edging behind a row of exercise bikes. Barton had to marvel at his physique. Even with a yellow cropped vest and matching tight shorts, he resembled an Adonis.

'The game's up, Lothar. I'm arresting you on suspicion of murder.'

'It wasn't me.'

Lothar didn't appear shocked by the accusation.

'You can say what you like at the station. Put the weights down and step over here.'

Lothar pivoted, twisted, and flung the weight in his right hand at the tinted window next to him as an athlete would throw a discus. It bounced off, leaving a long crack. Then he sprinted to the left, rushed towards them, and threw the other weight at Zander's shins. Zander dived up and forward to dodge the missile and fell onto his hands and knees. Lothar jumped over Zander's dropping head and, with his foot on Zander's back, looked to leap to freedom.

Barton swung his left arm in a bear swipe and clotheslined him. Lothar landed on top of Zander, cracking their heads. Zander collapsed. Barton grabbed Lothar's right arm and knelt across his hips, putting all of his eighteen stone through his knees. Zander and Lothar groaned.

'Get him off,' shouted Zander.

'I'm just cuffing him,' said Barton. 'You know, Zander, you really are a talent. Rookies won't find techniques like this in the manual.'

'Get him off!'

Mark appeared next to Barton.

'Can I help?'

'Tell the officers through there to come in, please. Oh, Mark,' said Barton. 'Is there CCTV in the gym?'

'Of course.'

'Excellent. I'd love a copy.' Barton put his hands under the now cuffed Lothar's armpits and lifted him to his feet. 'As I'm sure would the rest of the department.'

Zander groaned again.

88

THE HATCHET MAN

It's a ten-minute walk to Joan's house from where the taxi driver has dropped me. I considered asking him to wait, but it's not worth the risk. I haven't bothered putting the red coat on because she'll see it through the door glass and be alarmed. Just my old Spiderman mask, in case anything goes wrong.

It's lovely and nostalgic here with the contrast between the stone houses and Christmas decorations in the evergreen trees. I find myself whistling that Jona Lewie song about the cavalry as I approach her house, while checking if anybody else is around. There's not a soul about now it's dark. Maybe I'll move to the country at some point. There's nothing keeping me where I am now probate has finally come through. I wasted too much money trying to appeal her stupid will. Who the hell gives all their cash to charity when they have children? I suppose she could have given the bungalow to the bloody hospital, too.

Joan's little cottage looks picturesque in the gathering gloom. Her tree lights twinkle at the window. She hasn't pulled the curtains, no doubt to show them off. Well, Joan, you've obviously gone to a lot of effort so, good for you. I peer through the window and chuckle. Do old folk really still watch *Bergerac*? Actually, Joan's watching it through closed eyelids.

I make my way down the side of the house. The funny thing about people who live out in villages is they think they're safe, when they're anything but. I slip the mask on. She probably left the back door open. I softly press the handle. Bollocks. It's locked. I'd rather not ring the doorbell now she's asleep.

I sneak to the rear of the property. There's a line of pot plants on a raised concrete slab. I lift each one, getting more and more annoyed when my reward is only more woodlice. I nudge a porcelain gnome figurine over with my foot. Nothing. I stamp down and it cracks pleasantly underfoot, then freeze at my stupidity.

Nobody comes. I rest my hand against the kitchen window and scan the room. The key is in the back door. I breathe through my teeth, my breath whistling. Time is ticking.

I pull the hammer out of a new Manila envelope. This will mess with their heads. Obviously not as much as it's going to mess with Joan's. I grab a damp tea towel off the washing line, wrap the metal of the weapon in it, then return to the back door, which has four small panes of glass. I hold my breath and shove the metal end of the hammer at the bottom one on the right. The panel drops out, so I'm easily able to guide my fist through, turn the key and open the door.

The tinkling as the glass hit the floor was a little loud, but not too bad. I can hear the TV from here, so I'm probably okay. I step over the broken pieces and glide to the lounge door, which is almost closed. After easing it wider, I poke my head around the edge. She's stirring. Her hand comes off her lap and picks up the remote control. I stand behind her, breathing slowly, as she rewinds the programme.

She doesn't rewind for long, so she must have just dropped off. She puts the remote back on the arm of the chair, then leans forward and calmly lifts up an open box of chocolates from a small table. I flex my right hand, then slip the towel off the hammer.

Season's greetings, Joan.

89

DI BARTON

An hour after Lothar was returned to the station, an exasperated Barton stared across the interview table at him.

'Saying nothing isn't going to help your case.'

Lothar was sulking.

'Just tell us if you were involved,' said Strange.

Lothar frowned at his solicitor.

'My client has no comment.'

'I read your statement about the missing watch. Do you have anything to say about that?'

Lothar closed his eyes, reminding Barton of Cameron's behaviour.

'Interview terminated,' said Barton. 'We'll speak again in the morning.'

Lothar's scowling eyes followed him in the same way as a child who'd had their favourite toy taken from them.

Barton returned to his desk and slumped in his seat.

'It's not him, is it?' said Strange, pulling a chair up next to him.

'I'm struggling to imagine Lothar playing draughts, never mind planning a complex series of crimes like this. He could be protecting someone, though.'

'That would complicate things.'

'Yes, it would.'

'Maybe someone paid him to do it.'

Barton growled, returned to his computer screen and checked his emails. There was one from the Swedish police. It was a brief summary of Lothar's convictions. There were so many they were grouped into categories. Shoplifting. Common assault. Theft. Fraud. Domestic abuse.

Barton smiled. There were also a couple of outstanding charges. Theft from a partner's bank account and stealing from a business. Both amounts were for ten thousand Swedish krona. Barton checked Google and discovered that it equated to less than a thousand pounds. They were from a little over two years ago. Hardly cause for deportation. Barton could use the knowledge of them to gain Lothar's trust. He was behaving like a child, and children wanted to please.

Barton rose from his seat and went down to the cells. He nodded at the custody officer and slid open the observation panel and looked in. Lothar was chewing his fingernails while pacing the room.

'Lothar. I've just been reading your Swedish criminal record. I know about your previous, and I also know that you're wanted for further offences.'

Lothar shrugged.

'I'm innocent.'

'I don't think you're involved.'

Lothar held eye contact for the first time.

'I'm not.'

'Your outstanding crimes aren't serious enough for you to be deported. Look, tell me if you've even heard of these assaults.'

Lothar grinned.

'No, I've got no idea what you're talking about. I knew there was someone dressing up as Santa in Peterborough, obviously because of Maggie, but I don't have a TV. My landlord sits in the lounge watching poker on the one in there.'

'I take it you'll be leaving Maggie alone.'

'Yes. I'll also be looking for a new place to live.'

'Shame that you weren't able to exploit that nice woman.'

Lothar gave Barton a thin smile. 'I can go now?'

Barton had a brief moment where he wished it were still the seventies and they could keep him in on a whim, but the rules had changed. If he couldn't charge him with anything, he had to let him go.

'Yes. I'll arrange it.'

He walked back past the officer who was on the phone.

'We need to let him go now,' said Barton.

The officer raised his hand, then put it over the phone handset.

'Sergeant Zander called down here, guv. He left a message for you. He said to say 999 received a call reporting a prowler near a tagged address in Marholm. He only rang thirty seconds ago. Said he'd wait upstairs.'

Barton strode back to the office. Marholm was where Joan's house was situated. That didn't sound good, although it had been a long time since he'd heard the term prowler. Must have been an older person who called 999.

Strange and Zander were still there chatting next to a map. Zander heard Barton arrive and spoke first.

'What do you want to do?'

'I assume uniform are on the way.'

Zander nodded.

'Have you rung Joan?'

'Yes, took the number off the file. No answer.'

'Take Strange to see what's happened. I hate to say it, but you might have to secure the scene.'

'I'll take Leicester as well. He's been there before. It's up to you, though, because you could need bodies here.'

Barton took three seconds to realise what he meant. If there had been an assault on Joan, Anne-Marie was next.

90

DI BARTON

When Zander, Strange and Leicester had left, Barton tried Joan's phone. After eight rings, it went to voicemail. He rang Anne-Marie next, who answered on the second ring.

'Hello.'

Barton could tell from that one word she'd been drinking.

'Hi, Anne-Marie. Just checking in. Everything good?'

'You party pooper. I'd just relaxed.'

Barton heard an enormous cheer in the background. Then Anne-Marie's voice was muffled, but still audible.

'Get that bloody Quality Street tin off your head and pick them up.'

There was another burst of laughter.

'Sorry, Inspector. How can I help you?'

Barton reckoned it'd be a brave man who went uninvited around Anne-Marie's house tonight.

'There might have been an incident elsewhere,' he said, not wanting to worry her until he knew more himself. 'Just be extra careful tonight, and tomorrow night, okay? I'll be in touch as soon as I hear anything.'

'Auntie Doreen said to tell you she's been single for years. If he shows up when she's here, he'll have an evening he'll struggle to forget.'

Barton smiled.

'Happy Christmas, Anne-Marie. I'll have a police car outside your house for some of the night, so don't be freaked if you see it. Or there'll be a van driving past over the next few days, just to be safe, okay?'

'Merry Christmas to you too.'

'Be alert.'

'Oh, we will be. Drew's put a security light up that's so bright, if he comes here, all we'll find in the morning is a burnt crisp.'

Chuckling, Barton rang Maggie. She picked up. He could hear the echo of high heels on concrete.

'Hi. Are you checking up on me?'

'Of course. Where are you?'

'Church. They do a little nativity thing each year, so I decided to give it another go.'

'Another go?'

'Yes, Pippa shouted out that there was a man in a dress two years ago. I thought she meant one of the wise men, but she pointed at the vicar when he strolled past and laughed really loud. I explained to her yesterday that people can wear whatever they like nowadays.'

'That's a lesson for us all. Are you at home tonight?'

'Yes, after here. Amazon has done the job on the present front this year. My mum will be on guard. She loves Christmas Eve. It's just the three of us, as usual, but that's okay. At least we have each other. Sorry, but I'm here now and my battery is low, so I'd better say goodbye.'

'Happy Christmas,' said Barton, feeling dreadful as to what might have happened at Joan's. 'Which church are you at?'

'St Jude's in Netherton. I used to come here as a child.'

'I know it. Keep your mobile turned on if you're able. Send me a text when you get home otherwise.'

'Will do.'

As Barton put his handset down, something jarred about recent events. He was rewinding the conversation in his head when his phone lit up. It was Leicester.

'Yes,' said Barton.

'We're at Joan's house now. I'm not quite sure what to make of it. There's an ambulance on the way, but I don't think it's needed.'

'Oh, God. Is it that bad?'

'No, the reverse. Joan's talking and really pissed off. It seems someone's smashed her back-door window. She was watching *Bergerac* so didn't hear it break. Next thing she knows, someone bashed her around the head with a hard object.'

'Great. She's okay.'

'Seems so. She doesn't want to get checked out, but we should be able to persuade her when she's calmed down. There's quite an egg on her crown. She told me that she'd rather I buggered off and looked for the little turd who nicked her car.'

'Her car's been nicked?'

'Yep. It's a cheeky theft. I assume they thought they could sneak in and swipe the keys, but they were in her handbag in the lounge. The best explanation is that they coshed Joan over the head and took them.'

Barton let out a small sigh of relief, but no detective liked coincidences. It was a different MO from The Hatchet Man's. It sounded like youngsters. Very nasty youngsters, but not murderers.

'Okay, have you called in the number plate?'

'Uniform have already done it. Obviously, this isn't anything for Major Crimes as it appears, so Zander said to leave it with them.'

'Okay, that's fine. See you back here.'

Barton put his mobile down and drummed his fingers on the desk. He still didn't like it. Was that too much bad luck for one family in too short a time? The teacher in Anglesey was hit with something blunt, although he didn't recall anything about anyone's car being stolen.

He looked around at who was in the office. Hoffman and Malik.

'Hey, lads. Want some more overtime?'

Malik always wanted more money. He'd just bought a house and wanted it decked out to the nines. Hoffman seemed to have a penchant for fast cars. Young men like them could cope with a few days of little sleep.

'Yes,' they replied with perfect synchronicity. Barton explained what he needed them to do, then went to see Cox to update her. She steepled her fingers while he explained.

'You really are blowing our department's budget just before you leave. Nice work.'

'Pleasure. I've built up around twelve thousand hours of unpaid overtime during the last fifteen years. Is now the time to mention it?'

Cox rose from her seat and walked around her desk. He'd always thought of her as a young woman, but as she stood next to him he saw crow's feet, and there were deepening lines on her forehead.

'You're free to mention it as much as you like.'

She smiled at him, and he noticed that one of her front teeth had a small chip in it. There was a single grey hair in her fringe.

'I take it there was no uniform available tonight to sit outside the properties.'

'No. Apparently, around a quarter aren't at work due to Covid. Whether they have it, or a family member is infected, I'm not sure. It's a nightmare. If we have two incidents, we'd have to prioritise. I can only assume the other forces have the same problem.'

'It's all hands to the pump. We should be thankful your lot have escaped it so far. I appreciate the effort your team have put in over the last few weeks.'

'It's been nice to get my hands dirty again before I leave.'

Cox studied him for a moment.

'Thanks for the email accepting the division role, John. I think it's the right move for you. As I said, we'll gladly have you back if you choose to return.'

'Thanks, ma'am.'

'Zander is going to step up until there's time for an assessment and interview day.'

'Was Strange interested?'

'No. I'd say her focus is elsewhere. You know how this job can churn you up.'

'I do.'

'You're also aware I'm not prone to emotional outbursts, but I did want to thank you for your years of service and commitment. What else can I say apart from that you're a true professional? Now, help them catch this murdering bastard. He's making every single copper in the country look stupid. Don't forget, I've still got a few days left to fire you.'

91

DI BARTON

Barton was leaving for the day when the call came in that they'd found Joan's car. It had been crashed into a ditch at the side of a straight road. There was nobody inside. The doors and boot had been left open. The dashboard was broken apart, Barton suspected, with the same weapon that had been used on Joan, and the satnav and CD player had been damaged in an attempt to steal them.

He walked home, glad of the drizzle in his face to keep his mind whirring. He was missing something, it was lurking somewhere in the corner of his mind. If only he could coax it out. It was dark by the time he crossed the small bridge over the river. Sadly, the team had been down here numerous times, dragging people out. There had been many more suicides over the years than murders.

He watched an old guy operating the lock by torchlight. They nodded at each other. A heron launched into flight off a bare tree nearby as he crossed the railway tracks.

He was glad the lights were on when he reached his house, giving him a welcome sight. The heat met him as he opened the front door. Holly was in the kitchen reading a book. The radio was on low, and she had a glass of red next to her. He kissed her on the top of her head, getting a hint of her favourite shampoo, then walked to the fridge.

'Get your paws out of there. I fancy Domino's.'

'That's because you're drunk.'

'I need to be, living with you lot.'

Barton gave her a little smile.

'You all right?' she asked.

'Yeah, good. It all feels like the end of an era at work, which is daft. I might only do the project for a year. Then I can take that parachuting position I'm so clearly suited for.'

Holly rose from her seat.

'When you jump out of the plane, keep away from our house, please.'

Dina Carroll's 'The Perfect Year' came on the radio. Holly put her arms around Barton's waist and started to slow-dance with him. She placed her stockinged feet on his shoes and looked up at him.

'It's time, John. I want you back.'

'Has anyone ever said you're heavy-footed?'

Holly choked.

'You've got some cheek. Talking of heavy feet, have yours been in the fridge lately near Layla's Toblerone?'

'Hmm. I don't think so.'

'Any more lies and the love gates will be closed.'

'What about the pizza gates?'

92

DI BARTON

Wednesday 23rd December

Barton woke up in his favourite armchair with the large pizza box containing one slice on his lap and a half-drunk alcohol-free lager next to him. At least he'd slept well. The times really were changing if pizza was left. He ate the slice and left the beer. His mobile phone was on the arm of the chair where he'd put it, waiting for a call from either Malik or Hoffman, who'd spent the night parked outside Maggie's and Anne-Marie's houses. Those calls had thankfully never come.

After a quick shower and a bowl of All-Bran, he began his walk to work. It was a cool morning. The water had wisps of mist on it as he walked over the footbridge. He waved at the fisherman at a bank further down the river, as he'd become accustomed to doing, despite never having talked to him. The fisherman beamed and waved back.

It was a few minutes later, when Barton was crossing the road to the station, that he realised what was bugging him. Then, he gave a little fist pump as a solution dawned on him. He supposed he had Lothar to thank for that one.

After making a quick brew, he sat down at his desk to check his hunch. He ran through the details in his head. They hadn't really missed anything. If Barton was right, this killer had been ice cool, but not quite frosty enough. He also had a feeling that he was going to get concrete proof right now. Barton turned his computer on. After entering the website and checking he was right, he blew out a deep breath of relief.

Zander was the first of his team to arrive.

'Have you won a holiday or something?' he asked.

'Why do you say that?'

'You look ever so happy. Wait, you haven't tampered with my seat, have you?'

'Nope. I'm going out in a blaze of glory. I know who it is, or at least one of the people responsible.'

Leicester was next to show. Barton beckoned him over as well.

'Who?' asked Zander.

'You remember when I said there'd be an event that triggered a shift in behaviour?'

'Yes.'

'Who had a bereavement of an important family member?'

Zander frowned. 'Not Cameron?'

'Nope.'

Barton glanced at Leicester, who looked blank. Then Leicester remembered, and it hit him like a sledgehammer.

'Shit. Bloody Ken. Really?'

'I think so. He implied that his mum's death was a long time ago, but I'm guessing it was within the last few years, and that was the start of his drastic change. I bet that's why he lives in a bungalow. There was something else to all this that wasn't adding up. I was beginning to suspect his business was failing, yet he had an over-the-top BMW. I thought that if you were short on cash, the flash car would go back pronto, unless perhaps you were thinking strangely, or murderously, in his case.'

Strange had come in by that point and had been standing next to them, listening.

She clicked her fingers.

'He gave them bonuses, too. Both Anne-Marie and Maggie were pleased with them. He even gave employee of the year, Heidi, something extra.'

'Yes, I think the business is going well, despite what he said. It's a profitable company, but he's spending it. The complaints from his suppliers are likely due to the fact that Ken is distracted by his other interests.'

'That makes sense. Fitters and suppliers would be quick to complain if they felt they were getting stiffed,' said Zander.

'Also, only clued-up people have any idea how many road cameras and CCTV there are in the UK. We're one of the most surveilled places in the world. My daughter told me that London is third on a list surrounded by Chinese cities. Yet, we never found Ken's car anywhere suspicious. Nothing was seen of it outside Peterborough, but Anne-Marie said he was often out of the office. I'm betting if we check his bank account, there'll be big cash withdrawals for trains or taxis. Neither of which are cheap, but he understood driving wasn't an option.'

Leicester nodded.

'Peterborough's always had a few shady unlicensed taxis.'

'He's the connection to Maggie and Anne-Marie. I'll bet he has a hatred towards women, probably from some perceived humiliation or repression from mother figures.'

'Like his teacher,' said Strange.

'Yes. Maybe he decided to visit and threaten her, but instead he ended up hurting her. That was the messy attack. He didn't know how to use his chosen weapon, the hammer, so she survived. Practice makes perfect. Ken, with a hatchet in his hand, will be a dangerous man. We need to think this through.'

'Exactly,' said Zander. 'We don't want any Christmas trimmings.'

Strange slapped his arm and groaned. He smiled at her.

'Ken's showroom doesn't open until ten, so he probably won't have left for work yet. I'm going to call up the ARV and meet them down there.'

'We're with you, boss,' said Zelensky.

'Actually, I'd like you to go around to Anne-Marie's. Hoffman was there all night, just in case she was next, but there was nothing to report. He clocked off at six this morning. Let's get Ken into custody before we start relaxing. After all, there could be another party involved in all of this.'

'Any idea who?'

'No, but I'm still concerned. I've spoken to Ken numerous times, and he fooled me. Does he have something else up his sleeve? I reckon he might be a pathological liar. He told me his car had been vandalised and there have been silent phone calls. It'll all be bull shit. He told me he saw a young black lad in his back garden, which would make me think of Anne-Marie's son. I won't be happy until this guy's in custody.'

Barton's email pinged at him. He opened the most recent one. After reading it, he looked up at Strange.

'Can you go and visit the DJ, Tim Tibbles, at the radio station? He's pooping himself after he got to work this morning. He's received another note. This threat said the same as Anne-Marie's. "You're next but one."'

'Bloody hell,' said Zander. 'But you know what this means. Joan was probably the first.'

Barton tipped his head back and half barked, half laughed.

'Oh my God. He almost had us again. Ken is a genius. He staged that attack on Joan to make it look like it was kids, so we'd be confused, and our resources stretched. He even removed the radio from the car before he crashed it, although I've just realised, they said it was on an open stretch of road. How often are we out-driven by Peterborough's joyriders? They don't crash on straight roads.'

'Sneaky,' said Strange with a touch of admiration.

'Exactly,' said Barton. 'Zander, Ken Wade reported a crime years ago when someone smashed a window at his showroom. His statement is on our county's crime-recording system and holds some personal identification questions. You can use my computer to check.'

Zander took his seat and soon had it on his screen.

'What's Ken's place of birth?' asked Barton.

'Anglesey.'

93

DI BARTON

With excellent timing, a few minutes later, Barton received an email from Anglesey Police saying they'd spoken to the retired teacher who'd been assaulted and she'd remembered a very odd boy called Ken who used to be in her class.

An hour later, Barton and Leicester were parked up fifty metres from Ken's bungalow. His car was sitting on the drive. The ARV crew had just turned up. Barton was pleased to see it was Jules and Al, who he'd worked with many times over the years. Like him, they were both in the twilights of their active careers but were more than capable.

Barton ran through the pertinent case details with them.

'So, he could come out swinging,' stated Jules.

'Maybe, but I would say not. He's very bright. I doubt he'll want to give us a chance to shoot him. He probably thinks he can talk his way out of it. At this point, he won't know we're onto him either. Actually, that might be the best way to play this.'

'Go on,' said Al.

'If I turn up with Leicester, it'll look like we're just bothering him. He might even believe we're there to help him, which he'd most likely get off on. If you two sneak over the neighbour's fence, you can grab him the moment he opens the door.'

'Unless he opens up and throws his axe at you.'

'That's why I'm wearing a stab vest.'

'And if he throws it at your head?'

'Good point. I don't think he'd hurt a man. That might sound weird, but I reckon his rage is focused on women, and so far all of his attacks have been hit and runs from behind.'

'How about you walk up the drive and knock, then step out of the way? We'll take it from there.'

'That sounds much safer.'

'Yes, for you,' said Jules with a smile. 'We'll sneak across the lawn as opposed to leaping over the fence. We could try your now infamous fence-jumping technique from the Cold Killer case.'

'It's not my fault. I'm like an elephant. I need to keep one foot down all the time, which isn't great for jumping.'

Jules laughed.

'You know what? We'll be sad to see you go.'

'Who told you I was leaving?'

'Everyone knows. It's a hot topic when one of the big beasts moves on.'

'Charming. I'm moving to HQ, not the enchanted misty lands.'

'Well, me and Al wanted to say we haven't minded working with you. Isn't that right, Al?'

'Yep, you've been okay, John. Not at all unreasonable. I think you brought us sausage rolls once. We got you this as a thank you for your slightly above average performance.'

Al passed him an envelope. Barton opened it. The front of the card had a picture of a whiskery pig with a pipe in his mouth. There was a five-pound voucher for McDonald's inside it. They hadn't bothered writing a message.

'This is too much, guys,' said Barton.

Al slapped him on the back. 'We know.'

Ninety seconds later, Barton had knocked on the front door, then stepped out of sight. Barton's ears strained for a sign that someone was coming. There was nothing. Barton and Leicester returned to their car to let the riflemen do their jobs. Jules and Al went down the side passage and vanished from view. Shortly afterwards, they reappeared.

'Looks empty and it's all locked up,' said Al. 'Are we going in?'

'Yes.'

Barton watched again as they disappeared. There was the sound of broken glass, followed by the occasional shout of 'Clear!' Five minutes later, Jules came back out, shaking his head.

'We've done a preliminary sweep. If he's there, he's well hidden or in the loft. Is that likely?'

Barton shook his head.

'No, he didn't know we were coming. Bollocks. He is sneaky, though. I hate to say this, boys, but we'll need to do a full search, loft and all. I wouldn't put it past him to have some kind of hidden room, even if it was his mum's bungalow.'

'You might want to come around the back and check out the tree.'

Barton followed them to the rear of the property, then looked at the fir tree that Jules was pointing at. There had to be a thousand chop marks in the bark. Barton cursed under his breath and turned back to stare at the house.

Where are you, Ken?

94

THE HATCHET MAN

I can just make out Inspector Barton and the men in black jumpsuits as they head to the rear of my property. Christ. That was close.

'Phew!'

'What was that, Ken?'

'I was just looking out the window, Bert. Looks like rain. I was fortunate to come over when I did. Maybe I will have that cup of tea after all.'

Bert brightens considerably.

'Okay, that's great. I'll get the Christmas biscuits out. I got the same ones you said you liked last year from Aldi.'

'The Belgian cookies?'

'Yes, that's them. Shall I bring the whole tin out, or put a few on a plate?'

I glance through the net curtains down the road and see another police vehicle arrive.

'The whole lot. It is Christmas after all, and I'm not in any rush.'

'Brilliant.'

'I've found it's best to enjoy your pleasures while you can. Who knows what the future might bring?'

Bert doesn't reply. He's still in the room, but he hasn't heard what I just said.

'Is something bothering you?' I ask.

Bert wrings his hands in front of me, stepping from foot to foot. I know what he's going to ask, but I might as well let him suffer. He's a merry widower. Well, more drunk than merry. His wife died years ago, and he's never got over it. My mum used to invite him over for Christmas and Boxing Day. The pair of them would get hammered on the sherry, then spend all three courses waxing lyrical about what a bunch of wankers my generation were. I'd watch the Queen's speech on my own, while they sat side by side in a dense and spreading fog caused by overcooked Brussels sprouts.

Last Christmas, it was just the two of us. It was okay, to be fair. We slagged off the generations underneath me instead. I didn't even mind his sleep farting. It was kind of nostalgic.

'Have you made any plans for this year?' he asks.

'Yes, I've been invited to lunch with royalty.'

His crumpled little face falls. It appears my dark side has no end to it, although it's the truth judging by what's happening at my place. I'll likely be pouring the gravy under Her Majesty's watchful gaze.

'Maybe you'll find time for a drink or two at some point,' he asks with hope in his eyes.

'Only joking. I thought we'd do it at yours this year. I'm worried about receiving unwelcome guests at mine.'

'That's an excellent idea. I can nip to the shops and get most things. They're bound to have a chicken at least. You always joke that turkey tastes like old trainers.'

Bert is positively sprightly as he returns to his kitchen. My shoulders slump. I haven't got the cash or the energy to go on the run. It seems, appropriately, that my goose is cooked. I spare a thought for work and decide I don't care. Nothing matters much when you're on your own. My brother is a joint shareholder, so he can keep the business going, assuming it survives the loss of Maggie.

I think about her all the time. She's such a great woman. I spent hours watching her on the CCTV. The way she laughed at the customers' ropey jokes. Her giggle when they flirted with her. When she thought nobody was looking and adjusted her clothing. Although, I realised it was her voice more than anything that I enjoyed. It's like crystal. I can feel every word. That was why I installed the listening devices. Now that really was bittersweet, hearing men crack on to her, but she kept her distance. She was a true professional.

But then I heard her and Anne-Marie talking about the job offer at B&Q. Maggie was going to leave me, just like all the rest. She doesn't care about my feelings. Her career at Ken's Kitchens and Bathrooms is over, but not in the way she planned. I'll have the last say. That's the type of man I've become. More should pay the same price, but I've run out of time.

I hear Bert whistling. My face is so scrunched up in concentration that I have to rub it with my hands to change the expression. Otherwise, Bert will think a gargoyle has come around for tea.

The grand prize is still in my grasp, though. I'll do it tonight. With this cloud cover, it should be a dark night. Perhaps I can even stay here with Bert for a couple of nights. Enjoy a final pleasant Christmas. If he notices the police vans, which is unlikely with his eyesight, I'll tell him that I've been burgled, and need to sleep in his spare room.

It's funny to think this will be my last Christmas as a free man.

Ah, well. I suppose that'll teach me to be a murdering bastard. Bloody Barton must have solved it. I should have given him more credit. Still, he can't stop what I'm about to do. They'll send me to jail for the rest of my life, anyway. Another death won't give me more time.

I slip my large coat off and place it on the back of a chair. Lucky it was cold outside, or I might not have put that on. At least I don't need to return to my house to get the most important item.

It dawns on me that the police will knock on the neighbours' doors at some point. Bert's bungalow is a long way from mine, but I can't risk staying here for long.

'Bert. I'm going to nip out in a bit. Can I borrow your hat for the weather? I'll take your walking stick too, if that's okay?'

'No problem, my friend. Are we doing presents this year? Perhaps just a little something to open.'

'Of course. Christmas is all about surprises.'

95

DI BARTON

Barton glanced at his watch. He looked out of the window. The street lamps were on, as were the lights in the office windows opposite. Dusk had rapidly turned to dark. He ran his hand over his head and loosened the knot of his tie. Was there anything else he could do? Christmas was all about anticipation, but not this kind.

Leicester had agreed to be on duty this evening, so Barton sent him home at lunch to catch some sleep. His shift would start at seven, and he'd text Barton to confirm.

There had been no sign of Ken, despite every officer in the city looking for him, not to mention the council's CCTV controllers. Ken's face was on most news channels, and his description broadcast on every radio channel, PCR included. Malik and Hoffman were outside Ken's house, but he hadn't returned. Al and Jules were going to be on call tonight. Another ARV was currently parked at the front of Anne-Marie's house. Joan had been kept in hospital with a suspected concussion, so she was safe.

Tim Tibbles had got home from work that afternoon to find a walking stick thrust through his letter box. He'd taken that as confirmation his death was imminent. Zander drove to his house, but Tibbles had already left. When Zander rang him, he refused to give his location, and hinted that Zander was part of a conspiracy to send him loopy.

Barton was imagining heavy clouds outside when his desk phone rang. An operator told him that Ken Wade's brother was on the phone. Barton said to put him through.

'Detective Inspector Barton speaking.'

'Hi, my name's Eric Wade. I'm Ken's brother.'

'Excellent. Thanks for ringing in. How are you?'

'Concerned about Ken.'

'Yes, us too. What can you tell me about him?'

'Not much about his current state. I've barely seen him since his wedding, which was well over twenty years ago, and I'm only down the road in Thrapston.'

'Okay. We suspected he was a loner. He mentioned that he was widowed.'

Barton thought for a moment the connection had gone.

'Eric?'

'Yes, sorry. I'm stunned, but not completely surprised. He wasn't widowed. His wife is called Inga and, as far as I know, she's alive and thriving in Hertfordshire. She did a flit one night a long time ago. I got on well with her. We used to chat occasionally. I think she felt obliged to explain why she left afterwards by email with a bit too much detail.'

'Do you mind telling me what that detail was?'

'Incredibly, her wanting a family was a cause of some issues. Ken worshipped her, but struggled to perform. She fell in love with him because he worshipped her, but she began to realise it wasn't a healthy kind of loving. As the months went by, he unravelled rapidly, then she found out she was pregnant.'

'No way.'

'Yes, she didn't want him anywhere near her child, so she

vanished. She apologised for leaving me to deal with him. She blamed his extreme behaviour.'

'Extreme in what way?'

'I can't remember. Look, neither me nor Ken got much of an education, but I can probably blame him for that. The best way to describe him is stalkerish, if that's a thing. He was obsessive about Inga. He'd follow her to work, check her post, want to be with her all day, every day. He used to write letters to her all the time, take photos of her and videos. She couldn't stand it. She was a nice girl, though. Put up with it for years.'

'Did he ever hit her?'

'A few times. She rang me once and asked if he had mental health problems in the past. I told her what happened at school. Maybe I shouldn't have.'

'Was it to do with a teacher called Joslyn Torrington?'

'Yeah, that's right. Ken attaches himself to people. He needs them to want him. Our parents were selfish and should never have had kids. We were pretty feral. I just got on with it, but Ken was always hanging around my mum, trying to get her attention. He probably wanted some love. I knew not to bother. As he got older, she beat him with whatever was to hand, and told him to piss off out of the house. He had the odd bruise. My dad pushed him about as well.'

'Were your parents more than physical?' asked Barton.

'We got no more than most kids back then. There was nothing depraved going on. Trust me, Ken was really irritating. I used to thump him every now and again. He drove me mad over the years, following me around, and as for his barefaced lying, well, let's not go there. I always felt guilty, though, after I whacked him. It was a bit like kicking a puppy. That was why I part-funded his shop when he started Ken's Kitchens and Bathrooms.'

'Does he pay you a percentage of the profits?'

'No, we're fifty-fifty on ownership. I only put in six thousand pounds that I received from a whiplash claim. He said that when we sold the business, we'd be rich. I wanted to do a nice thing for him, but keep him at arm's length. I think he keeps away from me because he's worried about me getting involved or wanting my cash back. In a way, it was money well spent. My life's been much simpler without him in it.'

Barton remembered something Ken had said.

'Did you ever have acid poured over your Volvo?'

'I've never owned a Volvo.'

'Another car?'

'No, of course not. Ah, you've heard a few lies from Ken as well.'

'It seems so. How did your family end up moving from Anglesey to Peterborough?'

'The short story is I kicked him hard once after he blamed me for breaking the window with a ball when he'd done it. I left a mark, which got noticed by his form teacher, that Mrs Torrington. She'd kind of been looking out for him, not realising she was fulfilling a role that my parents weren't interested in. Ken told her our father was responsible for the bruise. There was a load of shit because of it. The social was involved. Our dad cleared off. My mum blamed Ken. Then Ken began to behave oddly to Mrs Torrington. I guess he ended up completely obsessed with her, too.'

'What did he do?'

'The usual. Bombarded her with letters and presents, which were apparently quite sweet, but they twisted into stuff about living with her and drawings of them together. He was only thirteen. The school called my mum in and she'd had enough. My old man had been a self-employed engineer who was in and out of jobs, but it paid well. My mother was one of those who felt that once she got married, she didn't need to work any more. My dad didn't leave a forwarding address or any dough, so we were soon miles behind on the rent.'

'And that's when you moved here?'

'Yeah, to my grandma's bungalow in Portman Close. I was nearly fifteen. I failed all my exams, left home, never went back. We kept in touch for a while, but my mum didn't give a shit. Never heard from Dad again. Ken put Mum on a pedestal as a struggling mother who was doing her best, but she was a total bitch. She threw him out when Grandma died and the property became hers. Ken got the arse when I said he couldn't come and stay with me. We stopped communicating except for the odd text and my yearly visit to see Mum, until I stopped them as well. I thought he was lying when he told me a girl called Inga had agreed to marry him. Women were always wary of him because he was too keen.'

'Did you go to the wedding?'

'Yep, best man. It was a sad affair. I took my girlfriend. An uncle and aunt came, but apart from my mum, who was already getting scatty and poorly, that was it for Ken's side.'

'Was that when you stopped speaking to them?'

There was another quiet spell.

'It wasn't an active decision, more a drift apart. I guess it was just easier not having anything to do with him or my mum. Felt like a waste of time and energy when you got so little back. Months became years, years came to all this. Maybe I could have helped.'

'Did you come to your mum's funeral?'

'Yes, there was only me and him at the crematorium, but he went over the top on the flowers. He even insisted on doing a long speech when I was the only one in the congregation. The guy doing the ceremony was freaked. I asked Ken if he wanted a beer after, but it was as though he had shell shock. I should have noticed he was struggling. He kept saying, "They all leave me."'

'No, this isn't your fault. Last few questions. Any thought to where he might be?'

'No, I've got no idea. Be careful if he is responsible for this. Ken might be mad, but he's not daft. He's crafty, like when he told the school my parents hurt him. That wasn't said on a whim. He'd have considered all the angles. If people crossed Ken when he was young, he'd get them back in the way which they couldn't prove it was him. They'd suspect, but that was it. He soon got a reputation as someone not to mess with because your luck changed.'

'Was he dangerously violent in any way?'

'Sometimes when he was pushed, he'd be vicious. To be fair to him, he's had plenty of rejection. I can see how that would make you unstable. People seem to tolerate a lot, then one day, they've had enough. Love, or maybe adoration, turns to hate. I've seen it myself. When you get hurt, you want revenge.'

Barton had seen plenty of that over the years.

'One thing I will say is that Ken will have attached himself to someone else after Mum died. It's what he does. They'll be his focus.'

'Is he liable to hurt that person?'

'No, I don't think so. Not unless they leave him.'

'Christ, what would he do if he found out he had a child?'

The line was quiet for a few seconds. 'Maybe that's what this is all about.'

Barton finished the call with a better understanding of Ken, but was no closer to finding him.

'Now who would Ken be most angry with,' said Barton out loud to himself. He typed Inga Wade into the PNC. There was an assault four years ago against an Inga Wade in Stevenage. The victim was beaten with a brick. He had a quick flick through the notes and saw that a career criminal had admitted to the crime and had received two years. It was tempting to ignore it, but he'd have to ring Herts Police and tell them. The system only worked if it was fair.

Barton left the office and walked outside into a heavy shower. He'd been hoping for a refreshing walk home, but he wasn't able to concentrate with raindrops bouncing off his bald head. He was plodding along the street when a car pulled up next to him. Custody Sergeant Donald lowered his window.

'Fancy a lift or are you practising for when you swim the Channel?'

Barton bent down.

'It depends on how much you're going to charge me.'

'It's a freebie, seeing as you're off.'

Barton grumbled as he walked around the Honda Civic and got in.

'How did you know?' he asked.

'Someone begged me to write something rude in your leaving card.'

'You're a class act, Donald.'

Donald grinned and pulled away. Barton smiled as the wipers swished rhythmically in front of him. He'd even miss this grizzled, grumpy sod.

Running Thorpe Wood's custody unit was one of the hardest jobs in the station. The process of booking someone in was a flash-point. Many wrongly believed it was their last chance to break for freedom. Not only that, but the health and safety of every single person in the custody suite was Donald's responsibility the moment he signed for them. He would be judged on any suicide attempts. Donald seemed to take it in his stride despite all that pressure. Barton could tolerate a bit of rudeness in exchange if that was how he handled it.

Donald knew the way, and soon parked up outside Barton's house.

'Nasty case to finish,' he said. 'It really is a nightmare before Christmas if you've got some loon running around with an axe. What do you reckon? Love or money?'

'It's not money.'

'We hurt the ones we love.' He paused with a sad smile on his face. 'Merry Christmas, John.'

Barton walked through the front door with those words ringing in his head.

96

DI BARTON

All the children were at home and Holly surprised him with a late family dinner, so they could all eat together. Chips, egg and ham. What Holly called an easy tea. It was just what he needed. As always, the older kids cleared off before the clearing up.

'Dad. Can you watch *Star Wars* with me?' asked Luke.

'Which one?'

'All of them.'

Barton chuckled.

'How about the new episode of *The Mandalorian*?'

Luke cheered and ran from the room to load up the Disney Plus channel. Holly smiled at Barton as she dried a plate.

'You like that show more than he does.'

'I know. I'll have to watch it on my own later because he's going to talk through every second.'

'You wouldn't have it any other way.'

She whipped him on the arse with the damp towel as he left the room. Luke and he watched the episode, which Luke talked through, then got stuck into a box of Maltesers that a neighbour had given him for the kids. Luke wanted *The Lion King* next. Barton heard nothing of that either, as Luke bombarded him with questions about whether a lion could beat up a giraffe.

Barton took Luke up to bed just before eight.

'Night, Dad. Two sleeps until Christmas.'

'Yep.'

'Is Father Christmas your size?'

'No, much fatter.'

Luke's eyes widened. Cheeky little git, thought Barton.

'You told me he uses magic to get down our chimney. What type of magic is it?'

'It's the most powerful magic of all.'

Luke's eyes bulged.

'What is it?'

'Christmas magic.'

Luke stared hard at him for a moment.

'Okay. I don't want a story. I'm too tired.'

Luke rolled over and closed his eyes. Gotta love little boys, thought Barton. He was halfway down the stairs when Leicester rang him.

'Evening, boss. I'm up and at 'em. Anything you need me to do, or should I just hang around at home in case I'm called? I'll go for a drive later past all the places of interest.'

Barton's brain had been whirring along in the background ever since he'd spoken to Ken's brother about attaching himself to women. Sergeant Donald had also made a comment about people hurting the ones they love. Barton remembered the job offer Maggie received from B&Q. It appeared she was going to be another to leave Ken.

'Maggie's not safe,' he said to Leicester slowly.

'Why? She's got decent security. Don't tell me she got a note saying she's next?'

'No. The fact she hasn't received a message is why. I keep

judging Ken on past cases, but the guy is much smarter than your average crim. If you were bright, would you say where you were going to be?'

'No. So you think the notes are another decoy?'

'Yes. A double decoy. I spoke to Ken's brother today. Ken's only attacked women, so this Tibbles thing is just something else to confuse us. Caring for his mother was probably the only thing keeping Ken rational. Maggie might be his prize because he loves her. Or perhaps it's now hate. Either emotion could trigger his wrath.'

Leicester frowned.

'That makes sense. She's nice enough to drive a man to distraction.'

Barton smiled.

'Exactly. And she's struggling with raising a child with special needs on her own. She's vulnerable. I'm not sure if Anne-Marie's in any danger. Glenn attacked her because he wanted his mum to get promoted. Anne-Marie doesn't fit Ken's type at all. She's feisty, strong and a long way from helpless. Not only that, but she's happily married and resides in a busy house.'

'Whereas Maggie lives on her own.'

'Exactly.'

Another thought popped into Barton's head.

'My son just said something to me that triggered my curious mind. He asked how Santa would get into our house.'

'Did you say chimney or magic?'

'Powerful Christmas magic. Now, Joan was attacked, but not killed. Why?'

Leicester tutted.

'To distract us from Maggie. To make us think that Anne-Marie was next. Then Tibbles gets a letter to say he's next, which takes our investigation further from Maggie as the next victim.'

'Excellent, but Ken, even though he might not look it, is a criminal mastermind. What else did he gain from taking the vehicle, although he could have found them in the cottage while Joan was stunned?'

Leicester remained silent. Barton pulled his shoes on while he waited.

'Sorry, I don't know.'

'I'd check the compound to be sure if it was daytime, but that'll have to wait until the morning. What do you keep with your car keys?'

Leicester replied immediately.

'Your house keys.'

'Yes. Joan has her own set for Maggie's property. The securest door in the world is worthless if an intruder has the key.'

'Bloody hell. Ken stole her vehicle, crashed it, but didn't leave the keys at the scene.'

'That's my guess. Although he may have slipped the non-car keys off the ring or fob so we wouldn't have noticed at first, seeing as he's that sharp. There's another point to consider. If he's desperate to get in, he could simply drive a car through the lounge wall and window. I've seen it done. He must know the game's up now. It's over. He has one last roll of the dice. Maybe tonight, maybe tomorrow. It's very hard to go on the run even if you're a wealthy mafia boss, and from what I gathered from being with him, he probably doesn't have any friends or family he can stay with.'

'Do you want me to drive around to Maggie's now? I don't mind parking there all night.'

'Look, I've got to walk the dog. I'll take him down there. It's not too late. Maggie might have some thoughts, and she'll be able to tell me if her mum has a key. I'll speak to Control and give you a call afterwards.'

'Okay. Talk soon.'

Barton disconnected the call and tugged his coat on. Gizmo was already waiting at the front door, tail wagging.

'Come on, boy,' said Barton. 'There's a damsel in distress. We're all that's standing in the way of mortal danger.'

Gizmo paused, looked up out of the corner of his eye, then wagged his tail ferociously.

Barton left his house and strolled down the road towards Maggie's place with the conversation he'd just had with Leicester replaying in his head. He didn't even notice the cool breeze and icy rain. By the time he'd reached Orton Longueville church, which was halfway there, Gizmo and he were running.

97

THE HATCHET MAN

Even in this sleeting rain, I find myself enjoying the walk towards Maggie's. I still have Bert's flat cap pulled low, but I can't imagine anyone stopping me in the street. I'm almost there now, anyway. Bert kindly lent me forty pounds until I could make it to a bank. I had to go to a hardware store on Lincoln Road where there was a big mark-up. Annoyingly, I had to buy the cheapest tool they had because I needed good pliers too. The hatchet is sharp enough, but the handle is flimsy. I might only get one attempt, whether I like it or not.

I turn into St Catherine's Lane and stride straight past her house to the end. Nobody else is out in this weather, so I walk back. Standing outside, I roll my shoulders. The Spiderman mask is in my pocket. Funnily enough, Judith bought it for me as a joke. Why don't I want her? I glance at the mask, then throw it in the bushes.

A car accelerates by close to the pavement and sprays my lower legs with surface water. I'm gasping when I have a sudden moment of realisation. That's it. That's what's wrong with me. I've ruined my entire life by wanting people who don't want me. Perhaps I should have gone around Judith's house one of those many times she asked. We work well together. Although, I suppose she'd have wanted sex and I've rarely been able to manage that.

I gently touch the sharpened edge of the hatchet and smile.

I can't see any point in delaying, so I grab Joan's keys out of my pocket. It can only be one of two. If the keys don't work, I'll use the axe on the back door, like in *The Shining*.

It's fair to assume that she'll have the phone close to hand to call 999, but I'll only need a few minutes. Let's hope the child is already in bed. We don't want Pippa getting in the way. It's such a pity. I'd have been a great stepdad to her.

There's a new flashing box on the wall, which must be an alarm, but that's fine. They deter burglars, not killers.

I push the first key at the lock, but it's clearly the wrong size and shape. The second one slips in smoothly. The pins click quietly as I twist the key to the right. I press the handle down and nudge the door back until it touches a chain. The hallway is dark, but I think I can hear breathing. My new pliers make short work of the thin metal.

There's a tapping sound in the gloom, which rises in a crescendo as I step in. With the door fully open, the security light from outside illuminates the hallway. What the hell is a greyhound doing in here?

98

DI BARTON

Barton had settled himself on the sofa and was looking forward to a slice of Maggie's yule log when he heard Gizmo's tail hitting the wall in the hallway. He'd been left there, so he didn't climb on Maggie's sofa. Barton hoped she knew not to give Gizmo any cake because of the chocolate. He was pulling himself to his feet when the door next to him opened and Maggie came in with a tray. Barton looked at her, then at the far door on the other side of the room.

He turned back to Maggie.

'I think Pippa might have come downstairs,' he said under his breath.

Her smile vanished in an instant. She whispered the words, but they came out loud.

'I just went upstairs. She's out for the count.'

'Then there's someone in your hall.'

Maggie's face lit up with horror. The cups rattled on her tray. Barton had explained his concerns to Maggie when he'd arrived, but she hadn't been convinced. She didn't think Ken was an evil person. Her eyes looked upwards at the ceiling.

'No. He'll look for you in here first because of the sound,' he said quietly, pointing at the TV which had *The Great Escape* on. 'Creep to the kitchen and ring the police. As soon as you hear shouting in here, race along the hall and run upstairs. Either go in the bathroom and lock it, or go in Pippa's room and drag a wardrobe or drawers in front of the door. Sit on it, and hold the door handle.'

Maggie blinked rapidly. Barton reached out and squeezed her shoulder.

'Hold that door to your last gasp, Maggie. Your lives may depend on it. Now, focus,' he urged. 'Keep it together for your daughter.'

Maggie gulped down a deep breath and began to withdraw from the room. Barton took his cup of tea and the saucer of cake off the tray before she was out of reach. He heard a dull thud and the yelp of his dog. Barton clenched his teeth, his knuckles white on the crockery. The door slowly swung open. Gizmo raced in and cowered on the other side of the sofa. Barton knew he should have got a Rottweiler, or at least a dog that barked.

'Ah,' said Ken, walking through the doorway. 'It's *your* hound, Inspector. I'm not a dog man myself. More a people person.'

'Touch my dog again, and I'll touch you.'

Ken's arm appeared from behind his back. The flashing lights from the tree reflected off the wicked steel blade as Ken moved it from side to side. He bared his teeth as he focused.

'Give it up, Ken!' shouted Barton. 'It's over. Nobody else needs to die.'

'Where's Maggie?' snarled Ken.

'Out,' said Barton. 'Gizmo and me are babysitting.'

A clatter from the kitchen behind him, which sounded like a dropped tray, shattered that illusion. Ken raised an eyebrow, then stepped towards him.

'Get out of my way, Barton. Move!'

'That's enough. I know you don't want to hurt me. I have children who count on me.' Barton searched his mind for a method of getting through to Ken, who had an almost lustful look on his face. 'You hurt women, not men.'

'Ooh, you're good,' said Ken. '*And* you're right. I don't wish to hurt you, but I do want to kill Maggie, and, unfortunately for you, I want that very much. Which means if you have to die to make that happen, so be it.'

Ken strode forward, brandishing the axe. Barton gulped, threw the tea and cake at Ken, then rapidly backed out of the lounge into the dining room behind him. He bumped into the table, then shuffled around it and made his way into the kitchen. He was relieved to see Maggie wasn't still in there. As Ken followed him towards the kitchen, he struck the dining table with his hatchet. He had to pause to yank the blade out of the wood.

Barton looked around the room. He began pulling all the drawers open in desperation, knowing that he was unlikely to find anything more deadly than Ken's weapon. Ken stopped two metres away from him. Barton held the flimsy carving knife that he'd found out in front of him.

'Step outside,' said Ken. 'I won't mention it.' He smiled, but the top half of his face didn't move. 'Maggie won't tell anyone; I'll make sure of that. Then I'll hand myself in afterwards. You've got me. Even I can't talk myself out of this.'

There was a thump upstairs. Maggie's anguished roars and screams of desperate effort reverberated around the house. Barton decided to try and delay so Maggie could get her defences up and hopefully the police shooters would arrive.

'Why, Ken? Why kill innocent women? Were you lonely after your mother died?'

Ken tipped his head back and roared with laughter.

'You think my mother's death set me off?'

'Didn't it?'

'Do you have children, Inspector?'

'I do.'

'Must be a nice feeling.'

'It is.'

'Well, let me tell you a story.'

99

THE HATCHET MAN

Four and a half years ago

I stare at Inga's Facebook page. It's a strange thing to finally have tracked her down after all these years of looking. I try not to think of the money I wasted on private detectives when she first left. Must have been thousands and thousands. The closest one got was that she'd entered a refuge for battered women in Hertfordshire, but the trail went cold. Eventually I gave up.

It wasn't until one of the women at work told me how great Facebook was for finding old school friends that I thought to give it a go. Inga Wade was nowhere to be seen, though. She never divorced me, so we've been married all this time. I suspect she never wanted to risk my finding out where she lived.

She used her full German first names without a surname. Ingrid Petra. My stomach rolls at the profile picture. It's some arsehole in a military uniform and her in a ball gown. I'm not sure if they're fancy-dress outfits or real. They both look very pleased with themselves and each other. Bastards!

I don't seem to be able to see any other pictures due to whatever security she has on her profile, but he's commented on the photo. I click his name. Lucas Kohler. His profile is slightly more open. I can't befriend him, but I could message him if I wanted to. He has about ten different profile pictures, which I'm able to see.

Great. He looks the real action man with his mountaineering poses and marathon gear. I suppose it would have been too much to expect her to have been single for all this time. There's a photograph of him next to a flash motor. I can read the registration. Bingo. You're mine, or at least you will be when I get an investigator to trace that car. My fingers tingle at the thought of seeing her again.

There's a final photo of them. It's a close-up of them and a much younger woman. It's so close, I can see their eyes. I just manage to turn my head to one side to stop the projectile vomit covering my computer. It's not a woman. It's a girl, and when I zoom right in, closer and closer, I can finally see that she has the same hereditary eye condition that I have, which causes the outer ring of the iris to be a different colour from the rest. Hers are green and brown.

I frantically race back through the pictures, but it's the only one she's in. The caption under it says, 'Happy eighteenth birthday, Amelie'. Jesus Christ. When Inga left me eighteen years ago, she was pregnant with my baby. She's hidden her away from me all this time. I break out into a hot sweat, bile burning in my throat. I roar the words out loud as I think them.

'I'm going to fucking kill her.'

100

DI BARTON

Barton listened to Ken's minute-long speech with growing horror. No wonder Ken had gone off the deep end. Barton had already been worried, but now he feared for his life. Where the hell were the others? His mind raced for solutions, but the detective part of it began to look into the puzzle.

'Ken, I know you assaulted Inga and someone else got the blame, but you didn't kill her. How come after what she did to you? You've killed others who've done nothing as bad.'

Ken tried to smile, but it came out more of a snarl.

'I couldn't kill her, could I? The PI found their address and I began to watch her. I would sit outside their house and imagine them playing happy families inside. One day, I followed her to town and watched her buying some boots for her daughter, and I lost all control. She'd taken everything from me. I picked up a brick and smashed it around her head. I ran away, expecting an imminent visit from the police, but they never came.'

'Because you took her belongings and hid them amongst a homeless person's belongings, except for a ring.'

'Yes,' said Ken, as he showed Barton his little finger. Ken rotated the ring he'd stolen that day off Inga. 'I gave her this ring shortly after we met. She loved it so much, but it was only on loan. Clever, eh? It felt good to get revenge. It felt great to hit back, but I had Mum to look after. When she was gone, I felt liberated. I planned to pulverise my old teacher but I got disturbed. It was too risky to return, so I thought I'd leave a trail leading to Stevenage, not London, as you idiots seem to think. I was going to finish Inga off, but I can't, can I?'

'Why not?'

'Because what will happen to my daughter? She'd be without a mother. I couldn't do that to my daughter. That is true love, isn't it? That I would sacrifice my own happiness for the sake of my daughter's.'

Barton wasn't sure what to say to that. If it was true love, it was an unusual version of it.

'My mother's death released in me a terrible rage, a seething fury, that struck down those awful women.' Ken finally did smile. 'Funny thing is, I really enjoyed it.'

Ken seemed to remember where he was all of a sudden and his eyes came back into focus. Barton crouched, even though nerves weakened his knees. With a few deep breaths, he composed himself. He was going to charge Ken the moment he raised his weapon. He had to hope that his legs were quicker than Ken's arm.

Ken swung the hatchet in a figure of eight with a calm confidence, as though it were a part of his body. Barton's hope evaporated. Ken leapt forward, swinging sideways so fast that Barton didn't even move. There was the sound of cutting fabric. Barton looked down at his ruined coat. He gasped as the sharp pain registered across his stomach. He retreated on unsteady legs as warm liquid leaked from his belly button, but his back soon hit the door.

After a pointless struggle with the handle, Barton turned towards the psychopath behind him. Ken had his hatchet raised high, his expression victorious.

101

THE HATCHET MAN

I feel a rush of affection as the door to the hall begins to open. It'll be wonderful to see Maggie again, and it's nice of her to save me a trip upstairs. A rapid blow for her, then a coup de grâce for Barton. I might even have time to get away before the police arrive.

A young-looking ginger-haired lad strides into the room. I think he's one of Barton's detectives. He certainly has a serious look on his face. I rush over to catch him by surprise. Snarling, I strike with the technique I've spent hours practising – the overhead chop. My aim is true and the blade flashes towards his neck. At the last moment, he sidesteps out of the way. As my arm continues its arc, I receive a stinging jab into my ribs.

I jump to the side, grimacing with agony, half winded. He appears to be standing on his tiptoes. I flash the hatchet sideways with the same technique that bloodied Barton. The lad jumps backwards, but moves quickly forward as my weapon passes by. I'm completely exposed. He spins, my vision blurs, a jarring crack, then white light.

102

DI BARTON

Barton, who was still pressed against the door, watched as Leicester's kick almost took Ken's head off. Ken appeared to be horizontal in mid-air for a moment, then he hit the floor, back first. His arms, legs, and head thumped simultaneously on the tiles. Ken lay still, sparked out. Barton glanced over at Leicester and nodded.

'You beat me to it. Check they're fine upstairs.'

Barton winced slightly as he stood up straight.

'Are you okay?' asked Leicester.

'Yes, go on.'

Barton waited until Leicester had left the room before he opened his coat. His shirt was red, the stain spreading. It was a stinging, searing pain that made him gasp when he moved. He rested a hand against the wall, swallowed, then pulled the shirt open where the hatchet had struck and stared at his stomach.

The Barton belly had a long, nasty paper cut. He breathed a sigh of relief. Gizmo came in whimpering and stood next to him. They both looked down at Ken. For the first time in his life, Barton was incredibly close to beating a suspect.

He heard the arriving sirens, then the sound of running boots as the firearms officers arrived at Maggie's house. Two armed women hustled in as he was rolling Ken into the recovery position.

'Situation in hand,' he said to them.

The first officer walked past him with her rifle pointing downwards. She glanced at Ken, who remained unconscious, then at Barton.

'Ambulance?'

'I suppose so.'

'Any others in the property?'

'DC Leicester's upstairs with the owner and her daughter, who are unharmed. There's nobody else.'

She stared down impassively at Ken.

'Is this him?'

'Yes. He doesn't look so nasty, but he was a devious bugger.'

Barton pulled his phone out of his pocket and rang Holly.

'I was wondering where you were,' she said.

'I've just got to visit the hospital to tie up my final case. I'll be late,' he said with a smile. 'For the last time.'

'Good for you,' she replied. 'Where's the dog?'

'Priorities, eh? He's asleep on the back seat of a patrol car.'

He smiled, picturing her grinning at the other end as she put the phone down. It had been a dramatic night. Would there really be no more investigations? He peered down at his ruined coat and shirt. The bleeding had stopped. He recalled Ken's scything swing.

Barton thanked his lucky stars he'd been breathing in.

103

DI BARTON

Christmas Eve

The following morning, Barton drove to Leicester's house well before his shift started. Leicester was now off until Boxing Day, so Barton wasn't sure he'd be at home, but after their recent chats, he imagined he wouldn't have gone too far. Leicester lived in a small but pretty terrace on Cardea; a new estate near Stanground at the edge of the city.

Barton shook his head as he squeezed his car on the drive behind Leicester's. Houses there cost over two hundred and fifty thousand pounds. Barton's first house had been a similar size, but given him change out of fifty thousand. And he'd got a drive that was fit for purpose. Barton knocked on the door.

The previous evening, Leicester had panicked when Barton hadn't rung him, so he'd got in his car and driven to Maggie's. Funny how life turned out.

A long minute later, Leicester opened it. He had a tracksuit on, and his hair was damp.

'Sorry, guv. I've been for a run, so I was in the shower.'

'I understand. If I'm going for a jog, I like to get it out of the way early.'

Leicester didn't look as though he knew how to reply to that, so he just smiled.

'Put your shoes on. Breakfast is on me,' said Barton.

It was noticeably warmer, so when Leicester nipped back into the house, he returned with a summer jacket. They got in Barton's car, and he pulled off the drive.

'Do you like McDonald's breakfasts, son?'

'Not particularly.'

'Not even the hash browns?'

'Especially not the hash browns.'

'Okay, let's go to The Apple Cart.'

The housing estate's only pub was a few minutes away from Leicester's place, and they were soon being shown to a table inside. The restaurant smelled heavenly to Barton. There was an overkill on the decorations that had them both glancing around and smiling.

'Feels like we should be pulling a cracker,' said Leicester.

'I'll see if they have one.'

A sleepy-looking lad came over for their order. Barton smiled at his Santa hat.

'Merry Christmas. What can I get you guys?'

'I could murder a large breakfast,' said Barton.

The waiter didn't even blink.

'What do you have that's healthy?' asked Leicester without shame.

The youngster squinted.

'I'm not sure. Porridge. Apples, I think.'

'Live a little,' said Barton. 'My kids love the pancakes here.'

'Okay, I guess it is Christmas.'

The lad looked relieved that he didn't need to ask the chef which seasonal fruits he had in stock. He wandered away to get their food and drinks and left them to chat. It was warm and cosy in the dining area. Barton stretched out and smiled, but his face fell as he watched a laughing couple at the nearest table with their teenage kids clapping their hands as their piping hot plates of food arrived.

'What's wrong?' asked Leicester.

'Looking at that family made me think of the Hulses. Heidi and Cameron and their children. It's hard to believe we put Cameron in the frame for these murders after all he's been through.'

'Cases like this damage so many lives. Cameron and Heidi really have had a lot of bad luck. Glenn at least will hopefully be in the prison healthcare department by now.'

'Yes, it'll take a while for them to move him to Rampton or Broadmoor, but that's where he'll be heading if he's seeing dead people. They probably won't send him until he's sentenced, so at least a few months.'

'I reckon he'll get a big chunk of time, though.'

'Yeah, me too, but the CPS will accept a plea of diminished responsibility.'

'Mental illness isn't a defence, it's an explanation.'

'Correct. Glenn still committed those crimes. He's very much a danger to others, and he put Maggie and Anne-Marie through horrifying experiences, even though they appear to have escaped relatively unscathed. Although it's perhaps their support network, their families and friends, that have given them that resilience. It's hard to progress through life on your own.'

Barton watched Leicester for his response to that statement, but he didn't seem to pick up on it.

'Do you reckon he'll spend his entire sentence in a psychiatric unit?'

'Potentially, he could be in an institution for the rest of his days, but he isn't frothing mad. If he continues to hear his brother's voice, which tells him to hurt people who he perceives are interfering with his life, then he needs to be kept away from the public, but I reckon that's extremely unlikely.'

'You believe he'll get better?'

Barton paused as they brought their food out. Barton's plate looked amazing, but the pile of pancakes in front of Leicester was impressive. To Barton's surprise, Leicester got stuck right in.

'Better's probably not the right word,' replied Barton. 'I think Glenn will be able to manage his condition because the trigger for his decline was his brother's death. He felt responsible for it. The early teenage years are a perilous time for development. Through the right drugs, combined with therapy and counselling, they'll eventually get Glenn back to a state where he can function normally. Although in a way, that causes him another problem.'

Leicester nodded, with his mouth occupied. Barton speared a sausage. Grease oozed out of it. He shoved it in and spoke with his mouth half full.

'If the doctors are successful, then at some point in the future, Glenn will be well again, and therefore thinking rationally. He's then going to need to deal with the fact that he nearly beat two innocent women to death.'

Leicester swallowed slowly. 'I never really considered that.'

'No. The public often think open-ended hospital orders are an escape from facing justice for those who've committed awful crimes. But in Glenn's case, if he pleaded guilty without any kind of diminished plea, he might only be sentenced to five years for wounding with intent due to his age. He'd be out after two thirds of that sentence. Whereas as it stands, Glenn might never be stable enough to leave a secure unit. If that was the case, it would in effect be a life without parole.'

'You're right. If he took a guilty plea, he'd rejoin society in a few years' time, whether he was better or not.'

'Yes. Chilling thought, isn't it? He's a juvenile after all, so he wouldn't get sent down for long compared to an adult. We know what psychiatric care is like in a mainstream prison. Glenn would probably rot in a cell for most of his sentence with very few interventions.'

'Which would make him even more dangerous when he got out. At least in a hospital, he'd only get released when he was no longer deemed a threat.'

Barton nodded as he made himself a bacon sandwich with his toast.

'Spot on.'

Leicester took a swig of his juice.

'I suppose we should be thankful it wasn't worse. We've seen people die from comparatively weak blows to the head. Glenn could have been tried for murder.'

'Yes,' said Barton with another mouthful. 'Imagine if your mental health fell apart so badly that you killed your children or your parents. When you were better, you would dwell on that moment for every second of your waking hours. It's one of the reasons why so many of the inmates in places like Broadmoor and Rampton are suicidal.'

They ate in silence for the next few minutes as they digested their food, and those shocking and heartbreaking truths.

104

DI BARTON

Barton leaned back in his chair, replete. Leicester had somehow finished his mountain of pancakes and looked slightly green around the gills.

'I could stay here all day,' said Barton with a smile. 'But I suppose I'd better go into work, seeing as it's Christmas Eve.'

Leicester studied the young family, who were leaving their table.

'It seems tough that the CPS are charging Heidi for criminal damage,' said Leicester.

'They'll only fine her, but that won't do her financial situation any good. It might be one of those cases that's quietly dropped in light of the so-called victim, Ken, being a mass murderer.'

'How about charging Cameron and Ashlynn for wasting police time?'

'No. There's no point. I'm not even sure we'll be able to charge anyone for that stabbing at 222 Benland. Remember, the law is not just about punishment. It's also ensuring the criminal behaviour isn't repeated.'

'And keeping the peace.'

'Exactly. Cameron's got a new job now, so maybe the Hulses that still have their liberty can pull themselves out of their slump. At least they have a chance.'

'It's Maggie I feel sorry for.'

Barton asked for the bill. He paused for the waiter to leave before he replied.

'That's because you lurve her.'

Leicester's face turned beetroot red.

'Would you like to see her again?' asked Barton.

'I would, but I doubt I will. I'm not very good with relationships.'

'You don't need to be good with many. You only have to be great with one, and you were.'

'I don't want to jeopardise my career by taking advantage of a victim when we're supposed to be providing support.'

Barton chuckled. 'That sounds like it came from the police manual. I don't believe that applies here. You haven't had a massive amount of involvement in her case, and you knew her beforehand from the parkrun. Besides, you don't have to go on a proper date with her. Go and do something weird like yoga together. She'd love that, as I suspect you might. If you find there's a connection, then let me know and I'll clear it.'

Leicester nodded, but he didn't look Barton in the eye, which made him feel sad. He tapped the table to get Leicester's attention.

'You know, a wise man once told me life has a way of picking up speed like the proverbial runaway train. One minute, you're wondering what's on the horizon, the next you're looking back. You need to step off at a few of the stations along the way, or what's the point?'

'I understand.'

Barton thought back to his youth.

'I can remember winning a swimming race for the school. Blood pounding through my veins. Big muscles straining, full head of hair, strong jaw tensed in concentration, then arm raised in celebration as I surged out of the pool. Now I'm more like a bedraggled, moth-eaten mammoth hauling itself out of a murky swamp.'

Leicester's eyes widened slightly.

'That's what Holly said to me on our last foreign holiday,' said Barton. 'We'd had a heavy night on the ouzo, and I was struggling to pull myself out of the hotel swimming pool the following morning.'

Leicester laughed loudly.

'I hope I meet someone like her.'

Barton didn't say that perhaps Leicester already had. After a moment of silence, Barton realised Leicester was thinking the same thing.

'Maggie didn't deserve to have two men want to hurt her,' said Leicester. 'It's hard to believe all that can happen to one woman.'

'Is it?' replied Barton. 'Do you consider humans are better than other animals in how we treat each other?'

'Most of the time.'

'Look at the Serengeti. The wildebeest are a big family, but imagine a female gets separated from the pack. The lions notice, and they attack her. She escapes but sustains an injury. Does nature say, right, she's had enough bad luck now, let's give her a break?'

'No, I guess not.'

'What happens the next time she's parched and limps down to the river for a thirst-quenching cool drink?'

Leicester shrugged.

'She gets chomped by a crocodile.' Barton laughed.

Leicester chuckled.

'Okay, although I'm not certain I completely get your reasoning.'

'Ken's one of life's predators. He might argue poor parenting was to blame, or that a teacher let him down, but at some point, you have to take responsibility for your actions and stop blaming your upbringing.'

Leicester nodded as Barton continued.

'Funnily enough, Ken got exactly what he wanted when his mother became ill and he moved back into her bungalow to look after her. She was trapped. I dread to think what a festering sore of a relationship that was. But imagine what it'd do to a damaged person if they found out a child had been hidden from them. His mum leaving him was the final straw.'

'Left him? You mean she died.'

'Yes, but I bet Ken saw it as the ultimate betrayal. The attack on his estranged wife was probably impulsive. Who knows what his intentions were when he assaulted his old teacher? But like many who resort to violence, he'll have enjoyed the power he felt. I'm guessing he turned his attention onto Maggie, a single mother as his mum was, then put her on a pedestal to be worshipped. Meanwhile, he took his revenge by targeting women who were struggling. Those who had been separated from their packs.'

'Or perhaps he just wanted to get away with it.'

'Maybe. Ken was probably already annoyed with Maggie for rejecting him. That would have turned to anger if he suspected she was heading to a competitor. Glenn's attack isolated Maggie further. Ken must have seen an opportunity to offend closer to home and still escape justice.'

'And now he'll die behind bars.'

'Yes, but isn't this a damning indictment of how society is at its worst? People experience terrible loss like the Hulses. It must be easy to give up. Zander will tell you the pain of losing a child never goes away. Families fall apart, like his and the Hulses' did, but only the lucky have friends and relatives who are really prepared to help.'

'There's a massive mental health crisis in this country.'

'Yes, it's often only when people completely crack up that they're noticed. Oddly enough, if Ken had gone to his doctors and told them he had the urge to kill, he'd have probably been helped straight away.'

'Glenn's mental health had deteriorated so much that he thought he was helping.'

Barton rose from the table.

'It's a salutary lesson about how many in our city aren't living. They're merely fighting to survive. People can't afford what we might consider the basics. They suffer in silence after shouting themselves hoarse for help that never arrives. They end up hungry and surviving in the cold and damp.'

Leicester looked guiltily down at their empty plates.

'While we sit on our fat arses and eat until we're nearly sick,' he said.

'Yes, talking of which. What are your plans tomorrow?'

'I'm going to enjoy a chilled day. Call my dad in the morning. I'll go for a ten-mile run at lunchtime, and I've been saving the new series of *The Mandalorian* to binge watch.'

'Fair enough.'

Barton put a twenty-pound note on top of the sixteen-pound bill that arrived. They left the pub and walked back to Barton's car.

'I mentioned to Holly that you were on your own this year. She loves having surprise guests over on Christmas Day for dinner.'

Leicester glanced at Barton, but didn't comment.

'I can't tell you it'd be plain sailing, though,' continued Barton. 'Luke, he's only seven. He'll hit you with a weapon. Plastic sword, probably, or shoot you with a Nerf gun. Bring safety glasses. Lawrence is back from university, so he's likely to give you some grief about the planet or the fact your shoes are made out of innocent animals. Layla's thirteen, so she'll flirt with you, which will be unsettling for everyone.'

Leicester gave him a nervous grin.

'Holly won't be happy until you've consumed at least five-thousand calories, then she'll get the cheeseboard out. Her Christmas cake is heavier than me. You'll be forced to play Luke at Top Trumps because, apparently, I'm crap at it. Bring a bottle, well, because I like to drink. Zelensky said she'll pop over for a few sherries in time for the Queen's speech, because she's on her own, too. I expect to be fast asleep in an armchair by then.'

Barton stopped when they got to his car and put his hand on Leicester's shoulder.

'Don't bother about buying presents, although Holly will get you a little something to open. Your company is enough. Be at mine by twelve. If you don't fancy it, or change your mind, don't worry. I know that kind of madness isn't everyone's cup of tea. Watching back-to-back *Star Wars* might drive you to distraction, too. What do you think?'

This time, Leicester looked at him directly.

'Sounds wonderful.'

105

DI BARTON

Barton had been at his desk for about an hour when he noticed how busy the office had become. There was a hum of chatter, much of which seemed non work-related. He expected there to be a buzz because of resolving the case, but it was more than that. When he looked up and around, he realised the admin team had come in, some uniforms were present, even grumpy Donald from custody was standing at the back with a grin on his face.

The room went quiet when DCI Cox and Chief Superintendent Troughton arrived. He was resplendent in uniform. Cox was carrying a huge box. They headed for Barton's desk and the office turned as one towards them. Barton felt a lump in his throat as he noticed Mortis and Sirena amongst the throng, and even his old DCI, Navneet Naeem.

Cox placed the box next to him and lifted the lid. There was a stack of different coloured envelopes beside an enormous rectangular sponge cake. On top of it was a picture of two ancient, giggling men. One was saying to the other, 'I got this new deodorant stick today. The instructions said to remove cap and push up bottom.'

Cox grinned at him.

'It was Strange's idea. Something to do with making your farts smell better.'

Troughton cleared his throat.

'Morning, all. This is a sad day, but it's also a happy one. John, I've known you for twenty years and I can honestly say you're the best detective I've had the pleasure of working with.'

There was an eruption of cheers from around the room, intermingled with a few boos from Zander.

'I sneakily asked everyone for their views on you. I wanted my speech to be personal, but I'm afraid it's too early for so many swear words.'

More good-natured abuse followed. Troughton took a piece of paper from his trouser pocket and opened it.

'In all seriousness, people like John are the backbone of the police. There's a level of commitment that is beyond just doing a fabulous job. I should think everyone in this room has him to thank for a part of their progress and learning. That's why he'll be such an asset working with our development team. We will all miss him, though. He is the most reassuring of presences at the most worrying of times.'

There was a smattering of applause until Troughton raised his arm.

'A detective has to see the worst of the world and carry it with him, but an inspector has to look after his team's morale and well-being as well as his own. To do it for so long is testament to John's strength and endurance, both of which we've all come to rely on.'

More applause. He paused to let the clapping subside.

'Thanks to Sarah for sorting the cake and bringing it in for you. She also did a collection, I suspect at gunpoint, judging by the amount raised.' Troughton passed Barton a brick-sized box. 'Good luck, John. Hip!'

'Hooray,' shouted everyone, followed by, 'Speech!'

Barton stood and put a finger to his mouth to quieten the room.

'Thank you. I hope you know I appreciate all of your efforts over the years. Ours is hard work, but we do it best together.' Barton pointed to the contents of the box in front of him. 'I must say, this is the best individual cupcake I've ever seen.'

Barton's joke got a huge laugh.

'I'll definitely appreciate eating that later. You lot can have some doughnuts. I won't make a big speech. That's because of the one thing that you've come to know, trust and love. The Barton belly.'

That gave rise to more shouts and laughter.

'It's telling me that this isn't the end.'

That got the biggest cheer of the morning.

'Now,' said Barton. 'Could someone go down and interview Ken Wade? While I open what I'm guessing will be a load of leaving cards, taking the piss out of how old I am and congratulating me on my retirement.'

Zelensky appeared with some plates and a large knife and did the honours. Sirena and Mortis came over to him.

'I've got so much on with all the different crime scenes that I can't stay too long,' said Sirena after kissing his cheek. 'But I couldn't miss this.'

Zander had pulled Barton's leg about Sirena liking him when she'd first started working with the police. It turned out that Barton wasn't even the right sex.

'Have you told your wife that we're going to elope together?' asked Sirena.

'I thought I'd leave it until Boxing Day,' replied Barton.

'I can't wait. There'll be a huge wedding. I want six children. At least.'

Barton's face dropped.

'Six?'

'At least.'

'Now's probably a good time to let you know I've a vasectomy booked in for this afternoon.'

'Ah, such a shame, John,' said Sirena. 'How about you, Mortis? Want any more kids?'

'The very thought of it is enough to have me wheezing.' He turned back to Barton. 'Fancy you sloping off like this. Who am I going to ridicule now?'

With perfect timing, Zander appeared with an immense grin. They all laughed, but he was in no mood to be disheartened.

'Opened your present yet?' asked Zander.

Barton pulled the wrapping paper off the box and lifted out the contents. It was a set of golden handcuffs linked together on a plinth. It was a beautiful gift. Strange came over with a serious expression. Mortis and Sirena disappeared to get a drink, leaving Barton with Strange and Zander.

'Did Zander tell you some relatively urgent information has come to light?' asked Strange.

'I'm not sure I want to hear it right now. You two can't have anything to tell me which is more important than my cake.'

'That's the news,' said Strange. 'It's no longer just the two of us.'

Barton looked back and forth at his beaming sergeants. He dropped into his chair. His mind scrambled and clicked into place.

'That was why you had a few days sick,' he said.

'Yes, morning sickness isn't too bad now, but it was brutal for a couple of weeks.'

'Oh, my God. And that's why you've been more cautious than usual about rushing into action. Zander's been overly protective as well. Was that why you were ignoring me?'

'I had a feeling you'd guess if I spent too much time with you. We wanted to shock you together.'

It was only then Barton remembered Strange had miscarried a

baby during the resolution of The Snow Killer case. She'd stead-fastly refused to talk about it ever since. That was her way of dealing with it. This must have been an extra worrying time for her. He experienced a massive rush of warmth towards the couple.

'How exciting. You're having a baby!' he said with the widest of grins.

Zander shook his head.

'No, boss. We're having two.'

Barton's eyes widened while they both nodded. Barton leapt to his feet.

'Yes!' he roared, causing everyone to stop talking and turn around, but Barton didn't care. He looked into the faces of his team, his friends. He thought of Holly at home with his children. Barton let out another cheer, feeling as if he'd just won the lottery. In the most important ways, he had.

Smiling, Barton looked down at the golden handcuffs that were still in his hand and raised them above his head. He noticed there was a small brass plaque on the plinth. It was engraved with one word.

Detective.

106

Boxing Day

Lothar indicated right and crawled into the road where he'd been staying and stopped well away from the property. He got out of his car and checked further up in both directions. Bai's driveway was empty. He'd told Lothar that he was spending Boxing Day afternoon at a friend's.

Lothar returned to his car, drove to the house and parked on the drive. He held the steering wheel for a moment and had a think. Bai had been pretty decent to him even after he'd got behind on his rent. He was still snippy over the missing watch, though. God knew why. Lothar only managed to get two-hundred quid for it.

He turned the engine off, left the car and walked down the path. It was quiet. Lothar debated not following through on his plan, but he liked money. Bai probably had loads, so fuck him.

He chuckled. What kind of fool told a thief they were going out for the day? Lothar had promised Bai that he would move out on the thirty-first of December and pay all the rent he owed before he left. Instead, he was leaving now and taking a few extras. He checked his pocket to make sure the screwdriver was still there.

Whistling to himself, he let himself in and went straight to the lounge. The house was quiet, but Bai had left the heating on. Lothar smiled and took his coat off. He looked behind the TV to check his tool was the right size for the bracket and began to undo the screws.

Then he was out of this city. When he'd found out Ken was The Hatchet Man, he hadn't been that surprised. He'd recognised in Ken a deficiency that was present in his own moral compass. No wonder they'd had a laugh, but only idiots risked long prison sentences. Lothar was too smart for that.

He was on his fourth screw when he thought he heard a door closing.

'Bollocks,' he said under his breath.

He grabbed the screws in a panic and stuffed them in his jeans pocket. When he turned to walk to the window to check outside, he realised he wasn't the only person in the room. Bai was in the door-way, shaking his head in disgust.

'Adjusting my TV?'

Lothar struggled for an excuse, then decided he didn't give a shit. Even though he was blocking the only exit, Bai was small and thin. What could he do to a gym tiger such as himself?

'I'm fetching my stuff. Nice knowing you.'

Lothar walked past Bai and deliberately knocked into him. When he got to the hall, there was a man at the front door. He was the tallest Chinese person he'd ever seen. He didn't look happy. The man took a step forward, then slapped what looked like a cosh into his left palm. Lothar pointed his screwdriver at him, then spun on his heels to escape through the kitchen.

Blocking his way was a white guy who was a little shorter than the Chinese man at the door, but approximately twice as wide. His face appeared friendly, but the motorbike chain in his hands did not. Lothar lowered his screwdriver.

'You're a poor excuse for a human,' said Bai behind him.

Lothar turned to him.

'Look, I'm sorry. I needed money, but I'm getting paid this week, so I'll give you everything I owe you then, and some extra. I'll get your watch back, too.'

'I thought you knew nothing about my watch.'

Lothar's mouth was so dry, he couldn't talk. His tongue flicked out to moisten his lips.

'I've spoken to a few of my neighbours,' said Bai, softly. 'They've had items go missing, too. Valuable items.'

'I know where your watch is,' gasped Lothar.

'I don't want it back. What I want is to make certain you never do this to anyone else. We're going to teach you a lesson you will not forget.'

The last thing Lothar saw before the swinging chain knocked him senseless was a pair of pliers in Bai's hand.

107

GLENN

Psychiatric hospital, a month later

I stare out of my cell window. Well, they use the term room here, but it's a cell if you can't leave when you want. It's always so bloody hot here, to the point of there being a permanent sheen on my forehead. Or maybe that's just the drugs.

When I lived with my parents, I was always cold, but right now I'd give up a year's pocket money to experience the damp, creeping cool of our house on my clammy skin. I sit back on the bed and glance around. They don't allow me much of my own stuff. Not now, anyway. Even my books are gone. Turns out it's possible to really hurt someone with a hardback.

I glance in the corner and smile at Ronnie. He smiles back, or at least I think he does. He's fading. His edges are a little more blurred each day. Sometimes I can't see him at all. It's time for him to leave, though, or I'll spend the rest of my life in here. I smile at the shimmering image.

'It's okay, Ronnie. You can go now. Our family is safe. You've done your part.'

As he waves his hand in a small gesture, I hear the key in the lock and my door opens. Ronnie has gone when I look back at him.

'Ready for your counselling session, Glenn?' says the woman, who is either a nurse or a warden. She's a heavyset, no-nonsense type and suited to both, but she stays outside.

Few come inside any more. The two people she's with, dressed in the same white uniform, are tall, wide men. Eyes narrowed. Hands open at their sides. I walk out of the room and follow the bigger of the two men as his jangling keys open a series of locked doors. The other guy falls into step and trudges behind us.

They take me into a large room where there are two people sitting behind a big desk. My therapist, Namita, sits there with another gentleman who introduced himself as a doctor some time ago. He has one of those names that's always on the tip of my tongue. In fact, there's a lot of that lately. I couldn't even remember my parents' first names for a while after I first came here.

'Sit down, please,' says Namita. The bruises on her face have faded now.

'Good morning,' I say.

'How are you today?' asks the doctor.

I glare at him, then at Namita. I turn to the left and see one of the large men has remained in the corner. The other has stayed at the door. Their arms are crossed. My eyes slip towards the corner to Namita's right for Ronnie, but he's nowhere to be seen. It seems a dim flame has sparked inside me, that has long been gone. I won't be seeing Ronnie again. Somehow, I know that for a certainty.

That makes me grin. A grin so wide that my face might split in half. I can't stop that silent smile, even when I'm no longer smiling inside, and it turns into an ugly cry. I will miss him.

The tears blur my vision, but I can still make out Namita and the doctor scribbling furiously on their notepads, then sharing concerned looks. And so they might, because I am The Santa Killer.

A single tear trickles out of each eye and my heart breaks.

'Are you okay, Glenn?' asks the doctor.

'Please, I just want to be a boy.'

108

ANNE-MARIE

Anne-Marie rolled the nylon hold-ups along her shapely legs and slipped a gold high heel onto each foot. She puckered up and took a moment to admire her garish lipstick in the mirror. She'd never go out with this stuff on her face, but it was Drew's birthday and he loved it. After a last look in the mirror at her matching underwear, she giggled and put a hand over her mouth.

She was smoking hot, even if she did say so herself. She jiggled her boobs in the bra to get them comfy and carefully opened the toilet door. Drew was about to have the time of his life. Under thirteen stone, and benching fifty kilos, Anne-Marie felt fabulous. In fact, she felt so damn good, she was going to break him!

She chuckled to herself, then put a hand over her mouth again. The kids did not want to wake up and see her dressed like this.

She crept down the landing, pushed the bedroom door open, then stood there purring in her gladiator pose. Drew, meanwhile, was fast asleep.

Anne-Marie crawled onto the bed beside him. Bloody men. Drew grumbled mid-dream. His hand reached out and found hers. As he squeezed it, his breathing slowed to a steady rhythm. Anne-

Marie's phone beeped on the side table. She reached over and grabbed it to see a message from Maggie.

Looking forward to our spa break next weekend!

Anne-Marie was about to text back, then decided she might as well ring. An earthquake wouldn't wake Drew now. Maggie answered straight away.

'Hey,' she said. 'What you up to?'

Anne-Marie looked down at her scantily clad body.

'Nothing, sadly.'

'No, me neither. Although, I do have some gossip for you.'

'Ooh, excellent.'

'Do you remember me telling you about that nice young detective?'

109

THE HATCHET MAN

HMP Whitemoor, Category A prison, male estate

I turn off my TV when I hear my cell door being unlocked, then step outside onto the landing. They kept me on an extremely secure wing when I first arrived here. I assume it's a time for observation when you first arrive. There were never any other prisoners anywhere near me unless they were behind a tall, solid, metal fence on a strange square exercise yard.

They must be a bit slow in the head here. I told them the truth during all my assessments. I'm a danger to women, not men. That DJ might disagree, but he'd be dead, not terrified, if I wanted to hurt men.

I stand next to the railing and look down through the thick netting to the landing below. It's a small wing with a lot of officers. The others don't seem so bad on here. The chatty Scotsman, Cromarty, from a few cells up told me when I arrived yesterday that most are inside for killing their partners. The real psychopaths are kept elsewhere.

I suppose that's something. They're never going to release me from here after what I've done, so I've said I'm innocent. There's going to be a full trial with twelve honest men and women. That way, the world will hear everything. I want them to know just how clever I've been, and how bad those women were.

I suppose I have that to look forward to, but it's likely I'll get a whole of life sentence. That phrase makes me shiver. It seems a remarkably casual term to mean I'll die behind bars.

Still, I assume there will be pleasures to be had along the way. I've seen the movies. There's always someone who can get you something. A few more prisoners amble past me without making eye contact. I grin. Maybe I can be a man of substance in here amongst these dim-witted losers. I'm probably the shrewdest person here. I can write letters for them in exchange for smuggled items. A mobile phone would be nice. It'd be good to have a peek at Maggie's Facebook page. Perhaps she'll even message me back. Women are always writing to condemned men.

I look down at the ring I reclaimed when I assaulted Inga, and spin it around on my little finger. She must have said she didn't want it because they let me keep it. Maybe she'd be pleased if I sent it back to her.

'Hey, Kenneth,' whispers a voice behind me.

I turn to Cromarty and give him a forced smile. I told him yesterday to call me Ken. Even the newspapers have finally got that right. He gets too close to me, which is unpleasant. Cromarty's breath is a crime in itself. Worthy of the gallows. Weirdly, he looks just like my Uncle Johan, who was a vicar. Johan was slim, average height, ruddy and bald, although unlike Cromarty, his teeth hadn't been filed down.

'Hey,' I reply.

Cromarty, constantly on the move, looks around as though someone can hear us, despite there being nobody else in sight on our landing. I feel his warm breath on my face when he leans in and whispers to me.

'The top gadgie in this whole place is on the wing next door. He's a wee demon. Pure evil. He runs all the drugs, all the betting, all the scams, and all o' the killings. No' just in this jail, either.'

'So?'

'I'm to give you a warning.'

The piggy eyes that I assumed were dumb now appear flinty and devious. He lets out a chuckle.

'You know that poor wee lassie you murdered in Leicester?'

'Yes.'

'She was his cousin.'

AUTHOR'S NOTE

Thank you to all the readers who have been with Barton throughout this series. The themes in this novel are dark, which made it a tough book to research. The Hulse family developed in a way that I never imagined, as did Ken. When I was about a fifth of the way into this book, a very nice man came and installed a smart meter. We got chatting, and he told me one of the saddest stories I've ever heard. He'd lost his son after an epic six-year battle with cancer. The bravery and resilience during that terrible time, theirs and his, was humbling, which tempered the kind of people Cameron and Heidi were supposed to be.

I hope you found them believable characters, because none of us are all good or bad. I even made it a little sweet and sugary for Mr B at the end as a contrast, but isn't that what Christmas is all about?

As for DI Barton? This feels like the right time to stop. It's sad writing that because I'd love to know how the team gets on with the changes in their lives, but I'd like a fresh challenge.

So, I'm going to write a new trilogy set in Norfolk where I've spent a lot of my holidays over the last five decades. I'll mix it up a bit, but hopefully there'll be an authentic cast you can grow to love and, of course, some twists that you'll struggle to see. Who knows? Peterborough's not far from Norfolk. Maybe my DS could pop in to Thorpe Wood police station and see how everyone's getting on.

Please leave a review. I read them all. Maybe you have a few ideas about where I could go with DI Barton next, apart from McDonald's.

Perhaps, in the future, Peterborough will once again need the help of big John.

Read on for a taster of Detectives Knight and Fade Book 1 now...

MORE FROM ROSS GREENWOOD

We hope you enjoyed reading *The Santa Killer*. If you did, please leave a review.

If you'd like to gift a copy, this book is also available as an ebook, digital audio download and audiobook CD.

Explore the DI Barton series.

ABOUT THE AUTHOR

Ross Greenwood is the bestselling author of over ten crime thrillers. Before becoming a full-time writer he was most recently a prison officer and so worked everyday with murderers, rapists and thieves for four years. He lives in Peterborough.

Follow Ross on social media:

twitter.com/greenwoodross

facebook.com/RossGreenwoodAuthor

bookbub.com/authors/ross-greenwood

instagram.com/rossg555

Boldw⦿⦿d

Boldwood Books is an award-winning fiction publishing company seeking out the best stories from around the world.

Find out more at www.boldwoodbooks.com

Join our reader community for brilliant books, competitions and offers!

Follow us
@BoldwoodBooks
@BookandTonic

Sign up to our weekly deals newsletter

https://bit.ly/BoldwoodBNewsletter